BANTAM BOOKS BY LOUIS L'AMOUR

NOVELS

Bendigo Shafter
Borden Chantry
Brionne
The Broken Gun
The Burning Hills
The Californios
Callaghen
Catlow
Chancy
The Cherokee Trail
Comstock Lode
Conagher
Crossfire Trail
Dark Canyon
Down the Long Hills
The Empty Land
Fair Blows the Wind
Fallon
The Ferguson Rifle
The First Fast Draw
Flint
Guns of the Timberlands
Hanging Woman Creek
The Haunted Mesa
Heller with a Gun
The High Graders
High Lonesome
Hondo
How the West Was Won
The Iron Marshal
The Key-Lock Man
Kid Rodelo
Kilkenny
Killoe
Kilrone
Kiowa Trail
Last of the Breed
Last Stand at Papago Wells
The Lonesome Gods
The Man Called Noon
The Man from Skibbereen
The Man from the Broken Hills
Matagorda
Milo Talon
The Mountain Valley War
North to the Rails
Over on the Dry Side
Passin' Through
The Proving Trail
The Quick and the Dead
Radigan
Reilly's Luck
The Rider of Lost Creek
Rivers West
The Shadow Riders
Shalako
Showdown at Yellow Butte
Silver Canyon
Sitka
Son of a Wanted Man
Taggart
The Tall Stranger
To Tame a Land
Tucker
Under the Sweetwater Rim
Utah Blaine
The Walking Drum
Westward the Tide
Where the Long Grass Blows
West of Dodge
With These Hands
Yondering

SACKETT TITLES

Sackett's Land
To the Far Blue Mountains
The Warrior's Path
Jubal Sackett
Ride the River
The Daybreakers
Sackett
Lando
Mojave Crossing
Mustang Man
The Lonely Men
Galloway
Treasure Mountain
Lonely on the Mountain
Ride the Dark Trail
The Sackett Brand
The Sky-Liners

SHORT STORY COLLECTIONS

Beyond the Great Snow Mountains
Bowdrie
Bowdrie's Law
Buckskin Run
The Collected Short Stories of Louis L'Amour (vols. 1–7)
Dutchman's Flat
End of the Drive
From the Listening Hills
The Hills of Homicide
Law of the Desert Born
Long Ride Home
Lonigan
May There Be a Road
Monument Rock
Night Over the Solomons
Off the Mangrove Coast
The Outlaws of Mesquite
The Rider of the Ruby Hills
Riding for the Brand
The Strong Shall Live
The Trail to Crazy Man
Valley of the Sun
War Party
West from Singapore

THE HOPALONG CASSIDY NOVELS

The Riders of High Rock
The Rustlers of West Fork
The Trail to Seven Pines
Trouble Shooter

NONFICTION

Education of a Wandering Man
Frontier
The Sackett Companion: A Personal Guide to the Sackett Novels
A Trail of Memories: The Quotations of Louis L'Amour, compiled by Angelique L'Amour

POETRY

Smoke from This Altar

LOST TREASURES

Louis L'Amour's Lost Treasures: Volume 1 (with Beau L'Amour)
No Traveller Returns (with Beau L'Amour)
Louis L'Amour's Lost Treasures: Volume 2 (with Beau L'Amour)

SKYRING WATER

LOUIS L'AMOUR

AND

BEAU L'AMOUR

SKYRING WATER

A NOVEL

BANTAM BOOKS
NEW YORK

Bantam Books
An imprint of Random House
A division of Penguin Random House LLC
1745 Broadway, New York, NY 10019
randomhousebooks.com
penguinrandomhouse.com

Hardcover ISBN 979-8-217-30246-8
Ebook ISBN 979-8-217-30247-5

Printed in the United States of America

1st Printing

First Edition

BOOK TEAM: Production editor: Ted Allen • Managing editor: Saige Francis • Production manager: Maggie Hart • Copy editor: Kathleen Fridella • Proofreaders: Adele Starrs, Barbara Greenberg, Al Madocs

Book design by Caroline Cunningham

The authorized representative in the EU for product safety and compliance is Penguin Random House Ireland, Morrison Chambers, 32 Nassau Street, Dublin D02 YH68, Ireland. https://eu-contact.penguin.ie

Dedicated to

Dr. Thomas O. Paine, Mike Demetre,

and Diana and John Lopez, inspirations all, in so many ways!

SKYRING WATER

CHAPTER 1

SPAIN,

1961 . . .

THE REAR END of the Lancia skidded sideways. Muddy gravel roared in the wheel wells and rattled off the undercarriage. Mike Fowler counter-steered, then held the accelerator steady, letting the torque of the six-cylinder engine do its job. As the tachometer hit five thousand rpm, he shifted into third gear.

Ahead of him the rugged peaks and ridgelines of the Pyrenees were obscured by low gray clouds. On one side the slope fell away with not much more than a slushy berm between his tires and the treetops; on the other rocks nearly clipped the sideview mirror. Watery wind-driven snow smeared under his wipers, blurring his view of the rutted road.

It didn't matter. In this machine, under these conditions, nothing could touch him. The car was a 1955 Aurelia B20. Though a few years old, it remained a wonder of Italian engineering. It was owned by Fowler's business partner, Anton Voss, a man who had an unerring instinct when it came to anything mechanical.

The fact that it was another man's car would not go over well if the Spanish police stopped him, and the situation was sure to go from bad to worse if they decided to search the trunk. But Mike Fowler had a considerably more serious problem than being pulled over by the Guardia Civil. And that was why he was tearing up a twisting mountain road headed into a storm that was sure to close the passes into France before morning.

Nearly thirty tons of gold bullion. Thirty tons lost to history, its existence the stuff of myth or the colorfully illustrated cover of a men's adventure magazine. A legendary treasure hidden in one of the most inaccessible places on the planet. Men were willing to kill to discover its location, and now some of them believed that Anton Voss knew where it could be found.

As the car roared past a stand of trees, Fowler saw what he was looking for: a long straight grade and, at the top, a tight curve disappearing behind a shoulder of the hill. He took it as fast as he dared while keeping an eye on the rearview mirror. There was no sign of pursuit.

He hit the brakes as he rounded the curve. The car slewed across the road, coming to a stop with its nose buried in the brush. Cutting the engine, he climbed out and, moving to the back of the Lancia, opened the boot.

Pulling away a greasy tarp, he removed a Sturmgewehr 44 assault rifle and a pair of pouches holding six curved magazines. Fowler dodged up the slope inside the elbow of the turn. Stopping at an outcrop of rain-slick rock he took cover behind the dead branches that had fallen from a small oak.

He spotted them a mile off. The driver of the black Mercedes was pushing it hard, fearing his quarry was escaping and desperate to catch up. Mike Fowler smiled grimly. He knew these mountains from long experience. He could outdrive his pursuers as long as he had petrol in his tank. But he couldn't allow them to know where he crossed the border. If they were as organized as he suspected, they could have a team waiting not long after he reached France.

What the men in the Mercedes didn't realize was that he hadn't been running, not since he'd left Barcelona. He had driven far and fast, but his plan had been to gain just enough distance to set a trap.

Adjusting the sights on the StG 44, he raised the gun. When the black car was about two hundred yards out, he fired. Once. Twice.

The first bullet went into the tank at the top of the radiator, the second lower down. The oil pan on the Mercedes was relatively well protected, and the 8mm Kurz cartridge would not penetrate like that of a full-power rifle, but he figured he'd try for it anyway.

Steam burst through the grill and the gaps around the hood. The tires locked up and the Mercedes slid to a halt, the vague form of the driver craning forward trying to see what had gone wrong.

The two men in the car didn't realize they were under fire.

Fowler squeezed the trigger again, putting a round through the windshield. Then he took out the left front tire and punched a pair of holes in the pontoonlike fender, searching for the distributor or fuel pump. The engine died.

There was a muffled shout of alarm. The front door on the far side of the Mercedes popped open and the men dove for cover below the edge of the road.

There was a flicker of movement just past the trunk lid and then pistol shots cracked up from below. He couldn't tell where the gunfire was aimed but it wasn't coming anywhere close.

Beyond the car, through a screen of wet, wilted grass he made out a black shape . . . the shoulder of a trench coat. Fowler fired a single shot. The man in the black coat twisted and cried out. Cursing in German, he crabbed sideways, painfully searching for better cover.

Fowler turned away from the road and bellowed, "On the slope! They're on the slope!" His voice echoed off the hill behind him, hopefully obscuring his location and confusing the men below as to how many attackers they were facing. It didn't work as well as he would have liked. One bullet and then another ricocheted off the rocks just to Fowler's left.

Mike decided he had played with them long enough. Thumbing the fire selector over, he loosed two three-round bursts. The bullets chewed up rock and weeds and mud. A ricochet whined off into the depths of the canyon. After that there was no more return fire, and he could no longer see either man.

Good. The plan had been to draw their pursuers' attention, giving Voss an opportunity to get away. Fowler wanted them to think that he and Anton were together, and he wanted them to report as much to their superiors. But if these men showed any more resistance, he would hunt them down and kill them. The shadowy group they worked for had destroyed everything he and Anton Voss had struggled to build over the last decade.

Fowler blasted a line of bullet holes down the side of the Mercedes. He shredded the left rear tire. He changed magazines and blew out the windshield and side windows. *Take this as a warning*, he thought. *Don't make me come after you.*

He changed magazines again and again, firing long undisciplined bursts. A pile of spent shells grew as he turned the grill into a pockmarked ruin and shot out the headlights, the mirrors, and then one of the door handles. When the stamped metal of the gun steamed and the foregrip scalded his hand even through his driving glove, Fowler stopped. Below him the almost new 1960 Mercedes 220 was a complete wreck. Only one patch of sheet metal remained bare, the driver's-side door.

He stood, a gesture of his contempt, challenging the men below to try something.

"You want to stop us?" he yelled. "Now's your chance!" His voice echoed off the hills and cliffs.

Nothing happened. He hoped they were listening but, if they were smart, they were halfway down the canyon. He slung the rifle and slid a handgun from his belt. It was a 9mm SIG 47/8, a gun their enemies knew was favored by Anton Voss.

Fowler found a position lower on the hill. He raised the pistol and fired, putting a tight group of bullets into the door and a few more into the rest of the body. He moved slightly, spreading out the pattern of ejected cartridges and smearing his footprints until they were hard to read. The gun locked open. Grabbing the heel release, he dropped the distinctive magazine on the ground, doing what he could to suggest there had been two shooters.

He didn't know how convincing the ruse was. But since he left Barcelona none of their enemies had come close enough to see inside the car. If he was lucky, they might not be aware that Anton owned a yacht or where, until just recently, it had been moored. He was risking his life and his freedom on what could very well be a fool's errand.

Deep in the mountains he pulled over at a wayside above a brush-choked ravine. Taking out the assault rifle, he removed the buttstock, recoil spring, and bolt carrier. He swung the barrel and receiver of the gun in an underhanded arc, sending it pinwheeling into the depths to his left. He tossed the remainder of the parts in the other direction. A moment later he had disposed of the SIG in a similar fashion.

Fowler opened a garment bag and a leather Gladstone. He changed out of his dirty clothes and into a three-piece suit of brown tweed. Then he replaced his muddy combat boots with a pair of handmade shoes. In the last light of day, he combed his hair in the reflection of the car window. He wasn't sure who he saw looking back: a nondescript forty-year-old man with a lean, disciplined body and a face that betrayed little. A man who had fought his way to the top of a profession that he could not discuss in polite company. And now he suspected he couldn't claim even that: his business was a smoking ruin that would probably be seized by the Spanish government. He was a wanted man. There was no way of going back.

He took a slow look around. Catalonia had been his home as long as anywhere on earth. If he ever returned, it was likely he would be arrested for murder. He slipped into the mud-streaked Lancia and fired up the motor. There was a storm coming, and he still had a long way to go.

FRANCE,

three hours later . . .

Mike Fowler crossed the border at a lonely outpost on a snow-frosted pass. Any traffic would be well-remembered, but it was also manned, on both sides, by members of an ancient family who had been in the profession of smuggling since the time of the Romans. They knew Fowler from the days when his business had not been quite so legitimate. His documents, along with a duplicate passport belonging to Voss, were accepted and stamped in the normal manner. However, the official record of their passing would be delayed by exactly twenty-four hours. Neither of the officials more than glanced outside at the Lancia with its breath-fogged windows. They remained behind their desks and warmed themselves while counting the piles of 1,000 peseta and 100 nouveau franc banknotes Fowler left with them.

Snow chased the little car down through the mountains, eventually changing to rain. Earlier in the day he had discovered that the airport and train stations in Barcelona had been staked out. It was not only the police; some of the men Fowler spotted were certainly private detectives in the employ of the group that pursued him.

Now that he was in France his first impulse was to ditch the Lancia and get to Paris. From there he could find a flight to London or the U.S. At some point the fiction that Voss was with him would dissolve, but the longer it took, the better. In a crowded airport it would be a lengthy process to verify that they hadn't slipped away on separate flights. Fowler was betting everything that he could still find a way to vanish even as he provided the distraction that allowed Voss to cover his own trail.

A cautious reconnaissance of the palatial Toulouse-Matabiau train station suggested that getting to Paris without the car might be difficult. There were no cops, but instead of the grubby middle-aged gumshoes he had seen in Barcelona, the men covering this station were young, fit . . . and distinctly Aryan.

No doubt they had come in overnight, alerted as soon as it was clear he had escaped Spain. The scope of the manhunt was a frightening indication of the size of the organization he and Voss suddenly found themselves up against. And if they had the train stations covered, then the airports would be, too.

Holding to the shadows, Mike Fowler pulled back to where he had parked. As he saw it, there was only one option left. If he could arrive in time, it would completely foil his pursuers. On the other hand, it might also put the whole operation at risk.

He started the car and headed for the coast. Fatigue clouded his vision and dulled his mind. If his adversaries were alert, they might realize what he was up to. It all depended on how much they had bothered to learn about Mike Fowler and Anton Voss.

One thing at a time, he thought, and drove faster.

Before dawn the Lancia grumbled through the gray, rain-wet streets of Marseille. Beyond the railyards at Gare d'Arenc, Fowler found the street blocked by a line of freight cars waiting on a set of tracks that led to the docks. Looking quickly around, he pulled diagonally off the street beside a pile of discarded packing materials.

Opening his bag, he lifted the false bottom. He removed a flat sap, black leather stitched around nine ounces of lead shot with a spring steel handle, and a compact Remington automatic. He tucked the blackjack inside the waistband of his trousers and dropped the pistol into a specially tailored hip pocket. Two loaded magazines went into his coat.

Mike left the car unlocked and the keys in plain sight. It would certainly be stolen before noon. He slipped the strap of the Gladstone over his shoulder and across his chest. Then he followed the boxcars to where the rails passed through an archway in a building and ran straight down the pier that was his destination.

The passage smelled like a latrine but, standing in the shadows of the entrance and with the dark mass of a railcar behind him,

Fowler could observe the activity along the quayside with little chance of being recognized.

It wasn't five minutes before he saw them. Two tall young men appeared out of the confusion of trucks and laborers on the pier. In contrast to the stained denim and leather aprons worn by the burly longshoremen and warehouse workers, this pair seemed dressed for a day at the country club. One of them even wore an argyle sweater under his blazer and held a raincoat draped over one arm. His companion sported a windbreaker and a driver's cap.

Just across the street from Fowler's position, a low-slung Opel Kapitän pulled out of the flow of traffic. Inside, two dark silhouettes peered down the dock. Over the roof of the car Fowler could see the man in the driver's cap catch the eyes of those in the Opel and spread his hands. It was not the elaborate shrug of a Frenchman, just a quick signal to communicate that something expected had yet to occur.

Was *he* the something they expected? Did they have men all along the waterfront, or were they aware of which ship he planned to take? If he waited, would they go off to search another pier?

The trouble was that he didn't have long. Beyond the roofs of the warehouses, he could see the signal mast of a freighter. A "Blue Peter," the flag indicating imminent departure, was hanging in the moist air. Maneuvering a ten-thousand-ton cargo ship out of port was a slow and tricky business. They would leave on schedule, and he had better be aboard.

There was a crunch of gravel behind him, and Fowler whirled. But it was just a startled pair of railroad employees in white vests and peaked caps.

"Pardon! Pardon, monsieur . . . le train. Dégagez la voie." The man pointed, indicating that they were going to back the train down the pier . . . It was an opportunity, if his luck held.

The railroad workers walked out into the thoroughfare along the quay, motioning for traffic to stop. There was a heavy clank as the slack went out of the couplings and the air brake cleared its throat with a hiss. The line of boxcars began to back slowly toward the pier.

Mike Fowler was in luck; the men with the Opel had parked and gotten out, but they were on the far side of the tracks. One of them had a powerful build that looked familiar but a bandage like a pirate's eyepatch obscured much of his face.

One, two, three railcars rumbled past, and Mike began to walk, pacing the train. Canvas-sided lorries and horse carts moved out of the way. The people on either side of the dock were forced more tightly into the space between the tracks and the warehouses. He looked around; he had lost sight of the two men ahead of him. That was not good, but he dared not slow down.

Mike checked off the numbers above the doors. It looked like he had about a hundred yards to go . . .

Then came the prolonged blast of a ship's horn. There was no time left.

Mike Fowler broke into a run. He cut off a man with a hand dolly, cleared the end of a truck carrying blocks of ice and racks of meat, and dodged around a cursing Frenchman like a football player who had just received an unexpected pass.

"Halt!" the bandaged man from the Opel shouted. Over the bed of a flatcar Fowler could now tell it was Heinrich Hartmann, last seen a little more than a day ago in a blood-spattered hallway back in Spain. Hartmann raised a pistol but was cut off by the slowly rolling tank car that was next in line.

Mike was almost there, almost to the door he needed. Expecting a bullet in the back, he made it into the echoing dimness of the warehouse—and came to a dead stop.

The athletic young man with the windbreaker was just inside the doorway, crouched and ready to take him. His companion was shaking the folded raincoat off his arm to reveal a Walther P38.

Fowler leaped to one side, palmed the sap, and swung, chopping with its thin edge across the muscles of the gunman's bicep. The man gasped and dropped the pistol. He staggered back, his face white with shock. The one in the windbreaker grabbed at Fowler from behind, but the Gladstone got in his way. Mike turned with the momentum of his blow, twisting inside the shoulder strap. He blocked a punch, shifted his heel behind his attacker's foot, and smashed the base of his palm into the man's nose. The German grabbed at him, and they went down together. But as he fell Fowler brought up a knee. It smashed into the man's diaphragm, the breath exploded out of him, and ribs broke.

Fowler never stopped moving. He rolled to his feet. The guy in the argyle sweater was scuttling after the gun. Fowler swung the sap backhand across one side of the man's head and then, as he went down, forehand across the other.

"Mon Dieu!" There were exclamations as the warehouse workers turned to stare at the sudden violence.

Fowler didn't look back, didn't worry about the men or the gun. He knew the damage a properly wielded blackjack could do. He ran out of the warehouse on the far side. Across the wharf two men from the MS *Orna* had just begun to winch up the collapsible stairs leading to the deck. At the bow a tug was churning the debris-flecked water, edging the ship back, away from the pier.

Mike jumped, grabbing the folding stairway and pulled himself onto it just as Heinrich Hartmann appeared in the warehouse door. There was an instant where it took all of Fowler's self-control not to draw the Remington and attempt to kill Hartmann on the spot. He could see the German was caught in the same dilemma; his pistol held half-concealed at his side. But a shooting now would solve little. It would not allow Hartmann to discover where Voss had disappeared to, and it would turn Fowler's getaway into an exploration of the French justice system.

Fowler relaxed. Then he lifted one hand in an ironic wave. Maybe next time, he thought. Maybe next time I'll have a clear shot and no witnesses.

"Hey, you! What are you doing there?" An officer frowned at him from the railing.

Fowler clambered up the stairs toward the deck. As he reached the top, he pulled a business card from his vest pocket.

"Mike Fowler. I represent Sistemas Militar. I am going to need to accompany my cargo."

He was safe. This ship carried over half a million dollars' worth of goods that were being sold by Sistemas Militar Internacional S.L. or International Military Systems, a company owned, courtesy of a minor manipulation of Spanish law, by Anton Andreas Voss and Michael Fowler. The cargo was made up of one million rounds of ammunition, seven Austin K2 ambulances, an assortment of surplus medical supplies, and five hundred tons of steel chevron-type track units for the M4 Sherman tank.

It would be a week before they made port. He could rest, gather his wits, and come up with some kind of plan. The one thing he would certainly need to do was to have his story straight when he arrived. He might be getting himself into a whole new sort of trouble. Only time would tell.

The men chasing him were Germans, part of an organization that seemed to have the capacity to influence politicians and private businesses all over the world. They were, not to put too fine a point on it, Nazis. Calling themselves the Brotherhood or the Invisible Reich, they had lost the war but somehow won the peace. There was one place, however, they could not go, a place where they were deaf and blind . . .

Above him a flag fluttered and snapped in the wind. White and blue with a star and stripes. It was the flag of Israel.

CHAPTER 2

SPAIN,

two months earlier . . .

MIKE FOWLER WAS not a philosopher. He had been hired as muscle, a man who had no qualms about using violence and a willingness to accept the consequences. Because of his extensive knowledge of weaponry Voss had eventually made him a partner. In the sunny days before the attack on Pearl Harbor, Fowler had been a Gunner's Mate, trained in the use and maintenance of everything from handguns to artillery. But, first and foremost, his responsibility was to watch Anton Voss's back.

His abilities had been tested not long after they met. The two of them had been jumped by a gang of thugs in the back alleys of Inchon. Their attackers had thought them foolish enough to have been carrying the proceeds from the sale of a shipment of refurbished Japanese machine guns.

The four Koreans had surrounded them, and Voss pivoted to defend their rear. "Kill them!" he ordered.

Fowler did. The men carried blades and clubs. Fowler had a V-42 commando knife. Voss had a leather briefcase he could use as a shield. When it was over, Mike lay on the ground, bleeding from seven wounds but surrounded by the bodies of their enemies.

Anton had carried him halfway across the port that night, forcing a Korean doctor out of bed in order to save his life.

Anton Andreas Voss was tall, well past sixty, with thinning hair and cold gray eyes. He rarely spoke about his time in the military, but Mike knew he had been an officer in the Kaiserliche Marine, the German navy of World War I. He claimed to have sat out the last conflict in a technical position at the Reichspost. However, it was hard to imagine him sorting mail; the man was a predator and watching him stalk a business opportunity made Mike glad they had fought in different wars, in different decades, and on different sides of the earth.

After the surrender of Germany and Japan, the world was rocked by a wave of expanding and collapsing empires. The Soviet Union had immediately moved to dominate the war-ravaged territories east of what Winston Churchill called the Iron Curtain. Simultaneously, in Asia, Africa, and the Middle East, the grip of the old European empires began to weaken. It was a time when entire populations could taste both freedom and fear. The future was suddenly torn between the forces of communism and capitalism, totalitarianism and democracy. Many believed it might descend into an existential struggle, fought beneath the looming cloud of atomic annihilation.

But the great game of the Cold War played out on many fronts. Although England, France, the United States, and Russia all possessed nuclear devices, the spectacular power of this technology, and the potential for deadly radioactive fallout, limited its ability to express political nuance. Traditional small arms and artillery remained the primary weapons in the struggles that ravaged the disintegrating colonies of an exhausted Europe.

The world was awash in the leftovers of war, so for Anton Voss, Mike Fowler, and many other small-time arms brokers, there was a good income to be made supplying the factions fighting for either freedom or repression. Although Asia was occasionally a lucrative market, it was far from Europe. The Middle East was dominated by the major players, governments and corporations so large that the public often forgot they also dealt in armaments. North Africa, however, was conveniently close to Barcelona, and its conflicts simmered at just the right temperature to provide a continual income for independent contractors like Sistemas Militar.

Among the native Algerians, there was the Front de Libération Nationale, or FLN. On the other side were, of course, the French army, the police, and a variety of unofficial militias including the secretive La Main Rouge: the Red Hand. These paramilitaries had the backing of a syndicate of French politicians and businessmen who wanted a deniable source of weaponry for their comrades across the Mediterranean. Early in their career, Voss and Fowler brokered a deal between certain contacts in Spain who were liquidating stockpiles of weapons and the French syndicate.

They were in the midst of their third transaction when the syndicate suddenly refused to continue the payments. Something had gone awry and, as the weakest link in the chain, Fowler and Voss had been chosen to take the fall. Caught short between the Spanish seller demanding what they were rightfully owed and the French buyer intent on hijacking the guns, Voss acted coolly and without hesitation.

He started by obtaining a large and frighteningly expensive loan from a pair of American mobsters based in Cuba. With that in hand Voss paid his suppliers and delivered all the guns, grenades, and ammunition to the French colonials, whether or not they had been paid for. Then he opened negotiations with the FLN and any other anti-French militia that could rub two francs together.

The Frenchmen were apoplectic. This time they threatened Voss with action by the Red Hand. Feared across North Africa, the infamous group of procolonial commandos was rumored to have been organized by SDECE, the French intelligence service.

But Voss had prepared for this move, too. Not a week after he received the warning, a series of anonymous telephone calls was placed to the members of the French syndicate. The caller informed each recipient how to locate an explosive device that had been cunningly hidden in their car, home, or office. One charge had even been placed in the bed of the mistress kept by a certain member of the Assemblée Nationale. None of the bombs had been armed—in fact all their trigger mechanisms had been clearly rendered inoperable. After each discovery the caller generously offered to withhold lessons in bomb making for all of the syndicate's North African enemies.

The payments resumed and, in a particularly worldly and French manner, the entire episode was put behind them. Mike Fowler had never done much breaking and entering, but he had been trained by the best the United States government had to offer when it came to infiltration, reconnaissance, and explosives . . . and he *was* a quick study.

The loan from the gangsters had been a curse all on its own, and the day it was paid off both Fowler and Voss breathed a sigh of relief. However, it did allow them to move from being middlemen, or brokers who made deals by connecting buyer to seller, to being dealers with warehouses full of their own inventory and the luxury of doing business on their own terms.

The new arrangement worked especially well because Voss had demonstrated an unerring ability to locate misplaced or poorly documented stores of high-quality weapons and other surplus. Occasionally what he had for sale was not even hardware, but information. In the mid-1950s a file of material on field-effect transistors, the prewar work of a German physicist, had quietly sold to an American company preparing for a patent application. That sale had allowed Voss and Fowler to pay their debts and to choose a better class of customer. Since then, they had auctioned more once-secret technology to various industrialists. Anton Voss was a man who understood the value of even the most obscure pieces of information.

One night, not too long before everything in their world went to hell, Mike Fowler brought a briefcase full of paperwork to his partner's favorite café. The new government in Tunisia was making a large purchase of guns and ammunition, and there were several contracts and letters of credit to be reviewed and signed.

In Barcelona a man was known by the café, bar, or restaurant he frequented. For many, these establishments functioned as both office and social club. Voss wasn't particularly social, and most of his business was conducted at the small factory complex the company owned in the Sant Martí district. However, he liked to observe the ebb and flow of humanity and he seemed to be particularly interested when professors from the Universitat de Barcelona gathered at the nearby tables to discuss science, politics, and the ever-changing state of the world.

Mike knew that his partner could have called himself *Doctor* Anton Voss. A diploma from Ruprecht Karl University occasionally surfaced as he shuffled through the stacks of paper on his desk, and his shelves were filled with dog-eared editions of scientific journals, most of them specializing in physics.

Education, especially at a prestigious university, counted for a good deal among both Germans and Spaniards. That his degree went unmentioned meant it was probably something Voss hoped would be forgotten. Even for its adopted citizens Barcelona was a city of secrets, and the past was often a package best left unopened.

Once they had finished with the documents, Mike and Anton sat over coffee and watched the traffic as it passed along the Gran Via. Even after more than a decade of working together Mike was never quite sure what made the older man tick. Anton Voss lived alone and was cautious in his personal relationships. The number of people he spent time with, unrelated to business, could be counted on one hand. Beyond the borders of their divided fatherland, Germans were often looked upon with suspicion. For the most part the only company they trusted was one another. Voss took his isolation even more seriously; he seemed to avoid his countrymen most of all.

Before they cleared the table to sign the contracts Fowler noticed that Voss had been drawing something in a small spiral-bound notebook. His engraved silver cigarette case was open on the table and at first Mike assumed Anton had been doodling copies of the elaborate art deco designs that covered its interior. But that was not exactly it—the casually drawn arrows and squiggles included numbers and symbols. It was hard to tell because the ring of moisture from the bottom of a glass had soaked through two of the sheets of paper.

"What's that?" Fowler asked.

"These?" Voss tore off the pages and wadded them into a ball. "They are nothing. A type of notation developed by scientists before the war. Wentzel and Stueckelberg were their names . . . a similar system is now promoted by Richard Feynman, an American physicist." He used the crumpled paper to mop the table, the ink running into a dirty gray blur.

"The conversation at the next table . . . it had me revisiting the past," Voss went on, describing how the university professors had been discussing quantum mechanics, the strange behavior of electrons, and the great men of science. The important part, the aspect he had found most interesting, had been a particular "thought experiment."

A cat was placed in a steel box along with a capsule of poison. Under certain circumstances the capsule might be broken. However, since it was unknown whether or not this had happened, the cat theoretically existed in a state that was both living and dead, at the same time. At least this was supposed to be the case—so long as the box remained closed, and the cat unexamined.

The idea seemed intentionally ridiculous, and Mike said as much.

Voss took out a Chesterfield before tucking his cigarette case away. The flat lenses of his round steel glasses reflected the lamplight, making his eyes invisible.

"Yes," he said. "It is just a story, an analogy. There are several levels. One illustrates the concept of these simultaneous states, 'superpositions,' and how they resolve themselves into a single outcome. Another is to suggest that what may be true at the level of the atomic particle is clearly foolish if you are talking about anything as large, and complex, as an animal."

Voss leaned back on the fading cushions, clearly confident in his opinions. "What they do not realize is this: the size of the object is unimportant. It is the quality of the isolation. The real question is not about the cat . . . it is about the *box*."

Mike wasn't sure if he entirely understood what Voss was talking about. He also wasn't sure that Voss knew more than the professors from a university established before Columbus set sail for the New World. He did know one thing, however. Unknown and unstoppable forces were always lurking just over the horizon. At any moment, a man might be consigned to one existential state or another without even realizing it.

And as a soldier, he sympathized with the cat.

The first time Mike Fowler had truly thought about the power of unforeseen events was on the second Monday in December 1941. Early that morning he had been dragged out of his bunk, along with a half dozen petty officers, and hustled across San Diego Bay to a gigantic PB2Y flying boat. No mention was made of where they were going, but all of them had just completed a one-month course in the use of diving gear aboard the submarine rescue vessel USS *Ortolan*. On Sunday he had been just another twenty-year-old sailor playing softball; by Monday the whole nation was at war with the Empire of Japan.

Pearl Harbor was a smoking ruin, its defenders still so gripped by the fever of battle that his plane had diverted to the other side of the island to avoid antiaircraft fire. Within days he was alone with his breath in a copper Mark V helmet. The dead drifted like silent commas in the dark corridors of the sunken ships.

He learned to overcome his fear and disgust, to ease them on their journey, gently passing them along to the burial crews. His heart cried out to these men, his decaying brothers-in-arms. In the night he dreamed that he could bring them back from the depths and give them new life, repairing their bodies as he had the ships in which they had once served.

Over the year that followed Fowler and the growing crew of divers raised three battleships. The work was dangerous, and they had made mistakes, but in the end those ships had taken their vengeance. In the final chapter of Mike Fowler's military career, he had watched as two of them, floating fortresses wrapped in the smoke of their gigantic guns, fired at enemy positions on Okinawa.

By then he had volunteered for the Amphibious Scouts and Raiders, a reconnaissance outfit that was rapidly evolving into the navy's Underwater Demolition Teams. In doing so he traded an intimacy with Pearl Harbor's dead for the immediate possibility of sharing their fate. Armed with only a commando knife, a notebook, and his skill at observing while remaining unobserved, he had swum ashore in the dark hours before three amphibious landings.

Crawling out of the water on a lonely beach wondering if he was going to trigger a mine or cross the sights of a Japanese machine gun made a man wonder about the narrow difference between the living and the dead. Treading water a mile offshore as dawn broke, fearing that he had somehow missed the boat that was supposed to pick him up, produced the same question. The less you knew about the mine or the machine gun or the missing boat, the more isolated you were, and the tighter that box became.

Mike Fowler had come a long way from those days. The world of arms merchants was full of colorful, and shady, characters. Voss, however, insisted they cultivate the opposite image, that of low-key success and reliability. Fowler had a modest savings account in a Swiss bank and, more important, 25 percent of the company was his.

For the most part, it was a good life.

And yet Mike chafed under the burden of office work and mild success. He could not forget the rush of bringing death and destruction to his enemies, of pitting himself against impossible odds and emerging alive. It was a feeling he had tried to leave behind, but it still beckoned to him in secret ways. And it had nearly gotten him killed the night Anton's mysterious past came calling, the night that became the turning point in both their lives.

Three to four times a week, in all but the worst weather, Mike skipped dinner and went for a run and a swim. From his building in the old merchant's quarter of La Ribera he took a meandering six-mile route. He dodged his way along the bustling thoroughfares, detoured down narrow alleys where Roman soldiers had once stood guard, and crossed dim and hidden plazas where the fragments of Fascist bombs still scarred the ancient walls.

From the towering Christopher Columbus monument Fowler turned north along the waterfront, the rubber soles of his trainers nearly silent on the damp stone. He zigzagged through the narrow apartment blocks of La Barceloneta, where the fishermen lived, a shadow fleeting and shifting beneath lines of laundry stretched from balcony to balcony like patchwork banners.

Slowing to a jog he made it to the end of the seafront promenade. This was a wide elevated walkway made of concrete and recently constructed as a symbol of the city's economic rebirth. It ended, abruptly and ironically, in the sandhill slums of Somorrostro.

The maze of block and driftwood shanties stretched up the beach. It was bracketed by the hulking silhouettes of cylindrical gasometers and the railyards with their forest of signal gantries. The area was home to Gypsies and pickpockets, but also to many of the workers who found employment in the factories along the coast.

At the tideline, Fowler slipped out of his shoes and sweat-soaked shirt, then waded into the low surf. He started off with a slow backstroke to keep his face above the polluted water along the shore. Once he was far enough out, he rolled over and slid into a distance-eating crawl.

The moon was rising over the dark sea and its light offered a point of reference, allowing him to ignore the diver's compass on his wrist. Once the dull glow of Barcelona and the twinkling of lights along the coastal range were out of sight, the moon and the radium dial of the compass would guide him back. If he came back. That was always the question.

There were pieces of his life he never spoke of, like the last days with his father, who had briefly made a good living running whiskey up from Mexico. Or a particular clandestine operation just before the end of the war. It had been a nightmare of death and destruction on a bleak, scrub-covered sandbar in the South China Sea. A place called Itu Aba. Out of the handful of men, only two, Mike and an Australian commando, had survived.

These long midnight swims, however, were Mike's last small secret. Voss, as cool a customer as he was, would be disturbed to learn how far his partner pushed himself. How much he risked to remember what it had been like when the closeness of death had given meaning to life.

Fowler swam until the sea chilled him to the bone. He swam until the moon soared higher in the sky and he knew he was at the point of no return. This was the test; this was the deadly game he played. Could he make it back to shore? He wasn't sure.

It was a long cold struggle, his mind closed, his movements robotic. From every direction water sucked the warmth from his body, a liquid vampire more dangerous than a shark. Finally a swell lifted him, and he saw flames, something burning on the beach just north of the promenade. He dug in, knowing that even when his body begged to give up there was always a hidden reserve of strength. If the Teams' hell week taught you anything, it was that.

A wave tumbled him onto the sand, grit and salty water rushing back into his nose and mouth. He coughed, spat, and stood. Another wave slapped him on the thighs. Then hands, hard bony hands, grasped his arm. A woman.

"Vingui! Si us plau vingui." She urged him on in muttered Catalan, pulling him from the surf toward a bonfire built just feet from where he had left his clothes and shoes.

There were three of them, not just the old woman. One was a familiar-looking middle-aged man; the third was a girl, young and pregnant. They wrapped him in a coarse, patched blanket, handed him his towel, and sat him down, shivering, close to the fire.

"The young one, she saw you go in the water. We are in the first house." The man gestured at the line of rock-walled hovels. Each not much larger than the place where Mike had grown up, a driftwood cabin on a beach just north of the Mexican border.

"Th-thank you." Mike could barely make out his own voice. He could see they had propped his sweater on a piece of driftwood so it would be warmed by the flames.

The old woman spoke rapidly in Catalan. The man struggled to translate, using both English and Spanish. "Señor, we were worried. We see you come to swim. So many nights. Perdóname pero . . . I—I think 'usted está loco' . . . you are crazy. You are gone a long time, and she is worried."

They were quiet then, comfortably sitting in the dark. The girl got up and came back after a few minutes with hot coffee, two tin cups and a mug with a cracked handle and the fading logo of a hotel on the side. Mike's shivering subsided.

"We worked for you before. In the summer. Me and her." He indicated the old woman and she cackled and mimed using a needle and thread. "She repaired uniforms. I was finishing the metal on Mauser rifles." The man grinned. "A good gun, but not *too* good . . . When I was young the Falangistas shoot at me many times, but always they miss!"

Safe and warm, Mike slipped into his clothes. He stood, his legs finding their strength, his heart and breathing calm. He looked down at the odd little group that had gathered, long after midnight, to help a man they barely knew.

"Thank you, again." There was little more that could be said. He had no money with him and no confidence that they would even accept such a coarse form of gratitude.

"De nada."

"Any time you need a job. You come and find me. Anytime."

The old lady toasted him with her dented metal cup. The girl held her belly and watched with large, dark eyes. The man shook his hand then turned away to pull the unburned ends of wood from the fire.

Mike walked home, a strange, hollow feeling at the base of his throat. It was an odd thing to realize you finally had a home, yet one so far from the country and culture of your birth.

It was a feeling that was not destined to last very much longer.

A distant ringing woke him. The room was dark, and Fowler lay in bed for a moment hoping the noise would stop. He had been dead to the world, unable to remember even crawling between the sheets. The ringing continued. Mike twisted, looking at his watch. It was 3:12 A.M. He staggered out of bed, through the door of his apartment, and down the stairs to the tile niche that held the telephone he shared with Aleixandre Porras, the accountant who was the third partner in Sistemas Militar. In the dim light he saw the door to the hallway crack open. Aleixandre's wife scowled at him . . . but then she closed the door, going back to bed. No one *she* knew would be so impolite as to call at this hour.

"Hello?" he said into the mouthpiece.

There was an intake of breath, then silence, only the sound of an open line, then something else. Tap. Tap. Tap.

"Hello!" He tried again, but he was afraid of what he was going to hear. He clutched the Bakelite handset.

Tap. Tap. Tap.

Suddenly wide awake and alert, he wasn't sure how to respond, what word to use . . .

"Okay," he said.

Mike Fowler bolted back up the stairs. He snapped on a light and ripped open the burlwood armoire that filled one end of his bedroom. Quickly dressing, he laced up a pair of boots and pulled on a leather jacket. He slid a knife, a short-bladed Alaskan Skinner with a slimmed-down handle, into a sheath that fit inside his waistband behind his belt. He had a snub-nose Smith & Wesson .38

stashed inside the artfully veneered case of his bedroom radio, but the Spanish authorities frowned on firearms. Mike didn't know what sort of trouble he was walking into, and he didn't intend to make it worse than it already was. The knife looked like an oddly modified piece of junk, but it was razor sharp and could be counted on to do a ferocious amount of damage.

The three taps on the telephone were a distress call. It meant Voss was at the office and needed help . . . help he could not discuss.

At the foot of the stairs Mike propped open the door to the alley. Then he rocked his BMW R68 off its center stand and muscled it down a single step and outside.

The building was on a corner, with some of its rooms above a small plaza. Mike had a careful look around. The tide was out and the stink from the drying sewers grated in his nostrils. No one was in sight in any direction. He pushed the motorcycle into the plaza before kicking it to life. Finally on the move, he made it to Calle de los Almogávares and opened the bike up, roaring over the railroad tracks into the Sant Martí district, headed for Poblenou.

The "new town" was an industrial area built up during Barcelona's manufacturing renaissance in the nineteenth century. All along the coast tall brick smokestacks reached for the sky and walled factory compounds were interspersed with low apartment buildings and small shops.

Mike switched streets, edging nearer to the shore. When he was close, he cut the engine and headlight and coasted, braking to a stop a half block away, near a narrow passage between buildings closed by a gate of rusting bars. After using his keys to open the lock, he rolled the bike inside. Walking to the corner, Mike could see down the streets to the north and west of Sistemas Militar.

As with many of Barcelona's aging factories, the place was built like a fortress. An entire city block, it was enclosed by a wall, fifteen feet high and built of soot-blackened brick. The main entrance, a carved limestone arch containing two huge wooden doors, appeared to be closed and locked, as it should be.

All was quiet. Wisps of fog drifted up the street. The only sound was the dripping of the brass faucet on the public fountain by the corner. Inside the wall, at the far end of the three-story office building, a dim light reflected in the mist. A lamp was burning in the office used by Anton Voss.

Mike did not try to approach the main gate. He returned to the passageway, unlocked a steel-wrapped door, and went down a narrow set of wooden steps. One of the great benefits of the old factory was that it included an air raid shelter built during the Civil War. The brick-lined tunnel was more than a hundred yards long and ran under the street and the first line of shops. Voss had seen its potential as an underground shooting range, a place to safely test weapons unbeknownst to the city officials. It also served as a hidden way in—and out—of the factory compound.

At the bottom of the stairs was another door, then a bulletproof backstop made of old tires packed with sand. Clambering past this barrier, Mike jogged down the length of the dank gallery to the concrete staircase behind the shooting benches. Using yet another key, he let himself out into the portico that protected the entrance to the office building.

The compound was silent and dark. The walls of the warehouses were covered with a meandering growth of ivy and sharp-thorned bougainvillea. Past the tall smokestack of the old powerhouse and the other centrally placed storage sheds, the south end of the property was full of military vehicles and artillery parked against the wall in tight rows. In the night it was a shadowed mass of camouflage paint and slanting barrels.

The security office, just inside the main gate, was closed and unlit. Rafeeq Farkhani, an ex-soldier from Spanish Morocco, should have been on guard. Also missing was the battered bicycle he usually rode to work.

Keeping to the shadows, Mike stepped away from the L-shaped building and looked up. The only rooms with any light were those in Voss's third-floor office. A slight breeze shifted the leaves of the palm trees that grew in the out-of-the-way corners of the compound.

The muffled slam of a pistol shot broke the silence. Then another. The two shots came from within the building, from behind those lighted windows!

Mike lunged for the door; caution forgotten. It opened, *unlocked*, under his hand. He sprinted down the main hall, past display racks of small arms on one side and cannon on the other. A wide travertine stairway led to the second floor, and an art deco doorway of brass and stained glass closed off access to the third . . . but *it* wasn't locked either. Mike slowed; he was making altogether too much noise. The top floor was a shooting gallery—he had designed it that way.

Across the landing at the top of the stairs was Mike's office, closed and locked. Mike dropped down and peered around the railing, looking back toward Anton's office. The door at the end of the hallway was cracked open three or four inches and light spilled out onto the tiled floor.

Mike stood and moved forward as quickly and quietly as he could. His right thumb slid around the slim handle of his knife, but he didn't draw the blade. He gave the door a gentle push, looking into the office through the widening gap.

The room was paneled, with a high ceiling and tall windows. Close to the door was a mirror-backed bar. At the other end was a heavy desk with banks of glass-doored shelves and wooden file cabinets against the walls. In the center, two chairs and a settee flanked a coffee table. Slumped in one of the chairs was a stranger, a short heavyset man in a black suit. Standing over the man was Anton Voss, a SIG automatic held in his right hand.

Voss turned. The gun came up.

Mike Fowler and Anton Voss stared at each other for a long moment. Voss appeared completely calm but a crackling energy emanated from him, an energy that brought Mike to a dead stop.

Mike knew what he was looking at: a man keyed up for a battle that had ended too abruptly. A man whose brain might understand that the need for violence was over, but whose body was still ready to fight.

Then the muzzle of the pistol wavered, lowered. The safety snapped on.

Mike relaxed. He stepped closer. The man in the chair had been shot twice. Once in the heart, the second time in the head. Mike turned.

"Mr. Voss?" he said. "What the *hell* . . . ?"

CHAPTER 3

Voss set the pistol on the edge of the desk then walked around behind it. He slid a drawer closed and sat down.

"Thank you for coming."

To Mike it sounded like the sort of thing a man might say at the end of a routine business meeting. The detached tone would have been amusing except a man was dead and Fowler suspected their troubles were just beginning.

"We are going to have to clean this up," Voss said.

The body sprawled in the chair, blood dripping into the carpet. It looked as if Voss had unexpectedly taken the pistol from a drawer and fired. No . . . Mike could see two ejected shells. From their position it seemed Voss had walked around the front of the desk before he shot the seated man.

"What happened?"

"He attempted to blackmail me."

"To do what?"

"That . . . is a long story. It will have to wait."

After a moment it was clear that Voss was going to say nothing more. Fowler silently cursed. Anton Voss was every bit the Prussian gentleman. He couldn't be pressed to speak or act until he had precisely calculated how he wanted to proceed. Mike often wondered if that quality had anything to do with coming out on the losing end of two devastating wars, but he wisely kept his own counsel.

"Okay." Mike was already cataloging the scene and considering their options. His employer, his partner, his mysterious mentor, had murdered someone in cold blood. It was a first, but it was not a problem that couldn't be handled.

"We might be able to make it look like self-defense. We could give him a weapon. You would have to come up with a story for the police."

Voss shook his head. "No. This must be a secret. No one knows he was here."

"No one?" Fowler could imagine a list that started with a wife and children and ended with cab drivers.

"No one in Spain. Possibly no one at all. We have a few days at least and, if luck is with us, much longer."

Mike looked at the clock. "Where is Rafeeq?" The watchman's replacement would come in at 7:30 A.M.

"I sent him home before I called you. This had to be a private meeting."

It wasn't long until dawn so they were going to have to move quickly. Mike went down the hall and unlocked his office. He dug a pair of gloves and a shop smock out of the closet. When he got back, he found Anton going through the inside pockets of the dead man's suit.

"Mr. Voss!"

The older man looked up. For a moment it seemed like he might try to hide what he was doing, try to slip what he was holding back under the man's lapel. It was a thickly folded piece of paper, a map in a colored card-stock folder. The first nine-millimeter bullet had punched a hole in the top and blood had soaked through the outer layers.

Mike pulled on the gloves. "You shouldn't touch any of this!"

"Get me an envelope."

"Look, whatever that is, it's too dangerous to keep it."

"Michael, in this case it is dangerous *not* to keep it. Now get me an envelope!"

Mike took a large manila envelope from its box on a shelf and Voss dropped the map inside. Voss turned the dial of the safe that squatted on the floor behind his desk. He slid the envelope inside and relocked the door.

Mike Fowler bent over the body, awkwardly searching with gloved fingers. "So, who is he?" he asked.

"Hanno Wuttke. A policeman. I knew him in Berlin before the war."

Mike pulled a mottled green folder from Wuttke's other breast pocket. He flipped it open. Wuttke might have been a policeman three decades earlier, but now he was something a good deal more dangerous.

"He's Stasi!" The Ministry for State Security was East Germany's brutal version of the FBI.

"Yes, I know. That is why I believe we have some time."

"Sir . . . maybe you had better tell me exactly what that means." Anton's terse replies weren't much help.

"He did not bring any backup . . . He was confident his position would protect him."

Mike left it at that. The situation stank to high heaven but trying to drag the details out of Voss was just wasting valuable time. "Get me another of those envelopes," he said. "Is there any reason we can't use your boat?"

Voss shook his head.

Fowler glanced around the room, assessing the situation. "Okay. Go down to the shop and get a tarp. I don't want to make a mess when we move him."

They took the body, the chair, and the rug. The pistol, both ejected shells, and Wuttke's ID were sealed in an envelope. Everything was wrapped carefully in tarps and loaded into the back of the Land

Rover 107 they used as a shop truck. It wasn't a clean sweep, but it was a start.

There was also the issue of the map Voss had put in the safe. Obviously, that was valuable, but it was a damning thing to have around even if it was locked up, blood-soaked bullet hole and all.

Just before Mike pulled the Land Rover out of the main gate Voss used the telephone to get Aleixandre Porras out of bed and tell him to come in and open up before the morning security officer came on duty. Like anyone who had survived the Civil War and the early days of Franco, Porras knew how to keep his mouth shut, even when he didn't know what was going on.

They drove carefully. Fog had now engulfed the entire coast and caused the headlights to blare back into Fowler's eyes. His hands strangled the wheel, and he fought the desire to mash the accelerator to the floor. He knew how early Barcelona's fishermen tended to set out. He could only hope that the lack of visibility would discourage them for an hour or two.

Finally, they pulled up on a lip of wet stone. Fowler killed the lights. He could just make out the forest of masts and lines where the yachts rested low in their slips. Squatting near the rear door, Voss helped him position Wuttke's tarp-wrapped body over his shoulder.

Mike staggered a bit then got his balance. He had always been strong but, after his evening run and the nearly disastrous swim, he wasn't sure if he was up to it. This was the critical moment, carrying a dead man the hundred yards or so down the slick and unsteady docks. If anyone got a close look at his burden it would be immediately obvious he wasn't struggling with a load of folded sails or anything else that made any sense.

They were in luck, however. By the time he got to the boat Mike was breathing in hard, fiercely controlled breaths. He unceremoniously dumped the body into the cockpit. It hit with a thud that made him shudder, and he and Voss looked at each other, each searching for words they couldn't find.

"I will ready her for sea," Voss told him. "You get the rest and park the truck."

The engine burbled to life and Fowler cast off, pushing the boat free of its moorings. Voss guided her as she drifted back, and then opened the throttle just enough to give her headway.

Sigune was a racing yacht, a flush deck cutter built in '28 by Anker & Jensen to compete in the International Eight Metre class. In the early days of Sistemas Militar she had seen hard use, allowing them to travel inconspicuously while making deals along the African coast. In the hands of a master seaman like Anton Voss she was a fast and agile craft.

Voss guided her south through the harbor using some trick of perception or memory unknown to Fowler. He seemed to sense the center of the channel and to unconsciously compensate for the force of the tide. They ran up a minimal amount of sail, but kept the engine idling, ready in case they encountered inbound shipping.

Once they had put several miles behind them, Mike cut the tarp open and wrapped the corpse in a length of chain. The mist was lightening and the wind was picking up, so they added more sail. Mike wanted to get out beyond any current that might cause their cargo to drift back toward the coast should it somehow come free of its shackles.

They emerged from the fog and Voss brought her about, tacking to the east. As they heeled over, he and Mike rolled the body of Hanno Wuttke over the side. The chair, rug, pistol, blood-spattered smock, gloves, and empty shells followed. Last of all, Mike tore the Stasi ID booklet into shreds and let them blow off to leeward. He hoped it would be the last they ever heard of the unfortunate agent, but he doubted they would be so lucky.

With the breeze picking up and visibility all the way to the southern horizon, Anton Voss tightened his sails and pushed *Sigune* to the limit, making her fly though the waves and spray. He tacked and tacked again, working the wind like the naval officer he once had been. Mike wanted to demand answers, but he knew he would get nothing until his partner had cleared his mind and made a plan for their future.

Like any good soldier, Mike Fowler knew how to make the most of his time: he went below, rolled into a bunk, and went to sleep. Back on deck Voss continued his mad tango with the wind and the waves, an Ahab in a three-piece suit and striped tie. But fast as she was, *Sigune* was just an aging sailboat; she couldn't outrun either the past or the future.

Mike woke to the smell of fish frying and the feeling of calmer seas. Voss stood in the galley at the foot of the ladder. He was in his shirtsleeves and carefully turning sliced filets of mackerel in a blackened skillet. Out past the sliding hatch Mike could see that the tiller was tied off and a fishing pole was still trailing a line in the water. Voss set out the pan of fish and a pot of heavily seasoned rice. He handed Mike a knife and a fork and the two of them ate directly from the cookware.

When they were done, Voss lit a cigarette and leaned back on the bench. "When you were a boy, did you ever read *Treasure Island*?"

Mike shook his head. Robert Louis Stevenson was one of those writers they pushed on you in school, but he had always been more interested in magazines like *Popular Mechanics* or *Outdoor Life*. By the time he was in his teens his days in the library were spent studying engines and electronics, things he often didn't understand until he had reread the books over and over again.

"Well, I will spare you the . . . literary allusions. There are no pirates in this story, just Nazis. Some of us were loyal to the end. But you have to ask, when is a war over? When is a soldier released from his obligations? To know exactly . . . ?" He shook his head. "It is hard enough when you are looking backward. At the time it was even more difficult."

Voss looked away, out the hatch. The fog had long ago burned off and the sky over the Spanish coast was blue and cloudless. Mike realized that he almost never heard Voss use the term "Nazi." Spain's expatriate Germans used other words, publicly skirting the distinction even though, in private, some of them were still known to one another by their political titles or what had been their military rank.

"So, the problem we have is a . . . 'treasure.' In the last days of the war, it was sent to South America by U-boat." Voss took a breath. "Twenty-three thousand, five hundred and . . . eighty-six kilograms of Reichsbank gold."

"That's—" Fowler started doing the math in his head but Voss already had the answer.

"Thirty million American dollars. It was to aid party members, and others, to escape. It was our mission to keep the dream alive, the dream of creating a *Fourth* Reich."

"Wait a minute . . . I thought you worked for the post office!" Mike was suddenly realizing how much of his partner's history he had taken for granted.

"Let us call it 'detached service.' Yes, I worked for the Reichspost. But you must understand, in Germany nothing was outside the war effort."

"So, this, uh, treasure . . . ?" The word felt awkward coming out of Mike Fowler's mouth. Voss was right, the whole idea had a theatrical aspect that separated it from reality.

"Do I know where it is?" Voss measured him with a careful glance. "That is the dangerous question."

Mike was tired of playing games. "Mr. Voss, we just dumped a dead Stasi agent over the side. After all these years, it's a little late to decide you don't trust me."

The older man looked away first. "I am pulled in many directions," he said quietly. "There is honor, my duty, my oath as an officer. People might question how any German can speak of these things. But when there is horror all around, a man has to discover what he stands for. I had to learn the difference between my country and my *government*, between our hopes and dreams, and the dark places they led us.

"There is also fear. What I know, it could be a death sentence. So, I am afraid. A man who is afraid to admit his fear is a fool and, ironically, also a coward."

Voss was quiet for a long moment and then sat up and squared himself to the table. "Those are my excuses. Now, I will tell you. Yes, I was there. There were a number of reasons why I had to go; much of it was because I had served in U-boats. The old U-boats from what we briefly called the Great War.

"We sailed for Argentina. We were told that our agents could unload the cargo, and no one would be the wiser. But the whole mission was ill-conceived. Once we arrived, the Argentine government—they were sympathetic to Germany but under pressure from the Allies, you see. They were afraid of being embarrassed by our presence. Your American navy was searching for us. So, we had to make another plan.

"We headed south for Tierra del Fuego. Have you ever studied a map of that coast? It is a labyrinth. A broken maze of passages, bays, islands. We were like the *Flying Dutchman*, a ship with no harbor.

"A fishing boat was sent to rendezvous with us. It was manned by true believers, Nazis who had lived in Argentina and Chile for many years. They imagined they were the future of the National Socialist cause.

"We located a—an Unterkunft Platze—a secret place, a hiding place. There was no consultation with anyone ashore. It was just the two boats, one crew exhausted by war, the other still idealistic . . . innocent. Stupid.

"We prepared the sub, and then we left it and its cargo on the bottom and started back to civilization. I have no idea where we were, the exact coordinates. Most of us had to remain below decks. It was dark, and cold. The weather was hellish. But, of course, this was also to maintain security.

"The plan turned into a disaster. Out of the crew of the U-boat and the fishing boat—only one other man made it to shore, and he lived but a few hours. They are all dead . . . all dead but me.

"Back in Germany there was such chaos, so many dead, displaced, or imprisoned. The old structures, they were torn apart, the authorities had fled or been discredited. There were things we had done, and things that had been done to us, all unspeakable . . . and so, few spoke of them. People did not ask for stories that no one wanted to hear.

"Of course, I had questions about the mission, but where would I go for answers? To the Americans? The British? One of these old blowhards who claims to once have been an important Nazi? Worst of all, should I go to those you and I both know are *still* Nazis?

"I decided to wait. They could come to me. I am not hiding. My name is on the door. But, you see, the secrecy surrounding this mission was extreme. I have waited fifteen years. Sometimes I thought I was the last one alive who knew anything at all."

Mike had become impatient as Voss told his story. "Sir, you need to tell me what went on with Wuttke. You said we have some time, but the Stasi aren't going to rest until they know what happened to their man. When they figure it out—and they won't need proof—they are going to come down on us like a ton of bricks."

"Herr Wuttke learned someone was searching for the U-boat, and he must have had some idea of what I had done during the war. He proposed that the two of us offer our services to those who were trying to find it. He did not intend to give me a choice."

Voss sighed and looked Fowler dead in the eyes. "You must understand, now that this game has started, it will not end. Some of what we know as the Cold War is real, some of it is manipulated. Forces within West German intelligence—General Gehlen's BND—play the CIA off against the KGB, always to the advantage of . . . other interests. In the East, many in the Ministry of State Security are also willing dupes. What one agency knows; the others will discover . . . if it pleases the puppet masters."

"Puppet masters!" Fowler frowned. "What in the world are you talking about?"

"Our Führer used to have delusions of the Jews as puppet masters, but this is not what I mean. Many look upon the Third Reich as an absolute dictatorship. They are blinded by Hitler, Hitler, the image of Hitler. One man; it is all *so* convenient. Well, that one man was everything they say and more. But alongside him there were . . . let us call them 'international supporters' and, more important, parallel structures of power. The most obvious of these was the SS, the Schutzstaffel. This was an elite military state within the confines of the German government and the German military. It had its own rules, its own ranks.

"But the SS is simply the most clear example. There were others, some that predated the Nazis. Old power, hereditary power, the secret power that always survives and thrives on chaos. There is a great deal of money in controlling change, controlling the process of history.

"More than a year before the end of the war it was accepted that Hitler, the Third Reich . . . even the concept of the state itself might be no longer useful. However, they saw a future for particular aspects of the National Socialist ideal, the fusion of government and industry, genetics, elite technocrats claiming to speak for the will of the people.

"Imagine a secret society whose members—some in business, some in other, more official, institutions—were dispersed throughout the globe . . . a hidden tribe making the most of their expertise, their connections. United by their old bonds of loyalty, possessing treasuries, patents, technology, investments, even entire financial institutions. They would become invaluable to their hosts and integrated into the fabric of every country. This time, they would remain obscure . . . behind the scenes, so to speak.

"The smart ones are not the obvious Nazis. They have given up the immature and overt symbolism. They call themselves by various names: Bruderschaft, the Brotherhood; Das Unsichtbare Reich, the Invisible Empire . . . I'm sure there are others."

Mike was suddenly aware they had probably touched the edges of this world several times. The whole idea was giving him a headache. "Sort of an *international* National Socialism?"

"Yes, yes. I am aware of the irony." Voss took a long drag, finishing his almost forgotten cigarette. "That U-boat and its cargo were part of their plans. I am almost certain these are the ones doing the searching. You've met some of them—"

"The hard cases from Madrid? All those old Nazis in Egypt?" In the past Voss and Fowler had dealt with a few notorious characters, once well-known members of the SS. There had been others, technicians and bureaucrats, who seemed more like corrupt middle-aged businessmen who had found a way to attend an unending convention, complete with belly dancers.

"They are the obvious ones, yes. Somewhat useful, supported out of a commendable sense of loyalty, but kept on the sidelines. There are others, less known but more powerful. Men whose reputations were carefully preserved."

"So, what can we do? Some of that Madrid crowd owe us favors. Could we make a deal?"

Voss was shaking his head. "Not one that I will survive."

The older man's choice of words got Mike's attention; Voss seemed sure the situation was dire. "Okay. How about CIA or MI6?"

"This is the same thing. They would want the gold, just as the Communists would. It is *gold*, very useful as a secret fund for covert operations. But none of the agencies will ever trust anyone not under their control. And it is too easy for, say . . . a pair of arms dealers to be killed or imprisoned."

Mike wanted to punch something. They had learned early on that the clandestine services might be just as quick to sacrifice their friends as they were their enemies.

Anton Voss leaned back, resting his head on the hull of the boat. The weight of the Mediterranean, of every ocean on earth, pressed against that thin layer of wood.

"We were in trouble before Wuttke ever arrived; we just did not know it." The older man closed his eyes. "I'm grateful to him for coming to tell me."

"I can move some money," Mike said. "We can be ready to run."

Anton Voss shook his head. "No. For me there is no more running. This has been like the Sword of Damocles. Every time I have met one of my countrymen I have wondered, 'Is this the one who will remember? Will I be forced to serve them again or will they kill me to keep their secret?' It is intolerable. I am going to solve this problem. It could be the last thing I do, but I am going to solve it."

"Okay. So, what are we going to do?"

"Not *we*. *My* fate is sealed. I'm going to try to locate the submarine and get there first. If I can remove and sell the gold before the people who are looking for it, or any of the intelligence services, can stop me . . . then it will cease to be an issue. On the other hand, if I am caught before I can complete the deal, I doubt I will live very long.

"*You*, however, have . . . options. You could stay here, try to keep what we have intact. There will be those who are sure you know my plans and they will use every ruse to damage the business. It will be a challenge: dealing with the finances, the banking, the lawyers." Voss examined him narrowly, as if this was some sort of negotiation, and he was about to win a deal point.

"Or?" Fowler said.

"Or we take this on together. We would be betting it all, my savings, the company assets, our lives. For me, this is all or nothing. You, however, must decide for yourself."

When they met, four years after the war, Mike had been diving for scrap with a ragtag crew of ne'er-do-wells in the South Pacific. He had been sunburnt, unshaven, and covered with sores from the primitive gear and the rusting, barnacle-covered, bombed-out wrecks they were salvaging. He and Voss had struggled to build a successful business. To go off and risk losing it now would be the height of foolishness. But . . .

"You are planning to salvage a submarine full of war loot, on the q.t., and you don't even know where it is? Mr. Voss, that's going to be damned near impossible!"

Voss shrugged. "Indeed. However, it will be less so if I have your help."

Mike Fowler stared at Anton Voss. Did he realize that life had become too easy, that some sinister desire called his younger partner out into the dark water in the dead of night? Mike cursed under his breath. Voss, generally cautious and calculating, had just hoisted the skull and crossbones and run out his guns. The man knew him, probably better than he knew himself.

"How deep?" Fowler asked. For a diver, that was always the first question.

CHAPTER 4

VOSS HEADED *SIGUNE* down the coast. If they ever needed an explanation for their brief absence, delivering the boat to the marina at Tarragona to have her hull cleaned and painted might suffice. As they carved their way through the light swells, Fowler did his best to enjoy the sparkling air and warm sunlight. He always approached ships and boats with a certain reluctance. They had a history of delivering him to places full of suffering and death.

Anton, on the other hand, was in his element. He lived for the freedom he found at sea, just himself and the interplay of hull and sails. He took pride in achieving a certain precision even as he slid into the harbor, bringing the boat about, directing Fowler when to drop the sails, and then allowing the last touch of momentum to deliver them to within jumping distance of the dock.

Once the negotiations for the work on *Sigune* were complete, Fowler and Voss walked back across the tracks and through the lower part of the ancient town. The day was ending, and shadows gathered in the narrow streets. Many of the shops had reopened after lunch and siesta, but only an occasional car or horse cart passed them as they walked toward the train station.

"We must get back and have a careful look at that map," Voss said. "I have no idea how Wuttke got it, but there were areas someone had marked, and they were dated. Whoever is searching is working their way down the Chilean coast from Puerto Montt, and they are methodically checking every possible anchorage. It seems they are very serious . . . but they have no idea where to look."

"Why Chile? You were supposed to deliver the sub to Argentina, right?"

"In that part of the world the best place to hide the U-boat was in a fjord. Almost all of them are on the Chilean side. A careful search of that coast could take them years, but we have an advantage. *I* know we were quite far south. I must do some research, there may be a better clue as to where we were . . . and I am sure I will remember the place when I see it."

"That would help. This idea is crazy enough as it is."

Voss paused at the curb in front of the long concrete block that was the Tarragona railroad station. He turned to face Fowler. "There is another thing: once we find it, we must be prepared to raise the U-boat to the surface."

"Raise it? Now *that* could get difficult." Mike had worked on the most extensive marine salvage project in history, but every crane, barge, air compressor, and water pump in the port of Honolulu and the Pearl Harbor Naval Shipyard had been available. The budget had been unlimited. "It doesn't make sense unless there is a very good reason."

"I can give you two: speed and safety. It will be faster. Fewer dives. There is also the fact that the boat has been extensively mined. Disconnecting the explosives and removing the cargo will be more quickly accomplished if it is dry and we have plenty of light."

"Alright. So, we have to deal with booby traps *and* getting into a pressurized boat without flooding it . . . Are there any other surprises?"

"These are not the things that worry me. I remember very well how the explosives were set, and demolition is a specialty of yours. In 1945 we left the boat with a plan in place that would allow us to return. It could be as easy as getting aboard and blowing the ballast tanks."

The station's public address system came to life with a crackle and hum, announcing that the train to Barcelona would soon be departing. Voss turned and motioned Fowler in the direction of the doors.

"I am much more concerned about obtaining the funds we will need without attracting attention. I am concerned about finding a government to take the gold off our hands, one that is corrupt enough yet won't simply try to kill us. You will need to find us a ship, and a salvage crew who can keep their mouths shut. Technical challenges can be overcome, it is the *people* that worry me."

Twenty minutes later the train rumbled north, the pantograph connecting the engine to the overhead wires striking sparks in the moist air. In the gathering darkness the ruined stone walls of Tarragona's Roman amphitheater loomed momentarily over the tracks, the crumbling arches choked with tall, cornlike Arundo reed. It was reputed to have been a place where gladiators and exotic animals had fought to the death for the amusement of the citizenry, but today it was just another outcropping of masonry to be photographed by tourists, a phase of history not yet buried by the more recent layers of the town.

Mike Fowler did not immediately get a look at Wuttke's map. He spent the next several days catching up with work and tightening security around the factory and the hillside home in Vallvidrera owned by Anton Voss.

The location of the three-story, turn-of-the-century villa was both a blessing and a curse. It was hard to find, on the inland side of the Collserola range and overlooking a disused reservoir surrounded by miles of wooded hillsides that reminded Fowler of his native Southern California. On the other hand, its very isolation made it vulnerable.

Mike had started carrying the Smith & Wesson .38 he usually kept in his apartment and Voss had already replaced the SIG automatic that had been thrown overboard from *Sigune* with three identical pistols. One went back into the drawer of his office desk, another was carried in a hidden holster that Fowler mounted under the seat of Voss's car, and the third he kept at his villa in the hills.

During the day, Mike began searching for any expensive lot of weaponry that might be for sale. Their best prospect was in Venezuela, which was selling off the last of its aging Mustang and Thunderbolt fighters. What Fowler needed was a cover, a story, one that in the small world of the arms trade would explain Voss moving money from one place to another. The deal would never go through, but the discussions would camouflage the transfer of enough cash to get their expedition off the ground.

Late at night, after their employees had gone home, Mike tore out the stretch of baseboard in Anton's office that contained the bullet hole and replaced it with an identical piece of millwork removed from an empty office down the hall. He used a stiff brush and cleaning solution on the floor to remove any lingering evidence of the crime. The bullet, recovered from the wall behind the baseboard, went into a pot of lead used for refinishing pitted rifle barrels. Within a few seconds it was part of a larger pool of silver metal, the only indication it had ever existed a rapidly dissipating whiff of smoke.

Years before, when Fowler had originally remodeled the compound, he had readied an escape route for Voss. Now Mike rigged an entirely different solution in case an attacker made it to the third floor.

After building several thick frames, he hung old promotional posters from the Belgian arms manufacturer Fabrique Nationale along the walls of the hall and the stairway. Mike also had the men in the woodshop build an oval crest with enough space behind it to hide an item about half the size of a hardback book. It was painted black with raised gold letters reading SMI . . . a bit gaudy, but it would serve its purpose. This he affixed to the front of the desk. Inside the kneehole, he set up a metal plate cut from the rear door of a Canadian armored truck. He ran hidden wires from each of his new pieces of decor to a series of switches under the rim near the right-hand drawer. If worst came to worst and they had to retreat to Anton's office, they would have one last, and very nasty, surprise for their enemies.

One evening, after the lights were out in the workshop and warehouses, Voss knocked on the door to Fowler's office. When Mike glanced up, he beckoned and, without explaining, walked back down the hallway.

Mike looked around at the mess of documents before him. He wasn't going to finish anytime soon. He stood, twisting to crack his spine, then buttoned up his vest, pulled on his suit jacket, and headed for Anton's office.

The coffee table and nearby floor were covered with cardboard tubes containing rolled up plans. A pile of folded charts and notebooks filled the remaining easy chair. Voss had cleared everything off his desk except the lamp and had unrolled several large sheets of paper.

"Come. Take a look." Voss picked a still-smoldering butt out of a divot in the edge of an ashtray and took a drag. He waved the smoke away as he exhaled.

It was a set of blueprints, construction plans for a submarine. In the lower right-hand corner a label read, UNTERSEEBOOT, TYP XXI. The pictured sub was blunt bowed, deep hulled, and menacing . . . and it was very different from the sort that Fowler had become familiar with during the war. There was no deck gun; in fact the entire vessel was so streamlined that there wasn't much of a deck at all. Periscopes, radar and radio antennas, and what appeared to be a snorkel to allow the diesel engines to run when the boat was at periscope depth, all retracted into the sleek shell surrounding the conning tower. The only features interrupting the tower's smooth lines were armored antiaircraft turrets pointing fore and aft. Unlike the typical submarines of the past, which spent the majority of their time on the surface and dove only to attack or evade detection, this boat seemed to be built to spend most of its time underwater. All in all, it bore a strong resemblance to designs that had become common in just the last few years.

"That's quite a boat," Fowler said.

"The goal of the Type XXI was to be the most advanced submersible in existence. It was intended to change the entire nature of war at sea. Like the V2 rocket and the Me 262 jet fighter, these were what our propaganda minister called 'Wunderwaffe,' wonder weapons. It was also a staggering failure. The concept was too complicated, too advanced, to be perfected before the war was lost. Only two ever sailed on combat patrols. Many more were nearly ready to be deployed. Hundreds were abandoned in various stages of completion, a fantastic waste of desperately needed resources."

Anton's voice betrayed both pride and bitterness. "I worked on what became the XXI. My program at the Reichspost was . . . well, it would have been like working at your Bell Laboratories. There were plans to utilize alternative forms of energy—"

Voss stopped abruptly, emerging from his memories to glance at Fowler. He looked away. "Um . . . there is the Walter turbine, for instance. Do you know about this?"

Fowler had no idea; he shook his head.

"As you know, the typical submarine is simply a torpedo boat that has traded high speed for the ability to dive and operate submerged for short periods of time. Many hours had to be spent on the surface running the diesels in order for the batteries to charge. At best they were a stealthy but extremely limited predator. All liabilities would vanish, however, if a U-boat could be built with a power plant requiring neither batteries nor outside air. We have precisely this situation with the modern nuclear-powered boats. For a country with an easily blockaded coast, like Germany, the XXI would have been the battleship of the future.

"Professor Helmuth Walter began building submarines before the war. He created innovative hull designs and an engine that would run on Perhydrol—hydrogen peroxide—and diesel. It developed a great deal of power and required no oxygen from the surface. Alas, Perhydrol is both explosive *and* corrosive. His streamlined hull, however, eventually became the Type XXI." Voss tapped the page. "These boats were reengineered to use conventional diesels but with a great many more batteries. The plans I have here are nearly identical to the boat we took to South America."

Mike looked at all the stacks and rolls of paper with appreciation. Two of the offices down the hall were used as storerooms. One contained their business records; the other Anton had stuffed with file cabinets and boxes full of musty documents, clippings from technical journals, and government reports. Some of them related to a subject that had become his obsession: atomic weapons and atomic power. There were files on nuclear bomb tests such as Ivy Mike, Mosaic, Gerboise Bleue, and Castle Bravo, along with articles on Edward Teller, Stanisław Ulam, Bertrand Goldschmidt, and Andrei Sakharov. Mike occasionally kidded the older man, asking him if they were going to go into the business of selling A-bombs. Voss was not amused. "War is a human condition. I, however, draw the line at apocalypse." Over the years he had continued to follow every development with ferocious intensity.

Most of the material, however, was just like this, esoteric information on different sorts of technology, much of it lifted from the archives of the Third Reich. Occasionally, they had even turned it into business opportunities. Anton's research had made them money, Mike would grant him that.

Five years earlier Voss had invited an exclusive group, representatives from a half dozen of the world's largest aviation firms, to a private auction in Monaco. They were allowed to view a small selection of what was on offer and told to ante up if they wanted to retain their seat at the table. Each additional round grew more expensive. The British representative dropped out, but soon a heated competition developed between the French and the Americans. This netted an additional half million. The prize was a trove of documents that Voss had dragged from a ruined building a decade earlier, files once belonging to the Rhön-Rossitten Gesellschaft, a German glider-building society dating back to the 1920s.

Though Mike hadn't realized it before he watched this drama play out, many of the great aircraft designs of the '30s, '40s, and '50s had sprung from the fact that the treaties that ended World War I had prevented Germany from building powered aircraft for several years. Forced to go back to the basics, meaning gliders, men like Alexander Lippisch and Theodore von Kármán had done the research no one else bothered to do. The inspiration for many cutting-edge developments, from the wing that gave the British Spitfire an advantage even over planes built by the Nazis, to modern delta-shaped supersonic bombers, had come from the German gliding societies. Everyone in the aerospace industry was concerned that there might be a few surprises still hiding in the Rhön-Rossitten archives.

Fowler squinted at the piles of blueprints and documentation on the submarine. "This is . . . impressive," he said.

"It is important to be prepared. What you cannot find here"—Voss gestured at the tubes and binders—"I may have here." He pointed to his forehead. "Our boat was off the books, so to speak, it never received an official number. The 'U-Null,' as we called it, was a platform for experimental systems. This is why it had a captain and a crew, and was ready for a long voyage when so many of the other Type XXIs were not. As liaison between the manufacturer in Danzig and the Reichspost Research Office, I was familiar with almost every detail."

"Okay . . ." Mike said. "It's been fifteen, sixteen years. I'm not going to count on there being enough air pressure to blow the tanks. And, no matter what you were thinking at the time, attempting to enter a boat that's been that long on the bottom sounds like a nightmare. Is there a salvage air system, an external connection that would accept a line from a compressor on the surface?"

Voss sighed. "No. Once the war at sea turned against us, what you call a salvage system was omitted as a potential area of failure."

Fowler shuffled through the pages of plans. "Alright. If I put my mind to it, maybe we can manufacture something that will work just as well."

Voss nodded.

Mike was already imagining lists of equipment, but he made himself slow down; there were bigger issues to deal with. "The most important thing is how do we find it? And then we have to get there before anyone can find *us*!"

"Yes. There are also many other problems . . . but let us attack this first one right now." Voss bent and spun the dial to his safe. He pulled the bloodstained map from its buff-colored envelope. "I have studied this carefully and learned a few things."

Voss unfolded the map. It covered the southern half of South America. He put on his glasses and indicated the handwritten scrawl of dates and arrows that pointed to various areas along the coastline. "Whoever is searching, they seem to have started last year. They made it quite a way down the coast and then quit for the winter."

From the dates Fowler could see that progress had slowed as the search reached the more remote areas to the south, but something else bothered him . . . "This is a cheap tourist agency map. They're just using it to make notes on their progress."

Voss nodded. "Or perhaps it was to relay the information to someone else. I have wondered if these were the notes of a spy, someone copying information off more detailed charts or out of a logbook."

Fowler straightened. "If Wuttke stole this, then whoever he took it from may be looking for him, as well as the Stasi."

The two men glanced at each other. It was a disturbing thought.

"All the more reason for us to act swiftly." Voss bent back over the map. "It is still winter in the southern hemisphere. But if they begin work at the same time as last year. . . . Well, we do not have very long."

Voss walked around the desk and picked up a stack of maps.

"These are from your American navy. They were compiled by comparing British Admiralty and Chilean charts, but I can tell you that they are *still* not accurate. Chilean Patagonia, Tierra del Fuego, however you want to call it, is one of the most poorly documented places on earth.

"Unterkunft Platze . . . 'an accommodation.' Do you remember when I used this term?"

"The other day. On the boat."

"Yes. Well, we made the decision to leave the U-boat near one of these 'places of accommodation,' using charts that you would call 'classified.' It just so happens that the lead cartographer on the U-Platze project was one of my mentors."

"So if we could find your friend, or if we had a set of these classified charts, we would be way ahead of the game!"

"Unfortunately, Captain Seegers is unavailable to us. He is still alive—in fact he is a well-known photographer—but he lives in a remote area of Argentina, a place where there are quite a few Nazis. His maps, however, are a different situation . . ."

"You know where to find them?"

Voss paused . . . "No," he said. "But I believe I know how to begin looking."

To avoid attracting the attention of anyone who might be searching for the same information, Voss reached out to Ernst von Holleben, a historian who had lived in England since the 1920s. The two had worked together several times in the last seven or eight years.

Professor von Holleben had established relationships at the German Federal Archives, or Bundesarchiv, in Koblenz. If necessary, he might even be able to access the German central archive in Potsdam . . . providing, of course, that the political situation allowed him to get into, and out of, East Germany.

For his part, Mike had to locate a salvage vessel and a crew. He was familiar with many of the top American divers. But divers, by their very nature, were a cautious lot. In this case, they needed someone who wouldn't get spooked by skirting the law. What Fowler needed was a pirate. And he knew only one.

Jack Johnson was a large, raucous, red-haired, and perpetually sunburned Australian. He was known for his unpredictable temper and hard-driving way of managing a job. In the salvage business he had the reputation of being a bandicoot, a claim jumper. If Johnson's crew was on the site, anything below the waterline was fair game, no matter what his contract read.

He billed himself as "Hydraulic Jack" Johnson. If it was in the water and you needed it elsewhere, he was your man. In true Aussie style he had a number of other nicknames. Among the commandos of the Services Reconnaissance Department he had been "Mad Jack." But his closest friends used the name given to him by his brothers: "Buckets."

Mad Jack Johnson was the other survivor of that misbegotten mission to Itu Aba in the final days of the war. At the time, they had known each other little more than a week, but they had fought back-to-back. They had hunted and killed together, and they had hidden in the waters inside the reef, wounded, burned, and traumatized, as the bombers came in with explosives and napalm, reducing the entire island to a smoking ruin.

Jack was also the man who had taken a chance on Mike after the war. Together with Johnson's crew of Australians and New Zealanders, they had stripped dozens of Japanese wrecks in and around Simpson Harbour, New Guinea. For all of them, the camaraderie and rough living, as well as the occasional danger, was a way to slowly return to civilian life.

Though he often seemed deaf to any interests but his own, after three years Johnson realized that Mike was yearning for greater challenges than a small-time salvage operation could offer and introduced him to a German who was buying up abandoned Japanese arms and ammunition to supply the South Korean military. That man's name was Anton Andreas Voss.

On the second floor of the Barcelona factory, just down the hall from where Aleixandre Porras and his assistants ran the day-to-day aspects of the business, was the switchboard and Telex room. Mike made sure the machine was set up to connect to the office of his Singapore sales agent, then typed out a paper Telex tape. He listed the names of port captains, ship's chandleries, and dealers of diving equipment from Brisbane to Hong Kong. He asked the agent to forward a message to each of them:

> IF YOU KNOW A CREWMEMBER OF MV BUSHRANGER II PLEASE COMMUNICATE THE FOLLOWING. BUCKETS CALL HOTEL ARYCASA BARCELONA TEL 220781 NINE PM TO THREE AM GMT. TELE CHARGES WILL BE REIMBURSED =
> RUMMY

The mission on which he had met Johnson started in Darwin, and an American PBY had flown the small commando team north. At some point, Fowler mentioned that as a child he had gone with his father to pick up boatloads of Mexican booze for the corrupt county supervisor who supplied the tourist hotels that dotted the beaches around San Diego, California. From then on, the team had called him "Rumrunner." For Johnson that had not been enough. Australian through and through, he had gone and shortened it to "Rummy."

After getting a room at the Arycasa, Mike returned to the factory compound to escort Voss home to Vallvidrera. He liked to check the property for any signs of intrusion or surveillance before heading back to the factory to put in a few more hours' work. He was burning the candle at both ends but, as the days and then weeks flew by, he had the terrible feeling that time was running out.

Voss started his Lancia and waited for it to warm up under the harsh lights of the factory courtyard. Rafeeq Farkhani opened the gates and Mike stepped out for a moment to look up and down the block.

A dark figure stood near the fountain on the corner to the north.

No one else was in sight and the man was obviously watching the compound entrance.

Mike motioned Voss to wait and started up the sidewalk on his side of the street, allowing Farkhani and his Mauser rifle a clear shot from the gate should he need to take it. As the man started toward him, Mike reached under his jacket and unsnapped the strap that held the .38 in its holster.

Then he relaxed. It was the metal finisher, the middle-aged man from the beach who had built the fire and helped to pull him from the surf. Mike and the heavyset Spaniard stopped in the middle of the street. The man glanced at the hip where Mike's revolver was concealed by his suit jacket.

"Is there trouble, señor? I am looking for work, but maybe I come at a bad time."

Mike almost laughed. "No, no. Exactamente lo contrario. You have come at the perfect time. Tell me your name."

"Zúñiga. Yo soy Fernando Zúñiga."

"Okay. Wait for me across the street."

Fowler turned and jogged back to the gate, refastening the snap on his holster and waving at Farkhani to stand down. He leaned into the window of Anton's rumbling Lancia. "All good. I've found someone who may be able to help us."

Mike climbed into the Land Rover. As he pulled out of the gate following the Lancia, he leaned over and popped the passenger door. Zúñiga climbed in and Fowler accelerated, trailing Voss inland. He glanced over at his passenger, gauging how to approach him.

"Can you drive?"

"Many years ago, I drove a Ford truck every day."

"I can offer you as much money as our shop foreman makes in a year. I will also give you a car, which will be yours to keep. If you wish, we can talk about full-time employment later."

Zúñiga shot Mike a calculating glance. "For this I have to kill someone?"

"I hope not. I want you to protect Señor Voss." The Lancia turned right and Mike followed, heading into the hills near the funicular railway and the baroque terraces of Parque Güell.

"Ah, el jefe." Zúñiga straightened a bit and pulled his shoulders back. But, as much as he seemed to feel honored by the offer, something else was bothering him. "He is a German, a fascist . . . ?"

"He is a German . . . but not a fascist." Mike wondered if this was correct. However, the reasons Voss had for keeping an arm's distance from his countrymen had become abundantly clear in the last few weeks. "It is possible our enemies are Germans, possibly Nazis," Mike said. "It is also my job to protect him, and I was in the American navy."

"You believe he is a good man?"

Mike shrugged and changed gears. Voss was dodging through traffic, drawing away from the slower and less agile Land Rover. Mike took an opening and accelerated. "You know our business. Good or not good?" He shook his head. "That's someone else's problem. He's an honorable man. That's enough for me."

"Honor is important, so is friendship and family. I have a mother and soon a grandchild to care for. What would you have me do?"

"Follow him to and from work. Protect the house when he is there. Stay at a distance. Don't tell anyone about your job and don't come into the factory. I'll show you a place to park in the woods near the house and a way in from the bottom of the garden."

As they wound up into the mountains, the towers of the white neo-Gothic Church of the Sacred Heart and the nearby pumping station appeared silhouetted in the moonlight beyond the dark ridge. On the empty winding road Voss drove hard, enjoying himself. Fowler tried to keep up, white-knuckling the wheel as the Land Rover heeled over in the corners, engine and tires howling. Eventually, the taillights of the Lancia were lost in the darkness.

Mike gritted his teeth. He looked over at Zúñiga, who was bracing himself in the passenger seat.

"With any luck the most dangerous thing you will have to do is try and keep up with him," he said.

CHAPTER 5

A PHONE JANGLED AND Fowler came suddenly awake. Dim light from the street filtered up through the window. It was an unfamiliar bell and he was in a strange room: high ceilings, gold wallpaper, dark wood trim. Mike threw off the covers and sat up; he had spent three days at the Hotel Arycasa and this was the first time the telephone had rung.

Pushing the chair out of his way, he reached across the small desk and snatched up the ivory-colored handset. A once-familiar voice bellowed at him from the far side of the world.

"Rummy! How're ya goin'? You've become the man of mystery, and now you're too good for us mudfish . . . Am I right?"

Mike stifled a laugh, taken back to when he had been one of a carefree gang of ruffians living on the *Bushranger*, a rusting landing craft that had been converted into a dive boat. The man's explosive energy could be both invigorating and exhausting.

"I'm good. I think about you guys every day—"

"Aww . . . Mate, you're makin' me blush."

Mike rubbed his eyes and sat in the chair; he needed his wits about him. "We have to talk, but there's a chance we're sharing this convo with a local shelf . . . you follow?" he asked. He had booked the room to avoid receiving the call at his own apartment, but "shelf" was an Aussie term for a police informer. American and Australian slang, spoken quickly, should be enough to confuse the hotel operator or anyone else who might be listening in.

"Takin' the James Bond routine seriously, I see. Alright, we'll bush 'em up."

"Interested in a gig? We'd need to start in the next month or two."

"Might be. We're in the Big Smoke for maintenance, but we should be back at it in a week. What've you got?"

In what had been the British Empire the Big Smoke could refer to any number of large industrial cities, the original being London. Knowing Johnson, Mike figured he was talking about Brisbane, Australia.

"It's a recovery op. Pigboat," he said. "Around ninety feet down to the superstructure, another ten or so to the deck. The bottom is maybe one thirty, one forty. When it comes to the location, think Vancouver or Sitka. You with me so far?"

"Sitka! That's twelve thousand miles before we can even get to work."

"It'll be less than that but pretend I can afford it."

"Alright. That's deep, and cold water's hard yakka. You reckon we're gonna do it this winter?"

"Not winter. It's in your hemisphere. Still, we're going to have to use dry suits if we're not in heavy gear."

They had trained with the black rubber predecessor of the modern dry suit in the military, but all of Mike's salvage work with Johnson had been in the tropics. When they needed insulation, they had worn thirty-year-old copper helmets and canvas suits, the primitive version of the heavy gear he had used at Pearl Harbor. In the last decade, however, Jack Johnson's fortunes had improved. Not long ago, Mike had received a letter containing a dozen photographs of an impressive salvage vessel, the *Bushranger II*, which looked ready for almost any situation.

"Alright, dry suits it is," Johnson replied. "Look, you've piqued my curiosity, mate. But the mileage, the op costs . . . unless you've forgotten, time is money. What's the swag?"

"What they found at Ballarat." Mike didn't know that much about Australian history, but he knew there had been a gold rush about a hundred years ago. "The amount is around thirty American."

"Thirty—?" Johnson knew Fowler was not talking about thirty thousand dollars, so he must mean . . .

There was a moment of silence, and Mike knew that Hydraulic Jack was suddenly more than just curious.

"Bloody hell! What are the terms?"

"We pay all expenses. Your profit is a percentage of the haul."

"Hold up—This 'we' . . . ? That's you and . . . the Kraut, right?"

Although Johnson had originally introduced Mike to Anton Voss, he had always remained cautious where the German was concerned.

"That's right. And we'll have to split with the 'laundry' . . . you know what I'm talking about?"

"I've read a crime novel or two."

"Yeah. Well, who's gonna be in that position is yet to be determined. There's no other way to do it, the swag is, uh . . . historically compromised."

"So how do you know it's . . . wherever it's supposed to be?"

"Eyewitness. The Kraut." Mike grinned; it was amusing to refer to his dignified partner in such an offhand manner.

"Coo-wee! And he's just been sitting on this since—"

"—It would seem so," he cut Johnson off, just in case someone was listening.

"Thirty American . . . Well, he is a patient punter, isn't he?"

Fowler wondered about that one. Voss had never spoken of any secret plan to fund his retirement; it seemed to have taken a major catastrophe for him to even consider going after the sub. On the other hand, he was no fool, and he knew how to wait in order to leverage information.

Mike changed the subject. "I have to warn you. There's competitions."

"Ahh! Is this where I demand a bigger percentage?"

Mike laughed. "Could be." Then he changed his tone. "I won't lie to you; you know the sort of people we deal with. There are at least two other players, and it's Rafferty's Rules at best."

"Me and the boys, we wouldn't have it any other way."

"Rafferty's Rules" meant no rules at all. Fowler hoped that Jack Johnson remembered what that meant. The Japanese on Itu Aba were a long time in their past. He knew that the crew of the *Bushranger* was up to a bar fight—all you had to do was show them the bar. But he wasn't sure they were ready for war.

"There's one last thing." Mike hadn't been sure how to broach this subject; he didn't want to get into any long explanations about Anton's engineering background or his work with the Kriegsmarine. "The, uh . . . target, we're going to try to raise it."

Again, there was silence, just the crackling of a line that ran across continents and through the depths of the oceans. Then, "Aww, cobber, you're talking like a crazy man."

"No. I'm not. I've got reasons I think it's possible, if we're prepared. I'll send you a list of equipment. You get in touch with the office that sent out my telegram. They'll forward an equipment list and a place to rendezvous."

"Alright. I trust you, mate, and told over a few beers this could be a great story, but"—Johnson hesitated a moment—"Rummy, you're gonna have to pay all the way in, *and* all the way out. It's a long trip, and, I've got to say, it also sounds like a bloody snipe hunt. A bloody *expensive* snipe hunt. You ready for that?"

"Let's get the paperwork and money settled. Then get your guys headed our way and you fly out to meet us. There will be a show-and-tell. If you don't like it, we pay your expenses, and you turn around and go home. This is serious. And I understand the costs. Alright?"

"Aye . . . fair dinkum."

Fowler hung up the phone. He sat for a moment staring at the instrument as the sky lightened outside the window and the doves that lived along the rooftops began to stretch their wings and call to one another.

He understood Johnson's reservations. The way he'd told it, the story sounded like the kind of tale you heard in a barroom once there were too many empties on the table . . . like the kind of tale that was used to separate naïve investors from their money. Johnson was his friend, but Mike couldn't say the meaningful parts out loud. He couldn't say Voss had murdered a Stasi agent and they had dumped his body at sea. He couldn't say there was a map with a bullet hole in it that showed they might only have a few months before others found the sub. And he couldn't say it might all be for nothing, that they had only a vague idea where the damned thing was or who else was looking for it.

Over the next several days, the international news, bad enough to begin with, turned even uglier. Tensions ran high over the surrounded enclave of West Berlin. The wall the Communists had built was unable to stem the tide of people, and credibility, fleeing from East Germany. Diplomacy failed repeatedly and both the Soviets and the Americans moved tanks into position on either side of the internal border.

Fingers were pointed and sabers were rattled. Premier Khrushchev announced the Soviet Union was withdrawing from the nuclear test moratorium and within days resumed atmospheric testing. Night and day American bombers loaded with atomic weapons flew a route along the Arctic Circle, as close to the Soviet Union as they could get without further escalating the talk of war. Voss closed himself in his office, listening to reports on the rack of high-performance radio gear he kept in one corner. Though he could coolly sell weapons to armies on both sides of a conflict, he seemed as concerned as anyone over the bellicose behavior of the

Warsaw Pact and NATO. Perhaps it was because he was a German and his fatherland would likely become a battleground yet again, or maybe it was just that nuclear war would be very bad for business.

Mike Fowler pushed forward with their plans, but the expenses had to be carefully managed. The operating costs for the *Bushranger* and its crew were going to run more than $30,000 a week.

Voss might be worth a couple million dollars, but most of it was tied up or committed to various deals. The previous spring, they had purchased several hundred thousand Enfield rifles and quite a few tons of .303 ammunition. The British military considered the Enfields obsolete, but they were still popular in less industrialized countries, and at around a dollar each, the price could not be beat. A sale to Pakistan was already in the works, but no money had yet changed hands.

On the positive side of the ledger, they had a shipment about to leave Barcelona headed for the Middle East. It carried a solid half million in ammunition and other supplies. But the vessel, and whatever it might eventually earn them, would be held up while loading additional cargos in Marseille.

Voss refused to take any money from Fowler's savings; liquidating real estate or taking out a loan could only be a last resort. There was a good chance the larger companies like Interarms and Merex might notice and start trying to figure out what Voss was up to. Sooner or later the cat would get out of its bag . . . or its box.

They had just enough cash on hand to get the operation set up in Caracas. By then Anton Voss was going to need a partner with an open checkbook.

Over Telex, Mike and Jack discussed the job as well as the capabilities of the *Bushranger II* and the equipment it would carry. Typically, submarines were salvaged using submersible pontoons and giant cranes, a brute force approach they couldn't hope to afford. In this case, however, they weren't dealing with a wreck. The U-Null had been intentionally submerged and should be in relatively good condition.

Voss and the original German crew had imagined they would

return within a year or two. Entering through the conning tower, which had been left open to the sea, they would access the control room. Assuming the tanks still held pressure, they could then blow the ballast and bring the boat to the surface. Given the equipment of the era it was a very risky concept. But even if it hadn't been, to think that the U-boat would now still be in good enough condition was a bit too much to hope for.

Fowler's plan was for the divers to remove portions of the hull and install connections to each of the submarine's ballast tanks. This would require cutting torches, nearly a mile of high-strength air hose, a compressor, and a large selection of hardware . . . but it was a far more reliable approach.

On his end, Mike went down to the warehouses and pulled out an assortment of the best military gear he could find: cold weather clothing, rations, medical supplies, camping gear, and radio sets. On the off chance that Mike's plan was not possible, Voss had even procured several hatch gaskets that matched the submarine's specifications. If necessary, they could be used to replace the aging elements originally installed on the sub.

Mike carefully checked over the diving equipment that he and Anton had occasionally used. The CRIS diving club in Barcelona had adopted the French-built La Spirotechnique Aqua-Lung early on, and Voss had suggested testing the newer versions of the system in case they wanted to carry the equipment for military applications. That business opportunity never developed, but Fowler and Voss were able to turn the club connection to their benefit by supplying their fellow CRIS divers with surplus fins and other accessories.

Mike Fowler enjoyed the freedom that the demand valve, or regulator, and tanks gave him underwater. Back when he had been a salvage diver, free-flowing air supplied by a hose from the surface meant you were rarely on the clock and allowed descents to great depth, but it also required a crew of helpers, and severely restricted movement. That heavy gear, the old-style copper helmet and rubberized canvas diving suit, was good for strenuous work, such as when a diver had to brace himself to use a tool, but mobility was not one of its strong points. On the other hand, the simple military "frogman"-style rebreathers that he had used on the later missions with Underwater Demolition Teams, were more compact but could only be used for shallow dives. The Aqua-Lung offered a useful compromise. In the moments when the business wasn't demanding all his time, Mike had enjoyed testing the limits of the new equipment.

The next consideration was weapons. Fowler selected what was probably the most versatile automatic rifle in their inventory, the Fallschirmjägergewehr 42. The FG 42 was engineered with the sort of flamboyance that typified Nazi-era weaponry. Extremely compact, it had a magazine that inserted horizontally into the receiver just behind the trigger. It was a superb compromise between an automatic rifle and a light machine gun. But it suffered from what Voss called "the German disease": overdesign. The gun was brilliantly constructed but complex, and its light weight made it fragile . . . not really up to the years of rough treatment it would face in the hands of the typical Sistemas Militar customer.

For this expedition, however, the FG 42 was perfect. With any luck they would not run into trouble, but if they did, the guns would give them plenty of firepower. Fowler disassembled his four best FG 42s, cleaned and lubricated them, then went down to the underground shooting range to sight them in.

Knowing Jack Johnson was familiar with the Browning P 35, Mike got out six of the Canadian-built version of the pistol and, with Voss in mind, laid out another SIG 47/8. All this plus magazines and holsters went into the packing cases their staff were assembling on the shop floor. For himself Mike chose a Smith & Wesson New Century "Triple-Lock" in .44 Special that had once belonged to an American general. The revolver had a four-inch barrel, Walter Roper grips, and an ingenious front sight that incorporated a small convex circle of chrome to reflect onto its brass bead, making it more effective in dim light.

Having no idea what was ahead of them, he also included a Belgian-built Blindicide RL 83, an improvement on the bazookas he had trained with during the war, and nine rockets in protective tubes. He also threw in a cut-down Browning A 5 shotgun. In the close confines of a ship at sea there might be no better weapon.

On the subject of explosives Voss had very specific ideas. "We must bring with us enough to destroy the boat completely. I want to make it unsalvageable."

Fowler had thought about it. "That's a big job. If I read you right, you want to do a lot more than just sink it."

"Correct. If we are discovered by our enemies, we may need to threaten to destroy the cargo. We must remove the old antipersonnel mines from inside the sub and dispose of them. Then we must replace them with something much more potent and reliable."

"You sure? Aren't we better off just trying to empty the sub and then make a run for it?"

Voss hesitated a moment; he seemed to be holding back an impatient response. "Michael, this is what I want: when we leave, there must be wreckage, nothing more. I want—I want it to be impossible to tell if the gold was aboard when the U-boat exploded. If someone else comes searching, I want them to spend a great deal of time trying to find the gold. Not looking for us. Do you understand?"

"Yes, sir."

Everything they were going to ship was wrapped in wax paper and tightly packed between wooden partitions, and then the cases were screwed shut. All the items were marked as SHIP'S SPARES IN TRANSIT TO THE M/V BUSHRANGER II. The destination was Talcahuano, Chile, the rendezvous point chosen by Fowler and Johnson.

Bearing the required documentation from Alfredo Larkin, Sistemas Militar's South American agent, the cases were driven to the port. As long as the paperwork could be properly filed, and therefore forgotten, the local officials didn't care what an export was or where it was headed.

The staff at Sistemas Militar might believe that all the activity over the last few weeks was just business as usual, but Aleixandre Porras was a different matter. He knew something was up and very soon he was going to be expected to keep the company running all by himself. Mike thought he deserved to be told something.

The day after the shipment departed for Caracas, Fowler and Voss knocked on the door to the accountant's office. A thin, balding man with a gray mustache, Porras peered at them over silver-framed half-glasses. Fowler turned the key in the lock to be sure they weren't disturbed.

Porras put down his pencil and took off the glasses. "Bueno. Will you now tell me what this insanity is all about, Señor Voss?" He gestured at the piles of bank statements and ledgers surrounding him. Mike guessed that he'd spent the last week or more scraping up every dollar he could find.

Voss pulled out a chair and sat. He lit up a cigarette. "No. I cannot do that."

When Aleixandre looked at him, Mike shrugged. Porras could be inheriting a lot of trouble, but if Fowler and Voss didn't make it back, he would be the sole owner of Sistemas Militar. The less he knew about their venture, the better off he might be.

"I believe you should take your family and run the business from the Monaco office," Voss told him. For tax purposes, Monaco was the company's official headquarters. However, real estate in the tiny principality was fantastically expensive, so their actual footprint there was minimal.

Aleixandre Porras looked back and forth from one of them to the other. Mike figured he was trying to balance the amount of trouble they were in against how he was going to explain the move to his wife. His children would have to change schools.

"Mr. Voss and I will be leaving in a few weeks," Mike said. "A month or two after that and it should be alright to come back."

"You are saying that whatever is happening, it is bad?"

Voss straightened in his chair. "I am saying that it is better for all of us for you to be in Monaco. Tell your wife it is a vacation. Stay at the Hotel Metropole, I will call Herr Scheck and tell him you are coming. Hire tutors and pay for it out of the company's earnings. Herr Fowler and I can forgo our pay for a few months."

"It will take some time for me to organize . . ."

"That's okay," Fowler said. "But you should go by car, no train or airline tickets. Tell as few people as possible."

Soon other details were wrapped up. The Tarragona boatyard was nearly finished with *Sigune*, and Voss would have to retrieve it before they took off for Venezuela. Fernando Zúñiga had obtained a driver's license and Aleixandre had signed over a blue 1941 Plymouth that had once belonged to the U.S. navy. Armed with a Colt revolver, Zúñiga was now able to shadow Voss as he drove to and from the office. During the day he would park not far from elegant Besòs water tower and nap in the car. He was little more than a block from the factory and Voss could drive past and signal for him to follow anytime he decided to leave. Mike was glad that they finally had someone on their side who was not obviously associated with the business, someone who could take care of any number of things with less likelihood of picking up a tail.

Mike broke out an StG 44 assault rifle and loaded seven magazines. This he stashed in the umbrella holder near his office door. It would be useful if he needed something more potent than the .38. Withdrawing several thousand in cash, he packed a suit in a roll-up bag and loaded his leather Gladstone with another change of clothes, a pair of boots, and a Dopp kit. The bag had a false bottom with several flat compartments built to hold his favorite undercover weapon, a slender Remington Model 51, in .380 ACP, several magazines, and a sap.

Aleixandre Porras soon left, his car stuffed with children and boxes of files. A "working vacation" was how it was explained to his staff. They asked few questions; it wasn't like he hadn't earned it.

Fowler wired money from accounts in Caracas to Jack Johnson via Singapore. Laden with equipment and drums of fuel, the *Bushranger II* was starting its long voyage across the Pacific. The list of things that had been accomplished grew steadily, yet the one of what needed to be done remained disturbingly long.

As the month drew to a close the temperature dropped and rainstorms stalled along the Catalonian coast. The sidewalks of Las Ramblas were covered in the yellow and orange of fallen leaves, and umbrellas, hats, and long coats appeared everywhere. The season of Spanish melancholy had set in; the sunny days of early autumn were over.

There were rumblings from beyond the eastern horizon, rumors that the USSR possessed a weapon capable of unbelievable devastation. Then there were reports of shattered windows in Norway and Finland. Seismographs in Italy shook as if they had recorded an earthquake. As the pressure wave circled the planet three times, the news broke: the Russians had tested the largest hydrogen bomb ever created. Its flash had been seen from Alaska, and the mushroom cloud towered more than thirty miles, higher than the stratosphere.

They called it Tsar Bomba, the emperor of bombs. Soviet officials bragged that they had intentionally throttled what could have been a 100-megaton explosion down to just over 50 megatons, 3,300 times the power of the Hiroshima blast. The largest thermonuclear device previously tested had been American, and just one quarter the size. It was true, the new bomb was not a practical weapon. It was so large that no existing missile could lift it, and even the aircraft that dropped the bomb had limited range. But as a message to the West, it was unmistakable.

"What fools!" Voss grumbled. Earlier in the evening Mike had driven him to his favorite café. The tall French doors were closed against a drizzling rain and the interior was crowded with customers who normally would have preferred the sidewalk. A haze of cigarette smoke hung low in the room.

"People say, 'What if there is an atomic war?' It is foolishness. This *is* an atomic war. It is fought by demonstrating one is willing to fight. The radioactivity, it is such a problem, they must control it, so they bomb *themselves* rather than each other! It is all crazy. 'The horrors of fallout,' they say. Well, I, for one, am thankful for it. Maybe it is the only thing causing restraint. The wrath of science has replaced the wrath of God."

Voss, who had been chain-smoking all evening, stubbed out one cigarette and lit up another. He glared around, as if seeking one of the local professors to continue the argument. "We pretend that these men of science, these doctors of physics, these doctors of engineering and chemistry, are wise. Most are crippled by arrogance. Now that such weapons are loose in the world, the great minds, they talk about the immorality of it all. Hypocrites. They are not above it. Each one would sell their souls for the facilities, the staff, the money to prove their theories, no matter how dangerous.

"It was only eighty years from your American Civil War to the invention of the atom bomb. We see what the Soviets have just done and we think we are looking at the future. No! We are looking at the past! Few have any idea what is now being created in secret laboratories around the world."

Mike Fowler had been scanning crowds for trouble since he left the crew of the *Bushranger* and sailed to Korea with Anton Voss. He had always possessed a sense that told him when something was off. It had been there when he was a child, running booze with the Old Man. It had kept him alive during the war, and more than a few times since.

He wasn't worried about atom bombs. There was trouble right here, somewhere in the café. His eyes flicked from the doors to the street, and then to the bar. The humidity-fogged mirrors that lined the walls confused his view, but he had seen something, a reflection of a face he recognized. A scarred face that could not be forgotten. Mike felt himself sit up straighter.

Voss noticed, and his bitter commentary came to an end. Then a group of patrons began to move toward the door and Mike was able to see past them, to spot a big man in a rumpled blue chalk-striped, suit. A *very* big man.

Voss saw him too and mumbled a curse in German. He reached under his coat, slipping the automatic out of its holster and covering it with his napkin. Mike slid out of the booth and stood with his back to the wall. If trouble was coming, he wasn't going to end up trapped behind a table.

And Standartenführer SS Otto Skorzeny was trouble incarnate.

CHAPTER 6

THE BIG MAN looked across the crowded room. He locked eyes with Voss, raised his chin in greeting, then strode forward.

Otto Skorzeny had to weigh 250 pounds. He was over fifty yet still fit, his height only apparent when compared to the other men in the room. One cheek had been laid open in a saber duel, and the jagged scar began near his left ear and continued past the corner of his mouth. His most distinctive features, however, were his eyes; he had a gaze so forceful it had always made Mike Fowler want to reach for a weapon.

"What are the chances this is a coincidence, eh?" Voss muttered.

Skorzeny had once been called the most dangerous man in Europe and was known far and wide as the officer who had personally led the force that crash-landed gliders on a steep mountainside in the Apennines to free Benito Mussolini from the remote ski lodge where he had been imprisoned. He had also stopped Germany's ally Hungary from surrendering to the Soviets, first by kidnapping the regent's son, and then threatening to destroy the Royal Palace with a company of infantry and Tiger tanks. It was rumored that a plot of his had caused General Dwight Eisenhower to go into hiding, forcing him to miss the triumphant Christmas celebrations that followed the liberation of France. These were but a few operations in a career that was still shrouded in secrecy.

From humble beginnings he had become famous as Germany's expert on unconventional warfare. By accident or design he had been at the center of a variety of political maneuverings and violence from the annexation of his native Austria in 1938 to the conversion of Hitler's Werewolves, specially trained saboteurs and terrorists, into an operation that helped important Nazis escape after the war. It was suspected that he and the ex-Nazi spymaster Reinhard Gehlen had recruited many of these same men into a network of spies reporting to the CIA and the BND, West Germany's intelligence agency.

Since then, he had become an advisor to both Juan Perón in Argentina and Gamal Nasser in Egypt. In all likelihood, Skorzeny's actual goal was to aid his comrades in exile. He offered his mercenaries to intelligence agencies worldwide; and though no operation had yet gone dramatically awry, he may have been particularly valuable because he was the perfect fall guy, as infamous as any villain Hollywood could create.

Beyond his flamboyant career, his ties to elite levels of power ran deep. He was married to Countess Ilse Lüthje, a woman rumored to have a background in intelligence, and to have attached herself to Hjalmar Schacht, the financial genius who had more than once saved Germany from economic collapse. Skorzeny was also involved in the arms trade, sometimes as a customer, other times as a competitor to Sistemas Militar.

"Herr Voss." The big man stopped in front of their table. "It has been some time. Since Egypt, when you did me a favor for which I am still in your debt."

"I am glad I could help." Voss hesitated a moment then gestured to the space beside him. "Have a seat. Tell us how you are, and why you have come to Barcelona."

Skorzeny eyed Fowler, who remained standing. The corner booth had two chairs and a built-in L-shaped settee against the wall. Skorzeny accepted the challenge; he took the other leg of the settee, placing himself between Fowler and Voss.

"I like your American," he said. "I never get the feeling he wants to kill me. But it always seems he is ready to try."

He arched an eyebrow and looked up at Fowler. "If there is trouble, you may shoot me here." Skorzeny patted the wavy hair near the top of his head.

"It's a deal," Fowler said, but he had his eye on a spot just inside the man's collarbone. At this range he was more likely to use a knife.

Skorzeny brought out a cigarette and lit up. "I come as an emissary. I have a business associate who would like to meet you. He happens to be interested in a company such as yours."

"I appreciate the referral. If we don't have what he needs, I'm sure we can find it for him." Mike struggled to hear Voss over the clatter and conversation in the café. There was something more to this. Skorzeny was a shark; he hadn't come all the way from Madrid to ask them to meet a potential client.

"Ahh . . ." The big man smiled slightly. "I haven't expressed myself adequately. These people are not interested in armaments. They wish to acquire your *company*. I suggested they should be prepared to pay handsomely."

Voss shot a glance at Fowler. "Acquire Sistemas Militar? Well, I doubt I would be interested, but I'm sure we can arrange a date to listen to their offer."

Skorzeny leaned in close. "Herr Voss, I am afraid this is a discussion that must happen tonight. They are coming in"—He checked his watch—"the next few minutes. I offered to make the introduction so that you would understand they are to be taken seriously."

Fowler caught a flicker of movement to his left. Fernando Zúñiga, who had trailed them to the café in his own car, lit a match and held it near his face so that Fowler could recognize him in the darkness beyond the glass doors. He gestured toward the main entrance.

Mike looked over; three men were just shaking the rain off their overcoats. He nodded to Zúñiga and motioned for him to hold on. Whatever was happening—well, they were just going to tough it out.

Skorzeny stood, making sure the newcomers could see him. One of the three, wearing a black overcoat, stayed by the door but the other two pushed their way through the crowd.

"Anton Voss, I would like to introduce Dr. Peter Anhaldt." Skorzeny gestured toward the shorter of the two men. He didn't bother with the other, and Mike classified the guy as some sort of flunky: he was young and yet didn't come across as muscle.

Anhaldt seemed to be roughly the same age as Voss. He was slightly built, with the pale, perfectly chiseled look of a silent movie star. He wore a suit of the latest fashion with narrow lapels and a tie to match. His silver hair was eccentrically long and carefully brushed back over his ears. Skorzeny offered him a chair.

"Professor Doctor Voss. Kapitän zur See Voss. It's interesting that we should finally meet. I believe portions of our work have intersected . . . but that was some years ago." Anhaldt's English had a precise mid-Atlantic accent that hid any trace of whatever his native language might have been. He offered a business card to Voss, who then pointed toward Mike . . .

"Michael Fowler, one of my partners."

Another card was handed over and Mike glanced at it before tucking it into the pocket of his vest.

MAGNETIC DATA CORPORATION
Solutions Through Information Processing
Peter Anhaldt Phd., President
666 5th Ave., New York, N.Y.
Quincy 3-4200

Anhaldt continued, focusing intently on Voss. "I moved to the United States in 1941, but I worked with Konrad Zuse in Berlin. We developed what became his high abstraction programming language. Before that I designed punch cards for Dehomag in the

Office of Reich Statistics. I have to say, we live in a time of such secrecy, it's only recently I realized that you were still alive."

"I'm not hard to find," Voss said. "Herr Skorzeny and I have known each other for several years."

Mike could see the muscles in Otto Skorzeny's back stiffen. Something about that comment bothered him.

"Indeed," Anhaldt said, and shot a look at the big Austrian. "In those days Zuse was preparing several programs for Admiral Rhein through the Reichspost Research Office. I believe some of them were for a project of yours, Dr. Voss. Remarkable work, truly."

Now it was Anton Voss's turn to look uncomfortable. "All of us have a past. Perhaps we should leave it behind and get on to the business at hand."

Anhaldt shrugged. "Alright." He snapped his fingers and the flunky stepped forward to hand over a slim black attaché case. He triggered the latches and brought out a document several pages in length and held together by a pair of brads at the top. "I've taken the liberty of putting together a Letter of Intent. My company would like to acquire Sistemas Militar Internacional S.L., specifically its client and subcontractor relationships, real property, inventory, and . . . archives. It is also a condition that you will remain in our employ as a consultant for the next five years. Your partners will be bought out."

Voss shook out his glasses and peered at the contract. Anhaldt indicated a clause several pages in. He glanced up at Fowler. "As you can see, the compensation will be generous."

Mike didn't lean over to look. Instead he asked, "Why does a computer company, or whatever you are, want to go into the arms business?"

"Efficiency. Computers are merely a tool. We deliver a full range of, ah . . . *solutions* for our clients. Different problems require different solutions."

Peter Anhaldt turned to Voss. "Ask yourself: where do I want to be in five years? You were once a gifted scientist. Our mission is to resolve the . . . contradictions between governments, multinational corporations, and nongovernmental organizations. Elite intellects offering global leadership. The future is not simply happening; we are creating it.

"A mind like yours should not be wasted. Do you really want to end up sitting in another filthy hotel somewhere in Africa waiting for a group of homicidal lowlifes to decide whether they are going to pay you or rob you? I believe you can do better."

"But only if we accept your deal, right?" Mike commented. He had faced plenty of homicidal lowlifes, and they weren't all in Africa, not by a long shot.

"Look at it this way, my boy, whatever plans you've made for your future, you could be living them by next week . . . if you accept our deal."

Voss sat back, looking from Anhaldt to Skorzeny. "Well, you have our attention. We will look this over and decide if we want to make a counterproposal. Shall I contact your office in New York if we choose to proceed?"

"You must understand the offer is time sensitive. I do believe we have overvalued your company by a fair amount. At Otto's request, we have been *extremely* fair."

"And *I* said I would think it over—" Voss replied.

Mike caught the door to the street opening. The newcomer was familiar, a muscular blond man in his late thirties. Fowler had last seen Heinrich Hartmann in Alexandria with Skorzeny, part of what the intelligence community jokingly called "the SS in Absentia." Since then, he had learned Hartmann was almost as notorious as his boss. He was nicknamed "Kuvalda," or Sledgehammer, because of the method he had used to torture Russian prisoners on the Eastern Front.

Hartmann spoke to the man in the black overcoat, then started across the room toward Anhaldt and Skorzeny.

"—the present value of my company is meaningless," Voss continued. "The question is, what will I make of it. The question is how much my partners want. The question is, Do I want to work for you at all, for any amount of time, or any amount of money."

When Anhaldt saw the new arrival, he pushed his chair back and stood . . . "Excuse me a moment." Hartmann, Anhaldt, and Anhaldt's flunky moved out of earshot.

Skorzeny leaned across the table and growled. "I am warning you, Anton: this is not simply a business transaction!"

"Yes? Then what *is* it?" Voss stared right back.

"Are you so foolish you do not understand?" Cups and saucers jumped as Skorzeny pounded a fist on the table. "I have tried. You deserve nothing more."

Anhaldt broke away from his colleagues and picked up his briefcase. "I apologize, I'm afraid we have been called away."

Skorzeny took a moment, seeming to gather his temper. Then he stood, and, aiming a sausage-sized finger down at Voss, snarled, "You have been picking over the corpse of the Fatherland for more than a decade. You sold our transistors to the Americans, aerodynamic designs to the French, and you simply *gave* a high-speed aircraft gun to the Jews, of all people! There is honor at stake, and you *owe* us!"

Mike stepped in, pushing Skorzeny back with one hand while the other slipped under his coat and gripped the butt of his revolver.

"Otto!" Peter Anhaldt stepped between them. "We have to *go*!"

Fowler dropped his arm and stepped back. The big Austrian glared at him with those crazy eyes, a look Mike was sure had intimidated many recruits and probably quite a few prisoners. They were now the center of attention for all inside the café.

Peter Anhaldt pointed his group toward the door. "Professor Voss, I thank you for your time . . . We'll give you forty-eight hours to discuss our offer and make up your mind. We will see each other soon, I assure you."

After the doors had shut behind them, Mike sank into the booth beside Voss. "Now what the hell was *that* all about?" he said.

"As you Americans would say, they are onto us."

"Clearly. But there was more to it than that." Mike turned to peer at his partner.

"Correct. There was a lot of history at this table." Voss surreptitiously slipped his pistol back into its holster. "The sooner we leave Barcelona, the better. And we will have to cover our tracks."

Fowler got the Land Rover started; he blinked his high beams as a signal to Fernando in his Plymouth. They were headed in the wrong direction, so he immediately turned right off Avenida Primo de Rivera and then right again onto a side street running back toward the compound. This section of the city, the Eixample, or Expansion, had been designed around the turn of the century. The blocks were uniformly straight and square, but each had its corners beveled off to allow for additional parking and so trolleys and commercial vehicles could make the turn from one narrow street to another.

Mike Fowler looked for Fernando's headlights as they made the first turn and saw another car swing in behind him. He kept an eye on the rearview mirror as they cut through the next corner. The new car stayed tight to the Plymouth's bumper.

"I think we're being followed," Fowler said. Voss turned to look back over his shoulder as Fowler accelerated. "Let's see what's going on."

The Land Rover was anything but powerful. Luckily, Zúñiga wasn't expecting Fowler to try to pull away. The distance between the two vehicles opened up. Mike glanced at the rearview mirror just in time to see the driver of the following car use the extra width of an intersection to put on speed and pass the Plymouth.

Fowler slowed down. "Okay. It looks to me like they don't care if we know they are there . . . and they don't know Fernando is part of our team."

Voss nodded. "Intimidation. I think we must give up on flying out. Unless you have a better idea, we should pack up the charts and plans then get to *Sigune.* Once we are at sea, they will never find us."

"Agreed. You're not tempted to take their offer?" Mike checked out his partner from the corner of his eye.

Voss paused a moment, then said, "No. It would be a deal with the devil."

The rain started again as the little convoy approached the block occupied by Sistemas Militar. Fernando Zúñiga had proved his worth by hanging back after the tail had passed him. Fowler pulled up near the factory gate without turning in. He honked his horn for entry.

He wasn't about to get himself bottled up in the driveway . . . but the tail car slid by behind him, a black Mercedes 220. In the side-view mirror Mike thought he recognized the man in the overcoat in the passenger seat. The Mercedes made a right at the corner. Zúñiga shot by, going much faster. As the gate opened to let the Land Rover in, Mike saw him pull a U-turn into his usual parking spot in the next block. Mike put the Land Rover in gear, cranked the wheel over, and started forward, then hit the brakes.

Something was wrong—

Gears ground as he slammed the vehicle into reverse. Dark figures appeared out of the rain and the courtyard was suddenly full of armed men. Voss had drawn his SIG, but the black Mercedes appeared again, skidding to a stop, blocking their ability to back up. Heinrich Hartmann tapped on Voss's window with the barrel of his pistol.

"Pull ahead and get out! *Schnell!*"

Mike hesitated. Two of the figures in the courtyard moved forward, each armed with a machine pistol. They were well and truly trapped. Any attempt to escape or fight back would turn the thin metal body of the Land Rover into the Alamo.

"No." Voss gripped Fowler's arm, keeping him from reaching for his pistol. "No. I doubt they would have allowed us to get this far if they weren't going to take us inside. We still have options."

They stepped out into the rain and were both immediately searched. Their pistols were pocketed, and Mike's knife was hurled off into the blackness where the trucks and cannon were parked. He looked quickly around; since their troubles began Fowler had doubled the security detail. Rafeeq Farkhani and his brother were supposed to be on duty every night during the week. But they were nowhere to be seen.

"Upstairs!" Hartmann ordered. "The Standartenführer isn't finished with you."

An older German who looked like he had never recovered from the battle of Stalingrad shoved Fowler through the doors into the office building. In addition to Hartmann, Mike counted six men.

Lying at the base of a display case, were Rafeeq and Salim Farkhani. They were bound and Rafeeq was gagged. His hands had both been smashed to a pulp and his brother's throat had been cut. A gore-spattered hammer was lying nearby. Rafeeq was alive, ragged breaths still whistling through his nose.

Fowler turned on Hartmann, who was leading Voss toward the stairs. Hartmann smirked. "You have something to say, cowboy?"

Voss quickly stepped between Mike and the German, blocking any attack. Hartmann was relaxed and he was ready, welcoming the chance to fight should it come. Almost gently he pushed Voss aside, looking Fowler directly in the eyes.

"Sometimes people do not believe they should take us seriously." Hartmann turned and, picking up the hammer, he swung. The blow struck like a lash, caving in one side of Farkhani's skull. The breathing stopped and the German tossed the tool onto the dead man's lap and carefully wiped his fingertips with a handkerchief. His eyes bored into Fowler's.

Mike's hands balled into fists; adrenaline tingled throughout his body. But Voss spoke quietly, "No! Not now."

Above them the door to the upper floors swung closed and footsteps descended toward them. Otto Skorzeny came to a stop a few feet higher on the stairway. He took in the scene, then reached inside his coat and pulled out a well-worn Luger pistol. He snapped off the safety. He didn't raise the pistol but spoke directly to Mike . . .

"Listen carefully—or die," he said. "I do not need you." He inclined his head toward Voss. "Only him. You are alive at this exact minute because it is *slightly* better if we all cooperate. If you understand, say, 'Yes, I understand.' "

Fowler took a breath. "Yes. I understand."

"Good. Now we are going upstairs."

Peter Anhaldt was sorting through the maps and submarine blueprints in Voss's office. His nameless assistant was pulling open the desk drawers, probably searching for weapons. Anhaldt looked up as Skorzeny led Fowler and Voss into the room.

"So, you gentlemen see how quickly events can accelerate." He held up a binder containing mechanical drawings of the Type XXI U-boat. "When I was informed you had all of . . . *this,* I had to come see for myself. I applaud your preparation, and I intend to take advantage of it."

Skorzeny stalked to the bar and poured himself a drink. He downed it quickly, then hurled the glass across the room to shatter against the wall behind the desk. He turned on Voss.

"You swine! We treated you as a brother officer! How long have we known each other? All this time and you never saw fit to tell me!" Skorzeny gestured at the tubes of blueprints. "And that is not the worst of it." He snatched up a U.S. Hydrographic Office chart of southern Chile and waved it at them. "Clearly you are planning some kind of *expedition.* Have you become completely mercenary? You should have reported in years ago, as soon as you returned to Germany! You should have told me!"

Voss's cold gray eyes narrowed. "Herr Skorzeny, you seem overwhelmed with yourself. You were never in my chain of command. You are not the leader, the Führer, of some government in exile. Your reputation has gone to your head!"

Skorzeny hooked a punch into Anton's gut and the older man jackknifed forward and fell to his knees. Fowler shook off the man who was grasping his arm, but the German was no fool; he moved back and drew his pistol.

Peter Anhaldt stepped forward. "Let's call an end to the drama, shall we? The situation is now much less confusing. There are no more secrets, and we all want the same thing. There will be rewards enough to go around. Our agreement remains open . . . for the moment."

Voss struggled to his feet, but he was still bent over and gasping for breath.

"Heinrich," Anhaldt said, "go get your hammer and a gag." He glanced down at Voss. "The two of you can sign. I suggest you do so before the terms need to change. Then we will go to work. The only amendment is that, now that I've seen this"—He waved his hand at the case full of plans and charts—"Mr. Fowler will have to accompany us, and Señor Porras and his family will remain under guard until we have succeeded in our mission."

"And if we don't?" Mike took a careful step closer to Voss and helped him to straighten up. The man with the submachine gun tracked them with its muzzle.

"If *you* don't sign, I'm sure Herr Hartmann will be delighted to use his hammer. It won't be long before you are useless. At that point there will be a change of plans. I will no longer need you or the contract, just the information held by Dr. Voss . . . the location of the U-boat. Our mission will be more difficult without him, but we will make do."

"The location. What makes you think we even have that?" Mike demanded.

"It is quite obvious!" Skorzeny threw a handful of charts on top of the pile on the coffee table.

Hartmann appeared in the doorway, the bloody hammer at his side.

Voss's hand tightened powerfully around Fowler's arm. He had not been as hurt by Skorzeny's punch as he was pretending.

"Okay, we'll sign your damned contract," Fowler said. He turned to look at Voss, eyes shooting to the far side of the desk and back, hoping his point would get across. "We might as well get something out of this, Anton? Right?"

The silent young man who followed Anhaldt around opened the briefcase. He extracted several copies of the same document they had been shown in the café.

"Get out of the way," Mike growled as he helped Voss to sit behind his desk, the desk with the crest proudly reading SMI attached to the front.

"Good!" Anhaldt rubbed his hands together. "Come along, Otto, we have to get to Monaco. We will return as soon as the situation there is under control."

Skorzeny glared at Fowler and Voss. "No foolishness, understand?" He turned toward the door. "Heinrich, it is your job to see this all goes smoothly."

"Jawohl!" Hartmann hefted the hammer. "There will be no trouble."

Mike held the desk chair so Voss couldn't roll it closer to the desk to sign the papers, but Anton didn't try, and he didn't attempt to put on his glasses. He knew what Fowler was going to do.

Unfortunately, Anhaldt and Skorzeny had already left the room. And unfortunately, Hartmann remained in the doorway. Mike gauged the distance . . . then he turned to the window ledge, picking up a curved rectangle covered in resin-coated fiber.

"Do you know what this is, Heinrich?"

"Just sign," Hartmann sighed. "You are wasting my time."

"Take a look. It's a prototype antipersonnel mine." The old guy who had been guarding Fowler raised his pistol and took a step back.

Fowler laughed. "Nothing to worry about, this one's disconnected. Inside are seven hundred quarter-inch steel cubes laid over three quarters of a pound of C-3 explosive. The American government wasn't very impressed with its performance in the field, so they're developing their own. We bought a few for testing."

Fowler set the mine back on the windowsill, then turned to spread the contracts out on the desk. Hartmann didn't move. He wasn't going to step out of the doorway. Voss leaned forward in his chair . . .

"But you know where they *are* effective . . . ?" Mike slid his hand under the edge of the desk, flipping the Power switch for the circuit he had installed weeks before.

". . . *Indoors!*"

Mike pushed Voss into the kneehole of the desk. The goon with the machine pistol jerked the gun to his shoulder just as Mike hit the first Fire switch and dropped to the floor behind Voss.

The gun roared; bullets stitched the wall.

Then the desk bucked and slammed backward. The Claymore mine that was built into the SMI crest blew out the carved wooden facing.

Steel cubes exploded in a widening arc, a hundred shotguns all going off at once, destroying, shredding, savaging everything in the room.

CHAPTER 7

Fowler's ears rang. He felt like he'd been punched in the gut. Ricochets rattled off the walls and ceiling. He pulled his head out from under the desk and sat up.

The room was full of dust, caustic smoke, floating bits of paper, and a settling haze of blood. The coffee table and chair had been turned to kindling. The maps and plans were confetti. The bar was shattered glass and splintered burlwood veneer.

The older German who had guarded Fowler was dead, his body pocked with bloody craters. There was little left of the man with the machine pistol and not all of him was in one place. His gun was dented and caked with gore.

Fowler coughed and stood, unsteadily helping Voss to his feet. His eyes welled up from the fumes.

"Can you hear me?!" Mike yelled into Voss's ear. Voss looked dazed but nodded. "I have to check the hall. Call Aleixandre! Warn him! Got it?" But Voss had already picked up the phone.

Fowler grabbed the Walther the older man had carried. He made his way to the door, crunching broken glass and kicking aside fragments of furniture. Hartmann lay there, face down in the hallway.

Mike Fowler ran toward his office. Over the ringing in his head, he could hear a commotion downstairs and had to assume that a counterattack was on its way. Without pausing to find his key, he smashed the glass panel of his door with the pistol. Reaching through he flipped the lock, tossed the dead German's gun away, and pulled the StG 44 out of the umbrella holder. Stepping to his desk he looked down to the courtyard.

He got a dim glimpse of Skorzeny hustling Peter Anhaldt into the backseat of a huge silver Adenauer model Mercedes. The gates were open and, as Skorzeny piled in, the driver took off. Clearly, they knew their plan had gone awry and were not waiting to be caught in whatever trap had been sprung.

Mike ripped open a drawer, snatched up a counterfeit passport he had maintained since his smuggling days, buckled on the harness of magazine pouches for the assault rifle, then poked his head back into the hallway. Down the stairwell, he saw motion behind the metal and glass doors that opened onto the second floor. Flipping off the safety, he fired two fast shots into each panel. He made it to the other side of the stairs, but curses and gunfire volleyed upward. The door crashed open.

"Anton!" he yelled. "Stairs!" A moment later the Claymore hidden behind the framed poster in the stairway exploded. Dust and fumes vomited toward him. Something ripped at his sleeve. His lungs burned. A man was screaming.

Back in the doorway to Anton's office, Heinrich Hartmann had rolled over. The side of his face was covered in blood and lacerations. He groaned and tried to sit up. Mike slung the assault rifle, then bent over and ripped Anton's pistol from Hartmann's coat pocket. As he stood, Hartmann grabbed his ankle. Mike pulled away and racked the SIG, coolly ready to kill. But bullets smashed the hallway window to his right. A gun flashed from the stairwell corner. He shifted targets and fired back.

Fowler ducked through the door to Voss's office, slamming it shut and locking it; this door was solid wood.

At the other end of the ruined room Anton Voss was yelling into the telephone in French. Mike locked the safety on the pistol and handed it over.

"You ready to go?"

Anton Voss nodded and, dropping the receiver, he reached behind his safe and produced the heavily knotted rope that was tied to its base. Clearing the broken glass away, he tossed the loop of rope out the window.

"The safe." Voss pointed. "Get the map, and the envelope next to it. Both! Understand?" He climbed onto the windowsill.

There was a commotion in the hallway, then a scraping noise and the sound of Hartmann cursing. His men were dragging him to safety. With unsteady hands, Fowler spun the dial of Voss's safe, and as he did a plan formed in his mind. He grabbed both envelopes, but he also took Anton's duplicate passport. He slammed the door closed and spun the knob.

There was a staccato concussion and a splintering of wood as someone opened up on the locked door with a burst from a machine pistol.

Mike Fowler grimaced: they weren't learning. He reached under the lip of the desk and flipped the last switch. The mine in the hallway detonated. Dust jumped from the walls. There was no more gunfire.

Mike wedged himself through the window frame, and climbed down to the rain-slick roof. Voss was already making his way toward the old powerhouse and the rusting steel rungs that led down the outside of the chimney. A few lights were coming on in the nearby apartment buildings but many Spaniards, still wise to the sounds of war, were probably taking cover. Lowering himself to the courtyard, Mike cautiously stuck his head out the main gate. He looked up and down the street.

The Mercedes that had followed them from the café was parked down the block, lights off. At least one man was taking cover behind its fender. Mike pulled back. The explosion had dulled his ears but he could hear sirens.

"Did you get Aleixandre?" he asked.

"I left a message. We have to get to *Sigune*. We can try him again from Tarragona."

Mike nodded, but he was working on a different idea. "Come with me . . ."

They crouched in the doorway to the bomb shelter as Mike fumbled with his keys. "You go." Mike pointed to the dark stairway. "I'll send Fernando to pick you up."

"What are you going to do?"

"Give them something to follow." Mike turned back toward the warehouse where their cars were parked.

Voss grabbed his arm. "You are taking a risk."

"They may know about your boat. It's better if I lead them in the opposite direction."

Anton nodded. "Alright. Meet me in Caracas as planned. We are not giving up!"

Mike handed over the envelopes but kept Anton's old passport. Then he ran for the cars. The siren's wail was growing closer. Fowler snatched the bags and his leather jacket from the back of his bike and tossed them, the StG 44, and the ammunition belt into the passenger seat of Anton's Lancia. The car liked to be carefully warmed up but there was no time for that. He slid in, put the gear shifter in neutral, and set the choke. He cranked the engine over. It sputtered and coughed, then caught. He gunned it forward and the car almost stalled. Stabbing in the clutch saved it from dying. Then, revving the engine madly, he accelerated toward the gates.

To the south, the street was full of flashing lights. Fowler crashed through the gutter and cut the wheel hard, flooring the accelerator. He straightened out heading up the block. A quick glance in the rearview mirror gave him a snapshot of a squadron of approaching fire and police vehicles . . . and the two Germans running back toward their car. He turned on his lights, shifted and, as he roared into the next block, he honked his horn and flicked the high beams.

Fernando Zúñiga was standing next to his Plymouth staring

down the road at the commotion outside the factory. Fowler slowed and, as Fernando crouched down to look at him, he pointed back toward the cross street.

"Voss! Bomb shelter!" he yelled.

Zúñiga nodded and jumped back into the Plymouth. Fowler pushed off the choke and accelerated away.

Behind him a police car had broken loose from the pack of emergency vehicles and was headed his way. That was not good. He had been hoping the Germans would chase him, not the cops.

He made a left at the end of the block and headed inland, flashing past occasional buildings interspersed with dark tracts of patchy farmland. He drove hard, rattling over washboards and dodging potholes, sliding the little car into intersecting roads. He needed to get turned around before he was trapped. There were only a few places where he could get across either the Besòs River or the railway.

The cops were still behind him, their lights distantly visible through the spray of water he was kicking up. Fowler started working his way toward the tracks. Then the gravel road pitched up and Mike slammed on the brakes. He skidded across a paved thoroughfare and down the far side. The Lancia slewed around. Mike shifted into reverse, cranked the wheel, then rammed it back into first. He launched himself up, turning onto the highway, and doused his lights.

In the distance the police car shot across the road behind him. He would only have a moment. Fowler slowed and made a left, crawling off the pavement into a muddy lot. Dark rows of partially constructed industrial or apartment blocks ran south toward the lights of the city. He coasted in behind a line of bulldozers and graders, and stopped. He waited. Five minutes passed. Mike got out and stashed the assault rifle, the magazines, and his bag in the trunk. Then he headed out again. He was still hoping to create a distraction to help Voss escape, but he also needed to get out of town before either Skorzeny's men caught him or he was arrested by the Spanish police.

By dawn Mike Fowler was hidden in the brush along the banks of the old reservoir beneath the villa of Anton Voss. Above him he could see lights in different rooms go on and off as men searched the house. He had changed clothes, thrown his ruined suit coat away, and pulled a pair of boots from his Gladstone. The airport and train station hadn't panned out; both were carefully guarded and if he had shown himself there would have been no opportunity to escape. Mike had been able to gas up the Lancia, and now he was going to see if there was one last chance to lead his enemies away from Tarragona and *Sigune*.

By a circuitous route he drove back to the crest of the ridge, past the buildings and the loop of streets around the top of the funicular railway, and then down, gliding by the turnoff to the villa.

Mike had hoped they would be watching the road but they were not. In the gray light, he made a U-turn and started back, taking Anton's spare pistol out of its holster and laying it on the seat beside him. He dipped down off the road into the dark path beneath the trees. As he coasted forward, he worked the clutch and put the gear shifter into reverse, ready to back out at top speed.

There was a hint of motion at the farthest edge of his vision, then someone shouted. Near the house, the lights of a car winked on. Mike took that as his signal and started backing up. He couldn't allow them to catch him, but he needed to be chased or followed. It was going to be a dangerous balance.

Fowler accelerated backward up the muddy track. He shot across the hilltop road in reverse, narrowly missing an early-morning bus whose driver swerved and honked furiously. He double-clutched and got it into first, pulling away as the black Mercedes turned in behind him. He roared between the houses and buildings that lined the way north, then held left and started his descent down the forested slopes behind the city.

Invisible in the cloudy distance were the Pyrenees and then

France. He set that as his goal and drove, downshifting into the corners and praying that the Lancia's unique radial tires could hold the road.

Mission accomplished. All he had to do now was to stay alive.

ISRAEL,

twelve days later . . .

THE MORNING AFTER the MS *Orna* docked at Tel Aviv was bright and breezy and cool. On his way through the lobby of the Dan Hotel Mike Fowler bought a copy of the *New York Herald Tribune,* then, ignoring a waiting cab, he headed inland on foot. The neighborhood was full of white concrete buildings festooned with streamlined balconies. Seagulls called in the distance.

Fowler had done his best to make his arrival in Israel appear ordinary. Using the ship's radio, he had sent a message to Hyman Lotz, a government contact who handled small-arms sales. The Israelis insisted that travelers obtain a transit or entry visa prior to arrival. A meeting with Lotz might allow him to circumvent that particular formality.

Mike had also tried to get in contact with Aleixandre Porras but discovered he had checked out of the Hotel Metropole on the night of the ruckus in Barcelona. A few days later the ship received a radio telegram. Porras and his family were safe in Switzerland. He was able to communicate anonymously through their banker, but he knew nothing about the fate of Anton Voss.

Mike had visited Israel three times before, always accompanying shipments. The Israeli government and Sistemas Militar had once had a serious, almost fatal, misunderstanding. Since then, they had developed what might be termed a special relationship. Mike Fowler smiled when he thought of it that way. The Israeli connection was personal, but the less said about that, the better. Fowler did not consider himself much of a gentleman, but there were some things he wouldn't talk about.

If everything worked as planned, he would talk a little business, enough to establish a cover and preempt any questions about his arrival. Then he would catch a plane for Rome or Istanbul and use his false passport to take additional flights. With luck he could make it to the rendezvous in Caracas faster than anyone could track him.

It was less than a mile to his meeting and he took off his jacket, enjoying the mild weather. Another taxi passed by but it didn't tempt him. There had been very few opportunities to exercise aboard ship.

He came to a sudden stop. It hadn't been *another* taxi . . . it had been the *same* taxi. The car was still visible a block ahead of him. Slowing, stopping . . . then it turned left. Instincts developed on the lonely beaches of the South Pacific suddenly began whispering to him, instincts he had not paid enough attention to back in Spain.

Mike unhurriedly walked until he came to the next cross street. Then he turned right. It was a narrow lane choked with piles of construction materials. Masons were at work and cement mixers were grinding away; more than one apartment house was going up.

He made it across the next street without seeing the cab again, but a light blue Fiat pulled up and parked half a block ahead. No one got out. Mike crossed the street behind the car and kept going. A sidelong glance as he passed caught two figures inside. A moment later the cab braked to a stop in the middle of the next intersection. A large swarthy young man leaped out of the passenger seat. From behind he heard a car door slam and turned. The two from the Fiat were headed his way. He was surrounded.

That was when the hood came out and the cuffs went on. That was when they took him to a silent, freshly painted cell . . . a cell where there was no indication of day or night. Though clean and bright, it was a box where one was held in limbo, a state where any outcome was equally possible. It wasn't the sort of place where they locked up criminals. It was the sort of place where they questioned spies.

After a few hours a pair of men showed up. One was a young civilian with scrawny neck and ill-fitting clothes, a kippah pinned to his hair. The other was a leathery older man in a military uniform but without any visible badge of rank or unit. His head was shaved, and his eyes were shark eyes, snake eyes. He wouldn't have a problem pulling Fowler into the corridor and shooting him in the back of the head. Yet of the two, Fowler trusted the military officer more. His rules would be consistent. He wasn't the sort of man who needed to rationalize his behavior.

They didn't ask many questions. While he was at dinner the night before, a team had searched his room and discovered the pistol in his bag. They claimed that was why they were detaining him. But there had been no formal arrest or charges.

"We know what you do. There are proper channels to go through for business, but there are no options for carrying an illegal weapon. That is breaking the law." The young civilian was there to rattle his cage. The old soldier just observed; he was probably the more important of the two, but he hadn't yet tipped his hand by asking any questions.

"I often travel to some . . . difficult places." Mike knew he wasn't going to get anywhere by denying anything.

"The questionable morality of your business is hardly an excuse. How in the world do you justify it? I can't imagine."

"I don't bother. But if I had to, I'd say that there are a hundred and thirty or so nations on earth. There might be a dozen that manufacture weapons. If no one ever sold any munitions, only those who made them would have them. Everyone else would be at their mercy. I deal in autonomy, freedom of choice . . . if you are willing to risk your life for it. Mostly, however, it just makes for good business opportunities."

"Our borders should not be open to those who traffic in human misery."

"Tell it to your procurement officers and sales agents. I sell

British, American, and Israeli weapons whenever I locate a buyer, or whenever those countries don't want to get caught doing it themselves."

The little man sniffed. "I will be discussing this pistol with the Ministry of Justice."

The military officer leaned forward. He placed a tablet of yellow paper and a pencil on the ledge that served as desk. "I'm going to need a list of everyone you have seen or intended to see."

Fowler pushed back. "I've done that already. When I went through customs at the port."

"Do it again. This time include everyone in the country you know. Everyone."

Fowler wrote. The names he remembered from previous meetings. The minister who had signed the draw-down of funds that paid for the MS *Orna*'s cargo. A few others. He stopped there. There was one more, but it was none of their business regardless of the risk to himself.

The deeply tanned older man peered over his companion's shoulder, scanning his way down the list. He seemed suspicious yet somehow approving. "Are you *sure* this is complete?" The officer looked up; his dark eyes boring into Fowler's.

"Very," Fowler replied, unblinking. If the man knew the details of his past, then they understood each other. The two men left, and he was alone in the silence of his cell. There was nothing more he could do, so he went to sleep.

He dreamed of the sea, of Alexandria and a beach resort. Arab children selling iced orange juice, bread, and duqqa. The feel of the water and sun against his skin. Better times. A world of possibilities awaiting him. It hadn't been like that, not really, but reality was never the important part of dreams.

When he awoke, he thought he might still be dreaming. She sat in a chair on the other side of the bars. She was still beautiful, with a dancer's posture, but no longer trying to appear glamorous. She wore little or no makeup, and her skin had been bronzed by the desert sun. Like the bald officer, she wore a military uniform without badges or rank.

"Hello, Michael," she said.

He sat up and smiled. It was her name he had not written down on his list of contacts. In those sunny days in Egypt, he had known her as Simone DeMaes. Sometime later, in Monaco, when the birds were singing in the dark before dawn, she had whispered into his ear and asked him to call her Nicole. He suspected she was originally Polish but both she and the state of Israel would be unhappy he even knew that much. That was yet another reason he hadn't written down her name for his captors . . . he didn't know it. "Nicole" was probably just as much of a fiction as "Simone."

"You didn't call." She shook her head and smiled a sad smile. "I worry that means you're up to something."

He shrugged. "It's good to see you," he said.

It took her only an hour to get him released. Israel didn't lack bureaucracy, so that was a testament to her rank—or connections.

They put the cloth bag back over his head, and when it was removed, he was in a dusty lot behind an apartment building. Across from the rutted entrance, Nicole leaned against the side of a silver Willys-Overland Utility Wagon. The burly young operative who had driven the taxi indicated that he was about to unlock the cuffs.

"Go ahead," she said. "He's my problem now."

Fowler's wrists were freed and the car pulled away. Waving the cloud of dust away from her face, Nicole got in and leaned over to open the passenger door. "Come on," she said.

"Your problem?" He laughed.

"Yes. You *are* a problem—" She looked around to see if anyone was watching "—and you're mine."

She slid across the seat and into his arms.

CHAPTER 8

SHE HEADED SOUTH up onto the bluffs of Jaffa, a port that had been ancient even at the time of the Jewish rebellion against Rome in 70 A.D. They stopped at a crowded hole-in-the-wall for musabaha, chickpeas and sesame paste; telkai, spicy sauce; and bread. Adding to the noise was a radio on a shelf above the door. Adolf Eichmann, one of the SS architects of the Shoah, or Holocaust, was making an appeal to the Israeli Supreme Court. The news report faded out, and a group of women began singing accompanied by accordion music.

"I just found this place. This is what the young people eat, some of those that I train." Her eyes smiled at him over a torn corner of pita bread. "The old Ashkenazim . . . like me—" She shook her head. "They would be horrified."

She wasn't as old as he was, but she was over thirty. During the war Nicole, or Simone, or whatever her name had been back then, had been part of a gang, or a group of resistance fighters, depending on how you looked at it. She and her older sister had fled with others to the forest. Their family had been modestly wealthy, but that had not saved them from the Nazis. All that survived were the two teenage girls.

They had studied ballet from childhood, so they were fit and hard and used to pain and privation. From the little Mike had been able to piece together their rebel band had done what was necessary to survive, and sometimes they had been able to fight back. The girls were young and pretty and their band used those qualities to lure Nazi officers and collaborators, to rob and kill them. The demands of survival and retribution turned them into wolves.

They had a dream of making it to Palestine, but her sister had not survived the journey. By the end of the war a few of their band had made it to Italy. There they were able to contact the soldiers of the Haganah, Zionist paramilitaries recruited by the British as translators and intelligence agents. In turn the Zionists formed an organization to sneak their people out of Europe and into Palestine, past the British blockades. And so Nicole had learned to smuggle Jews and counterfeit documents, and how to hide it all under the noses of the Allied officials. Eventually, after the formation of Israel, she had been recruited into its intelligence agency, the Mossad, a woman with a hidden past and an even more secret present.

After lunch they got back on the road, passing arcaded buildings with fading awnings on one side and a stone barrier atop the seawall on the other. Then they left the city behind and the road settled in between a series of coastal dunes occasionally covered with patches of scrub. Mike asked where they were headed.

"The beach, eventually. A place where no one is listening in."

He didn't press her. The rear seat had been removed from the Willys and the back held a folding table and chairs, a wicker hamper, bedding, and a galvanized water cooler. It looked as if they were going camping. A pleasant thought, but he wasn't sure if he was still a prisoner.

"I bought you some clothes, take a look."

He found an assortment of trousers, shorts, shirts, and a wool sweater wrapped in brown paper. In a box nearby there was also a finely woven panama hat and a pair of aviator-style sunglasses. He had no idea what her salary was but in Israel prices were surprisingly high for just about everything. He put on the sunglasses and grinned at her and she laughed. It was charming, almost as if they were a real couple off for a picnic by the sea.

They passed the turnoff to a village called Palmachim and continued down a straight dirt track until she slowed and shifted into four-wheel drive. Then she cut the wheel over and ground slowly to the top of a hill about thirty feet higher than the road. She stopped, looked at him, then inclined her head to the south.

"We shouldn't be here. And I shouldn't be showing this to you."

About a mile away, on top of another low rise, was a strange building. A massive multifaceted tower arose from a low block of dun-colored concrete. It was an imposing structure, stylishly executed, and surrounded by a few other buildings. Closer to the road there was a security checkpoint.

"That is the Soreq Nuclear Research Center. It contains a five-megawatt research reactor, donated by your president Eisenhower—thank you very much—but there is also a series of laboratories that develop projects dealing with physics, lasers, and gravity. Many things I do not understand."

She pointed toward the foothills out the left-hand side of the vehicle. "Four miles that way is the Weizmann Institute of Science, which was established in 1944. And, just so you don't think we are new to all this, to the southeast there is Yavne, or Yabneel, the town that protected the Jewish sages after the fall of Jerusalem. They called it 'the vineyard of Yavne' because knowledge grew there, and because the young scholars sat on the floor in rows, like grapevines. You will understand why I have shown you this later," she said. "But you mustn't tell anyone that I brought you here."

"Yes, ma'am."

Her serious mood dissolved and she slapped him on the arm, then put the Willys in gear and started back down the hill. They turned north and cut through the dunes heading to the beach. When Nicole got to the hard-packed sand along the waterline she accelerated, whizzing along to finally brake to a stop where the sand was blocked by a massive limestone promontory. In a protected hollow against the bluffs a large tent had been erected on a leveled wooden platform.

"We're here!"

"Is this your beach house?"

She ran lightly up the sand to the front, hopped onto the platform, and pulled back a flap of mosquito netting to look inside. "It's *our* beach house." Then she became serious again. "But you have to pay for it." She looked down at him, her eyes probing his, looking for an answer to a question he didn't understand.

"Some men are going to come tonight. It will be alright, I promise. You can say whatever you want, or nothing at all. Then I will drive you to Lod Airport and put you on a flight that was chartered by the Vatican. Once in Rome you can go anywhere you like."

It sounded perfect, too perfect . . . but last night he had been in a jail. Two weeks ago he'd been chased around Europe by a group of Nazis who wanted to kill him and torture his partner for information he didn't even have. If the cost of a brief vacation with Nicole and an untraceable flight to Rome was a polite interrogation by her superiors, who was he to argue? If they wanted to pull out his fingernails they could just as easily have done it in Tel Aviv.

"I'm not gonna swear to tell them anything," he warned her.

"Just listen to what they have to say. I don't believe it is what you are expecting."

They brought the hamper and cooler inside, then set up the table and chairs. In the back of the truck, he discovered his Gladstone. Pushing aside the clothes he found the remainder of his money but, tugging up the false bottom, he was not surprised to discover that the pistol, ammunition, and blackjack were missing. The forged passport remained. That was interesting.

"If we've got a few minutes, I want to take a swim."

"You go on then, it's too cold for me."

Leaving her at the tent, he went down to the water. When they had first met—no, that wasn't right . . . Mike smiled at the thought . . . when they first met, they had damn near killed each other. It was more accurate to say that soon after they first met, Mike had discovered she couldn't swim. Since then he had taught her the basics, but he doubted she would ever be comfortable in the ocean.

He took a breath and swam the first few strokes beneath the surface. Then he made his way up the coast, staying inside the reef and dodging past the occasional shallow spots where the tide sucked at the rocks.

Mike Fowler worried about Voss. In the few hours he'd spent at the Dan Hotel, he had missed his chance to contact their bank in Switzerland to get an update. Now he was itching to get to a phone, one that wasn't going to be monitored by the Mossad. But Nicole or her superiors had made sure that couldn't happen anytime soon. He wondered if that was on purpose.

He turned and, as the sun dipped toward the horizon, started back.

Nicole met him with a towel as he sloshed his way through the shallow water. Two vehicles had arrived while he was gone, a brawny Dodge Command Car with its canvas top and fitted side curtains, and its smaller cousin, a military jeep. A pair of young soldiers with slung Uzis kept watch, one on top of the bluffs, the other by the trucks. Pressure lanterns glowed from inside the tent and between the hush of wind and waves Fowler could hear a mumble of voices.

Nicole laid out some clothes for him on the seat of her Willys. "They are here. Come on up when you're ready." She glanced around to see if the soldiers were looking and quickly kissed him on the cheek. Then she left, picking her way through the rocks to disappear inside.

When he entered, Fowler found the table set for a meal. Three men faced him. They were not all strangers; one was the tough old army officer who had visited his jail cell. Nicole hung back, and the officer took the lead introducing the others.

"Ahh. Mr. Fowler. Tonight's accommodations may be more primitive but they are . . . less restrictive, eh?"

"Yes, sir. I appreciate the lack of bars."

"This evening we are going to use our first names only, for security purposes. You can call me Yaron; these men are Saul and Leonid."

Saul was a small man. Fowler couldn't tell how old; he was the type that seemed to prematurely age but then remain unchanged until they died. He had a ruffle of curly white hair around the back of his head and peered at them through thick glasses that appeared inadequate to the task. He wore baggy trousers cinched up over his belly by a thin belt and a sport coat that looked like he slept in it nightly.

Leonid was different. Once upon a time he had been big-boned and strong. He stood slowly and awkwardly and would not meet Fowler's eyes. One side of his face was constricted with scar tissue and, given his posture, that whole half of his body seemed to have suffered equal damage. He wore a thick sweater under a heavy coat and seemed to shiver slightly as he nodded a greeting.

"We have some questions for you," Yaron said. "But first we will eat."

Nicole and Yaron placed a series of covered aluminum containers on the table and passed out plates and glasses. Mike gathered that the two civilians were men of some importance. Yaron was at least a colonel, and probably a general, yet the other men remained in their seats and let him serve them.

The food was nondescript and the conversation equally lacking, but Fowler was able to pick up a few details. Saul and Leonid were academics, scientists. Mike's years of sitting with Voss in his café had attuned him to the type. And they didn't like each other. Saul appeared to be irritated by Leonid's presence. It wasn't anything to do with his deformity or slurred speech. It seemed to be that Leonid had ideas Saul found embarrassing. It was just before they finished eating when Yaron opened the ball . . .

"There was quite a commotion in Barcelona. Two men tortured and murdered, three more killed in some sort of fight. Explosives. Automatic weapons. Something else happened in France, a man beaten so badly they don't know if he will walk again. What do you know about all of this?"

"As an American, I'd like to plead the fifth." Mike glanced at Nicole. She arched an eyebrow and started clearing the plates. None of this was news to her, she'd probably been briefed before they let her see him.

"There are warrants out for you and Anton Voss, both in Spain and France . . . and reports, of a more secretive nature, that the Stasi and KGB are investigating. The KGB is pulling rank on the East Germans. That means whatever it is, it's important. One of our consular officers visited your facility. It has been cordoned off by the Spanish government. That's too bad. I'm sure there are intelligence agencies who would like to inspect your records."

Mike ground his teeth; this was supposed to soften him up for something. He wished they'd just get down to it. "I'd be happy to give you the keys, but I have a feeling that locks don't really slow down Mossad."

Yaron smiled thinly and placed a file on the table. The material in it looked like a haphazard pile of clippings, photos, and typed reports. He found a certain page and looked it over. "The dead, except for your two employees, seem to have been German. And neither West Germany nor the DDR is interested in investigating. I imagine it might be embarrassing. All were known to have once been members of the SS or the Hitler Youth."

"That's not a problem for you then, is it?"

"Not at all. But I believe it is a problem for *you*. You're in over your head. And your partner? In this case we don't know if your partner is the tail or the dog."

"What does *that* mean?"

"When we see our old enemies react in certain ways . . . Well, let's just say it arouses our suspicions." Yaron took a stack of glossy five-by-sevens from the file. "Tell me who you see."

The first photo was a portrait of a young man, clean-shaven and wearing some sort of athletic tunic, but the scar was a dead give-away.

"That's Skorzeny. You know we know him. You know we've done business with him."

"How about this man?"

Mike identified Heinrich Hartmann, looking arrogant and impressively fit in the uniform of an SS Scharführer, the equivalent of a sergeant. He gestured for another photograph.

This one was an older gentleman with bushy eyebrows, dressed in a homburg and scarf. It took Fowler a moment or two because, though he'd seen this picture before, he'd never met the man. "That's Dr. Wilhelm Voss, an industrialist. He used to be director of Škoda Manufacturing in Czechoslovakia . . . You might call him an arms dealer. No relation to *Anton* Voss, except they are about the same age."

Mike glanced at Nicole. She looked disgusted and rolled her eyes. She, or more likely people she worked with, had once confused Anton Voss with Wilhelm Voss. That confusion had nearly ended in disaster. But in an odd way it could be said that Wilhelm Voss had introduced Mike and Nicole.

The photos they had shown him so far seemed to have been tests. He certainly hadn't told them anything they didn't already know. Now Yaron set down another picture and, this time, Leonid leaned forward slightly, breath rattling in his lungs. It looked like a close-up of a page from a yearbook or a clipping from a newspaper. Fowler peered at the fuzzy rendition of a man in a naval uniform, and shrugged.

"I have no idea."

"That is Wilhelm Rhein, Konteradmiral Wilhelm Rhein. Do you know that name? He was chief of Research, Invention, and Patenting for the Kriegsmarine."

Now, *that* might have something to do with Anton Voss. The name even sounded familiar, but he couldn't remember why. Mike maintained a poker face and shook his head.

"Try this one." It was a rather good-looking man wearing an overcoat and bow tie. His pale hair was being blown about in the wind and it seemed as if he was about to light a pipe.

"No."

"Professor Walther Gerlach, director for physics at the Reich Scientific Research Council. Have you heard his name? Did Voss collect any papers or documents of his? He is still a renowned scientist. Think for us: he had interests in medicine, quantum physics, the effects of magnetic fields . . ."

Fowler shook his head.

"Call-called him 'the alchemist.'" Leonid cleared his throat. His accent might have been Hungarian, and his voice resonated hollowly. He coughed and then pushed against the table to stop his hands from shaking. "We made go-gold from mercury. Ionized mercury. Plasma spin. We ran, ran high voltage in isolation to cr-create . . ." He gestured at himself, his ruined body, and took a breath. ". . . Never elements . . . new elements."

"You *think*!" Fowler had expected Yaron to try and stop Leonid from saying too much, but he was surprised when it was Saul who spoke up, pointing an accusing finger at his colleague. "You do not know! You fill the air with confusion. Physics is not magic, no matter what those Nazi mamzerim were playing at."

"I was there! Do n-not scoff at what they were doing because of their ideology. The theory predates Nazism, and we cannot afford to close our minds!"

"Gentlemen, please! We have a mission; we must stick to it." Yaron produced another exhibit, this time a sketch, from his file . . .

"Take a look here. What about this object? Have you seen pictures, diagrams?"

On seeing it, Saul pushed back from the table. "Feh! I am tired of this Narriskeit! This what you brought me for? It is nonsense!"

"I brought you to ask the right questions should we learn anything useful," Yaron said.

The little old man stood, hiking up his trousers. "Well, I will be outside . . . if you learn anything at all, call me." He shot a baleful look at Leonid and walked out.

Mike looked down at the drawing. It was carefully done, an engineer's rendering of something that looked like a cylinder with a domed top sitting on a heavy base. Some sort of cabling ran into it from a rack with lights or dials. Though it was precise in its detail, down to the rivets or bolts and electrical connectors, the lines wavered as if it had been viewed through some strange distortion. Or perhaps they had been erased and redrawn. Mike thought of Leonid's shaking hands. Maybe redrawn by a talented technician whose abilities were failing. To one side, there was a series of arrows and squiggles, a form of scientific notation, almost a design, and some sort of mathematics. The equations had been crossed out with frustrated strokes of a pencil.

"I don't know." Mike decided to drop a line in the water and see if he got a bite. "Where would I have seen it?"

Yaron paused a moment, not as ready to give up this information as he had been about some of the people. "In a plan? A warehouse? Searching through archives for your partner? Think carefully. Perhaps you saw it in his files in Barcelona?"

Fowler pushed the sketch back across the table. "Anton has mountains of technical drawings and blueprints. There's lots of stuff I couldn't make heads or tails of even if it was in English. Can you give me a hint?"

"Do you recognize this word? 'Tychon.'"

"No. Is it a name?"

"In a way. Tychon was a nearly unknown Greek god. Either a god of chance, accident, or fertility: 'the producer.'" The officer stared at Fowler for a moment, but Mike had no idea what the man was talking about.

"How about 'Glasglocke'?"

"Nope."

There was a moment of silence, then Yaron said, "We will move on . . . Do you know this woman?" He turned over the last photo in the pile.

She was an attractive young lady, smiling and bundled tightly in an expensive winter coat. Behind her and slightly out of focus was what looked to be a Renaissance-era castle perched on a wooded outcrop overlooking a river.

But it wasn't the woman who grabbed Fowler's attention. At her side was a Kriegsmarine officer in a dark, elegantly cut uniform. There was an iron cross at his throat and, beneath the eagle-and-swastika national emblem sewn to his breast, there was another medal bearing a large swastika, the German Cross, a Nazi award for leadership. The officer was Anton Andreas Voss, and while he might have been working for the Reichspost, he definitely wasn't sorting mail.

Nicole glanced down at the uniform and the symbols on it. Then she grabbed a container full of dirty plates and silverware and carried it out into the dark.

"The woman?" Yaron prompted him.

"I've never seen her before. And, yes, I realize that's Voss. This was a long time before I came into the picture." It *felt* like a long time. A different age entirely. But in reality it might have been only four or five years before he'd met the older man.

"Alright." Yaron began putting papers back into his file. As he reached for the drawing, Leonid stopped him.

"Please, Yaron. Do no-not waste my time. I have not much left."

The officer glanced around, but it was just the three of them. "Mr. Fowler," he said. "You have Nicole's endorsement. That is something, but she is one person and there is a nation to protect.

"Here is what I can tell you: World War Two created the greatest looting spree in history. The Axis powers stole everything they could get hold of. Research from the universities, art from museums and homes, treasures many thought were hidden forever, the gold from our teeth. Then in victory the Americans, the Soviets, the British, and the French, they seized whatever they could find. Deals were made. Criminals walked free. Fleeing Nazis even stole from their own government, bars of gold from the Reichsbank, technology from military installations. It was done to preserve themselves, and it was done to preserve Nazism.

"Your general Eisenhower thought that German technology was twenty-five years ahead of the United States. Edward R. Murrow described it as 'malignant ingenuity.' Churchill called it 'perverted science.' Even today research done by the Third Reich is still paying dividends. The American National Aeronautics and Space Administration and other, lesser-known, efforts are led by German scientists, some of them once members of the SS.

"In 1945 we were not prepared to take advantage. Israel wasn't even a country. But there were things taken by the Nazis, and *from* the Nazis. Things that were paid for in blood. *Our* blood. By the right of that sacrifice, we would claim them."

"So, what is that thing?" Mike cut him off.

Leonid took a breath, but Yaron held up a hand, silencing him.

"I cannot tell you." He nodded in the direction Saul had taken when he left the tent. "Some would say it never existed or that it couldn't have worked if it had. Have you ever been to a dog track? Years ago, I saw this while visiting Florida. Like the horse races, but the greyhounds would run chasing a mechanical rabbit." He showed Mike the sketch of the odd device one last time. "Sometimes I think this is like that rabbit.

"Our enemies have been making plans. They destabilize the world to their own ends. You saw them do this in Egypt. Now for some reason they are after you and your partner . . . a man I think you realize is more than he seems. We need to know: what do they want from you? We might even be able to help."

Mike Fowler nodded, but not in agreement. "We" meant Israel, and Israel would kill him in an instant if it felt its interests were threatened. He looked Yaron straight in the eye. "You have your people to protect, and I have mine. Understand this: you're *overthinking things*. Doing business with Skorzeny is like doing business with the Mafia. Force has to be met with force. Our fight has nothing to do with these scientists or some machine that may or may not be real.

"You want to talk about what I saw in Egypt? I saw Israeli intelligence making this very same mistake. Yes, my company has sold military designs and information. We even *gave* you a working prototype just to get your business. If what I've said isn't good enough, you'll have to break out the rubber hoses."

Yaron sighed. "Alright," he said. "Then let me put it *this* way: if you were to catch this rabbit and bring it to us, we would make it worth your while. Israel is not a rich nation, but we pay our debts."

"Okay. If I see something, I'll consider it. But you have to tell me one thing . . ."

"What?" It was barely a question. The military man was not going to negotiate.

"Tell me who the girl is. The woman with Anton Voss."

Yaron looked to Leonid, and the old man drew a breath, tears welling in his eyes, "Doctor Elizabeth Adler. She was from the Al-Albertina . . . the um, University of Königsberg. A math-mathematician. A great mathematician."

"Is she still alive?"

"Oh, no." He drew a ragged, painful breath. "I—I certainly hope not."

Yaron called in his soldiers and went to collect Saul, who was standing in the moonlight a short way down the beach. The young men and Nicole packed up what was left of the plates and trays and stowed them in the back of the jeep. For a moment Mike found himself alone with Leonid.

The older man drew himself up, facing Fowler directly for the first time. "You are a lucky man. Healthy. A fighter. You have a nice Jewish girl. If you see that thing . . . and if you are a hero, you will destroy it. They have made you an offer, and they will talk about a beautiful future. Don't listen."

Then Leonid let out a long empty breath. "But if you are not such a mensch, just get away. Take her and go to the other side of the world. It will not keep its secrets forever."

Then Yaron came back, and the soldiers were helping the scientists up onto the running board of the Dodge. Its engine turned over and the sand and surf were lit up as the headlights came on. As they drove away, splashing through the rising tide, Nicole wrapped an arm around his waist and leaned her head on his shoulder.

"The old man, what did he say to you?" she asked.

"Not much. He told me you were a nice girl and that I was lucky."

Nicole looked up at him, her eyes invisible in the dark as the night pressed in around them.

"Be careful," she murmured. "I'm not that nice."

It was something to consider . . . Because on the night they had first met, he had thought she was very nice indeed.

CHAPTER 9

EGYPT,

five years earlier . . .

ANSON FORDYCE HAD been sitting in the lobby of Alexandria's Cecil Hotel when Mike Fowler and Anton Voss joined the short line of people waiting to check in. Fordyce hadn't changed much. He was a pear-shaped little man decked out in a seersucker suit with blue pinstripes and a red bow tie that made his collar look like it was choking him.

Fowler had always hoped he would never have to see Fordyce again. He was convinced that back in 1945 the man had attempted to send him to his death. Officially, Fowler and five other commandos had been on a secret mission. It was an assassination, a carefully prepared ambush, but it seemed the final element of the plan included the assassins themselves paying the ultimate price. Fordyce, along with an army general, had been in charge of the operation.

Mike Fowler was willing to risk death for his comrades, and for his country. But, as Anton Voss would later point out, he had never questioned the difference between his country and its government—or whoever controlled that government—until he began to suspect that Anson Fordyce had tried to kill him.

Even now, easily a dozen years later, he was sorely tempted to return the favor.

Irritatingly, Fordyce didn't seem to have aged a day. He stood up, recognizing Fowler immediately. A professional smile snapped into place.

"Mike Fowler! As I live and breathe!" Fordyce set down his briefcase and stuck out his hand as if they were old friends. The light, corrugated fabric of his jacket crinkled as it moved. In contrast to his pudgy appearance, Fordyce's grip was firm and his hand was hard as stone.

"You've gained quite a reputation! Truly impressive. Auctioning off the Rhön-Rossitten glider archives. From now on the whole world is going to wonder what you've got up your sleeve. So . . ." Fordyce tried and failed to catch Voss's eye. "Are the two of you here to buy or sell?"

Three months earlier, Egypt had engaged in a short, vicious conflict against the combined forces of Britain, France, and Israel. In the face of objections from the U.S. and nuclear threats from the USSR, the will of the old European empires crumbled and their attempt to seize the Suez Canal collapsed. Although Egypt suffered militarily, internationally it was beginning to seem like the regime of Gamal Abdel Nasser might have achieved a political victory. Now Nasser was planning on rearming as soon as he could pay his Soviet bloc suppliers. Fowler and Voss were there because the government was highly motivated to sell the remaining World War II–era British weapons still in its armories.

"We're always on the lookout for an opportunity," Fowler said. Fordyce had once claimed to work for the State Department. But Fowler was fairly certain he was now serving the CIA. Mike wasn't going to give this irritating little dandy any more information than he had to.

"Well, I'm here in the hotel." Fordyce gestured vaguely at the ceiling. "Look me up and I'll buy you a drink, for old times' sake . . . Maybe we can even find a way to work together again."

"Last time was enough for me. I remember a lot of napalm."

Fordyce made a motion, as if to wave away the circumstances of that mission to Itu Aba. He picked up his briefcase. "Mistakes happen," he said. "The fog of war and all that. I hope it can be water under the bridge. You always were quite an effective operative." Fordyce headed for the front doors and then down to the street.

Voss had made it to the front desk and was signing the register. Fowler handed his passport to one clerk while another checked their names against an alphabetized list.

"Oh, yes. Welcome back, Dr. Voss," he said. "I will inform the manager that you have returned."

"Mr. Voss, or Herr Voss, please. Not doctor."

"Of course. Very sorry." The clerk turned his back to search for their keys.

"This is the first time I have stayed here," Voss said as Fowler added his signature.

Mike chuckled. "Well, if they're going to send up champagne, don't argue."

Their rooms were a corner suite on the second floor. Voss pointed Fowler toward the slightly larger room overlooking the side street. "You take the one with the door to the hall."

The central sitting room had a magnificent view both up and down the Corniche. Across the crescent of the East Harbor Mike could see the Citadel of Qaitbay. Supposedly, it had been built from the remains of the great lighthouse of Alexandria, one of the Wonders of the Ancient World.

Mike checked the phone and was not surprised to discover a listening device. Egypt had two reasonably effective security services, the Mukhabarat al-Amma and Mabahith Amn al-Dawla. Each had their own operatives as well as a multitude of informers: taxi drivers, maids, street children, and beggars. It was a continuation of a system that had reached its height under the Ottoman Empire. These spies, however, had been reorganized by members of the Gestapo. Hundreds of Nazis had fled to Egypt after the war, and many had found work as advisors to the military and intelligence services.

Fowler whistled softly to attract Voss's attention and pointed out the bug. There was nothing they could do about it. Removing the device would trigger either an immediate "service call" by telephone company technicians to replace it, or a visit by some very tough men in dark suits who might replace you.

Voss walked over and took the receiver from Fowler. He jiggled the hook.

"Operator? When you bring our luggage, please be sure that the three wooden cases are sent up as well. They are very valuable gifts for . . ."

A hint of amusement could be heard in his voice as he mentioned the names of the general in charge of the police and an influential member of the Ministry of the Interior. That would certainly give the listeners something to think about.

Not surprisingly, their luggage and the long wooden cases appeared almost immediately, accompanied by a slightly-out-of-breath assistant manager. Fowler gave him a generous tip, and he backed out of the room bowing repeatedly.

"Thank you, and thank *you,* Dr. Voss."

The door closed and Mike turned to his partner, "There it is again."

Voss frowned. "Perhaps out of all the Germans here there is someone who remembers me from before the war . . ." he mused. He did not seem happy about it. "We will be seeing more than enough of my countrymen tonight. More of the past than I care to relive. But that is my problem, not yours."

Mike checked the cases the bellmen had brought up. He carefully removed the customs paperwork and opened the latches, verifying that nothing had been stolen. Each contained a customized Mauser hunting rifle complete with scope, cleaning kit, and carefully handloaded ammunition. Since there was no door to the hallway, he stowed the rifles under the bed in Voss's room.

"I'm going to take a look around, check the lay of the land." Fowler made a circling motion with one finger.

Voss nodded; he had lit a cigarette from his silver case and was now composing telegrams, following up on the work they had done over the last few days.

Alexandria's main thoroughfares were quite clean compared to some of the countries they had just visited. There were plenty of cars and people wearing western clothing, though it was sometimes mixed with traditional garb. On the backstreets and in vacant lots, however, there was a scattering of trash and debris. Donkeys and pushcarts edged through the crowd and there were more kaftans and vests on the men, and long wide-sleeved djubbehs and burqas on the women. It seemed almost like there were two Egypts, one that had long been part of the Europeanized Mediterranean, the other part of the exotic landscape of Arabia.

Fowler heard snatches of conversations in Greek, Italian, and Arabic, some English, but mostly French. It was a city of many nationalities, but some of them seemed to be in transition. Hand-lettered signs in English and French indicated moving sales, people who had found they were no longer welcome or were possibly being formally expelled by the government.

Mike walked quickly, staying ahead of the slim, fast-talking boys who tried to sell him tourist trinkets or services, some of which strained his credulity and sense of humor. By the time the call to prayer began to echo from the minarets and the streets emptied out, Mike had reached the large, modern freight facility that was the Western Port.

Up ahead there was some sort of commotion. A crowd was packed in behind a series of fences and lined up along the gangways leading to an Italian-flagged freighter. Soldiers stood on the outside; some of them had brought rugs and were praying facing the southeast. As he got closer, Fowler could hear a low hubbub of voices, some of them in a language he only vaguely recognized . . . Hebrew.

He could see that some of the men wore a short, poncholike garment with tassels attached to the corners under their coats. Other people were pulling up in cars and slipping the soldiers money for the chance to approach the wire. Once there, they clung briefly to a loved one's fingers, or passed small packages of money or valuables. The group within the enclosure, several hundred of them, were clearly being deported with no more than what they could carry.

Fowler walked into the street, skirting the idling cars. Ahead of him a man moved away from the fence, away from a young woman pressed up against the barrier with tears in her eyes. Mike recognized him immediately: one of the desk clerks from the Hotel Cecil. The clerk's eyes narrowed as he stared back at Mike, and he muttered something. Fowler knew the sound of an epithet in any language; all of the professional courtesy the man had displayed earlier in the day had vanished. As he turned the man said one more word, this one easily recognized . . .

"Nazi!"

Stepping through the door of Santa Lucia and out of the soot and dust of Alexandria's streets was like being transported fifteen hundred miles north, across the Mediterranean. It was a restaurant and piano bar expressly designed to make an expatriate feel they had returned to Europe. There was dark paneling, a staff that spoke several languages, and music that had probably been played in Paris, Berlin, and Rome before the war. The tall windows were frosted, sealing off the view of the street outside.

Mike could see Anton Voss tense as they crossed the floor. It was nine o'clock and the place was full of bustling waiters, and men and women dressed for the evening. As Voss followed the maître d' to their table, he did not glance left or right.

Mike Fowler, on the other hand, carefully scanned the crowd. There were quite a few Egyptian uniforms; the entire evening was organized as an opportunity to buy and sell military supplies. From a table on the mezzanine Anson Fordyce, now dressed in a dark suit with a flower in his lapel, caught Fowler's eye and gave him the Boy Scout salute. Fowler ignored him.

"Señor Voss? Señor Fowler? Hassan Ghorab, Colonel, Egyptian Ground Forces. Very pleased to meet you." They shook hands and sat down.

Colonel Ghorab looked like a recruiting poster for the kind of officer President Nasser was trying to promote, young and sleekly handsome. He was one of the Egyptian army's contacts for both the procurement and sales of military goods. The word on the street was that he was honest. Of course, the old generals and politicians would eventually get involved, each with their own way of collecting their due. To an arms dealer, however, bribery wasn't a problem. Many times the sole reason for a government doing business was so its officials could fatten their wallets through an unofficial markup, commission, finder's fee, or just a suitcase full of cash. The actual weapons were an excuse, a publicly funded prop in an elaborate play.

"Tell me, are you related to Standartenführer Wilhelm Voss? Until just recently he was the head of our military central planning board."

"Not to my knowledge. I know who he is, but the name means 'fox' in the Low German dialect. It is quite common."

They ordered drinks, then dinner, and talked about the tumultuous events of the last few months. Colonel Ghorab had flown in from Prague two days earlier. The Czechoslovakians were attempting to act as if all was normal. Yet every whispered conversation had been about the anti-Soviet uprisings in Hungary and Poland, the first signs of violent discontent since the protests in East Germany and Czechoslovakia in 1953. Egypt, of course, had recently faced what they were calling the "Tripartite Aggression." The British and French had only just withdrawn. A UN peacekeeping force, the first ever deployed, now stood between the canal and the Israelis who were still occupying positions in the Sinai Peninsula.

"So, how many rifles will be available?" Voss asked.

"Oh, twenty-some-odd thousand. Señor Fowler can get an exact count tomorrow when he does his inspection."

"Are all your new purchases from the Czechs?" Fowler scribbled a note to himself. "As long as you are selling .303-caliber rifles, we would be happy to buy ammunition, too."

"Yes, yes. We have to standardize when we can. The Americans and British, they claim we are falling into the hands of the Communists, but it is not so. There are simply fewer strings attached. No offense, of course."

Fowler held up a hand. "None taken."

"I myself would prefer American weapons, particularly the aircraft. But I believe the U.S. wants bases or other involvements, and we have just gotten rid of the English. Egypt must find a path between the U.S. and the USSR, between communism and capitalism."

"An admirable sentiment," said Voss. "Just be aware if you combine the two, you may achieve critical mass."

"Forgive me. I don't understand." A frown creased Colonel Ghorab's brow.

"My fellow Germans avoided the destruction of our economy under the communists, but the National Socialist Party was able to completely infiltrate our industry. It led to a . . . a rather unhealthy fusion of state and corporate power. I fear that people pay attention to certain parts of our history, yet they forget this one. All wars create government control of the economy, and the ones who benefit most are the biggest businesses."

Ghorab toasted Voss. "Señor Voss, I believe you are a philosopher."

"Ha! I sell arms. In some people's minds this makes me a villain. Well, perhaps. At this point in life I see myself as antiauthoritarian. It is man's nature one must beware of, not his tools."

It was a comment Mike Fowler had heard Voss make before, but he knew as well as anyone that at a certain point the tools did indeed become a problem. In just the last few months there had been tests of atomic weapons in Russia, the United States, the South Pacific, and Australia. Voss might affect an air of world-weary detachment, but the destructive power of the most advanced and expensive weapons had him as concerned as anyone.

Mike heard the door to the street open and looked over. Three tough young Europeans entered. The last of them, a powerful man in his mid-thirties with close-clipped blond hair, eyed the room. After a moment he was followed by a tall, broad-shouldered man who was somewhat older, a man whose scarred face Mike remembered from pictures in the Spanish press. Otto Skorzeny. Hitler's commando. The notorious hero of the Waffen SS.

The ebb and flow of conversation petered out. There was a shuffle and scrape as a number of men, and a few women, respectfully got to their feet. The man at the piano ceased fingering the keys. Except for the sounds from the kitchen, the room was silent. Those not standing glanced around nervously, wondering who the newcomers were and what was going on.

Skorzeny grinned, looking quickly around. Then he stepped up to the nearest table, where two paunchy bespectacled men stood, almost at attention, alongside a pair of seated women who might or might not be their wives. Skorzeny shook their hands and then moved on, greeting more and more people. Some went back to their meals; others crossed the room and clustered about the big man. The piano player struck up a new tune and the chatter and clatter of a busy restaurant again filled the room.

"Do you know Herr Skorzeny?" Colonel Ghorab asked Voss.

Voss shook his head. "We moved in very different circles."

"That was quite an entrance," Fowler commented.

"After the war, he helped recruit many of these Alemanni to be our military and political advisors," Colonel Ghorab said. "It will soon be announced that we have begun our own rocketry program. I believe he was involved with locating scientists and engineers for that, too."

Once their plates were cleared Colonel Ghorab took his napkin from his lap and announced, "I fear the plan for the evening requires me to visit some gentlemen from Poland who are just upstairs. Please, order coffee and dessert if you wish, the bill will be paid by my government."

Under the mezzanine, the powerful-looking man with the bristle cut who seemed to head up Skorzeny's entourage pushed back his chair. He crossed the room toward Voss and Fowler's table. Mike stood, though not out of politeness. Voss remained seated, smoking his cigarette. The man stopped at their table, clicked his heels, and gave a curt little bow.

"Herr Voss? Heinrich Hartmann." He glanced at Fowler, tangentially including him in the introduction, yet making it clear that Fowler's name was unimportant. Hartmann was roughly the same height as Fowler, but outweighed him by a good thirty pounds, all muscle.

"Standartenführer Skorzeny invites you to join us for further entertainments. Additionally, there is a business proposition to be discussed. Taxis have been ordered. Five minutes."

Mike had to stifle a laugh. In his opinion Germans fell into two categories, and well-oiled ramrods like Hartmann were the sort he didn't care for. Several others from Hartmann's group had spread out among the tables and at least a quarter of the people in the restaurant were collecting their belongings and getting ready to leave.

"You sure you want to do this?" Fowler asked.

Voss snorted. "Nein. But we will certainly become a topic of conversation if we do not attend." He stood and clapped Fowler on the back, a rare show of physical affection. "We must go, and we must make the most of it."

The swarm of taxis that had pulled up in front of Santa Lucia battled their way across town like a squadron of fighter planes intercepting the enemy. If they had been an attraction at an amusement park, the heartstopping ride would have required a premium ticket. Their destination was a building that crouched like a fortress between the sea and the corniche about three miles east of the restaurant. A stone bridge took them across a moat-like alley and surf crashed on the rocks below the circular concrete base of the building.

Côte d'Azur had long been a popular nightspot. It was said that, before he was overthrown, King Farouk had a permanently reserved table and would often play cards until dawn. Skorzeny's German exiles, the cadre of Egyptian officers, and a few arms dealers had arrived just in time for the belly dancing. It was a performance intended for tourists, but none of the locals seemed to mind. An additional commitment to buy or sell made under the influence of alcohol, exotic music, and seductive dance would be appreciated by their superiors.

With no plans except to see what Skorzeny had in mind, Fowler and Voss slid into a booth near the doors to the kitchen. There was a whine of strings and wail of pipes as the music started, and a spotlight picked up a girl in the center of the dance floor. She was perhaps a bit more scantily dressed than was traditional, but it made for a good show. As the drums joined in, she began to shake her hips and weave her arms, adding to the music with tiny cymbals worn on her fingers and a belt of bronze bells strung around her waist.

The dancer was attractive enough, if you liked the type, and clearly she was very skilled, but Fowler's attention was drawn past her, to the tables on the other side of the room. There, illuminated by lights from the arched hallway beyond, were three young women. While two of them were moderately pretty, neither held his interest for more than a moment. The third, however, was remarkable. She was dressed in a black-and-white ensemble that complemented her short dark hair and fair skin. The clothes fit her form closely enough to get his attention, yet, with the addition of gloves and a shawl, she was still dressed modestly enough for a night out in Alexandria.

The girl was not part of the crowd who had come from Santa Lucia. Fowler was certain he would have noticed her if she had been. Anson Fordyce had been in one of Skorzeny's taxis and

Fowler was irritated to see him stop, as he worked the room, to chat with the three women. They laughed as he made some joke, and he gallantly struck a match so that one of them could light a cigarette.

Mike shook his head as he thought of the young women being taken in by whatever line Fordyce was feeding them. They couldn't guess that Fordyce—cherubic, perfectly dressed, and obviously charming—was also the sort who would order an air strike on his own men. Struggling to be fair, Mike acknowledged that his own team had also killed dozens, including Japanese civilians, at Fordyce's behest. Life was full of ironies.

Fowler slid out of the booth and stood as a large figure approached. The lamp on the table illuminated the curving, branching scar and the penetrating eyes of Otto Skorzeny.

"May I join you?"

"Bitte . . ." Voss slid deeper into the booth; he gestured toward Fowler. "My partner, Michael Fowler."

Mike sat back down.

"Oh, yes? I have been warned that perhaps, just perhaps, you were the one who taught some of my French colleagues a lesson in bomb making." Fowler and Voss glanced at each other, wondering if the Red Hand's revenge was on its way, courtesy of the SS.

"No, sir. I have no idea what you are talking about," Fowler deadpanned. He carried a steel spike, designed for the OSS, in a sheath along his forearm. He crossed his hands on the tabletop, fingers touching the knurled end just inside his cuff.

Skorzeny laughed, a booming sound that cut through the cacophony of percussion and strings.

"Really? They were in the mistress's bed! And I understand the wife was quite pleased. Well, perhaps she wired them up herself. But you *were* a navy diver *and* . . . explosives expert, correct? My men could have used you when they attacked the pontoon bridge at Linz."

"I'll take that as a compliment. But I believe I was on the other side."

"Touché! Well, I for one no longer worry about 'sides.' Having faced the enemy in battle, it gives us a connection"—Skorzeny punched one big fist into the palm of his opposite hand—"a bond that others will *never* share!"

The man had an infectious enthusiasm; it was easy to see why soldiers would follow him. You found yourself wanting his approval.

"What can we do for you? That is why we are here, correct?" Voss obviously wasn't going for it. Maybe he'd had enough of charismatic Austrians.

"Always the practical businessman! Yes, of course. People say we are in the same line of work, you and I." Skorzeny indicated himself and Voss. "But though it is less glamorous, I fear I am much more of an employment agency. I don't have a stock of weapons on hand, and now I find myself having given my word, and yet unable to deliver. I need an additional thirty machine guns. MG 42s and spare barrels. I need them quickly."

Voss leaned back in his seat and offered Skorzeny a cigarette from his engraved case. The flame from his lighter flickered on both their faces. Mike could see that he looked relieved.

"Is five days too long? We can do it if you immediately forward an End-User Certificate." Voss looked over to check with Fowler. Mike nodded. The certificate was a polite fiction, assuring everyone the weapons would be bound for Egypt and not a third party. With that in place, the guns could be on a plane in two or three days.

"I can get one," Skorzeny said. "Not from Colonel Ghorab, mind you. What about price?"

"I will charge you fifteen percent over what I paid . . . because of this 'bond' we share. You will be billed for air transportation and a few bottles of wine which will support the widows and orphans of certain Spanish officials." Voss plucked a business card from his pocket and handed it to Skorzeny.

"Tausend Dank! My office in Madrid will contact your people in Barcelona tomorrow. I greatly appreciate the help."

Skorzeny extracted himself from the booth, shook hands with both of them, and moved off into the shadows.

"What do you think?" Fowler asked.

"He may have friends among the French right, but I would bet my sailboat those guns are going to the FLN or the Palestinian Fedayeen. The Egyptian army does not need a mere thirty guns."

"If it's the FLN, he's selling to both sides . . . just as we are."

"Yes. But Herr Skorzeny does not do it solely for the money. Just remember, he is often the most visible gear in a much larger machine."

CHAPTER 10

WITH A CRASH of cymbals, the music began again. This time there were two dancers moving in perfect coordination. Fowler peered through the darkness. The young women at the table opposite were almost invisible in the dark. At least Fordyce had stopped pestering them.

"How are you gents doing? Enjoying the show?" Anson Fordyce stood in the pathway to the kitchen. When Fowler and Voss looked over, he bent forward, resting his arms on the back of the booth. "Mike, you've never introduced me to your friend here."

Mike didn't do much more than grunt, but Voss extended a hand, "A. A. Voss. Mr. Fowler and I are the owners of International Military Systems. And you are . . . ?"

Fordyce accepted that as an invitation, coming around the end of the booth to join them at their table. "Anson Fordyce—"

"—Fordyce is with the CIA," Fowler interrupted.

"Actually, I represent an association of American businesses who—"

"—are a front for the CIA."

Fordyce sighed. "Well, regardless of who I work for, I believe I have an offer for the two of you." He glanced from one to the other and grinned. "Want to hear it?"

Fowler arched an eyebrow at Voss. It was not as if they had a choice; Fordyce was both persistent and thorough.

"Proceed," Voss said.

"A few months ago, you auctioned a sizable archive of aeronautic data to a French company. I will admit, it took everyone by surprise. Sometimes businesses—or governments—need a bit more time to consider and respond. So, if you are going to do something like that again, we would like to be informed."

Voss just looked at Fordyce, the sort of look he might have given a British merchantman back in 1917, right before he loosed a pair of torpedoes. Fordyce squirmed slightly, and Mike smiled.

"If we were to do it again, it would be the same. Everyone is given identical information and at the same time. I do not foresee any changes."

"Well, we were hoping you could find a way to give us advance notice . . . time to figure out which companies are in the best position to get involved. We'd also like to know the *entire* contents of the auction beforehand. Of course, we are willing to pay for these privileges."

"Hmm. I agree that this would be very useful . . . to you. However, I prefer to keep my freedom. In this way, I am somewhat like an American, yes?" Voss winked at Fowler.

"We could be *very* generous." Fordyce's offer sounded vaguely like a threat.

"I am sure you could."

"Say you'll consider it."

"Alright. I will consider it."

"Good! Thanks for your time."

Fordyce got up from the table, then paused a moment. "Oh, and Mike, I believe you must have some appeal that I lack . . . those girls over there told me they would like to meet you. They are secretaries on vacation from Belgium. Just beware—she may look like it, but I don't think the pretty one is actually the princess from *Roman Holiday*."

He wagged a finger in Fowler's direction. "Don't say I never did you any favors!"

Mike rolled his eyes as he leaned back in the booth. The music came to an end and the lights came up as the dancers made their way off the floor. Some of the patrons were beginning to pay their bills and collect their belongings.

Voss lit up another cigarette and took a drag . . . He gestured toward the table across the room.

Mike shook his head. "We're only going to be here till the day after tomorrow."

"Our lives cannot be all work all the time. This is why I gave you the room with a door to the hall."

Fowler laughed. Who knew, the next thing Voss offered might be the keys to the family car.

"Alright," he said. "Let's see what happens."

Mike walked around the dance floor. The whole thing would have been considerably easier if he wasn't sure that both Voss and Fordyce were looking on. The thought flickered across his mind that he ought to have an opening line. Then he told himself, To hell with it, they asked to see me. Either that or Fordyce was ambushing him yet again.

"Ladies. How are you doing this evening? Mike Fowler . . ."

He smiled, picked up a chair, and turned it around, straddling the seat and leaning his forearms on the back.

That was all there was to it. Two of them were Marta and Claire, and he instantly forgot their last names. The girl in the black-and-white outfit was called Simone DeMaes. Up close, she was truly stunning. She had dark hair, pale skin, and green eyes. When she adjusted her shawl, a mysterious scar appeared momentarily near her shoulder.

Simone offered her gloved hand, almost as if she expected it to be kissed. Mike held it for a moment, but then when the others did the same, he fussed over them a bit more. This wasn't going anywhere, so he could afford to see if he could make her work for his attention.

The tactic didn't get him very far. She was the only one who spoke English and his ability with languages ceased at his Tijuana-accented Spanish and a very limited ability to read German.

Simone translated. There was a lot of giggling, blushing, and going back and forth in French . . . so much so that he began to suspect that they were doing as much talking *about* him as they were talking *to* him.

"We saw you at the hotel. You were in the lobby and now here you are." They chatted on, and it was all easier than he had expected. In Mike's experience most girls, especially the attractive ones, would load a conversation with questions and comments designed to put him on the defensive, to rattle him if they could. It was like a sport, though he suspected they did it unconsciously. Yet none of that happened.

Simone seemed smart, classy, and strangely fragile. It felt good to talk to her, but it was just chatter. Mike was aware that while his female companions probably wanted to close the place down, he had other obligations. Voss was chain-smoking Chesterfields to amuse himself, and there was a full day of inspecting armories coming up, a day that was going to begin in just a few hours.

"Alright. I've enjoyed meeting all of you, but my business partner is waiting on me, and we both have to be at work in the morning."

Simone looked at him, the lamp on the table picking out the deep green of one eye while casting a slanting shadow across the other half of her face.

"Could I see you again?" she asked. "Maybe we could meet tomorrow at our hotel."

"I'd like that. But I have no idea how late I'll be back."

"Well, call my room. We can go for a stroll by the water. You can be my escort." She batted her eyes at him, and he had no choice but to agree that, yes, he would give her a call.

Voss kept his own counsel as they headed for the door. It was only while they waited for a cab that he spoke.

"That was an attractive woman. I hope you made arrangements to see her again."

"We'll see," Fowler said. She *was* an attractive woman, and that made him doubt that anything at all would come of it.

Behind them, inside the building, they could hear a piano playing from a private room on the lower floor; a chorus of drunk and off-key male voices were belting out the Horst Wessel song. In the movies he had seen on board ship that had often been the music that identified the Nazi villains.

At 7:00 A.M. Colonel Ghorab pulled up in front of the hotel in a bright red 1952 Ford convertible sporting a continental kit and whitewalls. It was a car that made Fowler wonder if Ghorab really was as honest as he was reputed to be. On the take or just a car lover, Ghorab grinned past a pair of aviator sunglasses and drove with a lead foot.

The morning was cool and the heat was on full, blustering and blown away in the slipstream. They cut through the farmland along the inside edge of the Nile delta, the road vanishing behind them at eighty miles an hour.

Ghorab wheeled through the checkpoint at the entrance to the army compound with a wave and a toot of his horn. They cruised past a rifle range on one side and a line of newly delivered Soviet tanks on the other. Ahead, rows of aging warehouses stood outlined in the morning sunlight. They pulled into the shade of one of these buildings and got out.

Inside, Mike found himself in a well-equipped machine shop. Several older men, their fingertips dark with grease and metal dust, were working on a pair of Bren light machine guns. They came to attention and Colonel Ghorab motioned for them to follow as he pressed on into the dim hallways of the armory. Lights flickered on to reveal a seemingly endless series of floor-to-ceiling rifle racks.

"The Number 4 Mk. 1 and Mk. 2 rifles are here. The older SMLE Mark III rifles are stacked in Building Five. How would you like to begin?"

"At the beginning, I guess." Fowler took off his sport coat and hung it over the back of a folding metal chair.

"I have several people I must meet. You are in the best of hands and I can be reached by telephone if there is any problem." Ghorab headed toward the door, and Mike started down the first aisle.

Out of every eighty or so rifles he would pull one out of the rack, open the bolt, and stick his thumb into the action, looking down the barrel at the light reflecting off his thumbnail to inspect the bore. He would then check the magazine tension, locking lugs, and bolt face. If he found unexpected wear or rust, he had the armorers pull the next twenty rifles for a detailed inspection. He wasn't accepting or rejecting individual guns—he and Voss intended to buy the lot—but his inspection would inform the price they would offer. Every purchase included some guns that would become scrap or spare parts, that was expected when dealing in volume.

The tin roof ticked and popped as it heated up in the sunlight or contracted when a cloud passed over the building. In the rafters a small colony of bats chittered nervously, reacting to the rare disturbance. The hours wore on and eventually two of the armorers went back to have tea in their shop.

Around 1:30 there was a sudden burst of shouted Arabic and then Colonel Ghorab came striding down the aisle trailed by the pair of armorers, both looking cowed and keeping their eyes on the floor.

"I have told these men that they are here to help you! They are not to be drinking tea and reading tabloids!" The colonel was carrying his gloves, and he slapped them into the palm of his hand. "This army needs discipline! Attention to detail! Discipline!"

Ghorab glanced around at the rifles laid out for inspection. "Are you done with these?"

"Just about." Fowler straightened from where he had just placed a battered Enfield back into the lower rack.

"Allow me to treat you to lunch before the officers' mess closes."

"Alright." Mike wasn't as hungry as he was thirsty, but the idea sounded good. He had been pushing himself, hoping to get back to Alexandria before too late in the evening.

Outside Fowler could hear someone else yelling, this time in German. They turned the corner of the building and headed past a series of berms that had been ploughed up to create individual shooting ranges. Standing in the third of these, fists planted on his hips, was a familiar figure: Heinrich Hartmann, Skorzeny's buzz-cut henchman.

A harried-looking Egyptian lieutenant was busily translating Hartmann's shouted German into Arabic. Around the two of them stood five fierce-looking young Arabs. A couple of them were struggling to fit pistols back into the shoulder holsters they wore under their patched and frayed jackets. Hartmann cuffed the slowest of his pupils on the back of the head. The man staggered forward. It wasn't a light blow.

"You see, it takes German discipline, English discipline. That is what these men must learn." Colonel Ghorab gestured toward the class, if that's what it was. Hartmann had turned to peer across at the two of them. He was sweating and sunburned yet still perfectly shaved.

"You! I saw you last night. The American, yes?"

Hartmann's students were a shifty-eyed bunch and, judging from their targets, not the best shots. That was comforting because they had the look of assassins, angry and expendable.

"So, what're you up to, Hartmann?"

"What does it look like?" He gestured, the shirt stretching across his powerful chest and back. "I am training these Dummköpfe to draw and fire. And I want them not to kill me in the process." A sly look crossed his broad features. "Hey, you are the cowboy. Give us a group. Prove your abilities." The German snatched the pistol from the holster under his arm, and fired twice. Hartmann looked over his shoulder and grinned.

Mike's ears rang and he cursed inwardly, but he wasn't going to let this bristle-headed goon see him flinch. Colonel Ghorab stood to one side with his fingers plugged into his ears.

Hartmann reholstered the pistol, and meticulously wiped powder stains from his fingers with a handkerchief. One of his trainees jogged downrange and returned with the target. The two shots had hit dead center and less than an inch apart.

"This is what I want. That is what I get . . ." The German pointed to the targets pocked with random bullet holes. "You show them. Show *me* that you are a cowboy."

Fowler looked at Hartmann's trainees. One of them tried to grin but only managed a sneer. There might have been soldiers, legitimate uniformed soldiers, that he wouldn't have wanted to show up, but this group deserved whatever they got.

Fowler approached the bench. On it were several Beretta M1951 pistols, a decent handgun widely adopted in the Middle East. He slipped a magazine into one and hit the slide release, chambering a round. Mike raised the Beretta, took careful aim, fired once and then again. He cleared the gun and set it down. One of the young men pulled the target and brought it back. He had hit about an inch out at two o'clock; the two holes were around two inches apart.

"Is this all?" Hartmann demanded. "Do better . . . Try harder."

What a jackass! Fowler thought. Well, he knew where the gun hit now, and he was familiar with the trigger.

He picked up the Beretta and closed the slide on an empty chamber. He reinserted the magazine, then stuffed it into his waistband. Fowler glanced over at Hartmann, who was squinting at him in the afternoon sunlight.

Mike faced the target. Then his right hand shot down to close on the grip of the pistol. He pulled it clear of his belt, pinched the slide between the fingertips and palm of his left hand, and punched his right hand forward, racking a round into the chamber as he extended his arm. As he felt the slide slam home, he pulled the trigger—one—and then, still firing, he started to walk—two, three, four, five, six—the gun locked open.

No one needed to check the target. There was one ragged hole chewed out of the center.

"Ha!" Heinrich Hartmann gave him a slow clap. "There! There is the lesson for these idiots. You *are* a cowboy!"

"Nope." Mike Fowler shook his head. "I'm a sailor."

The rest of the day was uneventful. The food in the officers' mess was acceptable, Colonel Ghorab refrained from giving his armorers another dressing down over their tea-drinking habits, and the Mark III rifles, which had probably been stored since Abd el-Krim had tried to drive the Europeans out of North Africa, were in the sort of shape he expected: bad. The sun was edging toward the horizon when they set out for Alexandria.

At the Hotel Cecil, Voss was still out. He had gone to Cairo for a meeting and then dinner, taking two of the three custom rifles they had brought as gifts. The third would be given to the colonel on their departure.

The room was quiet, and Fowler paused by the telephone, more nervous than he wanted to admit. There had certainly been other women. However, this girl was somehow different. He could easily say that the appeal was her looks, but he wasn't sure that was it at all. She had a strange mixture of vulnerability and watchful confidence. It was an odd and intriguing combination.

He took a breath, picked up the telephone, and asked the front desk to connect him to the room of Simone DeMaes.

"Oh! Yes, yes. Hold a moment, please," said the operator. The phone clicked a few times.

"Hello?"

"Miss DeMaes? Michael Fowler . . . from last night. You said something about going for a walk? Would you like to meet in the lobby, in, say . . . thirty minutes?"

"Of course! That sounds wonderful."

As he put down the receiver, he was already pulling loose his tie. He hopped toward the bathroom, wrestling with his shoes and socks, leaving a trail of discarded clothing. He wasn't in the shower long enough for the water to heat up, but that was good because it shocked some energy back into his tired body. He got last night's suit off the hanger, opened up a fresh shirt, and brushed the dust off his shoes. He combed his hair, tied his tie . . . and then, unhappy with the result, tied it again.

As the elevator descended to the lobby, Mike could see that she was already there, ready to go. How long had it been since *that* had happened? Making a man wait was another game that didn't seem to be in her playbook.

She was dressed more simply than the night before: a scarf over her hair, a skirt and blouse, the collar closed with some sort of cameo or brooch, and a light sweater over that. She turned as the gates to the elevator clacked open.

"Hello there." He felt like he was playing the part of a sophisticated world traveler with a stylish wardrobe. A man who moved from one exotic location to another making deals with governments and industrialists. The thought amused him because it was all true, except the picture didn't include spending the day in cobweb-filled warehouses full of greasy weapons or, until now, meeting with glamorous women.

"Mr. Fowler, how was your day?"

"Call me Mike. Mr. Fowler is the character I play at work."

She laughed and reached out to tap him on the chest with one finger. "How about Michael? 'Mike' feels like a tough guy in the American movies."

He winced. After all, he was wearing a steel spike designed for OSS assassins in a sheath strapped to his forearm. He offered her the other arm and said, "Shall we?"

They left the hotel and walked along the square to the corniche. There they waited for a break in the headlights and then ran across to the seaside walkway. She was fast and agile, skipping delicately over the curbs that outlined the parkway in the center of the street.

"So, Michael . . . tell me what is the business that brings you to Alexandria?"

"Freight forwarding. Import-export logistics. If you want to move stuff around the world, I'm the sort of person who makes sure it gets where it's supposed to go." It was the answer he gave when he didn't want to discuss the details of what he actually did.

She dodged in front of him and walked backward, narrowing her eyes in a mischievous way. "If I needed a hair dryer would you be the person to go to? Because my flatmate is getting tired of me borrowing hers."

He grinned and shook his head. "Maybe a hundred hair dryers. Would you have a place to put them all?"

"Actually, I'm not sure we have space for more than the one we have!"

"What did you do today? It has to have been more interesting than what I did." The less he had to talk about his business, the better. He generally didn't like lying . . . and he found he liked lying to Simone even less.

"You mean after sleeping so late they didn't want to give us breakfast?"

He laughed. "Yes, start there. Tell me everything."

"Well, we mostly drove around on a tourist bus. There was Pompey's Pillar, which I learned has nothing to do with Pompey the Great. The temple of Serapis. And we saw the catacombs! It's just a poor neighborhood and there are a few little mausoleum buildings, not really what you go all the way to Egypt for . . . but *then* you go underground, and it just goes on and on. It's like all the Greek and Roman and Egyptian ideas got mixed up. It's fantastic. You have to go!"

Her enthusiasm was infectious. It made him want to laugh, and there was nothing really to laugh about, except that she was excited because she had seen an ancient graveyard. The breeze hushed in the palms and her scarf fluttered like a flag as she loosened and then retied it. The lights of the city circling the bay glittered on the water. When they reached the sheltered corner where the fishing boats were anchored, they turned back.

She told him about her life before the war. An idyllic life where, in a modestly wealthy home, she had studied music and dance and thought the only possible future was marrying a young man of similar background and having a life identical to her parents. Then came the fighting. Many of the people she had known died, and she had fled to avoid the predations of the Germans, resentful neighbors, and then the Allied bombing. At one point in the story, he got the vague sense that she had lost a sister, but he didn't feel it was polite to question her about it.

Mike Fowler tried to return the favor by telling her about growing up south of San Diego. As he did, it all seemed to be a long time ago and very far away . . . except that some of the Egyptian countryside reminded him of home. To a kid, the estuary of the Tijuana River had been as vast and mysterious as the delta of the Nile.

"You and your father, you were fishermen?"

"On our good days. To be honest, for a while we were smugglers. The tourist hotels paid a lot more for whisky than fish."

She started to speak, but he grinned and cut her off, "And, *yes*, I do realize I'm still in the same business, except now it's legal!"

"No fair!" She slapped him lightly on the shoulder but then took his arm. "Were you in the war?" she asked.

"Yeah, I was. But it's not a good topic of conversation . . . and some of it I'm not allowed to talk about."

She nodded. "Very mysterious . . . but I understand." She gazed up into his eyes and then leaned her head on his arm for a moment. "Too many people have things they cannot say."

When they got back to the hotel, Fowler glanced behind the desk to see if Voss had returned. His key was still in the box for his room, so Mike and Simone took a table near the entrance to the restaurant. They ordered dinner, Simone discussing various items on the menu with the waiter in rapid-fire French.

Mike found himself hoping that Voss would stay out as late as possible, and that was probably what would happen; dinner with the Egyptians could drag on and on. Being an arms dealer had a dangerous sort of glamour, but it did not lead to meeting very many women. Especially the right kind of women. At Sistemas Militar they had managed to avoid most of the glitzy jet-setters and the femme fatales that came with them. Both tended to be more trouble than they were worth.

On the other hand, "regular girls," if you wanted to call them that, were generally horrified when they found out what he did for a living. And Fowler struggled to deal with their naïveté and hypocrisy. They granted themselves the privilege of judging the world from an ivory tower sheltered by many layers of civilization . . . each layer enforced and defended by violence. People had been killing one another since the dawn of time and the difference between taking a life with a gun or a rock mattered little if at all.

He was torn between wanting to see her again and the fear that this was just a pleasant but isolated evening. He didn't have any qualms about what he did for a living, but he didn't have much confidence in his ability to explain it. In Simone's case, however, the quandary resolved itself in a completely unexpected manner.

She was telling him about the details of her job, how her boss was trying to pull together the funds to help regional orchestras and the many roadblocks that kept popping up. The waiter poured her some coffee and as he did, Fowler looked across the lobby. Anton Voss was just turning away from collecting his key from the front desk. He caught Fowler's eye and indicated that he was headed upstairs.

But as soon as the elevator clanked and hummed its way toward the second floor, Mike noticed one of the clerks step out from behind the front desk and peer into the dining room. Not just peering, more like scowling. It was the same clerk who had called him a Nazi on the street near the port.

Like dominoes clicking over, a series of thoughts flashed through his mind: the hotel had been recently nationalized by the government. Its previous owners, the family who had built it, were Jewish. Any of the extended family or their friends who were still employed might harbor a good deal of resentment not only toward Egypt, which had been intermittently at war with Israel, but also toward the cadre of Germans who had aided in that effort.

"Can I call you in the morning?" he asked.

"What? What do you mean?" Simone didn't look perplexed. She looked shocked . . . or scared. It was a bit heartbreaking, but he didn't have time to concoct an explanation that would make her feel better.

"Something serious has just come up. I'm sorry. I hope you'll understand." He pushed back from the table. "I'll call you in the morning before we leave."

"No! Michael—!"

He paused only for a moment by the maître d's station to tell them to put the bill on his room's account. The clerk he was worried about was no longer behind the desk or in the lobby. He got his key, then took the stairs, not bothering with the elevator.

The passage to their suite was empty, so Fowler took a moment to look down the other hallway. Nothing there either. He moved to his door and quietly twisted the key in the lock . . .

The room was empty and dark. Nothing unexpected.

He went through to the sitting room. Nothing there either, except that the lights were on and Anton's coat lay over the back of a chair. From Voss's side of the suite he could hear the shower running.

Mike breathed a sigh of relief . . . and he felt like a fool. He realized that he had known Simone only a few hours, but she was truly one of the most charming women he had ever met. He wasn't sure he would ever get the chance to explain to her what had happened, or hadn't happened, or if he'd be able to do it without permanently scaring her off. Hell, he wasn't even sure it was worth trying.

There was a knock on the door . . .

Fowler cautiously moved across the room. The fingertips of his right hand slid inside his left cuff, touching the end of the spike strapped to his forearm. He stopped at one side of the door, listening.

The knock came again.

And then, "Michael? Michael, are you there? Please! Did I do something wrong?"

She started to knock a third time, but he opened the door.

And that was a serious mistake . . .

CHAPTER 11

HE CRACKED THE door. She was standing in the hall, a bit bedraggled and out of breath. Had she run up the stairs, too? One hand was inside her purse —

"Michael . . . ?"

Fowler heard a floorboard creak in the hall and knew he was in trouble. He moved to slam the door, but a large and very male body rammed itself into the opening, forcing him backward. They struggled for a moment, a desperate shoving match, but then someone else added their weight against the door and a man's arm, hand clutching a revolver, appeared.

Before the guy decided to just shoot through the wooden panel, Fowler moved. He twisted, rammed his back against the door, and drew the seven-inch spike from its sheath along his forearm. He struck downward, aiming at the gun arm. But the point hit the revolver and glanced off, burying itself in the door's molding. The man released the gun and Fowler kicked it away but in doing so lost his footing.

The door smashed open, and he staggered backward. He grabbed the first man and yanked him into the room. The guy punched, short body blows. He was hard and strong and knew how to hit. He knew how to grapple, too. They crashed into the settee and nearly went over it. Fowler could feel him going for a hold. He got a hand into the hair at the back of the man's head and another under his chin. Fowler forced the man's head backward and twisted. He went down and Mike rabbit-punched him at the base of his skull, bouncing his head off the floor. Then the other man, the desk clerk who hated Nazis, came at him, swinging wild and barely effective blows.

Mike shoved him off and kicked out, catching him just below the hip and sending him sliding across the floor and into the wall. He could feel the big guy's hands groping for a hold on his ankle, so he lashed out with a heel, catching him across the jaw.

That was when Simone attacked. She led with a big Italian switchblade and, as he ducked, it sliced through the padding in the shoulder of his jacket. She withdrew the knife and he blocked a blow aimed at his throat. Still backed against the sofa, he blindly stamped down, hoping to crush a hand or foot as the larger man tried to get to his knees. He got a grunt of pain but nearly lost his balance.

The glittering blade came in again and tore his earlobe. Mike Fowler had had enough. He slipped to one side as she thrust, took hold of her knife arm, and, using her momentum, scooped her up and threw her over the settee. She dropped the knife but hit the floor rolling, already getting to her feet. Mike snatched up a bronze ashtray, smacked the big guy over the head with it, and then threw it at Simone. He shoved the settee out of the way and glanced around. The clerk was trying to stand. Mike wanted that pistol, and he wanted her knife before he lost the advantage permanently.

His date from earlier in the evening circled him. The face that had been so entrancing suddenly radiated deadly intensity. The body he had found so seductive was coiled and ready to strike. He noted that her knife was on the floor by the drapes just as she rushed him. She threw a flurry of blows with her hands and knees, aiming at his eyes, crotch, and throat. One caught him, a whiplike lash across his Adam's apple. He coughed and gagged. It was all he could do to fend her off. He responded without thinking—as she pulled back to strike yet again, he punched her square in the face.

She staggered and went down like a broken marionette. But the two men were again on their feet, and the desk clerk had found the big man's Webley revolver and scooped it up. It was at this moment Mike heard a latch click open—

"Halt!"

Everyone froze. Anton Voss stood in the doorway to his bedroom. He wore a robe and was raising Colonel Ghorab's customized Mauser sporting rifle. He palmed the bolt closed and pointed the gun at the desk clerk. "Drop it!" he commanded.

Mike turned and picked up Simone's knife.

"Back against the wall! All of you!" Voss stepped farther into the room, pointing with the barrel of the rifle. "Mr. Fowler, are you wounded?"

Just my pride, Mike thought. "I'm alright," he croaked . . . then he coughed and coughed again. He crossed behind Voss and collected the pistol.

"Good. Now what is this? What is happening here?"

"I have no idea . . . Well, a slight idea."

Simone struggled to sit up; her head was cut and her nose was crushed and bloody. The big man who had forced open the door was staring at Voss.

"That's not him," he said.

"What?" Simone winced and spat a wad of blood on the floor. She stood up. *"What!"*

"It is!" The desk clerk backed away from them as if Simone and the other man had suddenly become the enemy. "It *is*! What do you mean? He is the arms dealer. He sold aircraft designs. We heard this from the Germans themselves! Dr. Wilhelm Voss, he's come back to help them build rockets to hit Israel!"

Voss chuckled. He glanced at Fowler and, seeing that Mike had their attackers covered with the Webley, lowered the rifle. He bowed his head slightly. "Excuse me, but I am Dr. *Anton Andreas* Voss. At your service, of course."

Simone moaned and collapsed into one of the chairs. She held her head in her hands.

Voss looked at Mike. "What do you think we should do with them?"

Fowler used a tea towel to soak up the blood from the cut on his ear. "I'm not ready to take any chances—" Simone had clearly been a carefully set honey trap to keep him away from Voss, or at least to get him to open the door, which he'd foolishly done. "Well, not ready to take any *more* chances. I want someone to take them off our hands."

"So, do we call the authorities?"

Mike thought about that for a moment.

"No," he said. "I have a score to settle. I know *exactly* who is going to clean up this mess."

When he arrived at the door, Anson Fordyce was wearing silk pajamas and a paisley robe. His hair was mussed and his eyes bleary. Mike had told him, in no uncertain terms, to get himself down to their suite, or he would come upstairs and drag him there.

Fordyce looked around, taking in the broken furniture, the assortment of weapons, and their captives. An expression of wry amusement crossed his face. "Well, my, my! Now, *this* looks interesting!"

"You set me up," Mike growled. "And it's not the *first* time." Then he stepped in and punched Fordyce in the gut.

The air went out of him and Fordyce staggered, but just like his handshake, the smaller man was a lot more solid than he looked.

"Oh! Whoa!" Fordyce bent over struggling for breath. But after a moment it became clear that, through the pain, he was laughing.

"Please, tell us, exactly what is so funny?" Voss demanded. His thumb toyed with the safety on the Mauser.

Fordyce sucked wind, then gasped. "I guess the date didn't go so well! Did it?"

"Very amusing." Mike ground his teeth. "Now why don't you explain what's going on here."

"I'm sure I don't know," Fordyce said. "At a guess, she used me to get to you." Then he indicated the heavyset guy. "But I think I recognize this one, and I know who to call."

Fordyce went to the phone and unscrewed the mouthpiece. He lifted out the phone's transmitter and pulled the security service's bug out from underneath. Then Fordyce reassembled the instrument and joggled the hook. When the operator came on, he spoke in Arabic and, after a moment, was connected with someone and spoke again, in Turkish this time.

Simone and the clerk looked nervously at each other.

Fordyce hung up. "We have to wait," he said. He moved around the room, searching inside the lamps and behind the paintings. He went into both bedrooms and returned to show them three more listening devices. Then he went to the bathroom and flushed them down the toilet.

"My associate will arrive within the hour, and we can figure out how we are going to approach this." Fordyce turned to the would-be assassins. "Unless one of you wants to start explaining . . . that way I can get back to bed."

There was no response. The big man, who seemed to be in charge, shook his head. Simone breathed raggedly through her mouth, her eyes running tears of pain. Mike tried not to look at her. He didn't know how to feel. She had taken advantage of him . . . hell, she'd tried to kill him. But he had never punched a woman before. He decided that if he was going to feel ashamed about anything it was that he had nearly let someone kill his boss.

Mike used Simone's switchblade to cut the curtain cords and began tying up their captives. When he bound her slender wrists, she wouldn't meet his eyes. Eventually, there was a tap on the door and a small dark-complexioned man entered. His face was pockmarked and partially bearded. He moved with the care of the elderly and leaned on a cane.

"We'll call you 'Sarkis,' if you don't mind," Fordyce said, glancing around at the others. "The men with guns are Mike and Anton, and we need some information about those three, over by the wall."

Sarkis peered at them, immediately barking out a laugh. "Hello, Avi. What have you gotten yourself into? Tied up and at gunpoint? This seems beneath your station, eh?"

"A case of mistaken identity. Get us out of here," the big man growled.

"Perhaps. In good time. Young lady? Look at me."

It was Simone's turn to stare defiantly at Sarkis. "Ooh, la, la! Do we happen to have any Nazis with us?"

Everyone but Mike turned to stare at Anton Voss.

Sarkis stroked his beard. "You are lucky to be alive. Ten—twelve—years ago, they called her 'der Todesengel,' the angel of death. Yes, yes. She is known to have killed seven German officers. Probably quite a few more." He glanced at the clerk and shook his head. "This one I have never seen before . . . but they are Zionist Jews, Israelis."

"We could turn them over to the Mukhabarat . . ." Voss glanced at Fowler and a cruel smile tugged at his mouth.

The clerk looked like he wanted to beg for his life—he was sweating with fear—but Simone sat there with a broken nose, blackening eyes, and who knew how many bruised or broken ribs. If she stayed silent there wasn't much he could say.

Voss tucked the rifle under his arm. "Or maybe we should we call Skorzeny's fellows," he mused. That was aimed at Simone. In the aftermath of the attempt on Adolf Hitler's life, Otto Skorzeny was reputed to have impaled suspects on meat hooks. The SS would gleefully torture a Jew who had stalked and killed seven or more of their own. Initially, Fowler thought Voss was purposely toying with their prisoners, but it was someone else he was testing . . .

Anton Voss turned to Fordyce and waved in the direction of the Israeli agents. "But you notice a lack of pleading. That is commendable. What happens to us if we let them go?"

Fordyce turned to Sarkis. "Do me a favor, old man? Step outside a moment."

Sarkis nodded and closed the door behind him.

"You have to face up to it." Fordyce rubbed his hands together.

"You are arms dealers working with their enemies. This time they thought you were VIPs, but you could be targeted again . . . *unless* you want to reconsider the offer I made. In addition, you would also receive the grateful protection of Uncle Sugar."

For a long moment Fordyce and Voss stared at each other.

"I think I'd rather take the risk," Voss said. "But it is always good to have some idea of what I can ask for . . . should I ever be so tempted."

"Let's try this," Mike added. He reached into the breast pocket of his jacket and pulled out several business cards. He crossed to Avi and shoved the cards into his pocket.

"I don't believe Mr. Voss is worth much to you dead. On the other hand, we are open for business. If you want to make a deal, however, send *her*." He pointed at Simone. "I'm going to need an apology."

Voss nodded, impressed. Mike cut the cords binding their hands and pulled them to their feet. "Everyone out!" he said.

Sarkis gave the group a bemused frown as they emerged from the room. Simone walked as straight and proud as she could under the circumstances, but as she headed down the hall she turned back to shoot Mike Fowler a darkly appraising glance.

Fordyce joined him in the doorway, hands stuffed into the pockets of his fancy robe. "I think she likes you," he said.

"Shut up." Fowler wanted to hit him again, but he ached all over.

Months passed. Summer scorched the vaguely malodorous streets of Barcelona. The deal with Egypt had been completed. In the wake of the Suez Crisis, British Prime Minister Anthony Eden resigned, and in the United States, Dwight Eisenhower had been reelected president.

The world's first nuclear submarine, the USS *Nautilus*, logged sixty thousand underwater miles, the same distance as its namesake in Jules Verne's novel *20,000 Leagues Under the Sea*. The British tested a hydrogen bomb. And from Africa to the Far East, empires continued to unravel. New governments and independence movements created potential markets for Sistemas Militar. The telephones rang and the Telex devoured rolls of paper. After some earlier setbacks, the company finally seemed to be on the road to long-term success.

Fowler heard Voss coming down the hall and looked up. The older man stopped in the doorway. He held a telegram in one hand and had an amused look on his face. He glanced down at the paper.

"'The state of Israel is prepared to consider an ongoing business relationship with Sistemas Militar,'" he read. "This is providing we can produce certain items. They include a list of ammunition, easy enough . . . but they also ask for steel chevron tracks for the M4 tank, and HVSS suspension modules. Do you know what these are?"

"It's an upgrade for the older Shermans. I can find them. Anything else?"

"They want us to impress them, to bring something special."

"What the heck does that mean?"

"It is a test. We have sold technological documents. They demand that we bring them such a gift."

"So, it's the price we have to pay to get access to their business. You willing to go along with that?"

Voss shot Fowler a devilish grin. "Oh, yes. I believe I have the perfect item."

"Alright. When and where?"

"Monaco. Two weeks."

The Sistemas Militar Internacional offices in Monaco were three small rooms up a staircase from a narrow street back of the port. The sole employee was Paolo Lorenzi, a grumpy Monegasque who Mike Fowler suspected was happier when the owners stayed away.

The Israelis sent one of their procurement specialists, Lou

Eckstein, a onetime U.S. Army Air Force fighter pilot who had lost his American citizenship when he flew a patched-together Messerschmitt Me109 in support of Zionist troops in the 1948 war. Notably, he was the only one who showed up . . .

"In Alexandria we made a deal," Voss said. "There was a requirement for this meeting."

"I don't know anything about that. I'm here to talk money, guns, and technology," Eckstein stated. "If there's something else, I'll go back to Tel Aviv while you work it out."

Mike was embarrassed. Extracting an apology from Simone, and Israel, or the Mossad, or whoever, had seemed like a good idea when his blood was up. He suspected Voss liked it because it gave him the moral high ground, a position he found amusing. But having to confront her, and his own foolishness, again, all the while having to sit through an afternoon of wrangling about financial drawdowns and delivery dates, was not something he had been looking forward to.

"It's alright," Mike said. "It was my condition, and I waive it. We're here to do business, so let's do business."

Lou Eckstein was a good choice for a negotiator. He was a tough, outspoken kid from Brooklyn who had become a proud Israeli. He looked upon Anton Voss with the disdain he had for all things tainted by the Third Reich, but not with the visceral anger or fear of many European Jews. He had the confidence of a man who had shot down Nazi fighters and blown up German tanks. Yet he was unable to restrain his interest when Voss unveiled the "something special" that had been requested in the telegram.

It was a gorgeous piece of design, the feed mechanism for an extremely fast firing automatic gun that had been developed by the HwaA, the German Army Weapons Agency. The mechanism could deliver a rate of fire of four thousand rounds per minute, and each round of ammunition contained nine separate projectiles.

"Thirty-six thousand rounds per minute!" Eckstein murmured. Fowler and Voss had lucked out; one of the few areas where such a high rate of fire was valuable was in aircraft and antiaircraft weapons, and this cigar-chomping ex-flyboy had seen that immediately. Voss had one example of the mechanism, two rounds of ammunition, and a notebook of mechanical drawings, some partly charred and water-stained. All the material had come from the bombed-out ruins of a factory in Leipzig.

As they walked back to their hotel Fowler said with a laugh, "Did you see his eyes light up?"

"We have precisely fulfilled their request," Voss stipulated. "It is a unique, seemingly promising technology. They can see it was designed by a genius. Now the Jews can entertain themselves for the next decade trying to get it to work. Who knows? They might even succeed."

"It doesn't work?" Fowler was a pretty good judge of military hardware. In his eyes the package they were offering looked pretty good.

"Ya, ya. The part we are selling them *works.*" Voss laughed. "Herr Zettl, the inventor, understood getting ammunition into, and out of, the gun. This was quite a challenge. But, you see, he never figured out how to keep the barrel from melting, not even with the finest steels in Germany. Just because you *can* do something, it does not mean you *should*. Especially when you do not know the cost of taking the next step."

Voss left Fowler in the lobby of the Hotel Metropole and Mike continued on, catching the elevator and riding it up three floors. When he unlocked his door, she was sitting in the easy chair. Dressed in striped capri pants and a sleeveless blouse, she had tossed a hat that resembled a flying saucer onto the coffee table.

He froze for a moment, taking in the scene. Simone had clearly posed herself to look completely at home. Behind her the windows were open to reveal an edge of the town and the wide panorama of the Mediterranean.

"What are you doing here?" He said it as coolly as he could manage.

"You said I had to apologize."

"Mr. Eckstein seemed unaware that was part of the deal."

"Lou Eckstein?" She waved away the suggestion. "Officially, the state of Israel does not apologize to Nazis."

"I'm not a Nazi."

"We don't even apologize in the same room with Nazis." She stood, a smooth, clean motion. The capris emphasized the slimness of her waist and long legs. "So, this is personal, just you and me: I'm sorry."

"I accept." He moved to one side. It was hot and he cautiously slipped out of his jacket, not the least bit certain what was coming next. "Is that why you broke in to my room?"

"Maybe. Maybe I also wanted to show you that while we identified the wrong Dr. Voss, I'm not . . . unskilled." They were standing close together, very close.

"I never doubted that. Tell me, did you lower yourself down the outside of the building?" He dramatized the question by the way he loosened his tie, but she reached out and, slipping her fingers around it, undid it completely.

"No. I picked the lock. Less cinematic, but more . . . effective. I opened the windows because I had to wait a while, and it was stuffy in here." Simone unfastened the button at his collar.

"So, you had enough time to go through my drawers?"

"An interesting turn of phrase. The answer is no . . . not yet." Their breath mingled.

"Be careful of my nose," she murmured. "It's been broken twice."

"Twice?"

"Once by you, and once by the best plastic surgeon in Antwerp."

He put his hands around her waist and asked, "Is it possible it looks better than before?"

"Sometimes you know exactly what to say . . ."

And then, for several hours, they didn't say anything at all.

ISRAEL,

five years later . . .

FOWLER AWOKE AS the sky outside the tent was growing light. Low surf rolled up on the beach, a horse's mane of curling water. In the years since the events in Egypt and Monaco he and Nicole had, somehow, managed to remain together. It had not always been easy; the keeping of secrets was built into both their careers. Israel, however, was not directly aligned with any of the great powers and in his job political ambivalence was almost a requirement.

Mike untangled himself and pushed the covers aside. He slipped out through the mosquito netting and walked down to the water.

He stretched and began deep breathing, slowly inhaling, quickly exhaling, then reversing the process. Then deep breaths, swallowing more and more air down into his lungs. It was cold, and after resting a moment he waded into the water, which was a good deal colder. The chill made his flesh want to pull back, made him want to breathe shallowly, but he fought that. After several long exhalations he charged his lungs and dropped below the surface.

He concentrated on feeling the water, listening as he shook the bubbles from his ears. He opened his eyes and blinked until the stinging lessened. He blew some bubbles out of his nose. He checked himself, noting how he felt when he had held his breath about half as long as he could. He held on as his body began demanding and then screaming for air. This was not only to remember how bad it could get, but to know he could always go just a bit longer than what felt possible.

Mike allowed more of the poisonous substance that was filling his lungs to escape. His heart hammered. He was light-headed. But this was easy. Easy, because all he had to do to avoid unconsciousness and death was stand up.

When the need to take a breath was overpowering, he stood,

water sheeting off him, the cold air clutching him. He staggered a bit and shook the water out of his hair, rubbed the water out of his eyes.

"I hate it when you do that. I think you're never going to come up." Nicole was sitting a few feet above the waterline. She was wrapped in a coat and had brought him a towel. "We have to leave as soon as we can pack up. They won't hold the plane for you."

The ride to Lod Airport was uneventful. They didn't talk much. Mike had no idea when he might return to Europe or the Middle East.

Nicole's identity card got her onto the tarmac, and she pulled up a hundred yards or so from the plane, a triple-tailed Lockheed Constellation that looked as if it was crouched, ready to leap into the sky. A group of black-clad figures milled around the base of the boarding ladder.

She kissed him good-bye, holding on a bit longer than normal, and then took the hat she had given him from his hand and set it on his head, tugging it into place.

"Don't *lose* this," she said, and there was a strange tension in her voice. "You look good in it . . . and it was *very* expensive." Then she gently pointed him in the direction of the plane.

One by one the engines coughed to life. The stewardess smiled at him and asked if she could take his hat. He handed it over. It truly was a beautiful hat, a glossy Ecuadorian panama. He was surprised Nicole had found it in Israel; it was more like something that would be for sale in a high-end men's shop in Milan or Paris. He wondered again about the price, and the fact that she had mentioned it. That was very unlike her . . . unless—

Mike Fowler started to laugh. The priest beside him looked over, smiling, and Mike shrugged. Even if they had both shared the same language, he wouldn't have explained the joke: the hat was intended to make him easier to tail.

It meant that there were Mossad operatives in Rome who had

been alerted to follow him and report back. Whether he had answered the questions they asked on the beach or not, they were figuring they could follow him to Voss. And Voss just might know something about the mysterious device that Leonid believed in, Saul did not, and Yaron thought was the mechanical bunny at the dog track. Mike got the feeling that Nicole had been as much in the dark about Yaron's questions as he was, but she had sent him a message nonetheless.

His world was populated by liars and informers, government agents, thugs, and con men. Loyalty was a rare and valuable commodity. When they first met, she had abused his trust and since then Mike had expected little. He had learned his lesson.

But now she had done something that brought back feelings he remembered from their first evening together, during that walk along the Corniche in Alexandria, before he knew she was anything more than a secretary. She had given him a gift more valuable than the hat. She had given him all the loyalty she had to spare.

CHAPTER 12

ITALY . . .

THE CHARTERED PLANE made a bumpy descent into Ciampino airport. As they circled, the seven hills of Rome were intermittently visible through squalls of rain. All around him the priests were buckling up and saying prayers. Mike got the feeling these guys didn't fly all that much.

Either the prayers worked or there was nothing to worry about. The pilots allowed the aircraft to misbehave until the last minute and then, with a typically Italian flourish, they took control and pulled off a textbook landing. Fowler was barely able to tell the exact moment the wheels hit the ground.

Inside the terminal, Fowler shook the water off his new hat, then put it back on his head. He handed over the counterfeit passport he carried. The name on it was Steven Tallent, but it sported the same photo that graced Fowler's actual American passport. An expert located in Tangiers, a man Fowler knew from the days when he and Voss had played fast and loose, had provided the documents and done the necessary work. There wasn't much to worry about; it was a real passport, Steve Tallent had been roughly the same height and weight as Fowler, and, more important he had the same-colored eyes.

Although he was tempted, Mike didn't look around to see who might be tailing him. He needed to leave a trail that would make them confident they knew what he was up to.

Walking down the length of the terminal lobby, he scanned the departing flights. If his plan was going to work, he needed to get the timing just right. When he saw what he needed he bought a ticket on a plane that left the next day for Geneva.

Then he got some change and found a phone booth. He placed a call to the Swiss bank used by Sistemás Militar. Their banker had long ago agreed to pass short messages to his account holders. Mike gave him the numbers for one of Aleixandre Porras's accounts, then the number of the booth and hung up.

Sitting there, Fowler had the opportunity to casually observe the people in the terminal lobby. He tried to relax and figure out his next moves.

The phone rang.

"Hello?"

"Oh! Señor Fowler?"

"Aleixandre! Are you okay?"

"Yes, so far. How are you? Have you heard from Señor Voss?"

Mike's heart sank. If Porras was asking about Voss it meant he knew nothing himself. "I just landed in Rome; I haven't had a chance to hear anything."

"What are we going to do?"

"Stick with the plan. I'm headed to the rendezvous point. If I don't know more in a couple of days, we'll come up with something new. What do you know about how much trouble we are in?"

Porras laughed grimly. "Oh, you know, there is the police, Interpol. You and Señor Voss they want to arrest. I have retained lawyers."

"Well, you don't know anything, so blame your partners. Listen, the authorities are one thing—stall them as long as you can, but try not to get yourself in more trouble. The real problem is Skorzeny."

"Skorzeny!"

"And some people he works with, or works for . . . I'm not sure.

I'm going to give you a name . . . Peter Anhaldt. Magnetic Data Corporation. New York City."

"Skorzeny is always bad, but who is that?"

"I don't know. See what you can find out. Look, stall the cops as long as you can, then let them know I was headed to Israel. It will check out, you will seem cooperative. Something tells me Mossad isn't going to spill the beans on when or how I left."

Porras laughed; he always found American idioms amusing. "What can I do for you? What do you need?"

Fowler had a half-baked plan. "Get someone to make a reservation in my name at a good hotel in Geneva. I don't care which one, it's just a ruse. Then get mc on a plane to New York. I want to leave from Fiumicino airport before three, understand? I'm using the Steve Tallent passport. I need to get to Caracas and you need to let Alfredo Larkin know I'm coming. Now, how are we doing financially?"

"Not good. The candle burns at both ends."

"Yeah. Anton needs to raise some money or this thing will be over before it begins. I have no clue how he intends to do it."

"I know you can say that curiosity killed the cat, Señor Fowler . . . but I *am* curious."

"Well, I need the cat to stay alive and out of jail, okay? You were out of town when the fireworks happened. The hotel in Monaco can verify that. Do me a favor: have the bank wire three thousand dollars to the Piazza di Spagna American Express office. To Steve Tallent. Take it out of my personal account. Got it?"

"Sí."

"I'll be in touch."

Finding a bank of lockers, Fowler picked one in an exposed location and stowed his mostly empty Gladstone. What he wanted was to be seen leaving it at this airport, an indication that he was coming back. Then he caught a cab into the city.

The Hotel de la Ville was centrally located in the hustle and bustle near the Spanish Steps and the church of Trinità dei Monte.

Fowler pushed through the revolving door and asked for a room. As that was being arranged, he noted that the bellman set outgoing luggage, the bags that were ready to be loaded into taxis, to one side of the revolving doors.

Mike Fowler headed back out into the drizzle and down the steps. At their base, rain dappled the waters of the Fontana della Barcaccia, which depicted a sunken boat. Pigeons crowded under the tables of the cafés and the awnings of the stores, waiting for better weather.

His first stop was the American Express office. Aleixandre Porras had moved quickly. The teller counted out the money and slid it under the brass grille along with a telegram form that had been sent from the bank in Geneva. On it were the letters AL and then PA plus a string of numerals. He was booked on Alitalia and then Pan Am.

Fowler headed to the Rinascente department store. He bought a bright blue Samsonite suitcase and some clothes, including a belted Norfolk-style sport coat with a pleated back that gave him a full range of motion and a tan trench coat. He also picked up a brown Borsalino fedora and a canvas rucksack. He wore the trench coat but he put his other purchases into the suitcase as he paid for them. He continued to wear Nicole's hat, even though it was beginning to sag from the rain. When he had gotten what he needed, he headed back to the hotel.

He *was* being shadowed. The stop-and-start process of shopping allowed him to verify that. His tail was a bespectacled young man who waited outside the store. The operative took his corners carefully, alert to overrunning his target, and carried a folded newspaper so that he could occasionally pretend to be reading. Fowler made the job easy; he didn't look back again, and he paused in front of the hotel to allow his clandestine companion to reach the top of the stairs in time to see him go inside.

He got his key from the desk but instead of going immediately to his room he wandered into the bar, then returned to the lobby.

Crossing the patio, he carefully noted the exits. After he had learned what he needed to know, he rang for the elevator and went to his room.

Mike Fowler awoke from an uneasy sleep at 3:15 A.M. He was worried about Anton, worried about Aleixandre, and worried that the entire operation was going to collapse for lack of funding as soon as they all reached Caracas.

And there was still the question of whether Voss was even alive.

He was also worried that considerably more was going on than any of them realized. There seemed to be some other aspect of his partner's past that might be in play . . . *was* in play, at least in the minds of the Israelis. At the risk of making things even worse, there was one thing he could do that might even the odds just a bit.

Bleary-eyed, he climbed out of bed and pulled an envelope out of the desk. He took Peter Anhaldt's business card out of his wallet and stuck it inside. Then he wrote "Israeli Embassy, Roma. Attention Simone DeMaes" on the front and fell back into bed. He hoped that using Nicole's old cover would alert the local intelligence liaison to who it was from and what it was regarding . . . If the Israelis wanted to hunt Nazis then they could spend their time chasing Anhaldt and Skorzeny and leave him and Voss alone.

Confusion to the enemy, he thought and drifted off to sleep.

Up early, Fowler ran through his plan. Rome had two main airports, Ciampino, where he had arrived, and Fiumicino, also known as Leonardo da Vinci, which was much larger and had just recently opened. Fowler had left as many clues as he could suggesting that he would fly from Ciampino to Geneva, the location of Sistemas Militar's bank. All he had to do now was convince the Israelis he was headed to Switzerland for long enough to catch the plane to New York. The most critical part was to leave the hotel as close to the departure time of the transatlantic flight as possible. In chaotic, traffic-clogged Rome that was always a risk.

Fowler opened the gaudy blue suitcase and stuffed in the trench coat, his rumpled suit, some other dirty clothes, and Nicole's expensive panama hat. He added the hotel's bedspread to give it additional heft, then locked the suitcase. He put on the new clothes he'd bought and packed everything else into the rucksack. Then Mike put enough money to cover his bill, and then some, into a hotel envelope, wrote "Manager" on the flap, sealed it, and called the front desk.

"Good morning, Signore Tallent."

"Could you send a bellman for my bag and get me a taxi? I need to go to the airport."

"Certamente. Which airport, please?"

"Which is the old one?" He wanted the clerk to say the name aloud in case anyone was listening in the lobby.

"Ciampino."

"That's it. I'll be down in a few minutes."

He set the suitcase in the hall with the two envelopes on top and closed the door. After a short wait he heard the elevator ping and then a polite knock . . .

"Will there be anything else?"

Fowler spoke through the door. "No, thank you. I'll be right down." He listened until he heard the elevator rumbling down the shaft. Then he grabbed the Borsalino hat and the rucksack and headed for the stairs. He went down fast, fast enough so that he heard the distant bell of the elevator arriving in the lobby. Mike waited a moment, imagining the bellman setting the sleek Samsonite case near the door. He prayed his shadow was confidently watching it, waiting for him to arrive, pay his bill, and climb into a cab. Then he went out the back.

He crossed the patio, ducked through another wing of the hotel, and made his way out the service entrance. A narrow path took him through a gate and into the well-manicured grounds of a school.

A winding driveway led him through a tall iron gate and onto the street. He cut across the intersection and hailed a taxi just as it made the turn in front of the Hotel Eden.

"Fiumicino! Velocemente!" Fowler snapped and handed the driver an American $20 bill.

The little man gave a manic laugh and burned rubber. "Velocemente" is not a term to be used lightly with Italian cabbies.

Mike Fowler was in luck. The driver, who probably could have won the Mille Miglia if a series of fatal crashes hadn't brought the famous race to an end, got him there on time and, as far as Mike could tell, without being followed.

He paid for his ticket, then found a phone booth that allowed him to observe anyone approaching the departures board.

Voss hadn't checked in with Aleixandre Porras. However, there was another person that Anton might have contacted. If the mission was still on, they had better know where they were going . . . so maybe, just maybe, Voss had spoken with the man they hired to see if the once-secret Kriegsmarine charts were filed away at the German Federal Archives. Mike checked his watch and pumped the payphone full of coins, dialing a number in northern England.

Boarding time was closing in but the unpredictable miracle of international phone service demanded two more tries, and the instrument ate his money with the hunger of a one-armed bandit. Finally, the call went through . . .

"Good morning. Manchester Institute of Science and Technology." A chipper female voice answered the phone.

"Good morning. I'm trying to reach Professor Ernst von Holleben. I've forgotten what department he is in."

"Professor von Holleben! Oh! Oh, yes. Will you . . . um . . . hold just a moment." The woman suddenly seemed considerably less cheerful.

The phone bonged and he fed it more change, and again checked the time.

"Hello, this is Herbert Gosling. Who am I speaking with?"

Fowler improvised poorly. "Um, I was a student of Professor von Holleben's. I'm trying to reach him."

"Well, young man, I regret to tell you that Ernst has passed away. It was all rather sudden."

Mike's heart beat a bit faster. "Can you tell me what happened?"

"I really don't know very much. He was in West Germany, some research project of his own. He was beaten, horribly. He died in hospital. Please tell me your name, I need to know who I'm speaking with—"

Bong. Bong.

Fowler let the operator cut him off. He hung up the handset, grabbed his rucksack, and headed for the ramps down to the tarmac. Heinrich Hartmann had murdered the Farkhani brothers with a hammer, a tool that had become his signature on the Russian front. Mike had never met von Holleben but he cursed himself for not warning him. However, there was something that concerned him even more. Heinrich "Kuvalda" Hartmann's hammer was not just cruelty: it was an interrogation technique. Had the professor's research discovered the location of the sub? Had Mike Fowler and Anton Voss already lost their one significant advantage?

VENEZUELA,

one day later . . .

MAIQUETÍA INTERNATIONAL WAS situated just outside Caracas and perched on a narrow strip of land between the lush green mountains and the sea. Stepping off the plane it was clear why people from the colder parts of Europe and the States vacationed in the Caribbean. The air was balmy and the temperature was warm, far too warm for the belted wool jacket Fowler had bought in Rome.

Released from customs, Mike scanned the crowd and felt his spirits suddenly rise. Standing at the far end of the lobby was Jack Johnson. Streams of smaller people washed past him and, over their heads, he caught Mike's eye and grinned. Johnson was dressed in jeans and a workshirt, its sleeves rolled up over his massive arms. He looked very much like many of the oilmen down from the States, at least until he spoke.

"Rummy! Look at you, cobber. With that backpack I thought you were a student!"

Fowler wasn't quite ready for what came next. Johnson grabbed him in a bear hug and lifted him off his feet. Then both of them were laughing and trading mock punches. Though they had occasionally exchanged letters, Mike hadn't seen his friend in more than a decade.

"So, when did you get in?" Mike asked.

"Four days ago. You're a lucky bloke—I was almost ready to go back to Oz. The *Bushranger*'s due in Talcahuano in about a week. Is the job still a go?"

Fowler looked around; no one appeared to be paying the slightest attention to them, but he had been on the run for too long. "Let's get out of here," he said.

Johnson led him across the parking lot to a gigantic bronze-colored Chrysler Imperial. He chucked the keys in Fowler's direction. "You drive. I damn near killed myself piloting this barge."

It *was* a monster, heavy-browed and bedecked with chrome and whitewall tires. Fowler pulled out of the parking lot and followed the highway up into the hills, heading for the city. He tried to gather his thoughts. The situation was considerably more complicated than when he had offered Johnson the job. For Voss the stakes had become life or death, and now that was true for himself as well. However, Jack Johnson was not yet involved in any way that would be dangerous.

Mike took a deep breath. "A couple of days before we were ready to leave Barcelona things kinda went sideways . . ."

He described what had happened as clearly and brutally as possible, relating the appearance of Skorzeny and his thugs, the mysterious German American businessman Peter Anhaldt, and the battle at the factory. He described their plan for Voss to escape by boat, and his own desperate flight to France and then Israel.

Mike said nothing about the Stasi agent, or that the Israelis and Anhaldt seemed to know things about Anton's past that Mike had never heard of. He had the uncomfortable feeling he was making up his own rules.

"Do you trust him—Voss, I mean?" Johnson had a knack for hitting the most sensitive spots.

"With my life. I *have* trusted him with my life," Mike said.

"Different stakes now though, right?"

Jack had a point. Thirty million was a lot of money. But more than that, the past was circling his partner like a school of sharks. Was Voss willing to risk all of them to get rich, or was it to save himself? A few months ago, Mike would have said the idea was impossible. But that was before Voss had murdered his old acquaintance Hanno Wuttke in cold blood. Fowler and Voss had played rough before, but that was a first . . . and things had been getting stranger ever since.

"You know, mate . . . back when he hired you, he said he wanted a diver."

"What?" Mike frowned at Johnson and the Chrysler slewed toward the right-hand lane. He straightened out and glanced over again.

"That's right. Your Kraut was looking for a tough, careful bloke who could watch his back . . . *and* keep his mouth shut. But, in particular, he came to *me* because he wanted a diver."

"You sure?"

Johnson nodded.

They barreled into a tunnel and Mike fumbled for the lights. Voss had gone into the arms business because he knew of the vast amount of surplus weapons that would be for sale around the world. And because he foresaw the dozens of new countries that the breakup of the European empires would create. Describing him as smart would be an understatement; he was always thinking a step ahead. Whose idea had it been to buy the Aqua-Lung gear and join the club in Barcelona? Mike couldn't remember. But Anton had pushed Mike to learn everything about the new technology, and that had given him an excuse to pick Mike's brain about diving in general.

Mike Fowler swore under his breath. "You think he was planning this from the beginning?"

"No idea. Only met him the one time. But he seemed like a crafty bastard. I reckon I wouldn't have introduced you otherwise. You've done alright, the two of you. I just want it to stay that way."

Mike didn't know if Johnson's suspicions about Voss held water, but if they did, he wasn't sure whether he ought to be irritated or impressed. The man often planned for a number of possibilities, what he referred to as superpositions. But picking a young salvage diver to be his protégé so many years before he was needed . . . that really took the cake!

They swept around a gracefully engineered curve and into Caracas proper, a city of modernist skyscrapers, construction cranes, arcing freeway overpasses, and dramatic parks and boulevards. It was set in a series of valleys between jungle-festooned mountains and wreathed in low-hanging wisps of cloud. At first it looked like the world of tomorrow, an architect's dream. But underneath billboards and bridges were terra-cotta block shanties and tin shacks: people from the countryside who had come to the city for either the work or the welfare provided by copious amounts of oil money.

The big car floated through a cloverleaf and as the road branched Johnson pointed out the direction they had to take. Mike still didn't know if Anton was alive or dead. He didn't know if the job was on or off. At the moment they were stuck between realities, between potential futures . . . and there was something he'd better say while he could, before his loyalties were even more divided between his friend and his partner . . .

"Jack . . . if Mr. Voss shows up—*when* he shows up—he and I, we *have* to do this. We're in so deep that it's the only way. We've got to take that gold off the playing field, and once we do, we'll need whatever money we can keep to buy our way out, or to pay for a boatload of lawyers. But you . . . you're not in it yet. You'd better think about that. I can pay to send the *Bushranger* home. I've got enough put by."

Jack Johnson laughed, the rough laugh of a pirate.

"Look, *if* the Kraut shows up, and *if* he's got enough cash to keep this whole circus afloat, and *if* he can convince me that the story is real, the kind of real you can dive on . . . then, you and me, we're gonna go get it. And the devil can take anyone who gets in our way, alright?"

Then he shot Fowler a hard look, waiting until Mike could take his eyes off the road to return it. "But if he *doesn't* come though, to hell with him. I'll take your money. And then the two of us, we'll find this U-boat on our own."

Fowler squinted at Johnson. There was a lot he didn't seem to be taking into consideration, unless he was thinking of making a deal with the Nazis, the Chileans, or the governments who'd lost the gold to begin with . . . none of whom could be trusted in a situation like this.

Mad Jack Johnson turned back to stare out at the freeway and the futuristic columns of apartment towers, but to Mike he seemed to be looking off into a distance of gray seas and snow-covered mountains.

"Fifteen years I've been diving salvage, Rummy. Diving for *scrap*. This is the first chance I've ever got at a *treasure* . . . real money, and a story to tell the nieces and nephews. No one's gonna keep me from it."

CHAPTER 13

ALFREDO LARKIN WAS the Central and South American representative for Sistemas Militar, as well as a dozen other companies. His house was made of concrete and steel and looked like the wing of a modernist aircraft jutting out of the overgrown hillside. The road passed thirty feet below the steel pillars and guy wires that supported it, then wrapped around the edge of the slope and climbed back to the same level as the house. In a town continually damaged by earthquakes, it was a monument to either optimism, or arrogance.

Fowler nosed the Chrysler into a large carport with walls made of decorative stone blocks. There were spaces for five cars and two of them were taken up by other Imperials, a '58 and a '59. The '58 was dusty, and the tires were going flat.

"Who else is here?" Mike asked.

"Just the help. Larkin said he'd be back this evening."

They walked down a pathway lined with flowers and shrubbery. Johnson rang the bell, and they were admitted by a small woman in a gray-and-white housekeeper's uniform. The foyer walls held large, colorful pieces of modern art, roughly painted squares and circles that Mike couldn't make heads or tails of. Piled under them were dozens of red boxes, high-end German cameras waiting to be shipped out. The ceiling sloped up and was dotted with light fixtures that looked like orbiting brass Sputniks. At the end of a hallway they emerged into a huge triangular living room, its plate-glass walls revealing a view of the city and most of the Caracas basin.

Johnson gestured, indicating the whole of Larkin's impressive home. "You sure this bloke hasn't got his thumb on the scale?"

Fowler laughed. "As long as we get our end, I don't care. Alfredo's a character, but he's got a lot of connections, and he goes where the money is."

Mike went over to the window. The hillside below them was barely visible. It was as if they were hanging in midair looking off toward the center of the city.

"Have you met the wife?" Jack kept his voice low.

Mike shook his head. He hadn't been to Caracas in two years and didn't know anything about Larkin's personal life.

"Well, the sooner we get out of here the better. That sheila's gonna be a problem."

The housekeeper made them a meal and they ate at a table beneath a painting done in explosive tones that might have been a sunset or a bomb blast. Johnson gave Mike a short version of what had happened over the last few years. Colin McLeod and Frank Jano were still his engineer and electrician, and Ihaka Waretini was first mate, but the rest of the crew, with the exception of Clarence Benham, who had retired from diving to take the job of cook, were men that Mike had yet to meet. With pride, Jack detailed the capabilities of the *Bushranger II,* a ship he had now owned for several years.

It was getting on toward evening when they heard the far-off sound of a powerful engine and the swirl of tires taking a corner. Fowler got to his feet and walked over to the glass wall. A big car, another Imperial, this time white and even newer, was coming up the switchbacks, powering through the straightaways and then braking hard into the turns. Mike gestured for Johnson to come take a look.

"Larkin," Jack said. "He's pushing it!"

The Chrysler roared along the road under the house, and they heard the squeal of rubber on pavement as it turned the last corner. Mike took up a brass poker from the rack of fireplace tools. He started toward the foyer. Johnson was right on his heels. They moved to either side of the door.

Jack glanced down at the poker. "It's like that, is it?"

Mike shrugged. He wasn't expecting trouble, but he knew it was out there, hunting them. Outside, car doors slammed. There was a mumble of conversation, and a sprinkling of female laughter. Footsteps approached and a key slid into the door.

The woman, a tall, shapely brunette tightly packed into bright, form-fitting clothing, entered first, almost running into Jack Johnson.

"Oh! Mr. Johnson." She laughed. "You are right here! You scare me." She reached out and patted him on the chest in an oddly familiar way. "It take my breath away." She fanned her face with a well-manicured hand. Jack moved aside, catching Fowler's gaze over the top of her head and arching an eyebrow at him in reaction to her comment. Fowler nodded, and leaned the poker against the pile of cameras.

Alfredo Larkin pushed through the door carrying a briefcase and several shopping bags. He was tall yet portly, the sort of build that passed as a sign of attractive affluence in many parts of the world. Turning to close the door he saw Mike standing behind him.

"*Miguel!* Amigo mío! Cómo estás?" Larkin beamed. The woman turned away from Johnson, and Larkin ushered her forward. "I got married. I told you that, right? This is my wife, Cordelia."

She looked him up and down, batting her lashes and displaying a formidable set of teeth. "Señor Fowler, welcome to our home. You are the favorite of my husband. Please, let us go into the living room . . ."

She started down the hall, but Larkin drew Mike aside. Johnson joined them. "I have messages," Larkin said in a low voice.

"Al-*fredo* . . . !" Cordelia beckoned, hand planted on her hip, clearly peeved that no one was following her.

"She wants to show off the house," Larkin whispered. Then, more loudly, he said, "It will have to wait, mi corazón. We have important business to discuss."

She made an irritated noise and turned, her spike heels clicking on the inlaid linoleum as she headed for the kitchen. Larkin opened his briefcase and handed Fowler an envelope with "All America Cable & Radio" printed on the front. It was from Aleixandre Porras. The first line read "Magnetic Data Corporation," and proceeded to list the names of the board of directors and then associated companies, many just the abbreviation used by stock exchanges. It was long and would take some time to figure out. The last line, however, got his attention. It was not good news:

> ALL PROPERTY INVENTORY AND ACCOUNTS IN SPAIN IMPOUNDED. MONACO OFFICE ORDERED CLOSED. INCREASED PRESSURE HERE NO MORE CONTACT THRU BANK. YOU KNOW WHERE I AM=
>
> P

Mike folded the pages and put them in his pocket. "What's the other message?" he asked.

Larkin grinned, waving another telegram under their noses. "Mr. Voss is arriving tonight with three other men. We must go get him!"

Mike almost laughed with relief. Anton was alive! His state had finally resolved itself and, with luck, they could get the operation back on its feet. Fowler glanced at Johnson. I hope you're ready for this, Mike thought, because it's not rough-and-tumble; it's dead or alive.

Larkin glanced from Fowler to Johnson and back. "This is good, right?" he asked.

Then Mike did laugh. "Yes, it is," he said. "It's very, very, good!"

They took both the white and the bronze Imperials, setting out just after eight P.M., heading south and then west along the Pan-American Highway. Their destination was the town of Maracay, on the shores of Lake Valencia. It was about an hour and a half west of Caracas.

They passed by several small towns, and then the moonlit valley opened up into a vast flat area filled with the lights of the city and then black empty space that Fowler assumed was the lake. The highway cut straight through town with only a few interchanges. They took the last of these, shifting onto a frontage road that headed toward a distant beacon making slow revolutions in the night.

Larkin pulled to a stop at a guard post. The sign above the gates read "Escuela de Aviación Militar." They waited under the moth-haloed lights for a jeep to arrive; when it did, all three vehicles headed off into the darkness. When they reached the end of a runway, they left the searchlight and the airport buildings behind. A bit further on, the jeep pulled down a short weedy drive toward the lake and stopped as a pair of decrepit buildings loomed up between the trees.

Fowler shut off the engine and got out. The moon slowly climbed over the hills behind them. In the soldier's jeep, a radio scratched. The driver replied, then put the handset down and walked into the shadows alongside one of the buildings. There was a creak of rusty metal and the snap of a heavy switch. A string of buoys leading off into the depths of the lake lit up and a set of fixtures attached to the corrugated tin structure came on.

After a few minutes a pair of landing lights dropped toward the water and then the distant sound of radial engines could be heard. Larkin motioned for Fowler and Johnson to follow him, and they edged between a building and the encroaching brush and then out onto a rickety pier.

The aircraft was a tarnished Twin Beech floatplane. The cabin door flopped open, and the copilot stepped down onto the pontoon, tossing a rope to the soldier who had turned on the lights. The engines sputtered into silence as the plane was tied up.

The first passenger to appear was Anton Voss, and even in the glare of the naked bulbs he looked tanned and rested. The second man to step down surprised Mike: it was Fernando Zúñiga. He must have sailed from Tarragona with Voss after their escape from Barcelona. Zúñiga began helping to unload bags from inside the plane.

Voss ducked under the wing and came forward. "Thank God! I was afraid you had been lost." He leaned forward, whispering, "We must talk . . . but not here, understand?"

Fowler nodded, but Voss had already moved on. "Mr. Johnson. It has been a long time."

Mike squinted into the glare of the lights. Following the luggage, two more men stepped from the float to the pier, two men he knew all too well.

"What the *hell*!" Mike growled.

Voss turned back, his grip closing tightly on Fowler's arm. "Remember what I told you. *Later!*"

Paul Sobek and Mel Paluso were the mobsters who had loaned Sistemas Militar more than a million dollars back when the company had gotten in trouble with the French syndicate. They had bailed out Fowler and Voss when the partners had needed it most, and their money had helped the business grow and to control its own destiny. But they were also the last people on earth Mike would have invited into this venture.

Sobek was now in his mid-fifties and a bit paunchy, but he had once been a gifted tennis player. He wore a flashy tropical suit, the color of gold, and his shirt was open at the collar. Of the two he had been the money man, a slick operator who used his contacts in Havana and Las Vegas to play the middle ground between organized crime and legitimate business. Superficially, Paluso appeared to be the enforcer. Short, brawny, and bullet-headed, he came across like a thug and generally allowed Sobek to be the public face of the duo. However, he was related to the old Mafia families in Calabria and Sicily and was not to be underestimated. They were a team, not employee and employer.

"Mikey!" Paul Sobek approached with a smile and a hand outstretched. Yet the man couldn't have forgotten or forgiven how they last parted company. "Here we are again, working together. Who would have thought, eh?"

Mike didn't take his hand. He wanted nothing to do with Sobek or his partner. There was an awkward moment, but then Sobek laughed and clapped him on the shoulder. "Don't worry. When you guys get in trouble, we arrive to save the day, as always!"

Paluso caught Fowler's eye and smirked. He didn't need to act like there was any love lost between them.

"Anton, I have to say . . . I'm impressed." Sobek spread his arms and looked around at the drooping foliage, the rotting dock, and the rusting seaplane hangars. "This is quite mysterious. I'm intrigued to finally hear the whole story."

"Let's get going. I'm hungry," Paluso growled.

Fowler turned to Voss and lowered his voice. "You're alright? Really?"

"Yes, yes . . . and you will understand everything, soon enough."

As much as Fowler had been silently praying that Voss would show up alive, and with a solution to their problems, Sobek and Paluso were not the answer he had hoped for. Not at all. Their involvement suggested Anton was desperate and out of options . . . or that he had lost his mind.

"Hola, mi amigo," Fernando greeted Mike.

Fowler grinned, moving to help him with the luggage. "You're becoming a world traveler!"

Mel Paluso stepped in and grabbed an old leather case that looked like it had arrived with his father at Ellis Island. Johnson took the last two bags. As they loaded the cars, Paluso set his case down out of sight of the soldiers and, undoing the buckles, removed a large nickel-plated revolver. Mike got only a glimpse, but the vented rib along the top of the barrel indicated it was a Colt Python, an ultramodern, and extremely expensive .357 Magnum.

Paluso winked at him. "*Now*, you can take my bag," he said.

They loaded up. Larkin, Voss, Paluso, and Sobek in one car and Fernando, Johnson, and Fowler in the other. At a building near the gate Larkin collected the newcomers' passports and went inside.

Mike turned, leaning over the back of the seat. "Fernando, how did you get out of Barcelona? Where have you and Señor Voss been?"

Zúñiga rolled his eyes. "It has been lo—no, it has been *crazy*, señor. I drove Señor Voss to Tarragona. I had to put him in the trunk. We were afraid of Los Grises," Fernando said, referring to the "gray ones," another name for the ruthless Spanish Policia Armada.

"From there we sailed to Tangiers, and then we took *airplanes*!" Fernando's eyes gleamed.

"To where?" Fowler asked.

"The United States, and then to the islands."

"You were in the Bahamas until you came here? Nowhere else?"

Fernando nodded. "Did I do something wrong, señor?"

"No. You did not. Just remember I hired you to protect Señor Voss"—Mike nodded toward the white Imperial and its passengers—"from *everyone*. Understand?"

Fernando nodded again, eyes wide.

"You don't like those two?" Jack Johnson commented.

Fowler shot him a glance. "You ever hear of an officer calling in an artillery strike on his own position?"

This time it was Johnson's turn to nod.

"Well, that's what Voss just did." Mike looked off into the darkness. "So, the answer is, no. I don't like them at all."

After a few minutes, Larkin reappeared and gave Zúñiga back his passport. Then, after a stop for petrol, they headed back to Caracas.

If Voss thought Sobek and Paluso were their only option when it came to financing the operation and laundering the gold, they were all in trouble. The mobsters had access to money, that was certain. Several years before, when Sistemas Militar had needed cash, Sobek and Paluso had delivered in less than a week. But paying them off and getting them to finally go away—two completely separate problems—had been considerably harder.

Sobek wanted to be a big shot. Maybe he was a big shot. He had been connected to Meyer Lansky and Lucky Luciano's gambling operations in Havana. And he regularly had dinner with Fulgencio Batista, the Cuban presidente who had made the gangsters welcome. He knew all the players in New York's five families, the Chicago outfit, and Las Vegas. But he wanted to be an even bigger shot, and he had seen Sistemas Militar as his ticket. In the mid-1950s, after lending Fowler and Voss the money they needed, Sobek and Paluso tried to move in and set themselves up as if they were part of the company.

It started with a visit not long after Sistemas Militar bought the factory in Poblenou. As soon as Sobek understood the amount of graft that circulated in the arms business, he and his partner jumped on a liner and headed to Europe.

Once Voss had access to Paul Sobek's cash and Fowler had solved their problems with the French, Sistemas Militar began to court a more legitimate brand of customer. That meant doing business directly with governments. There was still corruption and underhanded dealings, but most of the players observed a fairly straight forward set of rules.

Sobek and Paluso seemed to have bought into a romantic vision of gunrunning. Perhaps it was their way of reliving the old stories of smuggling whiskey during Prohibition, of midnight landings on remote beaches and payoffs in bags of untraceable cash. But that was exactly the erratic, fly-by-night existence that Voss was trying to leave behind . . . and any attempt to push them back in that direction infuriated Mike Fowler.

The arms trade might have been an excellent way to launder

large amounts of ill-gotten cash, but Sobek had trouble maintaining his focus long enough to learn how the game was played. When Voss became aware of this trait, he suggested that Fowler draw out the deals they had in the works, postponing meetings, contracts, and payments. It was easy enough; nothing in the halls of government moved quickly.

Sobek fidgeted, drank, and chased the local women. But Barcelona was not free and easy Havana, and even among the tourists, the pickings were slim.

Mel Paluso entertained himself in the bomb shelter that had recently been converted into a shooting range. He blasted through belts of ammunition with a World War I–era Vickers machine gun and played cowboy with a pair of single-action Colts. He was a good shot, but the range was dimly lit and, when Mike neglected to turn on the fans, poorly ventilated. After a few days of choking on powder fumes, he lost interest.

Grimly amused, Fowler called the process "boring them to death." Eventually, Sobek and Paluso returned to Cuba.

But the one area in which Sobek seemed committed to playing the long game was the loan he had given them. No matter how hard they worked, it was impossible to get ahead of the interest payments. Every time they got some extra cash, Voss hoarded it. He feared there was going to be a showdown over control of the company, and he wanted to be ready. Sobek hinted more than once that a better deal could be made if they would consider smuggling weapons from their inventory into Italy and the United States. But Fowler was certain that the terms wouldn't be much better, and that it would somehow turn into an ongoing and highly illegal commitment.

Then Anton Voss noticed a detail in one of the scientific or business journals he read. He packed a bag and did something he considered only when absolutely necessary. He went back to Germany.

He returned with a packing case full of files. These he sold to a major American laboratory that was researching field effect transistors. Whether the information Voss recovered led to the breakthroughs of the next several years was debatable, but it did provide enough money to finally pay off their debt.

But getting rid of Sobek and Paluso was not quite that easy. Voss did not wire them the money or even mention that he had it. He made careful arrangements. Then he and Mike Fowler bought tickets for Cuba. Just before departing Barcelona, they sent a telegram to Sobek requesting a meeting.

Sobek agreed to see them a few nights later in a special suite next door to the Cabaret Montmartre in Havana. Then he made them wait for more than an hour before finally showing up with Paluso, an enormous bodyguard named Sebastian, and a couple of American chorus girls from the club.

"We're looking forward to hearing why you guys decided to drop in. If you had let us know ahead of time we could have arranged a tour of the island. Anyone else want a drink?" Paul Sobek dropped some ice cubes into a tumbler he had picked up from the bar that was recessed in one wall.

"You'd better have the vig. No excuses," growled Paluso. The "vig," or vigorish, meant the interest on a loan.

"We have your money," said Voss. Fowler laid a suitcase on the coffee table and opened it. He did the same with a second one. Both were full of cash.

Paluso sat up straight. Sobek's eyes widened. After a moment he said, "Sebastian, take the girls downstairs, then come back."

"That's all of it," Fowler told them. "We are paid off. Finished."

"Well, let's not get ahead of ourselves." Sobek's eyes narrowed. "We'll have to count it . . . and there's still the matter of the guns that need to get to our associates in Reggio and Chicago."

"No. That will not happen," Voss stated.

"Look, it's great . . . and surprising that you can pay us so much money." Paul Sobek took a slurp of his drink and grinned. "But don't get the idea this deal is over before we say it is."

Sebastian quietly reentered the room and took up a position behind the low chair where Fowler sat. He cracked his knuckles and Mike almost laughed. The move was pure Hollywood.

"Tell him not to stand behind me. I don't like it." Mike pointed his thumb in the direction of the bodyguard.

"He'll keep you from getting smart. Nobody acts up, and there's nothin' to worry about," Paluso said.

Sobek went on, "There's lots of ways we can help each other. The two of you need to accept that our arrangement has been mutually beneficial. A continuing line of credit might be just what you need."

"We're out." Mike leaned forward in his chair. "We're done with you dirtbags, and good riddance!"

"Sebastian, make him shut up," Paluso ordered.

Sebastian grunted, his version of a laugh, and laid a meaty hand on Fowler's shoulder, jerking him back in the chair. As he bent down to lock his arm around Fowler's neck Mike rammed his left hand inside the choke hold and drew a slimmed-down skinning knife from inside his belt. He sliced upward, cutting across the muscles under the big man's arm, then stabbed down, jamming the blade into Sebastian's calf. Blood spurted. The arm went slack. Pivoting out of the chair, Fowler left the knife where it was and, as Sebastian struggled to keep from falling, he snatched the Colt 1911 from the bodyguard's shoulder holster. Racking the slide to be sure there was a cartridge in the chamber, Mike covered Sobek and Paluso.

Arm and leg useless, Sebastian toppled to the ground, taking huge gulping breaths as he realized what had happened to him, his good leg straining and slipping on the blood-slick tile as he tried to roll over.

The ice in Sobek's drink rattled as his hand shook. Paluso's eyes gleamed. His gaze was a direct challenge to Fowler.

Mike handed the gun to Voss. "Your man is going to need a doctor." He yanked off his bloody coat and threw it to the floor. "We've paid our debt! This is *over*!"

Voss removed several folded pieces of paper from his jacket. "These are copies of your agreement. Please write that it is paid in full. Then sign it."

"To hell with you! Sign it? You have *no idea* how connected we are." Sobek was regaining his bluster.

"You *will* sign. And I recommend you use a date from three months ago." Voss tossed a fountain pen on the table.

"You see," he said, indicating one of the pages, "*that* is a copy of a bill of lading. A consignment of weapons is on its way to Veracruz, Mexico. The recipients are agents of Colonel Ramón Barquín. They will be used in a coup against President Batista in the next few weeks. If he is successful, the influence of the Mafia in Cuba will come to an end. I suspect that your 'connections' may want proof that you had nothing to do with this.

"Leave us alone and you will have a document that shows you were not involved. Cause trouble and the entire paper trail, including the *quite recent* withdrawal of this exact amount of cash, will be delivered to *The New York Times*. In that case, you will become famous: the men who freed Cuba from the dictator."

Sobek cursed, and Paluso's eyes followed Fowler carefully, a grim smile tugging the corner of his mouth.

"You still want to count it?" Fowler asked.

That ended the most difficult period in the history of Sistemas Militar . . . at least until Hanno Wuttke had shown up with his demands and his mysterious map. Fowler never found out if Sebastian had lived or died. At the last minute he had pulled back. Had he cut higher, up the inside of the man's thigh, the move would have almost immediately been fatal.

Fowler, Voss, and Porras went on building their rapidly expanding business. Ramón Barquín's coup failed, possibly because Batista was forewarned. But eventually a second revolution, this one led by Fidel Castro, caused Batista to flee the country and forced the mob to relinquish its hold on Cuba. The gangsters scattered to

Florida and Nevada . . . and, apparently, the Bahamas. The dream of a headquarters just off the North American coast refused to die.

As Mike Fowler piloted the big Chrysler back toward Caracas, he tried to reason out just what it was Voss had planned. Sobek and Paluso were like vampires . . . and they would want some payback for having been outmaneuvered in the past. If Voss had gone directly to them, something was deeply wrong . . . or he was planning something Mike couldn't even imagine.

In modern warfare if a fortified position was under attack by an overwhelming enemy, a desperate commanding officer might radio for a nearby artillery battery to center their fire on his exact coordinates. Since his soldiers were dug in, they *might* suffer fewer losses than the exposed enemy. But it was still a nearly suicidal move, one that was justified only in the most dire circumstances.

Anton Voss always had a plan . . . but now Mike was wondering if they were all about to become the casualties of friendly fire.

CHAPTER 14

THE NEXT MORNING Mike Fowler was up before dawn. In the early light only the mountaintops were visible, a sea of white clouds filling the entire valley. After pulling on his socks and boots, he jogged down, descending into the mist, taking one switchback after another.

Below the cloud layer the city was slowly preparing for the day. Lights were coming on in the houses and smoke trickled from a backyard trash incinerator. A crew of gardeners in peasant clothing shared a cigarette near a horse cart, waiting to begin work. Mike circled a block of clean white apartment buildings and started the hard slog back up the winding road.

He was covered with sweat and the morning sun was beginning to break through the overcast as he reached the spot where Alfredo Larkin's house loomed over the hillside. Standing beneath the concrete platform, Anton Voss waited beside the road. Mike slowed.

"It is good you went out. We may not have another moment alone," Voss said.

"You mean away from those jerks?" Fowler specifically meant Sobek and Paluso. He bent over, trying to catch his breath.

"Away from everybody. But yes . . . I believe I owe you an explanation."

"I don't know that you owe me anything, but"—Mike coughed and laughed at the same time—"Mr. Voss, are you *crazy?* Those two are going to screw us six ways from Sunday!"

Voss stepped closer, lowering his voice. "Of course you are correct . . . they are going to *try*." Voss shook his head. "But we are out of time. It was bad enough when we were only trying to stay ahead of dates on a map. Now that Skorzeny and Anhaldt know who we are, this is the best solution.

"Sobek and Paluso, they are setting up casino hotels and a bank in Nassau. This gold could make their venture instantly viable."

Fowler straightened. "They're dangerous. Look, my friend is risking his life, his crew, and his ship. I *asked* him to help out. That's on my shoulders."

Voss glanced away and took a long breath. "I understand. Please realize I have thought everything through. We will make our world a better place . . . um . . ." Voss gestured with one hand, perhaps struggling for the right phrase in English. ". . . We must take some risks, then this threat will no longer be hanging over us all."

There was movement from up the road. Mel Paluso scowled at them from the turn where Larkin's gravel drive intersected the switchback.

"Hey! If you two are done scheming, we're gonna eat breakfast."

Fowler waved to show he heard. As they turned toward the house Voss asked the question Mike Fowler had been hoping to avoid. "Tell me, how did you get away?"

"I went to Israel."

That brought the older man to a stop. "You did *what*?"

"It was the only way to escape." Mike could almost hear the unspoken questions whizzing through Anton's head.

"That was risky, very risky." The German's eyes probed his. "But I can see how it might work."

Voss didn't ask any more questions. And Fowler didn't offer any further clarification. It was a standoff. Neither said nor asked the next thing, the thing that would reveal their actual position. The two men had trusted each other for well over a decade, but the secrets they each held were piling up.

Voss changed the subject. "Have you heard from Aleixandre?"

"He's hiding out in Switzerland. We're shut out of both Barcelona and Monaco. No more bank, no more money. We don't have much time. He sent us some information on Anhaldt; I'll show it to you."

Voss shook his head as if to clear it.

"One more thing." Fowler wiped the perspiration off his forehead. "Von Holleben's dead."

Voss cursed in German. "Now we have *that* to worry about. Did he find the information? Did they get it from him?"

"He was in West Germany. He was beaten to death. I wasn't able to ask a lot of questions."

"I have prepared as best I could, but that is going to be a problem when it comes to Sobek's money." Voss let out a breath. "Let me handle the explanations, yes?"

"Of course."

Fifteen minutes later they were all sitting down to breakfast in Larkin's dining room. Jack Johnson caught his eye, sensing something was wrong. But Mike gestured slightly, a motion that said, Hold off. He'd tell Johnson later . . . well, he'd tell Johnson *something* later.

When breakfast was over Alfredo Larkin told his wife to take the housekeeper and go downtown to shop. Then packing his briefcase, he headed to the office. Fernando Zúñiga was put on guard duty, keeping an eye on the outside in case anyone came up the road.

The previous evening some sort of feminine intuition had led Cordelia to decide that Paul Sobek was the richest man in the room. Mike Fowler didn't know if this was actually true; Sobek represented money that wasn't necessarily his, but he put on the front of a man of wealth and leisure. Over the last twenty-four hours Cordelia Larkin had shifted her attentions from the masculine form of Jack Johnson briefly to Mike, and now she was batting her eyelashes and smoothing her tight clothing around the gangster from Nassau. Johnson was right—she was a real piece of work.

When the door finally closed behind her it was Paluso who cast a skeptical eye on Voss and his associates.

"Alright. We're all here. So you'd better start explaining exactly how you want to spend our money."

Voss opened his suitcase. Inside there was a small pile of envelopes, two of which Mike recognized as having been in the safe in Anton's office.

"As you know, our departure from Barcelona was . . . abrupt." Voss opened the first envelope. "Many of the documents I collected were destroyed. I have done what I could to re-create the most important of these." He extracted a sheaf of papers and placed them on the Formica tabletop.

"Our project is the raising of a Type XXI submarine containing 23,586 kilos in gold bars. This gold was, at the time it was transported, the property of the state bank of the Third Reich—"

"—The Nazis," Paluso grumbled.

"Correct," said Voss. He looked the mobster in the eye, giving him nothing.

Paul Sobek lit a cigarette. "I know you want to plan out the salvage operation. But first things first, how do we know it's there?"

"I say it is. If that is not good enough for you . . ." Voss handed him a set of photographed documents sourced from the United States Forces European Theater Finance Office. On them were headings like "Recovery of Reichsbank Precious Metals," "Reconnaissance to Discover Further German Gold," and "Final Report—Gold and Foreign Currency Assets of the Former German Reichsbank."

He then took a book out of his suitcase and slid it across the table toward Sobek and Paluso. It had a red cover and was titled *Gold Is Where You Hide It: What Happened to the Reichsbank Treasure*.

"I procured some of this in New York. I wish there were more reliable sources. I can only offer you one piece of primary evidence. I hope it will suffice . . ."

Voss handed a photograph to Sobek. The gangster froze, then let out a low whistle and passed it to Paluso. Looking over the Italian's shoulder, Mike could see it was a picture of piles of what looked like gold bars being removed from heavy wooden boxes. Standing over the white-coated men handling the bars was a somewhat younger Anton Voss. He was holding a clipboard and dressed in his naval uniform. In the background, the light of the flashbulb had caught a slim young woman who was making notes at a table or desk.

Mike was surprised. He had never seen the photograph before, but the woman was familiar. It was Dr. Elizabeth Adler, the mathematician identified by Leonid in the camp on the Israeli coast.

"Okay." Paluso fanned the air with the grainy black-and-white photograph. "You promised us gold, now I see a picture of gold . . . and you. That's a start.

"We want to hear all the details. Not just bits and pieces. Why does nobody else know about this? Why just you?" Sobek drummed his fingers on the tabletop.

Voss took a careful breath; he seemed to be gathering his patience. "The gold is not a *secret*. As you can see, quite a few people know it is missing. The question is, Where did it *go*?"

"And that's where you come in, right?" Johnson leaned his big forearms on the table.

"Correct. I will tell you what I can, but you must understand, I do not know all the details. I doubt there is anyone alive who does. If they did, they would have found me, or the U-boat, much sooner."

Paluso cut in, "We *do* know it's still there, right? No one's already found it?"

Voss opened the map with the bloody nine-millimeter hole in it. "They are searching. Check the dates."

"This could be anything. Most of these dates—hell, all of these dates—are from last year!" Sobek scoffed.

Mike Fowler was getting fed up; if Sobek and Paluso were really that skeptical, they wouldn't have come to Caracas to begin with. "You know who Otto Skorzeny is? Well, his thugs were chasing us around Europe just two weeks ago. If they knew where to go, they wouldn't have bothered!"

"Alright, let's not get sidetracked. Start at the beginning . . ." Paluso said.

Voss nodded. "A year before the end, elements in the German government and industry began to fear the outcome of the war. There were meetings held to organize a plan to protect the interests of the Third Reich—allow me to correct myself—*some* of the Third Reich, in the event of defeat.

"Using intermediaries, shares were purchased in foreign corporations. Patents were transferred. Assets such as art and jewelry were carried abroad and sold. The money was hidden, more or less successfully, in accounts around the world. Some of these cargoes were transported to Argentina. Part of this process was called 'Aktion Feuerland.' This is a reference to Patagonia's Tierra del Fuego, or land of fire. I was told these stories in confidence; they are not something I can prove or know as fact. Versions, however, have appeared in the press.

"By the time of the last months, there was no more opportunity for such careful planning. Whole cities were on fire, neighborhoods turned to rubble. The dead and lost were everywhere.

"For years my business had been research. My office reported to the OKM, the high command of the Kriegsmarine. One of our programs had access to an early model of what was called the Elektroboot, a Type XXI submarine. We used it for testing new technologies. The boat had a captain, officers, and a crew. More importantly to those who ordered our final mission, this particular Type XXI was off the books. Perfect for a clandestine operation: it had never been officially commissioned, it was a ghost ship.

"Our technology projects were *extremely* secret. Each of us had been chosen for our loyalty and discretion, we had been investigated by the Reich Security Office, and our work carefully compartmentalized. Even with all of this, my entire research staff—with one exception, a man who had been taken to hospital and lost among those wounded in battle—were loaded onto buses, driven to the forest, and shot."

Jack Johnson cursed under his breath, and even Sobek looked a bit taken aback.

Anton Voss smiled thinly. "So, you will perhaps understand my reluctance . . . why I have not attempted what we are doing, until now. The plan originated at the very top. Probably not with the Führer, but the more practical circle just beneath him. These people still have influence . . . quite a bit of it."

"This Skorzeny, is he one of 'em?" Paluso asked.

"The decision makers? No." Voss seemed sure. "Skorzeny is the man who gets things done. On the chessboard he is the knight, not the king or queen."

"And yet, somehow you were spared . . ." Sobek was goading Voss for an explanation.

"Not *somehow*. I was placed in charge of the mission. The U-boat commander was not yet familiar with all the changes we had been making. The U-Null—this name was our private joke—had been modified so frequently it was a challenge for the officers and crew to keep up. During the voyage my function was that of a supervising engineer. In addition, because of my security status I was the officer directly responsible for the delivery of the bullion."

Fowler knew he should keep his mouth shut, but still he asked, "When was that photograph taken?"

Voss took a moment to answer. "Two or three days before we sailed. I was required to do an inventory of the gold when it arrived in Kiel. A series of tallies and photographs were taken as a security measure, to make sure nothing went missing. All the documentation was later destroyed . . . However, I was able to save this one print."

Fowler took a closer look at the picture on the table. He wondered when Leonid had lost track of Elizabeth Adler, and why the old man had been brought to tears by her memory. If Voss was telling the truth, the photo had been taken very late in the war, within days of the German surrender.

He wondered if Anton's superiors had ordered Dr. Adler's death. Had Anton been responsible? In all the thousands of photographs that must have been taken during the war, out of all the pictures that had been lost or destroyed, Mike had now seen two that placed Voss and the lady mathematician together. What *was* her involvement in this Aktion Feuerland, and how well had they known each other?

Mike had a lot of questions, but this wasn't the time or place to ask them.

Voss continued, "Our departure was delayed, and delayed again. The Allied bombing was endless. Outside shrapnel from the flak batteries fell like hailstones. And then one day there was no more antiaircraft fire; the guns ran out of ammunition or had been destroyed. Soldiers and tanks from the east and west were crushing Germany between them. Anyone found on the streets would be forced to join the fighting.

"That was when it was time to leave. We waited until nightfall and, shadowing a convoy fleeing to our bases in Norway, we carefully maneuvered through the wreckage and out of the harbor.

"The commander of the U-boat was Emil Zapp, a veteran, a young man who had shown a great deal of talent. He was also the son of a family friend. I chose him. I was trying to save him from almost certain death. In 1943 and 1944 nearly five hundred U-boat crews were lost.

"Emil took us north, running the gauntlet through the great minefield and into the Kattegat, the shallows between Denmark and Sweden. This was the hunting ground of the RAF. It was filled with reefs and sandbars. There was shallow water and changing currents. For many months only half of the ships had made it through.

"The convoy ahead of us was attacked. We could see the flashes and tracers through the smoke and hear the delayed sound of the guns. The planes circled in the darkness, sometimes invisible, sometimes shadows crossing the parachute flares they dropped to blind the gun crews. Using the battle as a distraction we slipped past, hugging the coast of neutral Sweden. We left them behind, but there were no more ships, just burning fuel on the water. Finally, we could submerge, but for days we heard the war being fought all around us, ASDIC pinging, mines and depth charges exploding in the distance.

"On May eighth we received a shortwave message, the order to formally surrender. This was the critical moment. If we were seen by our enemies, if we were detected by radar or sonar, we would be hunted down and destroyed.

"The original plan was that we would locate a secret radio beacon southeast of Buenos Aires and approach the Golfo San Matías. By night we surfaced and communicated with the shore by Blinkgerät: a signal lamp. However, we were warned off, told to return to international waters. The Americans were suspicious and patrolling the coast, there was political pressure . . . we had not come at a good time.

"This was unacceptable. We carried a cargo of staggering value . . . and every hour we were at sea we were risking our lives! I demanded answers, insisted on communicating directly with whoever was in charge. We were given a rendezvous point. Someone with the authority to make decisions would meet with us.

"It took a week. By that time, we were on half rations, sailing in circles, monitoring the radar and hydrophones, and fearfully watching the horizon. The weather, as expected in those latitudes, was terrible.

"Finally, the seas calmed, and a large trawler appeared. They hung a Reich Service flag over the side; it was the agreed-upon sign.

"We surfaced, and a boat brought over the captain of the fishing trawler, Raymundo Lommerzheim, and a young man called Gunther Könnecke. They had with them many crates of fresh food; it was a very welcome offering.

“Könnecke was a prewar immigrant to Argentina, a Party Gemeinschaftsleiter . . . a ‘community leader,’ and a member of the Sicherheitsdienst, the SD, the intelligence service of the SS. Könnecke possessed an air of enthusiasm I had not experienced since before the invasion of France. To him, defeat was barely a distraction. While our officers and crew were having their first good meal in months, he explained to me the problems ashore.

“Just days earlier another submarine, the U-977, had arrived at Mar del Plata and quite publicly surrendered. Before that, the U-530 had done the same. There was speculation in the gossip press as to whether they had brought with them Adolf Hitler, or Martin Bormann, or—as was actually true in *our* case—piles of Reichsbank gold. I assumed these crews had secret orders like ours, but the lack of coordination was unforgivable. It was a brazen disregard of the terms the Allies had given us. The war had been over for months . . . it was not surprising that the Americans were now extremely suspicious and followed up on every report.”

Anton Voss paused in his story and removed a cigarette from his case. “Könnecke may have had galaxies shining in his eyes, ready to build a new National Socialist utopia. Yet none of his South American allies was ready to take the risk, or the responsibility, of bringing what we carried ashore. Some alternate plan was needed.”

Anton Voss paused again, and he glanced at Paluso. “Now . . . this is the point that is critical for our venture,” he stated.

“That plan, the plan of what to do, was created then and there by Herr Könnecke, and it was enacted by the four of us: the two captains, Emil Zapp and Raymundo Lommerzheim, Könnecke, and myself. Out of this group, out of the entire crew of the submarine and the fishing trawler, I am the only one who survived.”

Sobek arched an eyebrow. “So, they may be looking for it, but you’re the last one who knows where the submarine is.”

“I do not.” Voss looked Sobek dead in the eye.

“What?”

Mike Fowler watched carefully.

"I do not know where it is . . . but I know how to find it."

"You were there. That right? You were there when they put that sub on the bottom?" Jack Johnson was frowning.

"Yes, I was there. Kapitänleutnant Zapp and I manned the controls for the final dive. And, if I returned to that spot, I would recognize the godforsaken place immediately. But this does not mean I know where it is."

Paluso looked exasperated. "You're takin' us on a ride here. Better get to the end of it."

"The other men, the crew of the sub and the fishing boat, you say they are dead . . . how do you know they're *all* dead?" Sobek asked.

"Because we killed them. Gunther Könnecke, and I . . . we killed them to keep the secret."

CHAPTER 15

Paluso cursed, and Fowler glanced over at Johnson, who slowly pushed himself back from the table.

When Mike Fowler went to face his god there would be lives to be accounted for, some taken quite recently. And he and his Australian friend had done what should not have been required of them during the war . . . but it wasn't like they had ever tried to kill their own men. Of course, someone—one of their people—had tried to kill *them*. That was another story.

Voss did not seem defiant; "resigned" might be a better description. He exhaled, and a haze of cigarette smoke surrounded him. "Think what you wish. But if these events had not occurred, you would not be here. The wealth that I offer would not be available to you." He went on . . .

"We decided the only course was to hide the U-boat and return once conditions stabilized. We would find somewhere no one would look . . . no one in their right mind, at least. Through the creativity of ignorance, Könnecke put forward the idea that the boat might be left submerged and yet still be recoverable. Kapitänleutnant Zapp, von Pollnitz, who was the chief engineer, and I discussed the issue . . . It could be done, it was a risk, but we seemed to have no other choice.

"Our project was considered Kriegsentscheidend, a title that indicated it was critical to the outcome of the war. Because of this we had been issued a number of secret documents, identification codes, names of contacts, and a special folio of carefully prepared charts that were only to be unsealed in case of emergency.

"The idea had been first developed in the days of the Kaiser and the Weimar Republic. Later, the Kriegsmarine, the navy of the Third Reich, improved and expanded the entire archive. The maps were vastly more accurate than the documents in common use and contained a list of the hidden anchorages, Unterkunft Platze. Using our copy of this notebook, Herr Könnecke was able to locate a place where the U-Null could be hidden.

"He insisted on compartmentalization. Emil would act as both navigator and commander, and the only others to know the destination, the location, were Lommerzheim and Könnecke. The plan was improvised, but as you will see, it is also probably the only reason I am still alive."

Jack Johnson shifted in his chair. "Seems like a lot of trouble. Why didn't you just transfer the gold to the trawler?"

Voss paused, stubbing out his Chesterfield. "Secrecy. Security. Only myself and Herr Könnecke knew what was on the submarine. The cases were stowed in the torpedo room, and that was off-limits, sealed." He tapped the cigarette case and put it back in his breast pocket.

"So, the two boats headed west into the maze of islands. Navigation was a nightmare. There were tides and kelp beds. At times we had to blow our tanks completely to float through shallow areas. The skies were dark through most of the day and there were squalls of snow. Once we had to quickly submerge when the trawler spotted another vessel. Our vocabulary became a litany of curses.

"The few times I was outside on the bridge told me nothing. It was raining, there were huge rocks, wind-blown trees, later snowcapped mountains all around. The route we took may have been to avoid shipping and patrols; it may also have been to leave us confused as to our actual location. For all his youth and open demeanor, Herr Könnecke was quite the devious character. Devious enough so that when we arrived close by, it was already night.

"We used the next morning to scout and decide what we would do. A heavy anchor was transferred from the trawler to the U-boat, and we proceeded slow-ahead into a narrow passage searching for the final hiding place.

"The water was black and still. There were steep slopes of gray rock, glaciers, and a stream that had turned into a frozen waterfall. It was both bleak and beautiful. If you had a romantic belief in the sort of German mysticism that existed before the war, you could almost feel we had arrived at ultima Thule, the frozen wonderland at the end of the world. It was the perfect hiding place for the last secret of the Third Reich.

"Könnecke took the charts and packed them away. We spent a week preparing to abandon the U-boat. All possible maintenance was performed, every valve and electrical connection was covered with grease to minimize damage from moisture. Then the crew was moved to the trawler and Könnecke allowed von Pollnitz, Emil, and myself to set sprengfallen—what you would call booby traps. Every hatch and door was closed, the compressed air systems were fully charged, and then the electrics were powered down. We waited for the tide to turn so the anchor cable would be taut and then we opened the valves to the ballast tanks. Emil waited to make a final adjustment . . . and that almost got us killed.

"I went up into the attack center, the tiny cabin inside the conning tower. As soon as Emil climbed past me, I closed and sealed the hatch down to the Zentrale—the control room. Emil and von Pollnitz made it up to the bridge, and they waited to help me through the hatch. The bridge of the XXI is surrounded by an armored fairing that comes above a man's chest, but some sections are completely covered over for streamlining. To move underneath you must crouch. The water came up faster than we expected. A boat was waiting to take us to the trawler, but before we could get free, the bridge was flooding.

"The water was freezing, and it trapped me under the covering. The shock of it, the hyperventilation . . ." Voss shook his head and glanced at Mike Fowler. "Well, you know how this is. For a moment I could not move. It would have dragged me down, but Emil swam back, pulled me out, and got me into the boat. We made it to the trawler, a warm cabin, blankets, hot-water bottles. We had discharged our final duty, and the next day, we headed back to civilization.

"It was a journey of two, almost three days. For security, the U-boat crew was kept belowdecks until we were in the northward reach of the Strait of Magellan. The wind was blowing so hard you felt it would peel the skin from your face. We were told Punta Arenas was closed because of weather, but there was a private landing about twenty-five miles south. It was near sundown when Captain Lommerzheim turned the boat toward several small inlets protected by fingers of land. He dropped anchor and Herr Könnecke came to get me, saying we must go ashore and see about transportation. Everyone else was to wait in the trawler.

"He brought a flashlight, a case, and a heavy canvas bag. We took the rowboat and made our way to the beach. There were no lights, no one anywhere. Near the end of a dirt road, we found a truck, but small, nothing big enough for the crew of two boats. The key had been left under the seat. Könnecke seemed nervous, he opened the bag, inside was a disassembled MG 34."

Voss paused and then looked at Sobek as he explained, "This is a machine gun with an ammunition drum that can be affixed to the side. The case he had brought held two more drums.

"'Can you put this together?' he asked. I could, so I did. My first thought was that he was intending to cover our disembarkation from the fishing boat. The last time I had stood on land there had been war all around. But here, there was no one, no planes in the sky, nothing but the dusk and blowing trees.

"'What are we doing?' I asked. He was constantly checking his watch. 'Bring that,' he said. He took the gun and pointed to the case with the ammunition drums. We ran back to a high point along the shoreline. He set the bipod and put the gun down. He grabbed me by the shoulders and over the gusts of wind he yelled, 'I'm sorry! You must understand, I have my orders!' He was going to say something else . . . but then the trawler exploded.

"Like any man who has lived with bombing and the presence of combat, I did not think. I found myself flat on the ground and crawling for cover. I heard the gunfire, two long bursts. I was rolling over and looking for enemies.

"Könnecke was firing into the bay, but there was no boat headed our way. His tracers were vanishing into the water or arcing off into the night. It took me a moment to realize: he was killing the survivors, shooting anytime a head or arm appeared above the surface. I threw myself on him and we struggled. But he was wearing a heavy coat, as was I, so our blows were mostly ineffective. He rolled away and pulled out a pistol.

"'Do you think I would do this if it was not *necessary*?' he screamed at me. 'It is *critical* to the future!'

"'*What* future?' I challenged him. 'You are insane!'

"'I would have *told* you,' he said, 'but I was afraid you would behave like this. Please realize, I *understand*. They were your comrades . . . mine too, yes? We have a higher calling. So, you *must* control yourself. The mission is not over.'

"He made me sit and he spent an hour scanning for life. Then he broke down the machine gun and stored it in the back of the truck. He carefully searched the waterline with the flashlight. There were no survivors.

"At gunpoint he put me in the truck, and we started north. I think I was in shock. I did not argue with him, I just drove. After a time, he began to talk. There was a detailed plan, he said. We were working to make a better world, for our brothers, our race and, through them, for all mankind. The gravity of this mission meant we were morally unconstrained. The U-boat had to be kept secret, and yet it would someday be raised. Therefore, *I* was the one who must be spared. My loyalty would be rewarded, and I would be given the honor of serving the new regime.

"The strategy had been carefully thought out. They would cast off the old theatrical accoutrements of Nazism, the indolence of the Latin fascists, the mindless brutality of our allies in the Balkans. Our creed would live in the hearts and the heads of those who understood our philosophy . . . The new Reich would become the true 'hidden masters,' a secret society that would infiltrate—in fact had already begun to infiltrate—every institution, every government, and business in the world.

"We would work from within until the day came to reveal ourselves. History, psychology, the economy, these forces were all in our favor. Capitalism would be aided in crushing Communism through economic forces. Communism would be used to demoralize democracy using cultural forces. We would turn race against race, men against women, those who were emotional against those who were practical. This time the fools would do the fighting and the dying. In the midst of disruption, our systems, the companies, the multilateral institutions that we had secretly colonized, would be called on to do more and more. They would dominate and supplant nation-states as we know them.

"'And this is where the dog is buried,' he told me. Authority will be required; it always has the need to centralize. Centralization leads to dictatorship, the unflinching leadership of the elite. Those best prepared to make decisions. Unlike the old Nazis who came from the street, we would be the most highly intelligent, educated, competent, and well-placed people on earth. Now that the old perverts and criminals had been purged by the fires of war, our ranks had been cleansed, purified. We would multiply in secret, preparing for the day when we will reveal ourselves again to the world.

"'But all of this takes patience,' he explained. 'Careful political, cultural, and corporate maneuvering, the ability to invest, introduce scientific developments to drive the economy, to control—

distract—the populace.' Above all, he reminded me, it takes money . . . not just dollars, and pounds, and lira, but the ability to anchor and control financial institutions.

"It was madness." Anton Voss shook his head. "Madness similar to what we had been asked to believe during the war. Political ambition combined with the romantic passion of a fairy tale . . . but I also knew that they could probably do it. My countrymen had marched into the fires of hell, the downfall of our civilization, of our own free will. All that was missing was the type of patience the last set of leaders had been unable to muster.

"I did not argue with him, I pretended to agree and understand. To his credit, Könnecke seemed relieved, thinking I might forgive him for what he had done."

Jack Johnson glanced at Fowler. "*Coo-wee!* You knew about all of this? The party will become 'hidden *masters*'?"

"Some of it," Mike said. "Remember, I warned you."

"Naw, mate," the Australian laughed. "It'll be a *pleasure* to take that money out from under their noses."

Voss unfolded a U.S. Hydrographic Office chart. He slipped on his glasses and rotated the page so that Sobek and Paluso could read it. Reaching into his pocket, he took out his fountain pen and used it as a pointer, tapping on one of two large nearly landlocked bodies of water.

"He was taking me to a headquarters, an estate concealed on the north shore of Skyring Water. His superiors would lay out the strategy in detail. Within the next year he, using his charts, and myself, with my technical knowledge of the boat, would return to recover the treasure.

"After we passed through Punta Arenas, he turned onto a dirt road that followed the edge of the sound. This is barren land; the port itself is a very small town. We stopped so that he could take over the driving. In the dark, along the side of the road, I killed him. I choked him to death while he beat at my arms and face. Then I burned his body with gasoline and left it there, on fire."

The old man relaxed back into his seat. The story seemed to have taken something out of him, sapped his energy, and maybe his pride.

"I am German. I have spent most of my life in the shadow of war. Inside, I was saying something I had seen painted on ruined walls in Berlin, 'Aus der Traum!' . . . The dream was over. Maybe, like a cancer, this new interpretation, not so much Nationalism, not so much Socialism, not the people, not the workers, but whatever our nightmare had evolved into, might metastasize and control the world. I did not care. I was going home.

"I drove the truck off a cliff into the sea. I hitchhiked and took buses until I could catch a train. I returned with many other German sailors on a ship called the *Highland Monarch,* under conditions where I never had to use my name. Everything had been so secret, our country was in such a state, sectioned into four pieces, bombed to rubble, starving, on the brink of civil war. I simply resumed what life I had left. No one ever realized I had been gone."

Sobek and Paluso glanced at each other. Paluso nodded. "Yeah. This is a story I've heard before. Those men of power who ruled the feudal states back in the Old Country, they didn't just go away when Italy was unified. They took their money, and their soldiers, and went underground. They kept their trade routes, their banking, and the control of their territory. They were an invisible government. La Stidda, Camorra, 'Ndrangheta, Cosa Nostra, Mafia, whatever you want to call them. It's a loyalty, a . . . country *inside* a country, and now inside *other* countries, wherever there are Italians. No one ever 'wins' a war, not unless you totally wipe out your enemies."

Sobek pointed to the chart that was laid out on the table. "So what happened to the maps? The ones that show where the gold is?"

"They are up in smoke. Burned with the body, I suppose. I never envisioned my life as it is now."

"Well, it's a great story." Sobek pulled the map with the bullet hole in it toward him. He pursed his lips, frowning as he looked from it to the chart where Voss had indicated the road to what had once been the Nazi headquarters. "But what you're showing me here is a wild-goose chase."

Fowler knew Sobek was thinking about the scale of it all. He suspected that Johnson was, too. Just the southern part of the archipelago, from a spot on the coast parallel to Skyring Water down to Cape Horn, was a semicircle of some four hundred miles. In many places the shattered crescent of islands and channels was ninety miles deep.

"That's a *lot* of territory," Paluso said. "A lot of chances things could go wrong, and that's if . . . *if* you can find the place at all."

"When I see it, I will know it." Voss appeared to have cleared his head and returned to the present.

Sobek pushed his chair back and stood up. "Mel's right. Let's say I'm convinced the gold is there—I'm not, but let's just say—and maybe we can find it before either your nouveau-Nazi buddies or the Chileans show up and try to take it from us. I *still* don't see odds conducive to that sixty/forty split you pitched us. The reward is tempting, but there's too much risk. It's the amount of time. The *exposure*."

Voss wiped his glasses and slipped them back on. "So, you are saying that the operation has potential, but the terms we discussed are not acceptable? That you now wish to renegotiate?"

"Yeah." Paluso leaned back in his chair. "Seeing this, I'd say twenty/eighty, our favor. You reimburse us for all expenses when we make the split . . . or no deal."

"When I do the math"—Sobek bent over the table and pointed to the map of South America with the dates scribbled on it—"I think you've got a choice. Assume they began searching at the same time they did last year . . . that schedule's going to overlap the area you're pointing at in about three weeks. Are you going to find a replacement for our financing in that amount of time? I don't think so."

"I hate to break it to you," Mel Paluso said, "but you're over a barrel, and you can't trust anyone outside this room. Take our deal, it's the best you're gonna get." Paluso turned to Johnson. "Unless *you* can do something to reduce our overhead?"

Jack Johnson glared at him. "I get paid in full, mate. That's the rule."

"Then you are working for us now." Sobek smirked. "I made a few calls before we left Nassau. If you have cashed our German friend's check, you may be in luck. But the return trip he agreed to? That's not going to happen. The Spanish government's seized his assets. Whatever Herr Voss has in his account here in Caracas, that's it. That's all he's got."

Sobek didn't have every detail exactly right, but he was close enough. Fowler clenched his fists, and a memory came to him, a memory from his childhood back in Imperial Beach. Dark shapes standing over his father as he peered through the moldering curtain that separated the rooms of their shack. Those men had tried to force the Old Man to sail back to Mexico, this time for heroin rather than booze. Mike had not been old enough or strong enough to stop what happened next.

"We talked about this." Mike Fowler shot a look at his friend. "You and the guys don't have to worry about your trip home. I can cover it."

Mike saw Voss suddenly sit up straight. Well, he *had* just offered to cover a bill that would clean out his accounts. Maybe Anton had been acting strangely, but Mike was his partner . . . and he had to protect Jack, who wouldn't have been in this except that Mike had asked him.

Jack made a gesture toward Mike as if he was toasting him with an invisible drink. "Now, *that's* a real mate." He glanced over at the gangsters. "Did Mike ever tell you that the two of us, along with some other cobbers who didn't make it, were sent to wipe out a whole mob of Japanese on the last day of the war?" He looked from one of them to the other, and the smile dropped from his face. "No? Well, I'll say this . . . blood brings you close." He demonstrated by intertwining his big fingers. “Better all around, when it’s someone else’s.”

Mad Jack Johnson let the statement sit there, a veiled threat. Then he said, “If I violated my rule, if I waived the return trip, went all in, Mike just might have the money to pay our way south and cut you blokes out, right?”

“Nobody cuts us out! We’re in this, whether you like it or not!”

Anton Voss’s eyes flicked back and forth from Sobek to Johnson. A hint of amusement played across his face. The men from Nassau had made their move, but now it was the Australian diver’s turn at the game.

“Really? I’m not seeing why we need you. I reckon we could strike a deal for the gold with the Chileans or some of those European countries the Nazis stole it from.” Johnson pointed from Fowler to Voss and back to himself. “Then we could split whatever they’ll let us keep. I’m betting Larkin could set up a meeting with a couple of ambassadors . . . maybe even tonight.”

Paul Sobek blinked, and Paluso made a noise like a growl.

“Alright! *Stop* this,” Voss snapped. The amused look was gone and strangely he seemed almost as disturbed as Sobek and Paluso. “We have come here to cooperate.” He pointed at Sobek. “You have had your fun, and you will get better terms than we discussed last week. But there will be none of this eighty/twenty foolishness. I appreciate that you are concerned about the time spent searching for the fjord.”

“I’m concerned with getting caught,” Sobek stated. “Expensive *and* dangerous does not equal profitable.”

“Ja, I understand. It is possible there is a way we can be more certain about where we are going. It is not *safer*, and it does not guarantee our success. But it could be quicker. And I understand *that* is your concern.”

“We’re all ears,” Paluso said. “Wow us with your plan.”

It dawned on Mike Fowler that he knew what Voss was going to say. And given that Otto Skorzeny and his mysterious superior,

Peter Anhaldt, were no doubt searching for them, it was a truly terrible idea. The equivalent, if you were Anton Voss, of crawling all the way into the belly of the Nazi beast and then hoping you wouldn't be chewed up and digested.

"I'm going to bring you the information regarding the Unterkunft Platze."

"The secret maps? You told us they were burned." Sobek frowned.

"Not the maps. I am going to recruit the gentleman who compiled them."

CHAPTER 16

URUGUAY,

two days later . . .

THE FERRYBOAT GRUMBLED through the dark, carving a long, slow arc across the muddy estuary that was Río de la Plata. The trip from Montevideo to Buenos Aires would take most of the night. Mike Fowler dozed in a grimy seat in the forward lounge while Fernando Zúñiga held down a table in the café. Anton Voss had a cabin, one that Zúñiga had purchased, surreptitiously passing off the key after they had boarded in Montevideo.

The three of them had flown south in a DC-6C chartered by Alfredo Larkin, packed in among a cargo of Zeiss cameras, American cigarettes, Scotch whiskey, and French wine. But Larkin had warned them about the passport inspections at Ezeiza Field outside of Buenos Aires. Since the abduction of SS Obersturmbannführer Adolf Eichmann by Israeli agents, air travel in and out of the Argentine capital was scrutinized in a manner that other forms of immigration were not. Voss had therefore decided that they would disembark across the river in Uruguay and enter Argentina in a more pedestrian manner. They would then meet up with Larkin and fly south to their final destination on what had become a domestic flight.

According to Voss, Konstantin Seegers, the captain commissioned by the High Command, or OKM, to compile the secret folios of Unterkunft Platze, had been one of his instructors at the German Imperial Naval Academy at Kiel. They had reconnected in Berlin during the time when the Reichsmarine of the Weimar Republic was being transformed into the Kriegsmarine of the Third Reich. Assigned to the Department of Navigation, Seegers was in charge of updating the existing cartography, while Voss was one of several officers with scientific training who were reaching out to the academic and technical community. In the days before Voss had been reassigned to the Reichspost research facility in Miersdorf, and a curtain of secrecy was drawn around every department, the two had been able to discuss Seegers's project, one naval captain to another.

Well before the outbreak of war, Seegers immigrated to Argentina. It was a place where he could indulge himself in his favorite pastimes, mountain climbing and photography, where there were still mountains that had never been climbed or photographed. He had settled near San Carlos de Bariloche, a tourist resort in the foothills of the Andes.

Throughout the 1950s Konstantin Seegers had published a series of photography books containing pictures of Patagonia's otherworldly landscapes. Using his network of connections, Alfredo Larkin had been able to track down a lead on how to find the reclusive photographer.

Fowler peered out the spray-flecked window but there was nothing to be seen, just the reflection of the dim lights and sleeping people around him. Alfredo Larkin had been highly motivated to get them out of his house, motivated enough that he moved up a shipment of goods to Argentina. What he truly wanted was to be rid of Paul Sobek. And even as Fowler and Zúñiga helped load Larkin's cargo onto the big four-engine aircraft, Johnson, Sobek, and Paluso were already on the first leg of a series of flights that would take them from Caracas to Talcahuano, Chile, to await the arrival of the *Bushranger II*.

Regardless of his attempts to renegotiate, Sobek had finally been convinced, or embarrassed, into parting with enough cash to calm the big Australian. That was the upside of the trouble that had eventually erupted between Fowler, Sobek, and Cordelia Larkin.

It had begun that afternoon. Fernando Zúñiga had come to the door to inform them that one of Larkin's cars was headed up the hill. Voss cleaned up the papers, the book, and the maps, locking it all in his suitcase. Mrs. Larkin wafted into the house on a gust of expensive perfume, purse in the crook of one arm, car keys dangling from her other hand. Behind her, the little woman in gray struggled to carry a pair of brown paper bags.

In the hallway she barked a series of orders at her servant in rapid-fire Spanish, then began bustling around the dining room, every movement subtly provocative. She sauntered up to Paul Sobek and tapped him on the nose. "Soon I will make entremeses . . . the appetizers," she said and then shimmied toward the back of the house.

Sobek waggled his eyebrows toward the other men. "I can't wait."

Mike and Jack shared a glance. Alfredo's wife was amusing to look at, and she was well aware of it, but clearly the time when the men could talk without being overheard was coming to an end. Voss, Sobek, and Paluso vacated the dining room so the women could set up for dinner.

"Well, it's five o'clock. Who's for a drink?" Sobek had tracked down the artfully concealed doors to Larkin's impressive bar the night before. He went to work making cocktails. A compact refrigerator contained frosty beers but no ice. Johnson and Zúñiga each took a bottle; Fowler just had tonic water.

In lowered tones, Fowler had finished outlining his plan to raise the submarine, then Sobek turned to peer at Johnson.

"What do *you* think of this?"

"Sounds right to me," Jack said.

"We were told *you* were the great salvage diver. Why're you taking a back seat to him?" The gangster pointed his thumb at Fowler.

Jack Johnson glanced at Mike and winked. "Me? I *am* the greatest! Hydraulic Jack Johnson: if it's in the water and you want it elsewhere, I'm your man! But Mike Fowler—? Well, he's a legend."

"Oh yeah?" Paluso took a sip of his drink.

"Mike raised the USS *West Virginia.* At Pearl Harbor she was hit by more than five torpedoes. After he was done with her, she fought the Japanese at Leyte, Luzon, Iwo Jima, and Okinawa. She was in Tokyo Bay for the surrender . . . and that's just one ship. If you want to talk about who's raised the most tonnage, all in one piece, Rummy here, he deserves the World Cup."

Fowler struggled to hold back a laugh; his old friend was laying it on pretty thick. "Jack's being modest . . . enjoy it while it lasts. And I was just one of a very large team. You need someone who has stayed in practice. You need the facilities and men to do the work. That's why *he's* here. My job's just to have a good idea every once in a while."

"Hmph." Sobek peered at his drink. "Anybody need ice?" He headed for the kitchen.

Mike Fowler's amusement didn't last long.

"Rummy?" Paluso asked. "That why you won't take a drink?"

"Rum*runner*." Johnson took a swig of his beer. "Could be Mikey was in the game before you were."

"At *what*, five years old?" Paluso looked Fowler up and down.

"More like seven. My old man had a boat. It was a long time ago . . . best forgotten about. You follow?"

"Ha! I guess I do!"

From the dining room there came some mumbled words and a curse, a shuffle of feet, and the ringing smack of a hand striking flesh. Then the clatter and crash of a plate breaking.

Fowler was up in an instant; he didn't know what was wrong, but instinct propelled him toward trouble. Voss and the others were close behind.

Cordelia Larkin and Paul Sobek were squared off on either side of the dining room table. Her blouse was mussed and her lipstick smeared. She scooped another plate off the table and, as Mike barged into the room, she cursed in Spanish and hurled it at Sobek. Sobek ducked and the plate smashed against the wall.

Seeing the others, the gangster straightened his shirt collar. "She's crazy!" he shouted.

Fowler slammed him up against the wall, a forearm barred across his neck. "Stop it! Whatever is going on, *stop*!"

"You saw her, she was asking for it! Was she asking for it?" There was a trace of her lipstick on Sobek's mouth.

Quick as a cat, Mrs. Larkin was around the end of the table. She snatched up a fragment of broken plate and attempted to cut Sobek's face. Fowler turned to fend her off and, as he did, the gangster crouched and slugged him in the ribs. Fowler threw an elbow that took Sobek on the side of the head. Mike pushed Cordelia Larkin backward into the table and Sobek collapsed to the floor holding a bloody ear.

Mike Fowler looked around. Paluso had dropped the bottle of tonic water and pulled the Colt Python from under his guayabera-style shirt. Jack Johnson stepped in front of him, fists up, ready to fight or take a bullet. Voss looked coldly furious and Fernando Zúñiga simply confused.

"Stop this!" Voss ordered and stepped between Johnson and Paluso, locking eyes with the Italian and pushing the gun down. Cordelia dropped into a chair and began to cry, and the housekeeper opened the swinging door to the kitchen and glanced around, eyes wide with shock.

At that moment the front door opened, and, with a rattle of keys, Alfredo Larkin entered. "Honey, I'm home!"

Anton Voss moved quickly to intercept Larkin and Mike turned to Paluso. Regardless of the fact that he had pulled a gun, it seemed he might be able to deal rationally with the situation.

"We are going out to dinner. Get your partner's ear patched up and let's move. We do not need trouble. Understand?"

Paluso nodded and stuffed the pistol back into his waistband, flipping the shirt over it. Mike looked at Cordelia. "I'm going to talk to your husband. We will be staying in a hotel tonight and we'll be gone as soon as possible. I suggest that you tell him nothing more than the truth. These people are rough customers, comprende?"

They moved out that evening and Alfredo had done what was necessary to start Johnson, Sobek, and Paluso on their way to Chile the next day, and to reschedule his next flight to Argentina for the day after. Mike did what he could to move the process along; the busier Larkin was the less time he would have to do something they might all regret.

ARGENTINA,

morning . . .

MIKE FOWLER'S FIRST concern was met with relief. There were no issues as they came off the ferry. Alfredo was waiting at the Buenos Aires docks with a driver in a newish Chevrolet. And as soon as they were in the air again, they sliced open a carton of cameras and began removing their weapons.

Larkin provided Fowler with a Ballester-Molina, an Argentine copy of a Colt 1911. There was a story, though Mike didn't really believe it, that the pistols had been made from steel salvaged from the *Admiral Graf Spee*, the German pocket battleship that had been scuttled not far from where their ferry had crossed the River Plate. The *Spee* had been badly damaged after a dramatic battle with three British cruisers in 1939.

Not having a holster, Fowler cut and bent a wire hanger so that it wrapped around his belt and then slid inside his trousers, forming a J-shaped hook he could fit into the muzzle of the .45-caliber handgun. On short notice Alfredo could only supply two additional magazines. None of it was ideal, but it was much better than nothing.

The DC-6 was uninsulated, and it was both cold and loud. Fowler used the noise, and the fact that Larkin was sitting with the flight crew, to his advantage. He dug Aleixandre's telegram out of his pocket and handed it to Voss.

The two of them examined the cryptic document. Magnetic Data Corporation and Peter Anhaldt as an individual seemed to be connected with a network of other businesses and organizations, many of them in the U.S. and Latin America. Voss put on his glasses and took out a pen, occasionally scribbling in the margins as he read.

"Here"—Voss pointed to one of Aleixandre's abbreviations—"Magnetic Data was once a division of Universal Tabulation and Processing. This is the key to everything on this page. But to understand you have to know the history of German industry."

Voss lowered the telegram and leaned close so that he didn't have to shout. "You see, for more than one hundred years the quality of education in central Europe has been very high. And the *scientific* education . . . excellent. The influence of hereditary aristocracy declined, yes? But because of this there was an increasing demand to have the initials of one or more advanced degrees associated with your name. Whether the person is called 'baron,' 'commissar,' or 'doctor,' people always create a market for some sort of social hierarchy. A way to say, 'I am better than you.' However, backed up by *actual* achievement, in disciplines that can improve people's lives, it is a powerful force . . . not mere snobbery.

"In Germany, the success of color-dye manufacturing drove the demand for scientists and technicians. Dyes created a focus on the discovery of new chemical formulas. This evolved into medicines, treatments for malaria, aspirin, Novocain, morphine. Then came photographic solutions and the fixing of nitrogen for fertilizer. Nitrates also had a role in the manufacture of gunpowder and explosives that were crucial for our survival in the 1914 war.

"We were already a culture where there was great pride in precision manufacturing, so the chemical properties of steel were important, as was the study of catalysts, electrical engineering, and nuclear physics . . . but the primary product behind all of this was *information*."

Voss pointed to another line. "You see here, this is where Universal Tabulation and Processing enters the picture. UTP was based in New York and founded in the 1890s. They produced a high-speed method of cross-referencing data points using punch cards and mechanical calculators and sorters. Their closest competition was another American company, IBM. Our friend Peter Anhaldt said that he once designed punch cards for Dehomag . . . this stands for Deutsche Hollerith-Maschinen, a subsidiary of IBM.

"So, in the beginning UTP, just like IBM, worked for the German states, creating systems for the census, documenting political party affiliation, who had what jobs, who was what race, who had firearms, and, in times of rationing, where the food should go. Precision and efficiency were the goal. UTP was the system that made the trains run on time, so to speak. By the 1930s it was also logical that this data and the means to process it should be shared with the Gestapo.

"From their census work, UTP made inroads into the police. From their connections to business, they found their way into science and academia. When the war came the giant steel works, weapons manufacturing, aircraft factories, chemical and pharmaceutical companies, all became essential to the state . . . but more than that, *fused,* you see? The influence of the National Socialist Party extended from the union men on the factory floor all the way up to the paneled offices. The center point to that circle was Universal Tabulation and Processing.

"It made complete sense for any group of organizations, in this case the UTP customers, to form an I.G., Interessengemeinschaft . . . an officially sanctioned trade organization, like the chemical cartel I. G. Farben. Then through one of its American subsidiaries the I.G. purchased UTP, the company that had provided the original service.

"You see here"—Voss tapped the page—"in 1941, UTP is purchased, and the new president is—"

"Peter Anhaldt!"

"Yes. The man who says he knew of me because we were both using the Konrad Zuse electronic computing machine! Well, it seems he was in the U.S. but kept a low profile during the war. So, here in 1946, UTP creates a list of new American companies. You see: aircraft, telecommunications, newspapers, chemicals, pharmaceuticals, and electronics. Then, with a 'mysterious' amount of newly found wealth, *those* companies begin to buy up their competitors, all successful medium-sized brands. In every case he retains the well-known American name. Unless you pay attention, you would hardly know it was happening. There are companies also in Argentina, Brazil, and Mexico.

"Finally, in 1956, Magnetic Data is incorporated, and Universal Tabulation and Processing is closed. This list, all successful businesses, has created what you would call an 'underground railroad' for cash, patents, and German scientists and engineers, and each can generate wealth on its own.

"What you see here is irony. It is the reverse of what occurred in Germany between the wars. In those days old European money, British money, powerful corporations in the United States, all invested in National Socialism.

"For a certain type of unscrupulous businessman, it would have been the opportunity of a lifetime: a dictatorship, one where the state and industry were deeply cooperative, financially desperate, yet also industrially advanced and with highly educated workers. I say unscrupulous because, whatever one might have thought of the Third Reich in peacetime, many of those same companies chose to maintain their holdings throughout the entire conflict."

"Wait . . . you mean *during* the war." Mike shook his head, tried to clear it. He should know better! It was very likely the Japanese businessmen he and Jack Johnson had been sent to assassinate on Itu Aba had stood in the way of a similar plot aimed at postwar Japan.

"Ja. In fact, my superior at the Reichspost tried to object to these foreign influences, to impound their assets. So, a prominent banker, a man with 'international connections,' placed the head of Gestapo counterintelligence, Walter Schellenberg onto the corporate boards. No one was willing to go up against the Gestapo *and* the bank that made National Socialism possible! Even a dictatorship must answer to someone.

"As soon as the war ended the foreign bankers, lawyers, and corporate executives were fighting to get back into Germany to reclaim their interests. And the world outside Germany was changing in ways that were very much to the advantage of those who understood the system we had established.

"Since the Great War, the First World War, our country had experimented with a certain . . . *interaction* between the roles of academia and industry, the military and government administrators. In an American context, your president, General Eisenhower, referred to it as the 'military-industrial complex,' a closed cycle of money and power. We knew it well. We could swim in its waters like a shark in the sea. Your system was . . . ripe for outside exploitation.

"War is a cultural exchange. If you are not careful you can become what you fight. Some, like Anhaldt, infiltrated your society before we declared war. Perhaps his goal was espionage or influence, I don't know. Afterward German scientists and managers were imported like so many cattle, and he was well-placed to help them pursue the American dream.

"Somehow Allen Dulles and his CIA were seduced into supporting the network of covert operatives controlled by General Reinhard Gehlen. Perhaps it is not surprising, Dulles had once been a lawyer representing a good deal of German industry. So, the question is: Are Gehlen's spies your spies, or do they work for their own ends? Do they manufacture crisis in order to increase the power of men like Anhaldt? I do not know . . . but I know what I suspect.

"Members of the Invisible Reich are now the experts, the top managers. Companies like Magnetic Data are the employers of many citizens. They supply products required for industry and national security. They use the fears of the Cold War, the arms race, as levers to manipulate the world of finance and politics. It is a risky game. A foolhardy game. The stakes are atomic war and the fate of the entire world. However, they are used to dancing on the brink and, with the Fatherland defeated, their web of connections has become their nation."

Voss took a breath, seemingly done . . . then, as if remembering, he added, "You have to wonder how much more successful they would be with a secret cache of gold."

After several hours tall mountains appeared to the west and soon they were flying over an area of dun-colored hills. They swooped past a tall rocky crag and descended into a wide valley containing a body of water that stretched almost forty miles to the north. The far end was lost in a scattering of hills that joined the snowcapped wall of the Andes. This was Nahuel Huapi, the largest of the area's many lakes. The big plane set down at what was clearly a busy airport. Two airliners were parked on the tarmac and a string of tourists was filing into the terminal.

While the rest of them waited near the plane, Larkin went to deal with the details of their arrival and the copilot was good enough to order lunch from the small airport café. The less Fowler and especially Voss were out in public, the better. Many of the Germans in Bariloche had arrived well before the war, some of them fleeing the changes that had overwhelmed their country. But the town had also become a hotbed of Nazism during the 1930s and, in the years since, the rumored sanctuary for war criminals.

The timeline Voss had laid out for Anhaldt's "invisible empire" raised more questions than it answered. Mike worried that there were things he needed to know, things he was not being told. The photo of Anton and Dr. Elizabeth Adler that Yaron had shown him in Israel was distinctly different from the one Anton now carried in his breast pocket. The first had seemed happy and hopeful while the second contained a sense of desperation. The contrast between the two made Mike wonder about a lot of things, but most particularly about how long Anton and Elizabeth had known each other and about the circumstances of her death.

Leonid, the scarred scientist, seemed to think Dr. Adler had died while the two of them were working on the device Fowler had been shown in the drawing. Yet Voss claimed his photo had been taken *after* his submarine had been commandeered, and thus after the other members of his research group had been shot. Mike realized he was straining at the boundaries of what his imagination could fit together . . . but still, something didn't add up.

He found Anton Voss near the taxiway, staring off to the south. "I have some questions," Mike said.

"And I will do my best to answer . . ."

"At the end of the war, what were you working on?"

"Hmm. You mean before I was ordered to come here?" Voss gestured at the panorama of mountains, the low haze hanging over the lake. "I have told you. Technology for the navy."

Fowler had heard all that before, and the moments he had alone with Anton were growing fewer and fewer. "Elizabeth Adler. Who was that?" he asked.

Voss sucked in air. He looked at Fowler with narrowed eyes. "Where did you hear this? Israel?"

Fowler nodded.

"Well, they are playing you," he snapped. "Always too clever for their own good. What did they say about her?"

"Nothing. They just asked." Even as he spoke, Fowler realized that wasn't exactly the truth. He was the one who had asked about Dr. Adler.

Anton Voss looked back to the horizon. The wind tousled the grass and he took off his hat and ran a hand through his hair. "She was my fiancée. Is that good enough? Please, I would like to drop this entire subject." Then he shook his head and walked away.

Over by the terminal one of the airliners started its engines, and the ground crew cleared away the boarding ladder. Mike frowned; he had crossed some line, a barrier between past and present, and he felt bad . . . he felt *guilty* for stirring up painful memories. But at the same time, he was aware that Voss had told him almost nothing . . . and he had a sudden suspicion that the older man had just misdirected him, used a painful memory as cover to escape giving a complete answer.

A half hour later a station wagon pulled onto the tarmac. Each of the front doors bore the painted logo DIEGO JARA—CAFÉ DE FOTOGRAFÍA. A young woman, who seemed to be of high-school age, jumped out of the driver's seat. She wore blue jeans and a colorful scarf and introduced herself as Valentina, the owner's daughter. She had arrived to pick up the shipment of cameras.

Mike and Fernando helped load the equipment into the back of her car while Alfredo introduced Voss. He explained that Herr Voss was searching for an old friend, Captain Konstantin Seegers. It would be good to say hello, but they only had a few hours before the aircraft would need to take off.

The girl had an electric smile. Yes, she had met Señor Seegers. His cabin was off the main roads and not easy to find. It seemed they had found exactly what they were hoping for: a local guide and transportation to their destination.

While Valentina moved a stack of mail, including several glossy magazines, so that Voss could sit in front, Mike leaned close to give Fernando a few instructions he didn't want Alfredo Larkin to hear . . .

"Don't let him out of your sight, understand? And for damn sure don't let him take off until we get back!"

The Spaniard nodded, and Mike clapped him on the back. Ever since the altercation between Paul Sobek and Cordelia Larkin, Alfredo had been acting strangely. Mike could hardly blame the guy, but he no longer completely trusted him either.

On the way into town Voss said very little. Valentina Jara made up for this silence by keeping up a constant stream of chatter. She spoke Spanish, English, and German, and was a remarkably well-informed tour guide.

Bariloche had been founded in the nineteenth century by German settlers who came through the Andes from Chile. In the beginning it had mostly catered to local cattle ranchers but, given the beauty of the countryside and the temperate climate, the tourist trade became important as well. Because of this, the Directorate of National Parks had remade the town in the image of a Swiss or Bavarian village, an idea no doubt promoted by the residents, many of whom were nostalgic for home.

Once the road left the desolate area around the airport the landscape truly did take on the look of the Swiss or Italian Alps, although on a much grander scale. Nahuel Huapi gave the feeling of almost being an inland sea. Low over the lake a sleek twin-engine aircraft was approaching from the west and sunlight flashed off of the small wind-driven waves.

The town itself did nothing to disappoint. All around were stone and timber buildings complete with chimney pots and clipped roofs. There was a Gothic cathedral as well as a clock tower on the village square. The lawns and flower boxes were tidy and the streets clean. Many of the cars they passed were made by Mercedes and Volkswagen. A hulking Mengele harvester lumbered down the highway. Well-dressed tourists snapped photographs.

On the other side of town, Valentina pointed out a large wooden gatehouse. The sign above the windows read CENTRO ATOMICO BARILOCHE.

"We have the Argentine Commission of Atomic Energy here. Scientists do research and make discoveries. We are one of the few countries with such a program."

Fowler glanced up the road into the facility. It was the kind of place he would expect Anton to be interested in, especially in a country like Argentina. But Voss was staring out at the islands across the lake as if there was something meaningful in that direction, something besides an attractive view.

They continued north, turning inland through a wilderness of roadside brush and tall trees. The only signs of civilization were a few dirt roads and the occasional timber bus stop. As they crossed a narrow bridge at the confluence of two smaller lakes the view opened up for a moment, revealing distant mountains. A half mile or so on the other side, Valentina made a sudden left turn onto a nearly invisible track. It was a muddy gravel drive that wound its way up the slope between tall conifers and the unevenly colored trunks of arrayán trees.

The car scraped its undercarriage on a hump in the center of the road and skidded a bit. The girl gunned the engine and laughed. "It is never good, driving here. Worse when winter comes." They emerged into a clearing with a parking area surrounded by log barriers. A decade-old Mercedes panel wagon sat covered by a dusty carpet of leaves and pine needles.

On one side there was a view that stretched thirty miles or more, across mountains and lakes, with the magnificent Llao Llao Hotel in the foreground, its white walls and red roofs resting like a set of Tyrolean caps on a low hill above the water. On the other side, past the rusting Mercedes, stone steps led up to a log cabin nestled in the shadow of the trees. Their guide ran lightly up the mossy stairs only to stop and loudly clap her hands. After a moment she clapped again.

"Hola? Capitán, are you home?"

By the time Fowler and Voss reached the door it had not yet opened. "Just wait," Valentina said. "He is here."

Fowler looked around; the cabin was hemmed in by the forest . . . It was not a big house. "You sure?" he asked.

"Oh, yes."

There was the sound of a lock ratcheting back, and then the door creaked. Captain Konstantin Seegers squinted into the daylight, his eyes moving from the girl to Mike and finally coming to rest on Anton Voss. He stared and his mouth dropped open slightly. Then he blinked to clear away what might have been tears.

Anton was also taken aback, but he recovered quickly. "Herr Captain. It is very good to see you . . . after all these years."

Mike took a breath, assessing the situation. It was clear that the plan to offer Seegers a quarter-of-a-million-dollar payday to come with them was probably not going to work.

The old man with the trim white beard who confronted them had big shoulders and strong arms, but from the waist down his body was withered, supported precariously on a pair of crutches.

CHAPTER 17

It was warm inside the cabin and the smell of coffee drifted from the kitchen. Mike Fowler could hear the bump and clatter as Captain Seegers moved awkwardly around, preparing cups and saucers, opening tins of biscuits and Belgian chocolates that looked as if they had been gifts from past holidays. The old man was as delighted to have company as he was unprepared for it.

While Seegers and Voss spoke of old times, Mike asked permission to look through the albums and boxes of photographs that covered every flat surface in the combination living and dining room that made up the front of the house.

"Please, you are my guest. All I have done in the last three years is work in the darkroom, printing. It is now my only way to visit these special people and places."

After accepting a foil-wrapped chocolate of indeterminate vintage, Valentina returned to the car to read through her stack of magazines. From the living room Mike could see her lounging behind the wheel, feet casually propped on the dashboard. The muffled voice of Dean Martin could be heard singing behind the rolled-up windows.

Konstantin Seegers was quite an artist, a master of controlling exposure and contrast to create glowing black-and-white images. He was aided by the fantastically rugged landscapes of southern Argentina and Chile, the twisted rocky peaks and translucent glaciers. His photographs were not only of vistas and wildlife. He had captured extraordinary candid shots of fellow mountaineers dangling from frozen waterfalls and driving pitons into the sheer faces of rocky cliffs to string their lines. Whatever accident had befallen the old captain, he had clearly been forced to give up an important aspect of his life.

"You move to a place like this—and you can see why one would want to—there is beauty all around," Seegers's voice carried from the kitchen. "When you are young—or at least not too old—it is all good. There are clubs for the skiing and mountain climbing, so there is a community. But if you can no longer ski or climb? Not so much, ja? You realize these people, they are mainly interested in the *activity*. Then you spend a lot of time thinking how far you are from home, your real home."

"Could you go back if you wanted? You can afford it, yes?"

"I have some money. Enough if I am careful. My books . . . I am world-famous in South America, you see?" Voss and Seegers both laughed at that, and Mike glanced around. He was hoping that Seegers had a map; this whole trip was going to be a waste of time if he didn't.

There were several wooden file cabinets with shallow drawers pushed in behind the couch and, on top of them, a stack of slim oversized books. Mike Fowler looked more closely. In the best of all possible worlds, the man might even have a photograph of the place. Down the hall toward the back of the house he could see a blacked-out room fitted with sinks and enlargers.

"I'm sure I could give all this up and have an apartment in some little town in Bavaria . . . and then I could be reminded that all the people I wish would come to visit me are now dead. Present company excepted, of course." Seegers chuckled. "When you are old, you grow apart from the world. It is just the way. Don't let it happen to you, my boy!"

"It pains me to say this, Konstantin, but I am not so pure of heart. I have come to ask you a favor." From the kitchen area Voss caught Fowler's eye and indicated that he should join them.

Seegers laughed. "Of course. If one moves to the end of the earth, one must accept it requires heroic circumstances to cause friends to visit. What can I do?"

"First, a compliment," Voss said. "During the war I was involved with a group that used some of your maps. The *special* maps. The mission was . . . cursed with troubles, but the one aspect that functioned perfectly was the navigation, and that was thanks to you."

The old man shook his head and, taking both crutches in one hand, dropped into a chair. When he spoke, it seemed that a touch of emotion caught in his voice. "When you do that sort of work, you are preparing for events you cannot even imagine. I like to think that what we did saved lives, German lives, at the very least."

Voss appeared decidedly uncomfortable. He took a drink of his coffee. The tragedy that followed the hiding of the U-boat wasn't the fault of Seegers or his maps, but they sure hadn't saved any lives.

"There was a place . . ." Voss took the paper napkin from under his cup, uncapped his pen, and sketched. "It was a fjord, leading northward, possibly northeast. There was a frozen waterfall . . . here." He turned the napkin and began drawing again, the absorbent nature of the paper making him work carefully. "The skyline may have looked something like this. The depths were twenty to fifty meters, or so. The location was near to an area designated Unterkunft Platze. There could not have been so many."

"A U-Platze?" Seegers suddenly remembered to be cautious. He looked from Voss to Fowler and back.

Fowler pulled one of several maps out of his rucksack. "Do you think you might remember it? Could you show us?"

Seegers shook his head. "It has been forty years since I sailed that coast. Almost thirty since I compiled my charts. Yes, we designated a few locations as U-Platze—but from memory? I don't know . . ."

"You no longer have your maps?" Voss asked.

Seegers shot a glance toward the living room. Fowler was beginning to think he had it right . . . those books and file cabinets shoved behind the couch might be where this particular treasure was buried.

"We must remember, Anton, all this was to be kept secret."

"Yes, it was." Anton recapped his pen. "But to whom do those secrets belong? Your survey was performed under the auspices of the Weimar government. It is gone. The German Reich is gone. Does your knowledge belong to the BRD in the West, or the DDR in the East? Neither of us has lived under either of those governments. Or does it belong to the German people . . . who will never be allowed to see it?"

Konstantin Seegers dragged himself up onto his crutches and turned to look out the window over the sink. There were things Mike was tempted to say, but he kept his mouth shut. As an American his presence seemed to be complicating things already. The books in the living room had been labeled with dried-out pieces of fabric-backed tape. They read *Revision 1932: Feuerland/Magellan-Straße.* The date was before Voss had been transferred to the Reichspost, but the locations sounded right. Were they the maps Anton was after?

"I would not ask if it was not critical, if lives—my own being one of them—were not on the line." Voss kept his voice neutral. He was not pleading.

"Your own? I don't suppose you are going to tell me what this is all about."

"I will if I must, but it might be best if you did not know. Would you accept that I might return, in person, to tell you the entire story, once it is completely resolved?"

The old captain struggled to look his friend in the eyes. "I am happy you have come. But I am so sorry you have wasted your time. Is there another way I could help?"

Voss motioned to Fowler, who reached back into his rucksack. This time he pulled out a six-inch stack of American hundred-dollar bills. While Seegers's eyes were on the money, Fowler glanced at Voss and inclined his head toward the living room and the area behind the couch.

"It means quite a bit to me, Konstantin. You could consider this a down payment," Voss said.

Seegers clenched his jaw; his sadness seemed to be shifting toward a darker emotion.

Anton's eyes narrowed. "If you did not have them, you would say so. Tell me: why did you bring copies with you? They are not your property. Were you thinking someday you might have to make some sort of deal with the Argentines? If so, I admire your caution and forethought."

"We swore our loyalty!"

"Says the man who emigrated in 1936! You were not there through the manic time, or the war. You were safe. Safe from the bombs, safe from the negotiations with your soul." Voss stood. "*Damn it*, the past is calling, Konstantin! I need to take this one piece and bury it as deeply as possible!"

Fowler heard the grate of tires on gravel, and the sound of an engine shutting off. He turned away from the kitchen table.

Seegers mumbled something in German. Voss pushed the pile of money toward him. "Help us. Help yourself . . . or not, whatever your conscience requires. Just know that if you do, my gratitude will be endless. It is a favor to mankind."

Mike wondered if Anton might be pushing it a bit too far . . . and then he looked out the window.

A Ford sedan with a two-tone paint job had pulled up. Four men piled out, leaving the doors open. One of them was Heinrich Hartmann, now wearing a black eye patch.

"Anton!" Fowler's voice was low and hard. He drew the .45 from the hook inside his belt. "Trouble!"

Voss also produced a pistol. Captain Seegers looked from one to the other of his guests. "What is this? What have you gotten me into?"

"Get down and be quiet!" Mike worked the slide of the Ballester-Molina.

Valentina had been resting her back on the passenger door of her father's car, lost in her magazines and music. One of the men jerked the door open and, with a cry, she tumbled onto the ground. Hartmann drew a knife. He buried it in the side of her neck.

Mike stepped back from the window, aimed, and fired. The pane of glass exploded. It was a good forty yards to his target. Instead of taking Hartmann in the side of the head, the bullet went low, punching through the roof of the car and breaking the window on the opposite side. Hartmann staggered. Then one of his companions opened up on the house with a machine pistol.

Fowler ducked and bullets whacked into the logs above the window. No one Hartmann worked with was that bad a shot. It was covering fire, intended to keep their heads down while his men got into position. Were they simply hoping to capture Voss . . . or had they discovered the connection between Seegers and the location of the sub?

"We have to get out of here!" Fowler yelled, but he knew that was going to be a serious problem. Unless they could escape down to the lake on the west side of the house, they were trapped. The only other way was going up the steep grade through the forest. Seegers couldn't make it, but sliding downhill might be possible.

The man with the machine pistol had taken cover behind Valentina's car. Mike shifted position and, getting a dark wall behind him, stood and put two rounds into the trunk lid and fender. He saw the gun barrel and part of the man's head appear, and fired again.

There was a shout, but then a long burst. He hadn't done any meaningful damage. Below, one of the men ran off to the right. Their plan was to encircle the house.

"Where are the maps?" Voss snapped at Seegers. "You can tell me, or these men will torture you for them!"

Seegers pointed, but Mike was already moving. Keeping low, he grabbed the edge of one of the large flat books behind the couch and pulled. The whole pile toppled to the floor. If they had to sort through it, they would be out of the line of fire.

"Keep an eye on them. I'm going to try and clear a way out the back." Mike clapped Voss on the shoulder and crawled for the back door. Pushing it open he looked left and right then sprinted a dozen yards uphill, sliding to the ground behind the trunk of a tree. There was a smattering of gunfire from the front of the building, but it devolved into regularly spaced three-round bursts. More covering fire, or at least that was what Mike hoped.

A man cautiously poked his head around the eastern corner of the building. He hesitated when he saw the back door standing open, his eyes shifting up into the trees. Fowler shot him. Once, and then again.

Fowler scrambled to his feet and swapped a fresh magazine into the pistol. The man he had just shot hadn't acted as if he had reinforcements coming up behind him, so Mike moved toward the west end of the cabin.

A tall man with pale hair in a plaid mackinaw rolled over the edge of the slope. He didn't try to stand, just came up on one elbow and started shooting.

Fowler fired, lost his footing, and hit the ground. Bark and splinters exploded off a fallen log and peppered his face. He rolled over and shot back. The blond man went down but was still struggling to get back behind the corner of the house. Throwing himself to his feet, Mike launched himself toward the door to the cabin, emptying the gun as he ran. If he was going to get Anton out, he had to do it immediately. Could he carry Seegers? He didn't know.

Mike ducked behind the cover of the open door and fumbled for his last magazine. He could feel it in his pocket, but he couldn't get ahold of it. Two bullets punched holes in the top panel of the door, and another came through the bottom. Mike felt something strange and looked down: blood was soaking through the calf of his trousers. He could smell smoke and burning plastic.

"Coming in!" Fowler shouted. Another shot notched the lower part of the door as he slammed it shut behind him and flipped the lock. A jet of burning gas was hissing from a rift in the side of the stove and flames were tickling the cabinetry. In the living room all the windows were broken. Voss and Seegers had retreated to the hallway leading to the darkroom. Seegers held a dishcloth to a torn cheek. His other hand had a tenuous hold on one of the bound volumes.

Voss stood, pulling an empty magazine from his SIG. But just as he did, the front door smashed open, Heinrich Hartmann's powerful kick nearly breaking it in two. He stepped aside and a young man, a boy really, in a leather jacket leaped into the room raising an MP 40.

"Anton!" Fowler dove toward Voss, tackling him to the floor just as the submachine gun fired. He felt the impact of the bullets, one a solid whack to the ribs, the other . . . he couldn't tell. He rolled over.

Voss grabbed at the wall and stood up. The kid was struggling to feed another magazine into the gun. Voss shot him in the forehead then scrambled backward, pulling Seegers deeper into the hallway.

Smoke poured from the kitchen, hanging like a ragged curtain across Mike's vision. He tore at his pocket, and a flicker of memory sent him back to the driftwood shack south of San Diego. His father on the floor. The hollow feeling of failure. Then his fingers closed on the steel of the magazine.

He punched out the empty as Hartmann stepped through the door. Mike threw himself sideways just as the German fired. The bullet picked meat off his arm. The magazine went into the gun, and Mike hit the slide release, then pulled the trigger. The bullet ripped along the floor and blasted the heel off of Hartmann's left boot.

Hartmann fired into the wall as he staggered, and Fowler pulled the trigger again. Nothing. The slide was jammed half open, a cartridge canted sideways, half into the chamber. He yanked on the oddly serrated slide of the Ballester-Molina. It didn't budge. The German lifted his pistol and Mike threw the .45 at Hartmann and lunged forward, following it in.

They collided awkwardly, and Fowler got behind him, slipping an arm around Hartmann's thick neck, locking him in a choke hold. The German struck backward with an elbow and Mike gripped him tighter. Mike had barely noticed when he'd been shot but now, even through the shock and adrenaline, his body was screaming at him.

Hartmann sidestepped and bent, a rough dance where he tried to escape and to get a leg behind Fowler's. Mike backed up against the wall and twisted, trying to smash Hartmann's head into the remains of the door. The man had a bloody gouge across his abdomen where Fowler's first bullet had ripped clothing and flesh, but he was still fantastically strong.

Hartmann broke away, colliding with the other side of the doorframe. He turned, and Fowler fired a right to the chin that connected too high; blood splattered and lips tore. The big man's head rebounded off the wood behind him. Mike punched again and they both went down.

Mike dragged himself out onto the doorstep and collapsed. Every time he sucked in a breath a stabbing pain overrode the burning in his side. He saw smoke pouring from the roof of Seegers's cabin. He had to get back, to get Voss, to save him while there was still time.

He tried to stand, or even sit, but barely succeeded in rolling over. Mike shook his head and nearly vomited. Then he heard distant gunshots, two of them, and glass breaking. After a moment Anton Voss appeared out of the trees near the lakeside end of the cabin. He was carrying one of Captain Seegers's books under his arm.

Voss barely glanced in the direction of the house. He calmly walked toward the cars. Mike tried to call out but could barely force out a whisper. Stepping over Valentina's body, Anton leaned in and checked the ignition of the big sedan Hartmann had come in. Then he tossed in the book and got behind the wheel. He put the car in gear and sprayed gravel and leaves, making a skidding three-point turn that headed him back down the rutted road. In the distance Mike could hear a siren approaching.

Mike Fowler had to get up. He had to get on his feet. He had to make Heinrich Hartmann pay . . . pay for the Farkhani brothers back in Barcelona, pay for the sweet teenage girl he had murdered just moments ago. And Mike had to get away, back to the airport, before Alfredo Larkin's plane left.

He was trying to stand when he was lifted nearly off his feet. Hartmann, eye patch gone, his face a scarred and bloody mess, dragged him up by the collar and belt and threw him bodily down the stone stairs. Fowler saw sky, dirt, and then stars as he hit the ground. The sirens screamed at him, then whined down into nothingness as he blacked out.

Hospitals echo in a particular way. Maybe it was all the linoleum, or the ceramic tile. Mike woke up thinking he might be back in the ward in Manila, starved, and burned, and shot, smashed into the coral by waves and bombs. But that wasn't right—Manila and before that the fishermen who had saved him from the hell of Itu Aba were a long time ago. What was real was the pain . . . and memories of other wounds.

"He is not awake?" It was Skorzeny's growl.

"No, Señor. Quizas pronto . . . soon."

"Well then, take me to Hartmann."

Footsteps disappeared into the background.

Fowler was lying on his stomach. He tried to move but he couldn't, not much at least. When he got his eyes open, he saw that his wrist was manacled to the chrome rail of the bed. A gentle tug told him the other arm was restrained as well. He lifted his head and turned to glance toward the windows, squinting into the light coming through the venetian blinds.

Peter Anhaldt was sitting in an armchair, as stylish as a movie star in a turtleneck and blazer. He watched Fowler with the barest smile showing around his eyes and on his lips.

"Otto is not patient enough."

Mike slid his foot over to the barrier that kept him from rolling off the bed. The handcuffs weren't coming off, but if he could break the rails from the bedframe, he might get free. He could feel the bracket flex, but it wasn't going to come loose. He was weak and woozy . . . He'd been given morphine; he remembered the feeling.

Anhaldt noticed Fowler testing his bonds but didn't seem concerned. "I would recommend you simply try to recover. We are negotiating with a local judge; he will allow our allies in the Federal and Provincial police to release you . . . to us, of course. Skorzeny has promised to give you to Hartmann . . . Ever since he lost his eye, he seems to bear you a peculiar animus."

"It couldn't have happened to a nicer guy."

The little man arched an eyebrow. "I never expected very much of you, but I'm sorry Dr. Voss is unwilling to join forces with us. Such a waste that he does not have the vision, the foresight, to understand our place in history. Is it because of the death of Elizabeth Adler? Is that the reason for his obsession?"

"Who?" Mike acted like the drugs were clouding his mind more than they actually were.

"The wife, fiancée, whatever she was. So many years later, has he decided to keep her final contribution for himself? That's insane. Everyone in the world is going to try and take it from him. Already the Soviets suspect the two of you killed their colleague from Berlin. Thank you for that, by the way. I have never been able to tolerate spies or traitors, and Wuttke was both. You have no comment, no snappy rejoinder?"

Mike said nothing. He had a whole raft of questions, but he wasn't in a position to demand answers.

"So, we know the two of you went to Seegers's house looking for maps. The question is, Which ones? I don't suppose you'd like to tell me?"

"Get lost!" Mike rasped. The very fact Anhaldt didn't know which charts Voss had taken was a relief. He guessed that enough of the cabin had burned so that they couldn't tell.

"Very well. We will have to question you more harshly. And you will tell us what we need to know. Shall we start right now?"

Peter Anhaldt stood and withdrew a surgical glove from a box on the stainless steel counter. He blew into it to clear the wrinkles, then slipped his hand in, theatrically stretching his fingers and smoothing the rubber tight. He flipped back the hem of Fowler's hospital smock, then peeled back a bandage on the upper part of his leg.

"My expertise is electronics. Data. Information. All very technical. Cold and hard. However, I find myself fascinated by human beings, their . . . inner workings."

He peered at Mike, a movie studio's concept of a wise consulting physician, then pushed his finger into the bullet hole and pulled sideways.

Even through the drugs the pain was stunning. Mike blew out and clenched his teeth, taking deep fast breaths through his nose. He was not going to allow this immaculate little sadist any satisfaction.

"So, which maps? Tell me and maybe we can send you back to the United States."

Fowler couldn't talk, he could barely think.

"Oye! Detén eso!" One of the clinic's doctors pushed Anhaldt aside. There was a rumble of voices from the hall, another doctor arguing with someone in German.

Not the least bit flustered, Peter Anhaldt stripped off the bloody glove and daintily dropped it into an enameled trash receptacle. Still taking stiff breaths, Mike turned his head. Otto Skorzeny loomed in the doorway. He glared at Fowler. Behind him stood a doctor and a pair of nurses.

"*You* . . . are a lot of trouble!"

"I'll take that . . . as a compliment," Fowler gritted. Anhaldt started out of the room, but Mike realized that he had a question they might answer . . . and he might learn something more about how much they knew about the maps.

"Wh-What happened to him? To Captain Seegers?"

"Ahh." Anhaldt and Skorzeny glanced at each other.

"Herr Voss executed him," Anhaldt said. "No doubt to keep us from asking any questions."

After they left, the doctor entered the room and checked Fowler's wounds. There was quite an assortment. His hands were torn and bruised, and in addition to the bleeding hole in his thigh, his arm and calf had both been grazed. Worst of all, a bullet had gone into his back. Traveling under the skin, it had entered near the outside of his ribcage and exited below his shoulder blade. Whenever the drugs wore off it was extremely painful. None of it was going to make an escape any easier.

They unlocked the handcuffs while the staff at the clinic worked on him. But there was always a policeman in the room, and another in the hallway. From what he had gathered, as soon as he was well enough, he would be transferred to the local jail. Unless Anhaldt and Skorzeny got him first. Mike had a feeling that they weren't going to waste any time when it came to leaning on their political contacts.

The afternoon passed away, and the night staff came on duty. His guards were replaced with a new set of policemen, one of whom came in to carefully look around the room. A few minutes later there was a commotion somewhere down the hall. An argument in Spanish, a clatter of footsteps, then a doctor in a lab coat and surgical mask stepped into the room followed by the two new policemen. A nurse seemed to be objecting to their actions, but all three men ignored her.

Fowler's IV was quickly removed, and his handcuffs were unlocked. He yanked his arms under his chest hoping he could push himself up, break away, and run. But one cop held him down, and the other levered one arm and then the other behind his back, manacling them together. His breath caught; his back burned.

"Okay. Up!"

Gripping his sheets, they lifted him off the bed and dropped him on a gurney. Then they pushed open the door and, at high speed, headed down the hall.

Wheels rattled on the floor. Fowler frantically arched his neck, trying to see where they were taking him. They swerved past the clinic doctor who was shouting something into a wall-mounted telephone, past another room where a rough voice yelled at them in German. Then there was a double set of doors leading to a circular drive, and Fowler decided that was going to be his chance. As the gurney slammed through, Mike rolled to his right.

"Oh, hell. There he goes!"

Fowler's bare feet hit the ground and he staggered, head spinning. He tried to run but got only a step or two before one of the policemen grabbed his arm. Mike cranked his head back and smashed it forward, attempting a Liverpool Kiss, but the Argentine cop was fast and Mike's forehead impacted the man's shoulder rather than his face. The other cop locked onto the opposite arm, and they lifted him off his feet, rushing him toward a cream-colored ambulance. The engine cranked over and the policemen all but tossed him through the large tailgate door.

"Hit it!"

The engine roared and one of the uniformed men crawled forward, dragging Fowler with him. The other struggled to pull the door closed as the big machine careened around the circular drive and headed for the road. Mike caught a glimpse of Heinrich Hartmann dressed only in a hospital smock stumbling from the building. Fowler knew he was missing something, but he was too fired up to care. He tried kicking at his guard and felt stitches tear.

"Mike! *Mike!*"

Fowler twisted, sending a dull stream of pain up his back. The doctor accelerated down the dark roadway. Then he reached up and tore off his mask.

It was Anson Fordyce.

"Stop fighting us! This is a *rescue*, dear chum . . . I do believe I've owed you one ever since the war."

CHAPTER 18

SOUTH CHINA SEA,

1945 . . .

THE P-38 LIGHTNINGS came down out of the morning sun, roaring along the southern shore of Itu Aba. The extraction plan had specifically called for a PBY Catalina flying boat. All the commando team had to do was fire off a signal flare, an indication that the mission had been accomplished and it was safe to land. Clearly, the single-seat, twin-engine fighters were not going to be their ride home, but in the wake of a disastrous mission, with four casualties out of a six-man team, they were ready to accept any help they could get.

Itu Aba was little more than a scrub-covered rock. Less than a mile long, it was the largest of the reef-encircled sandbars that made up the Spratly Islands. Plagued with bad weather and powerful currents, the Spratlys formed the western edge of a notorious hazard to navigation known as the Dangerous Ground.

The island was also the location of a secret, or at least not well-known, Japanese submarine and seaplane base. It was not too much more than a collection of flimsy buildings and long trenches dug in the sand, each containing hundreds of barrels of fuel. Ignored by the Allies, the base survived most of the war with a minimum of staff. As of that morning they were all dead. Dead, along with the crew of a Kawanishi H8K2 flying boat, three Japanese civilians, and their security detachment.

The security agents had been the unexpected element. They were fearsome warriors. Older men and insanely loyal, they were the sort who had made up the Japanese army in the rough-and-tumble days before Pearl Harbor, when assassination was a well-used political tool. Whoever they worked for, they had certainly been willing to fight . . . and die.

Of the commandos sent to infiltrate Itu Aba the previous evening, only Michael Fowler, Jack Johnson, and their commanding officer, Royal Navy Lieutenant Jerold Masterson, were still alive. But Masterson probably wasn't going to make it. He had taken a bullet through the spine and hadn't been conscious in hours. Using a Japanese stretcher, Fowler and Johnson carried him down to the tin awning near the foot of the dock. Masterson was as ready as he'd ever be when the time came for evacuation.

Fowler and Johnson knew their craft. Once they had set Masterson in the shade, they quickly searched the shack that served as the base office, the big aircraft, and the briefcases and pockets of the men they had killed. Anything with the potential to be intelligence was packed into rubberized canvas bags.

Most of it was written in Japanese, as impenetrable as code to the young noncoms. But the civilians had brought with them several meticulously prepared contracts, carefully typed out in English, that discussed serious amounts of money. Millions. Tens of millions. The sort of figures that made you wonder what else was at stake.

And that was when the flight of P-38s showed up.

"Oi! Rumrunner!" The distant sound of engines had drawn Johnson's attention. Mike turned, and Jack pointed. Drifting down out of the sky were the sleekly futuristic shapes of several Lockheed Lightnings.

Johnson snatched up their Very pistol and a couple of flare cartridges. He ran down the length of the dock, past where the Japanese H8K2 was moored. Waving his arms over his head, he yelled a greeting as if the pilots could hear him.

The first Lightning barreled in, firing a burst from the four .50-caliber machine guns mounted in its nose, a storm of jacketed lead that tore into the big H8K2 flying boat, then went on to shred a section of dock. In the moment of relative quiet that followed, as the big twin-engine fighter clawed its way high into the sky, Johnson's attempts to attract attention turned into a stream of enraged profanity.

Mike Fowler dropped the paperwork he had been packing away and ran out onto the beach. He could understand a pilot's obsession with destroying any enemy aircraft they saw, especially given that it might be his last chance to score a kill. But Mad Jack Johnson, six-foot-four, red-haired and sunburned, didn't look the least bit Japanese. These flyboys needed to tone it down!

Fowler was just in time to see the next P-38 release two cylinders from under its wings. Still keyed up from a night of violence, Mike reacted instantly as the canisters began to tumble toward the earth.

"Get down!" he screamed. On the west end of the island there was no cover back of the beach, so he ran for the water. For the next minute or so, that was going to be the safest place.

The incendiaries hit the structures at the foot of the dock, releasing a blossoming tower of fire fifty feet high. An instant later, Mike sucked in a breath and dove. He could feel the thud of the explosions in the water around him.

What was happening still hadn't penetrated. Not until the water to the right of him exploded in a boiling line of .50-caliber slugs. They are going to kill us, he thought. A quick glance at the shore showed him two more blurry fireballs rising into the morning sky. Then a black line of smoke tinged by red flame erupted from deeper inland. The planes had hit one of the fuel storage trenches.

"Jack?" he called out.

"Here!" Johnson was clutching a piling at the end of the flaming dock.

"The causeway! Before they come 'round again!" Mike grabbed a lungful of petroleum-tinged air and swam.

In their briefings the causeway was what they called the narrow bridge that had been built from the island out to the surrounding reef. The far end was easily a hundred yards away. The planes blasted over again, but the roiling clouds of smoke from the burning trench gave the swimmers cover. Then they huddled in the shadows, holding on to the concrete pilings as more napalm cascaded from the sky and the Lightnings strafed the buildings and the brush. The Japanese flying boat exploded, one wing pinwheeling across the shallow water.

"You alright, mate?"

"Yeah. Yeah. But, goddamn, I'm pretty sure they got Masterson."

Johnson cursed. "I'm gonna kill these bastards. Hunt each one of them down. You mark my words."

Two endless minutes later the fighters were disappearing out to sea. They didn't seem to be turning back, but there was another rumble of engines, more aircraft coming in from the east.

"Look!"

Approaching, at much higher altitude, was a formation of six heavy bombers, B-24 Liberators. "What the *hell's* going on?" Fowler demanded.

Johnson looked at him through haunted, bloodshot eyes. "SNAFU? Someone puts out the word: they want this place taken care of. Our friends with SOE and OSS, they offer us. The Air Force offers bombers. Same mission . . . different tool. Then maybe some tosser, he forgets to call the flyboys off."

Fowler nodded. "We're going to need better cover . . ." They edged into the protected space between the last set of pilings and the reef. The Liberators relentlessly ground their way forward.

"You ready, Rummy?"

Mike shook his head. Mad Jack Johnson, a man Fowler hadn't known a month ago, offered his hand. "See you on the other side, mate."

Whistling metal cascaded from the sky. Explosions tore the earth. Shockwaves compressed Mike Fowler's chest, tore at his ears and sinuses. The air crews professionally walked their pattern down the length of the island, a vengeful giant stomping his way along the narrow spit of land. Rocks and dirt, torn and flaming palm trees, and bucketloads of sand rained down. The planks above them splintered and caught fire. The concrete piles cracked and shook.

Through it all, Mike Fowler wondered if there wasn't another explanation. He couldn't stop thinking about the makeup of the team: he was an American, Masterson British, and Johnson Australian. The three others, the men who had been killed in the fighting the previous night, were Arend Boekman, an officer with the Netherlands East Indies Forces Intelligence Service, Corporal Francois Coville, a Frenchman from New Caledonia, and Harry Ma, an OSS operative born in Nanking.

For men who had only the briefest time to train together, they had fought well, but such a mixed team was never the best choice. There might be many reasons why each had been chosen. But the cynical side of Mike's nature caused him to wonder if someone was trying to make sure that accountability for the mission was evenly distributed among the allied governments.

And *that* begged the question of whether duplicate missions had been allowed to go forward by mistake, or if it was intentional . . . an insurance policy. Insurance that the mission would succeed, one way or the other, and insurance that, when the bombs ceased to fall, there would be no one left alive to talk about the details.

AUSTRALIA,

1945. Two weeks earlier . . .

THE MISSION TO Itu Aba started out at the old medical quarantine station across the bay from Darwin, Australia. The place was a rough collection of corrugated tin buildings slowly corroding in the tropical dampness. By afternoon the metal siding had absorbed enough sunlight to scald flesh, and the local ANZACs would tell you that your only hope for relief was to sit on the veranda come evening and wait for "the Darwin doctor." The "doctor" was a cool breeze that never arrived, but it did allow the Aussies to get the first spots in line for evening chow.

Like thousands of other American soldiers, Fowler spent the weeks following the fall of Okinawa wondering if his next stop would be an invasion of Japan. He became certain that would be his fate when he received orders to fly to Northern Australia and report to a location called the Lugger Maintenance Section. The name suggested it was a boatyard but, in reality, it was the local headquarters of what was called the Services Reconnaissance Department, a secret commando unit. Something was definitely in the wind, but there was no telling what it was . . . The whole world seemed to be holding its breath.

There had been rumors of a special bomb, something so destructive it was hoped the Japanese might choose to surrender. By the time he'd checked in at the old hospital, the story was that another of these bombs had been dropped, this time on the city of Nagasaki.

Fowler had expected orders to scout landing sites for the largest naval invasion in human history. Now, with a quiet afternoon ahead of him, he let himself think of returning home . . . another world, a place he rarely allowed his imagination to dwell. When a man didn't know if he was going to live or die, it was wise to keep his mind locked in the present.

Long after dark Fowler came suddenly awake, knife in hand. Someone had tapped lightly on the frame of his bunk and, without thought or hesitation, Mike rolled out from under the mosquito netting, coiled and ready. A tall slim figure stood at the foot of the bed.

"You Fowler? It looks like they've drawn our chits, old boy. Meet me outside."

A few minutes later Mike joined a small knot of men who stood silhouetted in the moonlight. It was too dark to make out their faces, but the sound of their voices told an interesting story. One was Dutch, one French, and another American . . . a Chinese American. The Englishman who had gotten him out of bed was the only one who was completely turned out; he wore his cap, KD jacket, and a canvas belt with a pistol. Mike could see the shine of two pips on his epaulettes, a lieutenant. After a moment they were joined by a large man who was struggling to tuck in his shirt and cursing under his breath.

"Evenin', mates, what's the dope?"

"Follow on, and we'll find out." The lieutenant led them through the bush to one of the smaller buildings where a guard stood on the veranda.

"Got them," the Britisher said, and the soldier turned and opened the door. The windows had been blacked out, but inside the lights were blazing. As his eyes adjusted, Fowler could see three men waiting for them . . .

"Ten-*hut*!"

Two were officers: a Royal Navy lieutenant commander in tropical whites, and an American major general with an array of ribbons on his chest and, of all things, a monocle pinched between thumb and forefinger. The third was slouched in a rattan chair, a paunchy young civilian nattily attired in a linen suit.

"At ease, lads." The lieutenant commander allowed them to relax. "You have been brought here to execute what we hope will be one of the last combat operations of the Pacific war. However, before we go any further, I need to verify that none of you have any qualms about doing what must be done, and that you are aware of the risks . . . We are, as they say, rather late in the game. So, I must know that you still freely volunteer."

"Volunteer for what, sir?" the big red-haired Australian sergeant spoke up.

"This is a combat mission." The American general had a rather alarming German accent. "You are either a volunteer, or you are not. If not, you will be asked to leave. That is all you need to know."

"Happy to volunteer, sir. And no . . . qualms."

"Excellent!" The general tucked the monocle into his breast

pocket. "Upon the conclusion of this operation, it must never again be discussed, or even mentioned. To do so would cause exceptionally grave damage to each of our allied governments. You will be required to sign documents to this effect before you leave the room. No further explanation will be given, but please understand this: your actions will be instrumental in transforming the future of Asia. Good luck!"

The general came to attention, saluted, and . . . clicked his heels. There was a moment of silence as the man turned and left the room. Then, with a crackle of rattan, the little guy in the linen suit got out of his chair.

"Alright chums. Now that we've got that out of the way, first we have the paperwork, then we'll run though all the details . . ."

And that was the first time Mike Fowler met Anson Fordyce. He met him again while recovering at a hospital outside Manila eight weeks later. Fordyce seemed perfectly sincere as he thanked Fowler for a job well done and reminded him that any mention of the mission to Itu Aba was strictly classified. But there were no apologies, no mention of the other men, or the fact that Mike and Jack Johnson had been stranded on an island of the dead, eating bomb-blasted Japanese rations and bird's eggs, until a Filipino fisherman rescued them.

The United States government had spent a great deal of time and money teaching men like Petty Officer Mike Fowler how to kill. And it had selected the best, or worst, of them for operations like the one he had just returned from. But they had been so well conditioned to think of certain people as the enemy that it was only after Fordyce had left the ward that Fowler began to wonder if they were actually on different sides of something . . . a divide much less clear than all the flags and uniforms might suggest.

The meeting in Darwin wasn't the last time Mike ran into the strangely Teutonic general either. A dozen years later there had been an event in Madrid. Present were army officers, diplomats, and yes, arms dealers, both men like Fowler and Voss and those who were more socially accepted, the heavy hitters in aerospace, precision manufacturing, and electronics . . . many of them from the United States and Great Britain. In a receiving line, standing alongside Generalissimo Francisco Franco, Spain's aging fascist dictator, was another old man, the American major general. He was dressed in a civilian suit, and he shook hands with Mike Fowler, looking directly into his eyes. There was no recognition. Mike, for his part, also remained expressionless. This far down the road that was how the game was played.

ARGENTINA,

1961 . . .

MIKE AWOKE. IT was cold and he had a vague memory of a crackling fire and voices speaking both Spanish and English. He'd been pretty well out of it since the escape from the clinic in Bariloche. That was a day ago, maybe more. His back hurt, so did his leg and shoulder, but the pain was tolerable . . . more tolerable than the hunger the smells managed to trigger, the very American smells of bacon and coffee. He sat up.

He had been lying on an army cot in a big room with a series of picture windows looking out at the lake. A pair of M1 Carbines leaned against the wall near the door. The walls and floor were made of wide planks, hand-adzed but beautifully fitted and finished. A bed of coals still glowed in the large fireplace at one end of the room. A couch and several leather chairs were arrayed before the hearth, and against the walls were more cots covered either with blankets or sleeping bags. Although there were dusty electrical fixtures, several unlit pressure lamps were hanging from nails driven carelessly into the beams of the ceiling. The place gave off a feeling of decaying rustic grandeur.

With a rapid clicking of toenails, a small black-and-tan hound trotted into the room, cocked its head, and barked once. Fowler grinned and patted his thigh, which was still covered by his hospital gown. The dog ran to greet him, wagging its tail. He was fending off its attentions, and its interest in the smell of his bandages, when a man stepped into the doorway. He was an African American, well into his forties, and with the posture of a drill sergeant. He was dressed in blue jeans and a work shirt.

"Howdy, sailor. Welcome to the Beagle's Nest."

"What?" Fowler tried to stand. He made it, but he had to go slowly.

The Black man moved to his side, ready to help if need be. "The Beagle's Nest. It's what we call this place, on account of our rat killer there." The dog quickly patrolled the room, carefully smelling each corner and doorframe. "You can call me Nix. You need something for the pain? Water?"

Fowler laughed, then stopped because his ribs hurt. "I'd give just about anything for whatever you're cooking!"

"Well, come on then . . . that's a good sign!"

Once out of the living room, he found the house was cold and larger than he expected. In the white-tiled kitchen a pair of portable barbecues had been set up in front of an open window. There was an enameled stove but, just like the light fixtures, it seemed disused. Bacon snapped and popped in an iron skillet and a coffeepot slowly perked through the glass cap on its lid.

"Here. Sit." Nix pulled a chair over to a rickety table and went back to his cooking. "Mr. Fordyce, he's at the dig, but he'll be back shortly."

"The dig? What's that?"

"Oh, we're down here digging for hidden treasures. Maybe they'll tell you about it, maybe they won't. This operation is all very 'need to know.'" He deposited a plate containing bacon, eggs, and toast on the table. Then a cup of coffee and another cup containing a small pile of pills. "That's an antibiotic, vitamins and minerals, and a secret remedy that's good for what ails you. You're healing nicely, but you'll have to continue with the pills for the next four days."

"Thanks. Can I ask who you are, what sort of operation this is?"

"Again, that's up to Mr. Fordyce. But you're among friends. Don't worry."

After he'd eaten, Nix, whose actual name turned out to be George Albert Nixon, helped Fowler outside to sit on a log bench with a view of the lake and the mountains beyond. Mike still didn't have anything to wear except his drafty hospital smock, but he was given a pair of heavy blankets to wrap around his legs and shoulders. Except for occasional visits from the busy little dog and the sound of Nix cleaning up in the kitchen, the place was deadly silent. The dark waters of Nahuel Huapi barely lapped at the shore of the tree shrouded cove.

Looking back toward the house he could see it was a huge rambling construction of carefully fitted rock and timber. More than anything it resembled a European hunting lodge. The place was incredibly peaceful, and yet Mike knew that just beyond the horizon events were continuing to unfold. Soon the *Bushranger II* would be arriving in Talcahuano. Anton Voss had been acting strangely, so strangely that, for Mike, it had finally reached a precipice in their relationship. If Anton had killed—murdered—an old and trusted friend . . . well, that was something Mike Fowler had trouble understanding, or believing. More and more he had the feeling that he was a cat, trapped in a box of Anton's creation, isolated, and worried that reality was going to resolve itself in some unanticipated and unpleasant manner.

About noon he heard the moan of a distant engine. A painfully shiny craft skimmed over the surface of the water at amazing speed. It slowed as it turned into the small bay between the heavily forested islands, then glided up to a pier that jutted into the lake to the right of the house. It had the classic lines of a dual-cockpit wooden speedboat, but it seemed to be made of polished aluminum and boasted a pair of large outboard motors. Three men scrambled out and Mike could see that the leader was his old nemesis. Anson Fordyce grinned and waved like a guest newly arrived at a picnic.

"Well, look at you! Already up and about!" The CIA officer was dressed in a khaki safari jacket with a silk scarf, or ascot, or something of the sort, tucked into the neck. Sporting a slim mustache, he looked like a young version of an old Ernest Hemingway.

"Where the hell are we?" Mike squinted up at him.

"Thirty miles or so up the lake. Your friends won't bother us here. Their Argentine associates become very nervous every time the word 'Nazi' is bandied about. Ever since Perón was ousted and Eichmann was kidnapped by the Israelis, the government has been more than willing to show how cooperative it can be."

"How in the world did you find me?"

Anson Fordyce laughed. "Could it have been the trail of destruction that follows wherever you go? Sometimes I wonder if all I need to look for are explosions and burning buildings. But to tell the truth—and that's not something I do lightly—I got a call from Alfredo Larkin. If you guys didn't think he was in someone's pocket you're not—ahh, I *get* it."

"Get what?" The sun was comforting, but Fowler was beginning to feel a chill in the air.

"You thought Larkin was *your* man. Well, it all depends on how much you have to spend, doesn't it? There was also Skorzeny. When he flew in the other day, I knew something was up. We arrived in Argentina about a year ago and ever since Otto's been a man on a mission. If he's chasing you, then there's a pretty good chance you're a big part of it."

Fordyce dusted some imaginary lint off his sleeve. "Let's go inside, old man. The boys and I picked up some clothes, and you need to get your strength back. I'm sure you understand that we're going to have a lot of questions."

For several days Mike Fowler was left to stew in his own juice. Fordyce had bought him three changes of clothing. The labels indicated the stuff came from a store in Bariloche that catered to the wealthy tourists who came to fish and ski. In addition to the basics, there was a sweater, a short-waisted parka with diamond-shaped quilting, and a duffel bag. It seemed they might be planning on taking him somewhere . . . a fact that gave Fowler confidence he wasn't going to be simply interrogated and then dumped in the lake.

Every morning the men made breakfast before dawn, then three of them loaded the boat and headed down the lake. Though someone always stayed behind to keep an eye on him, Mike was allowed to roam relatively unsupervised.

At first he took it easy, reading some magazines they had left by the fireplace or throwing a stick for the dog. Bending to tussle over the well-chewed branch hurt. Mike was recovering, but it was going to be a process.

Over the next few days, he pushed himself to repeatedly climb the stairs to the dusty second floor, and then to explore the rest of the property. Slowly hiking farther afield, Fowler discovered an eerie ghost town of barns and houses surrounding a circular stone water tank about a kilometer away. Towering over it was a slim radio antenna held against the wind by guy wires. While it was not terribly far from Bariloche, the estate was extremely isolated, and it had been carefully designed to be self-sufficient.

The two other men were named Gonzalo and Ray. Given the way they spoke Spanish, Mike was fairly certain they were Cubans. They had been the ones who had posed as Argentine policemen during his rescue.

It was at breakfast on the fourth day that Anson Fordyce opened the ball . . .

"So . . ." He casually gestured with his fork. "First question . . . tell us what you're up to."

Mike didn't say anything. He knew he was going to have to pay a price to get out of this, but he wasn't going to give up that easily.

"Seriously, you need to tell me . . . I already know most of it, these Nazi types think they are a lot smarter than they really are. But if you *don't* tell me, you're going to be up the proverbial creek."

Fordyce took a bite and went on, "The local police want someone for murder and arson and there are warrants for your arrest in

Spain and France. On the other hand, if Skorzeny and his crowd get you, they will have more questions than I do—you won't survive that. And then there's your boss, your partner, or whatever you think that relationship is all about. It's safe to say he's abandoned you to take the heat."

He wiped his mouth with a paper towel. "We're all you got, paisan. Make the most of it."

Fowler held Fordyce's gaze. The man had him over a barrel. "I have people I need to take care of," he said.

"Are you saying you want to make a deal?" The CIA man's eyes lit up, as if he was trying to contain his enthusiasm . . . or amusement.

Fowler nodded. He didn't really mean it, but lying to Fordyce wasn't a sin that would keep him up at night.

"Done!" Fordyce grinned and clapped his hands together.

"Don't you want to hear my conditions?"

"Not interested. You're in trouble. Voss is in trouble. The two of you have gotten *other* people in trouble. If Skorzeny doesn't get you right off the bat, the rest of the world is going to be hot on your trail. Anyone who had an intelligence agency operating in the European Theater: the Soviets, the Brits, the Frenchies . . . well, the only thing they are going to want more than what you're after is to keep everyone else from getting their hands on it. You alight anywhere long enough to try and make a sale, you'll be overrun.

"Tell me what I want to know. Do what I want you to do. I'll try to arrange a get-out-of-jail-free card for you and Voss, no more warrants, no investigations. It may take a while, but we'll get your bank accounts and property back. It will be like all of this never happened."

"You'll *try*? What are you going to want me to do?" Mike asked.

"Whatever I say. But instead of being a free agent, you'll know that Uncle Sugar is on your side. I'll give you a way to call for the cavalry."

"Unlike last time."

Fordyce shrugged. He wasn't going to get into that again.

Mike leaned back in his chair. Fordyce might be conning him, but even if he wasn't, Sistemas Militar was still on the rocks. Johnson was expecting a solid six figures and if there was no payday Sobek and Paluso were going to want loan shark rates for any checks they had written.

"We're all in this for the money."

Fordyce laughed. "See, you're still trying to negotiate. You really don't understand the size of the arena you're playing in."

"You make Skorzeny go away. We get to keep twenty percent of what we recover. Everybody gets paid and protected. That's *my* deal."

Fordyce's eyes narrowed. He sighed and turned to Ray and Gonzalo. "Amigos, take it in the other room."

When the two had left the table, Fordyce locked eyes with Fowler. His gaze was like his handshake, unyielding.

"You are an idiot. Answer this: just what do you think you are after? Believe me, you *want* to tell me. Now, tell me or be damned!"

Mike Fowler didn't trust Fordyce, and he didn't know what to think about Voss. But it was certain he was going to be held here or somewhere else if he didn't make a move, so he gave the safest answer he could, the one he'd been told to believe . . .

"Nazi gold. Tons of it."

Fordyce stared at him.

Then a smirk twisted the CIA man's mustache, and he laughed and laughed and laughed.

"Honestly," he said, wiping tears from his eyes, "it's good you have me to look out for you." He picked his plate off the table and started for the kitchen. After two steps he turned back and said . . .

"Anton Voss is full of it. And you're a sucker. I'm going to show you something . . . so, bundle up, it's going to be a cold ride."

CHAPTER 19

TWENTY MINUTES LATER the boat was rocketing along, engines howling. It was too loud for easy conversation, but Fordyce couldn't contain himself. He worked the wheel back and forth, spreading a wide wake and kicking up shining veils of spray.

It was almost two hours down the lake, even at top speed. The trip was uneventful and the scenery beautiful. Forested slopes rose out of the water, the shoreline was spotted with attractive homes, and the mist-shrouded Andes stretched off into the distance.

As they closed in on a pair of islands Fowler could see that they were near the outskirts of Bariloche, roughly parallel to the spot where the big government lab was housed. Anson Fordyce turned the boat toward the low end of the larger and more heavily wooded island. There was a house just above the waterline and, to the left of it, an L-shaped pier. As they tied up, a pair of large young men appeared to greet them.

They were in their twenties with crew cuts and dressed like construction workers, but their boots were U.S. military issue and they were packing Colt 1911s under their jackets. After a minute of banter with Ray and Gonzalo, they went about emptying the boat of supplies and then led the way up an overgrown road into the brush.

"Take it slow," Fordyce said. "We're not going far, but it's all uphill."

"You gonna tell me what this is about?"

"We are going on a tour, then we'll get down to brass tacks. Time is running out."

Fowler took a breath and started up the road.

"You and Voss did business down here, so you know Juan Perón had a lot of ambition and wanted to modernize Argentina as quickly as possible. He was tight with the unions and nationalized a lot of heavy industry. As a practical matter you might call him a populist socialist. But he found himself in bed with a bunch of influential Argentine Germans, many of whom were Nazi party members. At the end of the war, Perón welcomed both refugees and fugitives. From his perspective, he was using the Germans to acquire technical experts, scientists, and competent administrators. He hoped to bolster his country's economy—I can't blame him for it; it's not well known, but we did the same thing . . . and we paid a price for it.

"There was also a boatload of money," Fordyce continued, "a lot of it hidden away in accounts held by Eva Perón. That led to a good deal of wheeling and dealing when the Nazis tried to get it back. Your pal Skorzeny may have played a role in that.

"Anyway, Juan Perón had dreams of a New Argentina, and he pushed hard on the technology front. Initially, several of these projects seemed as advanced as anything coming out of the U.S. or USSR. One was an extremely efficient steam locomotive, not something we'd use in North America or Europe, but applicable to many other parts of the world. Another was a jet fighter, a design smuggled out of Germany at the end of the war. But the most important attempt was Perón's focus on finding a way to develop atomic energy.

"He briefly tried to recruit Nobel prize winner Werner Heisenberg to be part of a military bomb project. When that created an outcry, Perón reconsidered. He didn't want to be criticized by the international community, but his pride was at stake. That was when he was introduced to an Austrian named Ronald Richter.

"The jury's out on Richter's abilities, but he sold Perón on the idea of developing nuclear fusion technology. Civilian power plants, nonmilitary. You know the difference between fusion and fission?"

"Vaguely." Mike had heard Voss go on about it often enough, but his leg hurt and he wasn't up to being quizzed on the subject.

"You can think of the differences in the two processes as if they were opposites. In fission an atom is split into smaller elements, releasing energy. This can be done suddenly, using explosives, like in the Hiroshima bomb, or in a controlled manner, like a nuclear power plant. On the other hand, fusion is what happens when atoms are forced to combine, or fuse. It's a whole different ballgame power-wise; everything's bigger and it takes a lot more energy to get it started. If you want a *fusion* bomb, meaning a hydrogen or thermonuclear bomb, you have to use a regular old A-bomb, a fission bomb, to set it off... In fact it's the dirty fission part that causes all the lingering radiation.

"If you could build a fusion reactor for an electrical plant, it would be vastly more powerful and efficient than anything else. There's an absolute minimum of radioactive waste, and no need for heavy metals like uranium or plutonium. But the trouble is, the most likely way of creating fusion requires an extraordinary amount of heat, millions of degrees, and some way of suspending that super-hot reaction magnetically so it doesn't burn through its containment. And *that* requires a hell of a lot of electrical power and an extraordinary ability to fine-tune the process.

"A couple of years ago we started sharing information with the Soviets. They are clearly ahead of us with an experimental design they call a 'tokamak.' But, if they are telling us the truth, it doesn't work... *yet*. The bottom line is, no one's figured out how to balance all the elements needed to control the reaction . . . except, *maybe*, Ronald Richter."

Fowler paused to rest, and Fordyce gestured back down the hill at a pair of big vine covered buildings and a collapsing Quonset hut. "So that's where we are. This place was Ronald Richter's secret island laboratory."

"It's seen better days."

"That is true." Fordyce nodded. "A lot of people think fusion power is a pipe dream and always will be. A lot of people think Richter was a kook and a fraud, and that he took Perón and his government for a ride."

When Fowler was ready, they headed farther up the shallow valley that formed the center of the island. Ahead, a set of brick walls loomed over the trees. Somewhere a compressor hummed. The sound of jackhammers echoed like machine guns, and dust drifted on the wind.

"To his credit, Ronald Richter seems to have been a protégé of Manfred von Ardenne, a legitimate genius. Von Ardenne was rich and mostly self-educated. He received his first patent at age fifteen. In the 1930s he developed German television technology and electron microscopes, then went into radar and nuclear physics. During the war he ran his own laboratory financed by the Reichspost. We suspect he didn't hire second-rate talent.

"Even before the fighting was over, von Ardenne had cut a deal. In Russia he worked on various methods to produce 'heavy water,' or deuterium, which can be used for fission reactors, or . . . *maybe* . . . controlled nuclear fusion. For his contributions to their atomic bomb project, he was awarded the Stalin Prize . . . You can see why anyone he worked with might be of interest to Uncle Sugar, right?"

Though Mike Fowler didn't know what the punch line was, he was beginning to see the outline of the joke. It was the echo of something he had heard on a lonely beach in Israel. The shadow of a mechanical rabbit no one could catch.

Fordyce pointed a finger at him. "Right now, we can crack crude oil and make everything from food preservatives to plastics. You can fill your Cadillac with Ethyl and drive it down the road. But if you look at the big picture, burning petroleum for electricity is the waste of a valuable resource.

"Controllable fusion is the Holy Grail. Forget bombs. This is the key to the future, free and clean electricity, worldwide prosperity, flying cars, a chicken in every pot, total utopian Tomorrowland . . . the modern equivalent of man discovering fire. It is *very* important. Maybe more important than anything. You got that? *Any. Thing.*"

"Okay. Great." Fowler stopped. His back and leg were hurting. "So, why don't you tell me what the hell we're doing here?"

Fordyce laughed. "Patience my friend. Follow me." He led the way into a blocky building, one that was in better shape than many they had passed. In the huge unfinished hall, a room where one wall was broken by the gaps once intended for tall windows, he stopped. "A lot of people think Ronald Richter was a con man. But we don't *know*.

"In 1951 Perón announced that Argentina had achieved a controlled fusion reaction. Richter reran his experiment with local scientists looking on, but no one was one hundred percent sure what they had seen.

"Realize, this was almost two years *before* the United States detonated the first thermonuclear—meaning fusion—bomb in the South Pacific. It's been clear for quite a while that using fusion to blow stuff up is a heck of a lot easier than building a power plant. Needless to say, there was a lot of skepticism.

"Meanwhile Richter, who was very secretive, began behaving erratically. He had ordered the main reactor torn down before it was even finished and began building a newer, supposedly better version. No one had any idea why the reactor containment had to be demolished. It was a concrete cylinder, thirty-nine feet in diameter with thirteen-foot-thick walls. Destroying it was nearly as difficult as building it had been.

"The new reactor was to be underground, and his construction crews, all paid for by the Perón government, of course, began excavating a forty-six-foot-deep chamber, perfectly round, down into the solid rock. Maybe something was done down there, maybe it wasn't, but not long after they finished they were ordered to fill the cement-lined hole back up again . . . with construction-grade concrete. To a lot of people, it seemed Richter was delusional . . . or he was hiding something.

"The Argentinian scientific community hated Perón. And Richter was a temperamental outsider who had been given anything he wanted. When the eggheads got the opportunity to critique his results, they did so. Harshly. Physicists around the world piled on. Right or wrong, scientists can be pack animals, and discredit is their weapon of choice. Perón shut the project down, Richter was placed under house arrest, and everyone tried to put the whole affair behind them.

"After Perón was deposed—well, that's what the new regime thinks of Perón, his Nazis, and what went on here." Fordyce pointed, and Mike turned to read a large chart painted on one wall. In Spanish it itemized the costs of Project Huemul. The last line read: SPENT WITHOUT ANY BENEFIT $17,000,000.

Fowler leaned against the dusty plaster. "You're telling me that the government *and* the scientific community think this is all bunk, but you don't? And you're banging away at something up there and calling this place 'the dig' . . . like an archaeological dig."

"That's right." Fordyce grinned. "And you think Anton Voss is chasing *gold*. You're either lying, or a dumbass. The Nazis were chasing *fusion*, maybe for bombs, maybe for electric power. Hell, they still are! And I've got to wonder if somehow Anton Voss and his partner Michael Fowler aren't in on it.

"We settled in here more than a year ago and, before we started with the jackhammers, we turned over every rock and pebble. It's not just what was built here, it's the people who lived nearby . . . or were reputed to have lived nearby. We interviewed everyone we could find. And surprise, surprise, you know what happened next?"

Fordyce wanted him to ask, but Mike just stared at the little man.

"A bunch of international businessmen, ex-Nazis, *influential* ex-Nazis, *untouchable* ex-Nazis, started turning up the heat in Washington. 'Get off the island. Leave Argentina alone.' When you start taking flak, it means you're over the target.

"Then they brought Otto Skorzeny into the picture. And ever since they've been sailing up and down the Chilean coast, and . . . chasing *you*!"

Anson Fordyce leaned in close.

"Somebody's scared. And Voss *knows* something. *Just* like the transistor deal. *Just* like the glider archives. So, if he's told you he's after gold, he's lying. *Lying!*"

Fordyce led Mike Fowler uphill again to where a huge concrete-and-brick blockhouse stood like the ruins of an ancient fort. A breeze had blown the dust away and, just before they entered the roofless building, Fowler glanced over and saw a rough hole in a nearby patch of pavement surrounded by excavation equipment and piles of broken concrete.

Inside, Fordyce's men had set up a barbecue, just like the ones at the big house up the lake. The two Cubans, the young men who had met them at the dock, and a pair of older fellows were preparing lunch.

"Hola, compadres!" Fordyce gestured Mike to an aluminum camp chair. "Sit. You want some food?"

Within minutes Fowler was biting into a hamburger with all the trimmings. On the ground at his side was a cold bottle of Coke. Carrying a paper plate and his own soft drink, Fordyce dropped into a nearby chair and carefully tucked a napkin into his collar.

In between bites he continued, "I've been studying military technology since the end of the war, and I've heard all sorts of stories about why the Nazis didn't build an atomic bomb: they couldn't achieve a successful chain reaction. They never realized that graphite could be used as a moderator. Some of their top scientists either fled the country or were imprisoned in the camps, others were conscripted into the army. Antisemitism caused the work of Jewish scientists, like Albert Einstein, to be ignored. Theory after theory. But these were the greatest minds in physics, and the best engineers. Atomic science wouldn't have been developed at all if it wasn't for the work of men, and women, from Central and Eastern Europe.

"Hell, I've seen what purports to be an Austrian patent from 1938 for what they called a 'molecular bomb.' It looked a lot like an early attempt at a fusion weapon. At the same time Arthur Ruhlig observed deuterium-tritium fusion for the first time and Peter Thonemann came up with a design for a fusion confinement device. The theory was there, right from the beginning. There are references to experiments with subatomic particles, *exceptionally* heavy subatomic particles, but exactly what that means we don't know."

"So, if they could have built a bomb in '44, why didn't they?" Mike asked.

"No idea. All this is just a way of showing you that what I'm doing here isn't entirely a wild-goose chase.

"I'm pretty damn sure that deals were made. By the end of the war Nazi 'wonder weapons' and their designers were more useful as bribes to the victors than in creating some suicidal Wagnerian Götterdämmerung. Manfred von Ardenne and his colleagues went east. Maybe they took a German A-bomb design with them. All their spying aside, it would explain how the Soviets built one so quickly. Wernher von Braun and the V-2 rocket came to the U.S. Other technologies, more secret technologies, better suited to benefit a Nazi organization trying to survive after the war . . . Well, let's assume they kept those. They smuggled them out to places like this.

"So, if Richter was working on something serious, and it isn't here, where did it go? Or was he trying, with fragmentary information, to re-create something that never *arrived. That* is the question of the day." Fordyce looked at Fowler and arched an eyebrow. There was a moment of silence.

"I have no idea." Mike wasn't going to learn anything more unless he played into Fordyce's agenda. "But I agree. Voss was lying. He got whatever it was he needed at Seegers's house and left me to take the fall."

The CIA man set down his drink. "I'm not sure I believe you, but it doesn't matter. Larkin reported that Voss was in contact with your Aleixandre Porras as soon as his plane touched down in Chile. Our sources tell us that he is opening a bank account in South Africa, and he reserved seven suites and a private dining room at the Mount Nelson Hotel in Cape Town."

Fowler shrugged; it was all news to him.

"You know what I think? I think Voss is setting up one of his damn auctions . . . Well, he's *not* going to get away with it! And if you're lying to me, the *two* of you are not going to get away with it. *I* won't let you! I told you my deal, it's time for you to do the right thing. Get onboard or go home for an extensive debrief . . . as in we might be done with you by 1970!"

He stood and, looking down at Fowler said, "Given the current state of science, controlled fusion is the ultimate discovery. Whoever owns it, owns the future. I'm not going to let that be a bunch of Nazis, and I'm not going to let it be a bunch of Commies either. So, if you have anything to say . . . *Now* would be the time."

Mike looked him straight in the eye. "Voss said it was gold." He glanced around. "This is a lot to take in. It makes some sense, but I don't know anything beyond what you've told me."

Fordyce narrowed his eyes. "And it's a *salvage* operation? Don't mess with me. We know your background and we know what Seegers did before the war."

Fowler sighed; this last secret wasn't very secret.

"Yes. A submarine."

"Okay. Larkin said you were meeting a ship in Talcahuano. If you can't tell me anything more, then I want to get you back into the operation. You agree to be a good soldier, be my special agent, protect the interests of our government, and I'll keep my end of the deal."

Fowler finally saw an opening, the reason Fordyce was admitting things he probably shouldn't and keeping him on ice. "Back at the house you said you could get us out of trouble, get us our property and our accounts back, and that you could call in the cavalry.

Well, if you've got the juice to rescue us or shut down our operation, what in the world do you need me for? Get out there and find the damned thing yourself!"

Fordyce looked uncomfortable. "Time," he admitted. "What we're doing here is a fool's errand. Skorzeny's closing in. Voss is closing in. There could be other players for all I know. Rustling up ships, airplanes, diplomatic cover here and in Chile . . . That's going to take me flying back to Washington and doing some politicking. Skorzeny's bosses have contacts in high places. Hell, they *own* some of the high places. We were able to resist the pressure to stop work here. But to get the resources I'll need I'm going to have to do an end run.

"We're going to want to know exactly where you are. I'll give you a beacon. If you activate it, and if I get the plans, or the gadget, or whatever it is, I'll find a way to protect you and your friends. Hell, I'll even sweeten the deal: six million dollars. Split it any way you want, everyone can go home happy. But if you *don't* activate it, and you don't deliver, you're *all* expendable. Got it?"

"And what if *you* don't show up?" Mike was still unsure if Fordyce's past behavior was untrustworthy or just incompetent.

"I'll give you a name in naval intelligence. He's outside the channels I have to go through. If you can deliver it to him, you get the same deal. But let me warn you: the word is out. We wouldn't be here desperately digging holes in concrete if it wasn't. This is the biggest prize in the book. If you're still thinking you can sell it on your own, well . . . it's very unlikely you'll live that long."

CHAPTER 20

A de Havilland Otter arrived a couple of hours after Mike Fowler returned from his tour of Huemul Island. It buzzed the big house to alert them, then landed out on the lake, taxiing into the cove. The pilot unloaded boxes of provisions for the dig . . . but he also brought news: the *Bushranger II* was docked in Talcahuano and taking on supplies.

"The fueling pier is within sight of the naval base," Fordyce said. "Unless I miss my guess, they are not going to be there any longer than they have to."

He glanced at Mike Fowler. "It's time we get you back into the game. Want to see what Nix has cooked up?"

George Nixon's radio beacon didn't look impressive. It was a small box covered in gray hammer-tone paint. Several colored wires protruded from a hole in one corner. The wires were about a foot and a half long and ended in alligator clips. There was a switch on one side and a miniature flashlight bulb under a faceted plastic dome. The parts had come from a series of streamlined aluminum cases Nix had stashed under his cot.

"You familiar with radios? Professional gear?" Nix looked at Fowler over the rims of his reading glasses.

"We sell them. I couldn't build one, but the guts don't scare me."

"Okay." Nixon indicated one wire, then another. "This is power, this is ground. Are we good so far?"

Fowler nodded.

"Here's the tricky ones . . . once you hook them up, they will hijack the ship's radio to send out our signal. We're playing a few games with the broadcast frequency so it can't easily be detected. The power lead needs to come off *before* the transmitter's power switch, understand? We want our device on all the time. The light is a test circuit; it lets you know you're hooked up and running. The switch turns off the light so it's less noticeable. If you have time, it's better to solder the connections."

Fordyce took the device, wrapped up the wires, and placed it in the hollowed-out shell of a cheap Webcor transistor radio. He snapped on the back and handed it to Fowler. "Starting a week from tomorrow I'll arrange for a Canberra to do a daily overflight of the entire archipelago. If they pick up anything, and weather permits, they'll come in at lower altitude to get a precise location. Don't hook this up until you've found the sub. Are we clear?"

Fowler nodded and stuffed the gutted Webcor into the inside pocket of his jacket, then followed Fordyce and Gonzalo down to the moonlit lakeshore where the float plane was anchored not far from the pier. Soon they were pounding their way down the lake and slowly lifting into the dark sky. He wasn't sure what he was going to do, but as soon as he got out from under Fordyce's thumb, he'd have a few options.

The first leg of their flight took just over an hour. Landing on a lake alongside a small commercial runway they taxied close to where a sleek Lockheed business jet with the logo SOUTHERN AIR TRANSPORT painted on the side was parked on the tarmac.

As the engine wound down, Fordyce put a hand on Mike's shoulder. "I'm getting off here," he said. "You two are going on to Chile as soon as the crew can refuel."

He reached inside his jacket and handed Fowler two passports. Both Mike's legitimate document and the Steve Tallent identity had stamps showing an arrival in Santiago two days earlier. There was also a train ticket south that had already been punched by a conductor.

"Two things," he said. "First, you can solve a lot of problems if you play ball. The Spanish are attempting to extradite your partner, Señor Porras. He has been to court, but I don't know how long the Swiss will hold out. We can help, but he'll likely go to prison if we don't.

"Second, this is becoming a serious operation. It will require ships and aircraft. I'm going straight to Washington and I should be able to meet with the right people in the next few days. But preparing an expedition like this will not be quick even if there is no opposition. If the closest warship is in Panama . . . Well, that's a minimum of a week at sea to get to southern Chile. It's going to be expensive and if it fails heads will roll, chiefly mine. So, I'm warning you: don't screw us over. Not only will we kill you . . . we'll also send you the bill!" Just before Fordyce ducked through the hatch he winked and said, "Have a good flight."

Mike Fowler had never thought much of the CIA man's sense of humor, and the flight was anything but.

The plane banged and sideslipped through increasing wind and rain. Gonzalo, the only other passenger, looked pale in the dim lights of the cabin. He handed Fowler an oxygen mask. Mike's palms were sweating and strangely numb. Years spent at sea weren't going to prevent this case of motion sickness. They finally topped out at nearly 17,000 feet. For a few moments the peaks of the Andes loomed around them and it was clear as they crossed the spine of the continent.

At low altitude the air over Chile was calm but the pilot continued to tempt fate, putting the big plane down on the deck, and roaring along a valley just above the treetops. At a wide stretch just past the confluence of two rivers he eased toward the shining black surface and then brought the nose of the plane up to allow the rear of the pontoons to make contact with the water. The Otter slowed, but it was only once it pulled out of the current and dropped an anchor that Fowler relaxed.

He and Gonzalo rowed ashore in a rubber boat, their landmark being the lights of a car parked well back on the gravel shore. The driver handed the keys to Gonzalo and then clambered into the inflatable dinghy. They drove west along the river, passing through a couple of small towns before heading south beside Bay of Concepción to Penco. The car trip took well over an hour.

Originally founded as Concepción de María Purísima del Nuevo Extremo, the settlement dated back to the sixteenth century. Twice sacked by the forces of Lautaro, a native Mapuche war chief, it was then destroyed five times in succession by earthquakes and tsunamis. In 1751, Concepción was relocated to a less vulnerable area a half dozen miles to the south. The site of the old town, on the inland side of the bay, was settled again in the mid-nineteenth century and renamed Penco.

On both sides of the road were piles of broken masonry and the shadowed outlines of construction equipment, signs of the ongoing cleanup from a series of much more recent quakes. The Valdivia earthquake of 1960 was the most powerful in recorded history, creating tsunamis as high as thirty-five feet in Hawaii, and up to eighty feet in some parts of Chile. Cracked pavement, collapsed buildings, and other signs of the devastation continued as they drove down through the edges of the "new" city of Concepción.

With its back to the low ridge of the peninsula, Talcahuano was the commercial and naval port. Pulling up on a sloping residential street, Gonzalo doused the lights and pointed along the hillside to the north. "We walk," he said.

They picked their way down an alley where it seemed every second house was abandoned or being reconstructed. Shifting a tarp out of the way, his guide motioned Fowler up a creaking set of temporary wooden steps. Deep inside the framework of the building they came to a heavy door. Gonzalo knocked. A muffled voice said, "Wood."

The Cuban grinned at Mike. "Natalie."

A bar was withdrawn and the door opened. Beyond was a dimly lit room. A pair of sleeping bags lay on the floor and there was a pile of magazines in one corner and an ice chest and water jug in the other.

"Qué tal, hermanos?" Gonzalo shook hands with the two men in the room. One of them had the look of a former OSS man. Fowler knew the type, well-educated but incapable of office work, an aging and hard-drinking man of action. The other was young, a Boy Scout in a tight T-shirt that emphasized his powerful muscles.

The young man nodded a greeting and slipped out through a pair of canvas shelter halves set up to form a light trap. On the other side was some sort of observation post.

"This the one?" the OSS man asked.

Gonzalo nodded. "We have to get him on the ship. It is still here, yes?"

"Yeah. But there're some complications." The older man glanced at Fowler and didn't seem inclined to elaborate.

"Go ahead, give us the sitrep," the Cuban prompted.

"There're other operatives in town."

"Who?" Mike demanded.

"People we have dossiers on."

"What does *that* mean?" Fowler asked.

"People *known* to us. Multiple nationalities. I'm not cleared to talk to you about it." The OSS man gave Mike the cold eye and went on, "Something spooked our targets on the boat. When they first arrived, they were docked and took on provisions and fuel. There was a bunch of coming and going. Then there was a commotion onboard. Yelling, cursing, that sort of thing. Once it calmed down two of them stayed ashore, but they cut off fueling and moved the ship into the middle of the bay. They've been out there all evening. As far as we can tell a lighter has been hired to deliver a shipment of packing cases from Spain and more fuel in drums."

"Did they make us, or one of these other teams?" Gonzalo asked.

"Uncertain. It'll be daylight in a couple of hours. Our sources may have some more info."

"I have to get out there, onto that ship," Mike said. "What are we going to do about that?"

"He's right. Orders from the man himself," Gonzalo said.

"I don't care. My people don't move until I understand what's happening." OSS pulled a crumpled pack of cigarettes from his pocket and lit up. "You don't like it? Tough."

Mike indicated the canvas barrier. "Can I have a look?"

"Be my guest."

Mike Fowler slipped through the folds of canvas and onto a half-repaired balcony. The kid in the T-shirt was lying on a sheet of plywood and squinting through a spotting scope. The night was cool but that didn't seem to bother him. "Not much action," he whispered.

Mike picked up a pair of binoculars from the railing. He adjusted the eyepieces. The ship was dimly outlined against the waters of the bay.

The *Bushranger II* had begun life as a Cohoes-class net tender, a 168-foot, 775-ton-displacement naval vessel designed to lay and service the massive steel nets that had once been used to protect harbors from infiltration by enemy submarines. The most notable feature of a net tender were the two thick steel "horns" that protruded from the bow, giving it the look of a Chinese junk. Besides the twelve-ton derrick that serviced the foredeck, each of those horns could function as a fixed crane with a lifting capacity of twenty tons.

"What's going on out there?" Fowler asked.

"Nothin'," the Boy Scout replied. "All crew members as well as targets identified as Johnson, Zúñiga, and Voss are on board. Sobek and Iannucci went ashore before dark. They have hotel rooms."

"Iannucci? Who's that?"

"Don't know, sir. Our informants say he and Eduardo Suarez, arrived before Sobek, Paluso, and Johnson. The origin of their airline tickets was Miami."

"When is the delivery scheduled to go out to the ship?"

"Don't know that either. They were still trying to set it up when the shift at the warehouse went home."

"Thanks."

Mike went back inside. Gonzalo arched an eyebrow at him. "Welcome to our world, amigo. Get some sleep. I'll let you know if anything happens."

There was a squeak of brakes, the sound of feet going down the stairs, and a mumble of voices in Spanish. Daylight filtered through cracks in the siding. Mike was alone in the unfinished room; he had fallen asleep sitting against the wall. He blinked his eyes and tried to move. His back was stiff, and his leg wasn't much better. Gritting his teeth, he was about to try to get to his feet when the voices from the alley resolved into words.

". . . much drama at the hotel. One operative was captured. There were members of the staff paid to keep quiet. I think they are going to the ship now."

"What about the cargo?" the rough voice of the old OSS guy asked.

"The barge began loading ten minutes ago."

"And the others?"

"Well, one of them just made their move. But the Russkies? I'll bet they're waiting on orders, just like us. They don't have many assets in country. On the other hand, the Brotherhood has plenty of allies and a lot of them are in the Chilean navy. If the military gets involved there won't be a way to get them uninvolved . . . not the best way to keep secrets."

Fowler slipped the strap of his duffel bag over his shoulder and rolled onto his hands and knees. His leg hurt and he knew he couldn't move quietly on his feet until he stretched a bit. He crawled toward the canvas partition, pushing it aside to squint out at the bay. Whatever was going on, it didn't sound good. Not for the crew of the *Bushranger*, not for Fordyce's plan, and not for him.

A small launch was making its way toward Johnson's ship. Mike peered through the telescope. Aboard were a boatman, Paul Sobek, and another man he had never seen. The new guy had his hand on a long bundle wrapped in a tarp. Closer in, alongside a line of fishing boats, Mike could see a small crane lifting several wooden cases in a cargo net. He grinned; they were the cases he had helped build back in Barcelona.

Some indistinct words drifted up from the stairway, then Gonzalo spoke more clearly. "I need to get him down there."

"You wait! He's not one of ours, just somebody Fordyce strong-armed."

"He's all we've got!" the Cuban insisted.

"Look, I'm not putting him in there with an agent of some foreign government—an agent who is *in his file*—unless I clear it with the chief of station. This thing is looking screwier by the minute! And when the KGB shows up, I *know* it's time to double-check my orders."

Mike decided he wasn't going to wait or trust his handlers to manage the situation. He unlatched the strap of the duffel bag and refastened it around one of the posts that supported the balcony railing. Then he grabbed the strap, slipped off the edge, and fell. His grip on the strap brought him up short, about four feet above the hillside leading down to a street. The bandage on his back tore loose and pain ripped up his side. He grunted and let go, hitting the sloping ground and rolling.

"Hey! *Hey!*"

"Damn it! He just jumped off the balcony!"

Through the maze of studs and masonry that made up the first floor of the building the others had either heard or spotted his escape.

Fowler staggered to his feet and ran. His wounded leg rebelled, and he caught himself. Gritting his teeth, he straightened up and put on speed. He looked back to see the Boy Scout vaulting a fence and sliding down the slope. Mike ran out into a wide boulevard. He dodged a truck, changed his angle to avoid a pair of oncoming cars, and then awkwardly jumped the curb between a parking lot and a warehouse. The loading area with the crane operator was just ahead but he could hear the slap of boot soles closing in behind.

He slammed to a stop, crouched low, and braced himself. The young man hit and flew through the air. The impact nearly knocked Mike over, but he got his footing, turned, and kicked the Boy Scout in the stomach.

"Sorry, kid," he said as he limped away toward the barge.

Using a ladder set into the seawall Fowler dropped to the deck. The two crewmen were unhooking the heavy net that contained his crates. More boxes and fuel drums were already aboard. Mike dug around in his pocket. He handed thc bigger of the bargemen an American twenty-dollar bill.

"I'll give you another when you get me aboard that ship." He pointed at the *Bushranger*. The man's eyes lit up.

That was when Gonzalo, the old operative, and the still-gasping Boy Scout appeared at the edge of the wharf.

"If you want me, you're gonna have to come down here and get me!" Fowler gestured toward the Chilean gunboats anchored in the distance. "And if this turns into some sort of 'incident,' I'll make sure *you* take responsibility for it." He pointed at the OSS man.

On the deck behind Mike two men of the barge crew stepped up, one hefting a heavy wrench . . . They wanted to earn that other twenty.

Gonzalo looked at his companions and laughed. "Better let him go. Like I said, he's our only chance."

Out on the *Bushranger* someone saw them coming and swung the derrick boom over the side in anticipation of loading cargo. The man at the controls of the barge slowed, easing in under the hook until the worn-out tires that acted as fenders gently bumped against the cladding on the ship's hull.

"Hey! Trajiste nuestras cosas?" A tall, suntanned guy in a sport shirt and fancy loafers, the man Fowler recognized from the boat with Sobek, demanded to know if the bargemen were making a delivery.

They handed him an invoice and, after looking it over, he tossed down a pair of lines to secure the two vessels.

Back behind the derrick mast there was a clank and grind as the stranger engaged the winch motor. Fowler handed the pilot of the barge the other twenty, and then, as the net lifted, he stuck a foot in one of the rope squares and grabbed onto the line above it. Leaning forward, Mike caused the load to rotate enough so he could step off as he came level with the foredeck of the *Bushranger.*

"*You!* Hold it! Put your hands up!" The winch slammed to a stop and the stranger charged across the deck, yanking a nickel-plated automatic from his pocket. The guy made the mistake of amateurs and thugs: instead of stopping out of reach where the gun was an advantage, he barreled in, shoving it toward Mike Fowler's face.

Mike grabbed the gun hand, pivoted, shoved a leg backward, and hurled the well-dressed tough over the side. The move didn't do his back any good, but the look of surprise on the man's face made up for it. There was a satisfying splash as he hit the water.

Fowler made sure the safety was locked up and was tucking the pistol into his waistband when he heard someone clapping from the bridge wing. He looked up to see the grinning face of Ihaka Waretini, Johnson's chief mate. His deep voice boomed out, "They told me you were dead! Ha! Such fools. I'll be right down." The huge Māori ducked out of sight into the wheelhouse.

It wasn't only Waretini who showed up on deck. Jack Johnson was the first one out the starboard hatch. "Rumrunner! I told that Kraut *I* wasn't gonna leave without you . . . and just when I was about to throw these bludgers off my ship, here you are!" The Australian leaned close and spoke in a low voice. "There's trouble brewing. Just play along till you see what's up."

Fernando Zúñiga, Colin McLeod, the *Bushranger*'s engineer, his electrician Frank Jano, and even Mel Paluso crowded around to either greet Fowler or simply to verify that he was still alive.

Fernando in particular was deeply apologetic for leaving Bariloche without him. "So sorry! So sorry! Dios me perdone, I thought you was dead!"

Paluso helped Tony Iannucci, the guy Mike had thrown into the water, back aboard and introduced him. Iannucci was soaked to the skin and angry, but he grumbled something that might have been an apology when Fowler handed him back his pistol. Of course, everyone wanted to know what had happened. Voss had reported that Fowler was dead or captured by Skorzeny.

"Not exactly. The police showed up. I escaped from the hospital before Skorzeny and Anhaldt could pull any strings and get their hands on me." At least that much was true. Before Jack could get fired up about Voss having left him behind, Mike deflected further conversation by saying: "Look, if we're going to sail, we need to get this load onboard. I don't know the whole story, but this town's crawling with spooks, and we've got to get out of here!"

"You hear *that*?" Paluso glared at Johnson. "It's like I've been saying, we've been *made*! How much clearer does it have to get? Your buddy's here. We got our fuel. We're gonna end up in jail or worse if we don't move!"

"Keep your shirt on," Jack snapped. He put a hand on Mike's shoulder. "Stick with me, there's a mess we've got to get sorted."

Johnson turned to McLeod and Waretini. "Warm up the engines. Ihaka, get that cargo stowed, but don't let the barge go. You tell them there's someone who may be going ashore."

"Aye, boss."

Mike glanced up to see Anton Voss narrowly watching him from the boat deck. Beside him was another man, a face Fowler vaguely remembered from Sobek's operation in Havana. Anton tilted his head, indicating that Mike should join him. He didn't know what to think about Voss, but sooner or later his partner was going to have some explaining to do.

"Come on." Johnson nodded toward Paluso. "We were just about to get into it with these blokes." They headed toward a ladder on the starboard side of the deckhouse.

"We've sure as hell got someone riled up." Johnson pulled a folded telegram from his pocket. "I got this damn thing yesterday. The drydock in Briz is suddenly claiming we didn't pay our bill. Now Port Authority anywhere in the world can impound this ship. That's insane! No drydock *ever* let a ship go without getting paid in full!"

Mike cursed under his breath. If someone was putting pressure on Johnson it was likely Fordyce. The CIA man would be motivated to create a situation where the Australian couldn't turn back. But if Jack found out who was pulling his strings, even a decade and a half after the mission to Itu Aba, he'd go out of his mind.

"Thank the gods you made it, Rummy. I paid them once. Unless we're successful I haven't got the swag to fight a claim, let alone a seizure."

A hatch, hidden behind the tube of a ventilator, admitted them to a narrow chart room equipped with both radar and sonar consoles. Another door led into a cramped space Fowler assumed was Johnson's private cabin.

"Here's our other problem . . ."

The compartment had a bunk built into the outer wall with wooden cabinets and a small desk across from it. Paul Sobek sat in the desk chair with a gun in his hand. Anton Voss leaned against the far wall.

On the bunk was the tarp-wrapped bundle Fowler had seen from the CIA's observation post. Mike paused in the doorway. Something about the tightly bound roll of canvas made him think of how he and Voss had disposed of the body of Hanno Wuttke not so many months ago.

"Come on in." Sobek shot a suspicious glance from Mike to Voss. "You're the last person we expected to see. However, we have a bit of a situation on our hands, and *you'd* better have an explanation."

Cautiously Mike stepped into the room and Mel Paluso closed the door behind them. It was a tight fit. Sobek stood and handed his pistol to Paluso. Then he took hold of the tarp on the bunk and flipped it back to reveal a face . . .

It was Nicole.

CHAPTER 21

She was gagged with someone's shirt, and the look she gave Mike Fowler was veiled . . . She wasn't asking for help, and she wasn't giving anything away.

Fowler glanced quickly at Voss; he didn't seem to have let on that he knew her. It looked like this was going to be Mike's play . . . He hoped he was reading that correctly.

"Something's going down here, and I don't like it!" Sobek turned on Fowler. "Fritzy," he said, indicating Voss, "claims you're dead. Then we run into this babe in town. She demands to see you, and suddenly here you are! And she brought a bag, a *suitcase*, as if she expected to be welcomed aboard! So explain it. Sing a song that makes me understand and make it quick!"

"Is that Iannucci guy yours? And I saw another of your goons from Havana on deck. What are you up to?" Mike needed a minute to get his thoughts straight.

"Ah, they've been flashing guns around and telling us to set sail." Johnson cursed. "I said shoot me, see if you get off this boat alive! I didn't ask for any new crew members, and they look like a couple of shark biscuits to me."

"Yeah. Well, they're both certified divers and, if I'm bankrolling things, I want a better balance of power around here." Sobek turned back to Fowler. "Now, answer my question. Who is this?" He pointed to Nicole. "And what the *hell's* going on?"

Mike Fowler knew if he was going to improvise, he would have to use both truth and fiction. He took a breath and dove in . . .

"Her name is Nicole . . . DeMaes. She's an officer in Israeli intelligence and"—Mike indicated Voss—"we've known her for years."

"Oh? Is that right?" Voss, it seemed, had indeed neglected to mention that fact.

Fowler looked Nicole dead in the eye; she was going to have to take his lead here . . . "The Israelis know about the *gold*. I was questioned about it before I got to Caracas."

Mel Paluso cursed explosively.

"And you just *forgot* to tell us?" Sobek snarled.

"You were threatening to take your ball and go home. I'd be a fool if I didn't keep another offer in reserve."

"So, you told them all about it?"

"No, they told *me*." Fowler answered Sobek, but he shifted his gaze to Voss.

Anton winced. Well, now he could worry about how much the Mossad knew . . . and he could worry about how much Mike knew, too.

Fowler turned back to Sobek. "We discussed this. What we're doing here isn't a secret. We're just hoping we can get ahead of everyone else."

"Alright. As soon as we get out to sea, she goes over the side."

"No. That's *not* going to happen," Fowler told him.

"I reckon we put her ashore," Johnson said. "Nobody dies on my ship without my say-so."

"Not a chance. She knows too much," Paluso growled.

"You looking for a war, Paluso?" Fowler turned right into the gun the Italian was holding. "Right here? Right now? Anyone touches her, they're gonna die."

Mel Paluso looked at him, and Mike recognized his expression from all those years before in Havana . . . The man was measuring him, wondering what would happen if he decided to pull the trigger.

"Remove the gag," Voss spoke up. "Why don't we see what she has to say?"

That brought the blustering to a halt.

"She is a dedicated operative, willing to give her life for her country. She approached us for a reason. I, for one, do not wish to put her ashore, or to kill her . . . until we discover why she is here." He bent beside the wooden cabinet that held the bunk and began to untie the sleeves of the shirt that had been jammed into her mouth.

Fowler wondered what was going on. Did Voss want Nicole along for some reason? He had left Mike behind. Was he now trying to buy himself some goodwill by protecting her, or was this just the best way to keep track of what she was up to?

"Ach!" Nicole spat out the wad of cloth. She coughed. "Somebody, get me a drink." She struggled to sit up, but the tarp was still firmly lashed around her.

Johnson handed over the battered knife he wore on his belt and Voss cut through the ropes, quickly returning the blade to its owner. Sobek reached inside his jacket and pulled out a flask. "Have one on me," he said. "Then make your case. Every minute we sit here is an unacceptable risk."

She took a pull, swirled it around in her mouth, and swallowed, shuddering involuntarily. Then she backed into the corner of the bunk, pulled her knees up in front of her, and glared at them.

"I'm *not* going ashore. My country sent me to claim this"—she glanced at Mike—"*treasure*. We demand a position in the outcome of your mission."

"Ha!" Paluso laughed. "You *demand*?"

Nicole's eyes shifted back and forth, then she grabbed at an argument and ran with it: "Some of that gold came from Jewish teeth, some from our safes and bank accounts. Yes, everyone deserves a profit if we succeed. But if Skorzeny gets his hands on it he will use it to help a new generation of Nazis consolidate their power. My government will do whatever it can to stop that."

Sobek shook his head. "Listen, doll, as much as I'd like to know you better, I'm just not seeing this *'we'* you're talking about. You're not in any place to dictate terms."

Johnson spoke up. "I say she goes ashore. I won't have a woman harmed . . . but I don't want her on my ship neither."

"I second that," Mike said. She glared at him and shook her head.

Fowler didn't doubt Nicole was committed to whatever her mission was, but he also didn't want her in the crossfire when everyone aboard realized they were being screwed.

"Nicole, you may think you know what you're getting into . . . but you don't. There are *too many players*." Mike gestured at the others in the cabin to hide the fact that he was really trying to warn her about Fordyce . . . and himself. He had no idea how the Central Intelligence Agency would react to him bringing a competitor along for the ride.

"I didn't come to South America alone," she said to all of them. "You take me along to protect our interests, or we will protect them whether you like it or not. And without me you're not going to like it. When the time comes, you're going to have to launder your Nazi . . . 'treasure' or whatever you wish to call it. These are the facts: if Israel accuses you of stealing it, you won't survive the reaction. But if Israel helps you, uh . . . make the most of it, your lives will be a good deal easier."

She moved out of the corner to sit, more confidently, on the edge of the bunk. "You don't have a choice. But I can't help until you recover it, and my team aren't the only intelligence operatives in Talcahuano. I *guarantee* that you are under surveillance right now. Mossad is trained to take the initiative and organized to function with a minimum of bureaucracy. We need to sail before those others figure out how to leverage you like I just did."

Mike almost laughed, but Sobek was quick to realize he was losing control of an operation he'd thought of as his own. "We'll see about that! We're in first position here, and I'm going to be there when we make the split. I'm going to be there with reinforcements! Nobody gets away with cutting us out."

Voss kept his eyes on the floor, but a sad and cynical smile touched his lips. Mike realized that he and Nicole and Anton all shared a secret. But none was truly aware of the extent of the others' knowledge . . . and their mission was destined to become vastly more difficult when the others found out.

"I believe Miss DeMaes must sail with us." Voss pulled out of his reverie. "No one is cutting you out. Your money has been useful, but the situation is fluid and I suspect it will become even more so. The way you will earn your share must continue to evolve."

"You forget who's got the guns," Paluso said. "We can take what we want if we have to." As Mike turned to face the Italian, he caught Johnson's fingers closing on the haft of his knife. He wouldn't have to worry about Sobek. If the mobster moved, he was as good as dead.

Fowler felt a rising impatience with the entire situation. There were too many agendas, and no one was taking charge. "I don't want her coming along," he said. "But she's insisting, and Mr. Voss agrees. So, it's a done deal. No one stays behind. No one goes over the side. We are *all* going south." There was a moment of silence. No one challenged him.

From beneath their feet there was a blast of compressed air and the rumble of diesels as Colin McLeod started the *Bushranger*'s engines. It was as if the ship itself had decided their fate.

They hauled anchor and headed out of Concepción Bay, making for the open sea rather than following the coast. The first stage of their plan was to lose themselves in the vastness of the Pacific.

There was a lot of cargo to be sorted and correctly stowed. The drums of newly delivered diesel were lashed down around the deck-load of coiled air hose they had brought from Australia. An astute observer might recognize that a war surplus net tender would make a first-class salvage vessel, but the amount of hose they carried was more likely to be the tip-off to their actual mission.

Wind-blown spray washed the decks and the wake spread out

astern. Mike walked from the oddly shaped bow back to the fantail, studying the equipment they would have to work with once they arrived at their mysterious destination.

The Cohoes net tenders had originally mounted several 20mm antiaircraft guns as well as a three-inch cannon. Of course, the armaments had been stripped prior to its sale, and Johnson had gone further, removing the antiaircraft emplacement above the flying bridge entirely and cutting away the steel parapets that surrounded the other gun positions to replace them with pipe railings. This weight reduction increased the ship's stability and slightly lessened its vulnerability to the wind. The remaining 20mm mounts were modified to become pedestals for an additional set of high-powered searchlights.

The interior of the superstructure had been significantly remodeled. A well-equipped machine shop, crew's cabins, and the mess, or wardroom, were now all found on the main deck. There were still bunks below—indeed Colin McLeod refused to sleep more than twenty feet from his precious engines—but since the *Bushranger* sailed with a much smaller crew than during wartime, the alterations freed up a good deal of space for storage and additional equipment, such as the high-pressure compressors, air purifiers, and the many tons of chain and hawser that were used when the ship was working a salvage site. Updated wiring allowed a number of functions that had once required additional crew to be remotely controlled from the bridge.

With eight additional bodies aboard, cabins and supplies also needed reshuffling. Frank Jano, who had a stateroom with its own bath, was good enough to give it up so Nicole could have some privacy. He functioned as chief electrician and as McLeod's assistant engineer, so bunking belowdecks in the old engineering quarters put him closer to his duty stations. The rest of the newcomers found themselves crowding into the crew's fo'c'sle directly across the passageway.

Making his way forward, Mike thanked Jano as the man cleared out the drawers beneath his bunk and the contents of his tiny bathroom. "I never thought there'd be no woman livin' in here," he grumbled. "I'd like to spend a few hours cleanin' up the place." Jano stripped the mattress and flipped it over. He laid out a set of threadbare sheets. "Are you and her . . . an item?"

Fowler was unhappy that question was already being asked, but he *was* the one helping to move her in to a private cabin. "We've known each other for a few years. Let's leave it at that," he said.

"And she's some kinda spy?"

Mike shrugged. He didn't know what to say that wouldn't make an awkward situation any less so.

Frank shouldered a seabag full of his belongings and eyed the narrow bunk. "Will you be stayin' in here, too?"

Fowler shook his head. "Belowdecks. I think that will create less suspicion."

"That's wise. We go way back, so you know I'm sayin' this out of friendship: be careful. There are men on this crew, they weren't here in the old days. They got questions about what we're up to . . . about what *you're* up to."

Mike had already been getting a lot of side-eye from Nikos Cacoyannis, one of Johnson's new divers. "I can understand that. What about you?"

Jano snorted. "Trip of a lifetime, mate. You just be sure to watch our backs, 'right?"

The electrician headed down the passage. His request didn't make Mike Fowler any more comfortable; he didn't even know how he was going to watch his own.

A moment later Nicole came down from Johnson's cabin. She had indeed brought a suitcase. He tossed it on the bunk, then turned to close the door behind him . . . but immediately decided against that and left it open. They'd just have to speak carefully.

"You shouldn't have come," he warned. "I don't think this is going to turn out well."

She arched an eyebrow. "You mean the hunt for your mysterious 'gold'?"

"Did your people tell you what Anton is after?"

"In general, but it's beyond my expertise. I was given protocols to follow depending on, um . . . how much you discover."

Fowler pointed at the deck above him. "Look, this situation is very complicated, and it's going to get worse. I don't know what you think you're going to be able to do about it."

"Michael, I have to try. The people who were after you, Skorzeny's people, Anhaldt's people. They can't have it. That's the first priority. They are connected all over the world. To give them the keys to the future . . . ? It puts too much power in the wrong hands."

"Agreed."

She sighed. "I have my orders, but I don't like feeling expendable."

"What are they—your orders?"

"We get it. They don't."

Mike shook his head. "How in the world do your bosses expect you to make that work?"

"I'm supposed to ask sweetly. Improvise. I'm authorized to make certain offers under certain conditions. I meant what I said, there's a chance everyone can get something out of this." She lowered her voice almost to a whisper. "Obviously not what they expected, but something."

Mike changed the subject. "How did you find us?"

"The card you sent. The president of a company can move unseen using private jets. But the jets . . . they are not so easy to hide. After he left Europe, Peter Anhaldt flew into Puerto Montt, Chile. We just worked our way up the coast until we heard this ship had placed an order for fuel. The *Bushranger,* Captain Jack Johnson: these are things I know about you."

"Right." Mike checked the passageway again. "I've got to get Anton alone, get to the bottom of whatever he thinks he's doing. How the hell does telling all these lies make any sense?"

"Michael . . . *don't.* I don't know what he's up to either, but we're on our way, and we can't *do* anything until we find the sub."

"Yeah. But he has to come clean. Buckets—I mean Jack—it's not right that he doesn't know the score."

She took ahold of his collar and, going up on tiptoes, kissed him. "Please, wait," she said. "Please?"

He looked down at her. The kiss had been nice, but he suddenly wondered if it had been personal or professional. He was far from certain they wanted the same thing.

"I'll think about it. No promises," he said.

She bit her lip, frustrated but trying to hide it. Then she turned to her suitcase. "I have something of yours." She pulled out the Remington .380 and spare magazines that had been confiscated from him in Tel Aviv.

"Keep it. I'll sleep better knowing you're armed."

Nicole nodded. She took an elegant but effective-looking pair of hiking boots out of her case, and dropped the slim pistol and magazines down inside. As he went out the door she threw him a wink.

Mike Fowler found Johnson in the wheelhouse. He was running through a list of repairs with Waretini. A breeze buffeted its way through the open hatches leading to the bridge wings. Behind them, the continent had diminished into a bright line of haze.

"Alright, mate. What's cooking?" Johnson handed the clipboard back to Ihaka and looked at Fowler.

"Show me how to access the hold. I want to give you something. But it's for your eyes only."

The big Australian took him out to the bridge wing and down a ladder, then down again to the main deck. He undogged an oversized hatch, clearly one of his many modifications to the ship's original design, and led the way through a darkened workshop and past the drum-like gyrocompass. He pointed aft toward a wooden door. "The deckhouse cabins and mess are through there. Originally, this boat wasn't designed for rough weather. A lot of water comes in over the bow. I made it so we can button her up but everything's still accessible."

"You got screwdrivers?"

Johnson rummaged in a drawer. “That’s a damn good-looking woman,” he commented. “Funny you never mentioned her before . . . seein’ as how you two seem to have known each other quite a while.”

“Yeah, well, I didn’t exactly know how to explain it. Especially since you’re always razzing me about spies and all.”

“Fair dinkum. But you are the man of mystery, mate. Here . . .”

Jack handed Fowler two long Yankee ratcheting drivers. Then they headed down another ladder.

At the bottom of the steep stairs a corridor led aft to the crew’s quarters, where the new arrivals were still settling in. Johnson headed forward, opened a hatch, and switched on a light; he closed the hatch behind them.

“I’m looking for my shipment, the one from Spain.”

They threaded their way around reels of hose, racks of pressure tanks, and containers of supplies. In a dim corner they found the cases. Removing the lid from one of them, Fowler pulled out a smaller box. He stripped off the wax paper and handed Johnson a Browning P-35. He set three magazines and a box of 9mm ammunition on a nearby fuel drum.

Jack hefted the pistol. “Strewth! I like having friends with connections.”

“There’re a lot of guns on this boat. We shouldn’t be left out.” Mike unwrapped his Smith & Wesson .44. He loaded it, placed a handful of cartridges in his pocket, and stuffed it into a holster that fit inside his waistband and secured the heavy clip to the right of his belt buckle. He zipped the bottom of his jacket to cover the butt of the revolver.

There was an electronic click, and a speaker on the bulkhead hummed as the 1 Main Circuit came alive: “Captain to the bridge! Captain to the bridge!”

Fowler and Johnson looked at each other. Johnson frowned and moved toward the hatch.

They found Ihaka on the port bridge wing; he was scanning the sea behind them with a large set of binoculars.

"Hey, boss. Take a look at this." He handed the glasses to Johnson. Jack didn't lower the binoculars for a long moment, then he passed them to Fowler. He pointed aft.

Mike adjusted the width of the lenses. Just below the horizon were two splinters of white: speedboats. Rising behind them was a faint tinge of exhaust fumes.

Johnson spoke to the middle-aged Japanese man who had the helm. "Koji, head her dead south."

After a few minutes it was clear the two boats had changed course to cut them off. Fowler took up the glasses again. "They're not official. At least I don't think so." The pair were mismatched; one had a red cowling and an enclosed helm, the other seemed to have a blue stripe down the side. Mike pointed at the microphone for the PA system. "Can I?" Johnson nodded.

"Mr. Voss? Please come to the wheelhouse." Fowler's voice rang throughout the ship.

It wasn't only Voss who showed up, but at least he showed the proper etiquette before stepping through the door, "Captain, may I?"

Johnson nodded. Hard on Anton's heels were Paul Sobek and Mel Paluso.

By then no one needed the glasses to make out their pursuers.

"Can we outrun them?" Sobek asked.

"No chance. We can do fourteen knots, if we push our luck. They're good for more than twenty. They can intercept but they can't follow, not in the long run; they don't carry enough fuel."

"Does anyone care what they have to say?" Fowler asked.

No one spoke up.

"Well, this is why I packed that box of toys." Fowler turned to Sobek and Paluso. "Can you deal with it if anyone gets inside?"

The Italian patted his hard belly and Mike assumed that meant he had the Colt Python under his shirt. "Close quarters is where I'm best, pal!"

Voss turned to Johnson. "Captain, if it looks like they are about to come alongside, steer parallel with the swell but be ready to cut across it. With our size we'll do better than they will. There is no reason to make boarding easy."

Fowler led Voss down through the machine shop. The packing case he and Johnson had opened contained enough weapons for a full-scale commando mission, but there was no time to load magazines. There was only one alternative. Mike pulled out a heavy wooden box and handed a bundle of three reinforced fiber tubes to Voss.

They raced back up the steep internal steps, Mike banging the case on the railing and bulkhead in his haste. In the chartroom, just behind and slightly below the bridge, he laid the box on the deck and flipped open the latches. From the door to the wheelhouse, Paul Sobek peered down, mumbling, "What the hell . . . where did *that* come from?"

"Jack? How are we doing?" Fowler yelled.

"They're coming up on us!" he heard Johnson call out.

"I need a minute!"

"Righto, but that's all you're gonna get!" Johnson said something to Koji that Mike didn't catch. Then: "Hold fast! We'll make 'em back off!"

The Japanese diver spun the wheel and the *Bushranger* heeled over to port and then swung back. Bracing himself, Fowler unbuckled the leather straps that cinched the contents in place.

Voss dumped two of the tubes into the now empty box and struggled to open the third. He glanced at Fowler. "Do not wait for me! I will be ready!"

Mike slammed through the hatch leading to the upper deck and staggered forward just as Koji Yamada veered in the other direction. Off to his right he saw the red-decked power launch sheer off, nimbly avoiding a collision. Mike shielded the weapon from their view with his body. This would work much better if it was a surprise.

Fowler took shelter between the pair of winch motors and the case of signal flags directly beneath the wheelhouse portholes. He pivoted the two halves of the Blindicide RL-83 and locked them together, then snapped on the blast shield. Still kneeling, he hefted the long tube.

Voss tapped his shoulder. "Behind you."

The boat with the blue stripe accelerated into sight. In the cockpit a man crouched behind a belt-fed machine gun mounted on a tripod.

The gun rattled and red tracers streaked across their bow, visible even in the sunlight. It was the age-old command to heave to and be boarded, but Johnson wasn't slowing.

Fowler heard the arming ring drop to the deck, and he felt Voss slide the rocket into the barrel of the Blindicide and twist off the rear safety. "Ready!" he said and leaned in, pressing his chest to Fowler's back.

On the motorboat, the gunner traversed the machine gun upward and fired a four-round burst that struck just under the portholes to the bridge. Chips of paint, ricochets, and metal spalling flew.

Mike straightened and pivoted to align the smaller boat over his sights. Voss knew the dance and expertly remained close behind him. As the ocean's swell began to peak, Fowler squeezed the trigger.

There was a bang, a jet of fire belched from the rocket launcher, and an instant later the entire bow of the pursuing boat vanished in a splintering concussion. The rear half continued on, engine screaming, digging in and flipping over to bob upside down on the waves.

"Reload! Coming around!" Fowler yelled. Voss expertly ducked under the barrel as Mike shifted his aim toward the red-decked cabin cruiser on the opposite side.

But the remaining launch cut sharply away and a moment later was well out of range for any shot from a moving deck.

Fowler turned and looked at Voss, who still had a finger curled around the arming ring of the next round. "Hold up . . ."

Their enemy was heading back, maneuvering to rescue the survivors of the first boat. Mike breathed a sigh of relief and grinned. For a moment he and Anton had once again been a team.

Voss arched an eyebrow and hefted the stubby rocket. “Works just as advertised, eh?”

CHAPTER 22

SPECULATION ABOUT THE identity of their attackers was the main subject of discussion over dinner. Voss discounted the idea of the KGB: their tactics might be brutal, but they were much more likely to set up a sure-thing ambush or nothing at all. Nicole agreed; chasing the *Bushranger* out of port and attempting to waylay it suggested that Anhaldt and Skorzeny's Brotherhood had finally caught on to Johnson's involvement, as well as that of Sobek and Paluso. From now on there was no turning back . . . for any of them.

Mike kept his own counsel. He was fairly certain she was right, providing Voss had told the truth about everything except the exact contents of the submarine. Only an organization that was confident they could eventually find the sub's hiding place would attempt to stop them; anyone else would be more likely to try to track them to its location.

"So, we're back in action, just like during the war." Paul Sobek looked around the table and winked at Nicole . . . as if she had forgotten he recently wanted to dump her into the sea. "Mel here was in the OSS. I was a cargo control officer for the army. The Port of New York, then England, France, and Holland . . . Now, that was a job with potential!" He rubbed his thumb and index finger together, an indication there had been some sort of graft.

He pointed across the table. "You two fought the Nips, right?"

Mike shrugged, and Johnson said, "Damn straight!"

"But now you've got a crewman who's Japanese—what's the story there?"

"Koji's a top bloody diver. We all gave as good as we got. The war's over."

"Maybe. Maybe not for everyone." Sobek pursed his lips and glanced at Nicole. "How about it, doll? Is the war over for your people? Six million Jews, you've got to bear a grudge, right?"

Nicole gave him nothing. "Israel seeks justice when and where it matters. But the future is more important than the past."

"Very enlightened. A lot of people I know, they can't give it up: the war, the Nazis, revenge."

He turned on Voss. "So, what was it like, Fritz? You were there. The Beer Hall Putsch. The Reichstag fire. How'd you let it happen?"

"Shut up, Sobek—" Fowler said, then stopped himself. Defending Voss had become a habit, but it had been a long day and his back hurt.

Voss had barely picked at his food; now he lit a cigarette. The tobacco glowed as he drew in a breath . . . and then for some mysterious reason he went ahead, stepping into Sobek's ambush.

"People look at what happened during the Third Reich, they say: 'Only the Germans . . . only the Germans could do this.' Well, they are fools. If our mistakes cannot be a lesson, then millions of lives have been tragically wasted." A rueful smile twisted the corner of his mouth. "This is our gift to humanity." He turned to look at Nicole. "However, for many, it is not what they wish to hear."

She shook her head. "I didn't ask. But say what you want. It should be interesting."

Anton Voss rolled the Chesterfield between his fingers. "Your dreams, they define you, yes? Identity, knowing who you are, is critical. The picture you have of yourself, however poorly developed, *that* becomes your future.

"What people call 'Germany' has always existed in chaos. In antiquity it was simply an area: Magna Germania, home of the warring tribes. Then it was the Holy Roman Empire of the German Nation: the First Reich. Impressive-sounding, but if one wishes to quote Voltaire: the Holy Roman Empire was not holy, nor Roman, nor was it an empire. In the end it was merely a fragmented collection of Kleinstaaterei, hundreds of small, disorganized states, duchies, and independent cities.

"While Spain, England, France, and Holland all became colonial powers, financial powers, the German states were a battlefield. There were decades of plague, starvation, and slaughter in religious wars, civil wars, all with the rest of Europe throwing fuel on the fire. Once Napoleon invaded the last traces of our thousand-year Reich collapsed as if it had never existed.

"After the French were defeated, the remnants of the Old Empire became an uneasy confederation. But there were still more than thirty independent states and an ongoing battle for dominance between the largest of these: Austria and Prussia. For centuries we had been the victims of one conflict or another. Therefore, it is not surprising that certain elements, wealthy groups that operated behind the scenes in trade and politics, founded a tradition of, um . . . hedging their bets. It also follows that our society became students of warfare, its philosophers . . . and then its masters.

"In 1870, France again declared war, and they were quickly defeated. This success led to the creation of a Second Reich under Kaiser Wilhelm the First. The pieces of our nation were now more or less unified yet, even so, there was little . . . Zusammenhalt . . . cohesion.

"Science and industry, both developed very rapidly. The speed with which we moved from a life unchanged since the Middle Ages into the modern world created a mixture of arrogance and dislocation. The slow wealth of a landowner and the yearly delivery of crops suddenly became the fast-moving world of political turbulence, economic speculation, and scientific development. Many considered the agents of this remarkable and uncomfortable modernism to be the Jews."

Nicole glared at Voss. She crossed her arms and leaned back in her seat.

Anton shook his head. “Do not look at me that way, young lady. You may blame me for many things, but at that point in history, Prussia and other German states were a haven for your people.”

“Yes, because for hundreds of years we were persecuted in Russia and Eastern Europe!”

“Hardly a surprise, eh?” Voss tapped the ash off his cigarette. “Anywhere in the world those who present themselves as different are held in suspicion. Political differences, religious differences, racial differences.”

“Oh really? Do *I* look so ‘different’?”

Nicole was on the attack, and Fowler stifled a grin; she was pushing Voss as only a woman could. It was doubly amusing because she possessed a classical beauty that could just as easily have modeled for Thutmose’s bust of Nefertiti or an ad produced on Madison Avenue.

Voss sighed. “Now you are just being argumentative. Of course you do not. Even under the National Socialists there was constant confusion, ugly caricatures on one hand, yet on the other the sense that secretly *anyone* could be a Jew.

“Your religion, the way it is practiced, hones the intellect. And because they had no better path to improve themselves, your people excelled. But the next step is to realize that the success, and eventually the financial power of the Jews, created a great deal of envy . . . the most simplistic explanation for antisemitism.”

“I hope you aren’t gonna tell her that they brought it on themselves?” Sobek wasn’t done trying to stir up trouble.

“Didn’t they?” Voss said. “It is logical that if an immigrant population remains useful, subservient, and invisible, perhaps it can avoid conflict.”

When Voss said “subservient” Paluso laughed, and Nicole clenched her jaw, but Mike caught her eye and tiredly shook his head. Anton had a defiant streak that made him ready to play the villain if there was someone willing to oppose him.

When no one took the bait, Voss waved the idea away. "But that is not human nature, is it? I suspect your family did not arrive in America on the *Mayflower*, Herr Sobek. My guess is they came from the same part of the Europe as Miss DeMaes and myself . . . and they did whatever they had to."

Nicole frowned at Mike. He had never discussed what little he knew of her background, but she didn't know that. Voss caught her look and scoffed. "Your accent is imperfect, mloda damo. I have always known you were not from Belgium."

Sobek, it seemed, didn't want to go into his family background either. "You were making excuses for the Nazis," he said. "So, let's hear it."

Anton Voss finished his cigarette and stubbed it out in the ashtray. Fowler expected a biting remark, but it didn't come. What he saw instead might have been a smile, and Mike wondered if Voss was setting a trap.

"An explanation is not an excuse," he said. "There is a moment when you realize the future is like a switching yard for the railroad. There seem to be many paths forward, but then the possibilities . . . they collapse into a single outcome. Suddenly you are on the main line, headed toward the horizon at high speed.

"I have a memory, a summer evening in Berlin, 1914. The kaiser gave a speech. 'Today we are all German brothers.' For perhaps the first time in our history, it was true. Aristocrats, the middle class, laborers, Saxons, Prussians, Bavarians, Protestants, Catholics, and Jews, all had come together. But that night, that speech . . . it was the declaration of war, to honor our treaty and defend our cousins in Austria-Hungary.

"Our Great War quickly decayed into a collision of ambition and bad decisions. By the end, only the struggle held us together. To survive, a form of 'war socialism' took over. It was effective enough to become an inspiration for Vladimir Lenin; it also animated the dreams of every Marxist in Germany.

"In the spring of 1918, the Russian army collapsed. They returned home to fight among themselves. This freed our forces to launch a major offensive . . . one last great effort. There was a hope that a significant victory might force an acceptable peace before the overwhelming number of American troops finally arrived.

"But, just at the critical moment, there was a series of mutinies, or perhaps one should call them strikes because it was the socialists and labor unions who led them. We who served in the Unterseeboots were called to stand against the mutineers. It was ironic, our final battle was not against the English, but rather with our own people!

"Much like what had happened in Russia, this revolt swept across the nation. The government fell, the kaiser abdicated, and soon the Social Democrats were struggling with the right and the out-and-out Communists over the conditions of the armistice and who would control what eventually became the Weimar Republic.

"There were more than fifty political parties, many of them violently opposed to one another. Politics were discussed in the Reichstag, but they were settled in the street with pistols and explosives. We did not know who we were, or what we wanted to be.

"Then, in 1923, inflation struck like a meteor. The government had long been printing too much money but until wartime price controls were loosened, it was not recognized for what it was.

"It seemed bad when the exchange rate was five hundred marks to one dollar, but then it was twenty thousand to one. Then it was a million, then a billion. Rich and poor lost everything. Theft and violence were everywhere.

"Finally, the treasury ran out of zeros . . . They simply stopped printing money. The government collapsed. Political leagues, which had been little more than social clubs, had armed themselves. Unreliable comrades were found floating in the river. An entire collection of Messiahs offered solutions. Hitler was one of them, but it was not yet his time.

"Then suddenly it was as if the clouds had parted to reveal the sun. New money was issued. Everyone was broke, but the days of dog eat dog seemed to be in the past. It was time for rebuilding, and for an economy that advanced like there was no tomorrow. Some even found the prosperity boring. Until then we had lived such dramatic lives.

"I went back to university, filling my head with science and technology rather than ideology and violence. It was a wonderful time but, of course, it ended in 1929 with the stock market crash and the Great Depression.

"Again, the boat went over the waterfall. There was more poverty and suicides. *Now* people talked of Hitler, his endless speeches, his incredible energy. They spoke of him as if he might have an answer."

Paluso leaned forward. "So what was it? What did Hitler have that gave him all that power?"

Voss eyed the Italian carefully, but the question seemed genuine. "I think we were waiting for him. We felt angry and unappreciated, blamed for events beyond our control. We were searching for the chance to come together and prove ourselves. And we were surrounded by enemies who refused to allow us to do so. Some of these things *were* true, but they were also myths, and *that* is where the danger lies.

"Our history of chaos had led to . . . well, let us call it a lack of confidence. German self-doubt has always been held at bay by bravado and a devotion to perfection. We are always overcompensating. On one hand we have our military traditions: discipline, technology, classification. On the other, we are romantics who wish to commune with nature, who believe in chivalry, mysticism, and fantastical, fanatical heroes. This is our conflict, the mentality of Prussia versus Austria, the north versus the south.

"Ours might be an old culture but, as a *nation*, we had all the insecurities of an adolescent. And young countries are like young men. They are vain, they have belligerent energy, and they *will* test their boundaries.

"Hitler created a pathway for that energy. The country was sick of half-hearted compromises. It was conditioned by war, and it was ready for ruthless action.

"Many of the ideas put forward by the Nazis were not new. Certainly not antisemitism. Of course, many Jews were accused of being 'international Marxists,' those loyal to a movement rather than their country. It was said that they had sold out the Fatherland with the Treaty of Versailles. Yet they were somehow *also* exploitative capitalists, profiting obscenely from their usurious loans and willingness to speculate in the market. People were encouraged to believe whichever accusation suited them . . . or both at the same time. The ironies abound."

Nicole winced. "*Ironies?* It was a bit more than that!"

"We were allowed to choose the excuses for our prejudice, ja? Could we have avoided what happened?" Anton spread his hands. "Totalitarianism grows from a loss of legitimacy, and Hitler and his followers had spent a decade preparing the ground.

"The National Socialists spoke of a German renewal . . . not just politics, a *spiritual* renewal. They were young and optimistic, and they made the traditional parties seem out of touch. They bothered to come to the beer halls and the students' clubs. They were willing to fight, to put their lives and freedom on the line.

" 'From I to We,' they would say. They promised what they called 'Soziale Gerechtigkeit'—social justice—food for everyone, anticapitalism, profit sharing for workers, the expansion of social security, public health, and an end to real estate and stock market opportunism. They infiltrated the halls of industry and government to the point where survival required acquiescence but, unlike their Communist rivals, it was a revolution that did not completely alienate those at the top.

"The party's ability to do what it claimed, to bring back the feeling of togetherness from the August Experience of 1914, was stunning. The economy was a shell game, but soon everyone had enough to eat. The autobahn linked one end of the country to the other, and mobile cinemas brought entertainment and newsreels to rural areas. All of this was salted with propaganda, but it contributed to a sense of connection and progress.

"Most crucial was reuniting the Old Empire, the communities of ethnic Germans. At first it was just the Rhineland, the territory on

Germany's western border. After that there was the incorporation of the Saar region, and then 'Anschluss,' the dream of joining Germany and Austria. Hitler spat in the face of Versailles, moved like lightning, and no one had the backbone to object. Even people who looked down on his methods cheered what they were doing for the Fatherland!

"Then there was what the world called 'the Crisis of the Sudetenland,' a section of Czechoslovakia also populated by Germans. Although Britain and France attempted to intervene, they were cowards. By this time our country's finances were suffering. The momentum of the Third Reich could easily have been broken. Hitler was negotiating from boldness, not true military strength. But the old allies convinced themselves they could not go to war over a territory that, like Poland, had not even existed prior to 1918. The Czechs were well fortified and armed, but they were informed that, should they resist, it was *they* who would be held responsible for war in Europe! The surrounding countries, not just Germany, descended like vultures, snatching up whatever territory they could get.

"Inspired by the West's weak-kneed response, the Soviet Union formed an alliance with the Reich. Ultimately, this led to both Russia and Germany invading, and then dividing, Poland. All these conquests were audacious uses of political maneuvering and overt military power. However, it turned into a complete disaster once Russia was betrayed and invaded. Until then, it had seemed there was nothing the Third Reich could not do—"

"—You were *not* just an observer!"

"Eh?" Voss came to a stop.

Nicole pounced. "*Excuse me*, but you were *part* of the Third Reich. The briefing documents I received showed you were a party member. Schichau-Werke, the shipyard where you were a consultant, used slaves. Most of them died of exposure and starvation."

Voss paused, tilting his head back to peer at her through the lower half of his bifocals. "Yes. I am well aware of that. It was war and we took all the workers we could get. In my department, a technological development program, however, we required the utmost security and expertise. Therefore we used no forced labor. You are welcome to inform your superiors of that fact."

"But you *were* a Nazi, a party member?"

"The details are significant. I served my *country*. First in the Imperial Navy, then Reichsmarine of the Weimar Republic, *and* the Kriegsmarine of the Third Reich. We took pride in remaining strictly apolitical. However, by the time I was coordinating projects between the Kriegsmarine and the Reichspost Research Institute, party membership was required for career advancement."

"So, you did it for your career . . ." Sobek smirked.

Voss gritted his teeth. "I am willing to have this conversation this *one* time. And I accept that I owe Miss DeMaes a debt of honesty, if nothing else. I am not sure I owe *you* anything."

"Except a piece of that mother lode of gold you've promised us."

Mike shot Nicole a look. Paul Sobek might be trying to stir up trouble, but there was going to be a detonation of atomic proportions when he discovered Voss had been lying about the gold.

But that was a subject Anton didn't want to explore, and he used a flash of anger as cover. "I became a Nazi for my career, yes?" he snapped. "Okay, good! Do we have this over with now?"

Anton took a breath and turned to Nicole. "You must realize, we have a generational difference. What happened to you, as a Pole, must have seemed like a tsunami, an invasion devastating to your childhood. For me, a German, it came later in life and was a slowly rising tide. What happened evolved from something unethical, to inhumane, to completely murderous, but it took a decade or more.

"Eventually, crowds of people were put on trains. There were stories of camps that brought in vast numbers, yet very little food . . . not a good sign. The authorities did not *tell us* what they were doing, but they also did not hide their actions. Perhaps they wished to activate our imaginations, to send a message: 'Today it is the Jews, but tomorrow it could be *your* family . . . so keep quiet, be obedient.' Perhaps their intention was to make us all a little guilty, to dip us in their sin but not so far that we would drown . . . or object.

"We had been promised that our empire would be self-contained, that it would be 'just us,' the ancient ideal of an Aryan Europe, united by blood. *Family* . . . does that sound familiar? One of the goals of National Socialism was to create a new mythology, an elite tribe within an ancient tradition. Of course, much of this was made up, and *poorly* made up at that . . . but you, of all people, can comprehend the power of that concept."

Nicole drew back, her eyes narrowed.

"Herr Voss." Her voice was as cold as an arctic morning. "My tribe—my *religion*—are as old as time. We survived slavery in Egypt, forty years in the desert, exile in Babylon, the Cossacks . . . and we have survived *your* Third Reich. We mourn our dead, but we have become as strong as the steel in our knives and our guns. Whether you like it or not, we are the well from which the culture of the West is drawn, and we will *still* be here when our enemies have been reduced to the dirt in our fields!"

Nicole's intensity caused Paul Sobek and even Mel Paluso to shift uncomfortably in their seats. But Jack Johnson laughed his pirate's laugh. "You give 'em hell, sister!"

"And there it is." Anton Voss was unfazed. "Another reason for friction between Germans and Jews that is never admitted. Germany was unsure, posturing, struggling to prove it had a unified identity. But inside its borders, its towns, were a people who could trace their history to Abraham, who insisted on their own culture, language, and religion, who clearly knew who they were, no matter what threatened them.

"I was attending university when I became aware of the Nazis as something beyond the stories in the newspapers. They were social climbers. Many young people had come to the cities for the college degrees they imagined would improve their lives. But then the economy collapsed. It is a catastrophe for a society when there are a great number of students who have high opinions of themselves yet are underemployed. Frustrated in their aspirations, they brought politics into the classroom, disparaging and bullying the older professors. They demanded their vision of the world be accepted and were willing to take to the streets if they felt resistance. Their influence was such that the universities would order the police to stand down.

"They attempted to extend their politics into science, discrediting what had become known as 'Jüdische Physik,' Jewish physics, the work of Albert Einstein and others. Academics like to pretend the goal is truth, yet too often they have little interest in fairness, or even honesty."

Nicole was shaking her head. "And the laws for physics are different for Jews? These people were supposed to be intellectuals!"

Mel Paluso took a last bite, tossed his fork onto his plate, and said, "If you're gonna go to war with half the world, seems to me you'd want as many people on your side as possible. Especially scientists."

"Yes, but you are speaking like an American. You have a unique way of defining your nation . . . a contract. We Germans were also obsessed with discovering what could define us. Our borders had changed so many times, there had been so many governments, the question was . . . how do we decide who 'we' are as a nation? The Third Reich chose race. The inspiration was fantasy, mysticism, but we told ourselves it was logical, *scientific*. It is the devilish word of our age.

"There are always those who say, 'If only everyone would do this or that.' Well, *everyone* never does just one thing, so utopia can be created only by force. The Russians wished to manipulate human psychology creating the 'New Soviet Man,' the ideally obedient Communist. The National Socialists promoted 'racial improvement.' More than just breeding a better form of man, the idea was the ultimate embodiment of the unified nation: a tribe, fulfilling our destiny, stemming the degradation caused by other races, all in order to become the mythical heroes we imagined ourselves to be.

"To find employment with the government one had to have a

genealogical certificate of Aryan heritage. To join the party, as I did, there had to be proof of pure German blood going back decades. This was also an early step in the removal from the political arena, and from the possibility of intermarriage, of those we thought of as inferior.

"But you must understand, years before Jews and Gypsies were sent to their deaths, the National Socialists required the elimination of our own Aryan Germans, those who we thought might weaken the nation and pollute the gene pool. Even before he came to power, Hitler discussed culling a 'million burdensome lives,' leaving only the strong. While this may have simply been exaggerated rhetoric, practicing the 'science' of eugenics *was* common in many countries, and it still is. What we eventually did was not new, it was simply more thorough.

"In '33 or '34 medical officials began issuing certificates of genetic health. The unfit were sterilized. This included any determined to be mentally ill as well as chronic 'asocials': alcoholics, drug addicts, criminals, the merely rebellious. Teachers gave schoolchildren the assignment of creating tables of their ancestors. The horror, in this case, was subtle: they were required to innocently pass judgment upon themselves.

"Hitler assumed this level of commitment, the willingness to sacrifice rights, morality, even lives, would be his great achievement. He bragged that he had taught the world the difference between the means and the end. We were asked to see one another as racial comrades participating in a great project to deliver a shining future, the nation unified in a manner that was both ancient and modern, tribal and progressive.

"After the invasion of Poland, the process of 'preemptive intervention' went even further. In order to minimize the wasting of resources precious to the war effort, those considered 'useless eaters' were euthanized. The numbers should not be confused with the entire populations that were killed later on, but rather than doing it to others, rather than doing it out of racial animus, we did it to ourselves!"

"That's mad! Totally bonkers!" Johnson shook his head. "I'd heard all that 'master race' tripe but, well . . . not the details!"

" 'The ends justify the means,' " Nicole stated. "A perfect example of what happens when you allow monsters to ask that question."

Anton's eyes sharpened, and Mike saw a look that he recognized from many hours of watching the older man negotiate business deals. His partner had somehow turned the conversation to the point where he could use it to his advantage.

"Perhaps. It was a frenzy of becoming, of defining ourselves. Except for the scale, it was little different from the witch burnings during the Holy Roman Empire, an extreme case of mass hysteria. But considering whether the ends justify the means? *That* is legitimate. Hitler was tragically mistaken, but he thought he was saving his people." Voss looked at Nicole. "What would it be worth for you to save *your* people? What could it be worth to the future?"

Nicole opened her mouth and blinked several times. Before she could reply Voss broke in: "—Quite a bit, yes?"

He turned to Fowler. "Is there an end that justifies the means for this mission we are on?" There was a bite to the older man's voice that had not been directed toward Mike in many years.

Mike stared back at him. What the hell was Anton up to? Was he challenging him to spill the beans about the fusion device? Voss had no idea what he knew, just that he'd met with the Israelis and they had felt it important enough to send Nicole. If anything, Voss should be thanking his lucky stars Mike and Nicole weren't pressing him for the truth!

"We need to get what we're after and vanish." Mike avoided the exact question. Yet, even as he spoke, he was thinking back to Argentina, to the two gunshots he had heard and Peter Anhaldt informing him that Voss had executed his old friend Konstantin Seegers. Mike looked around the table. No doubt everyone in the room had taken a life, but was the end they were after worth *any* means?

"I ask this because those we are up against are ruthless." Voss turned back to the others, and Fowler felt he had just been tested, but had no idea what the test was, if he'd passed . . . or even if he wanted to.

"The National Socialists took a kernel of science," Voss warned, "in this case genetics, and used it as a lever to manipulate, to implicate, and terrify legitimately patriotic Germans. But *within* the ranks of the Nazi machine there were others, those with a vision of exploiting the currents of history no matter what the outcome. Some of them were true believers in the Nazi cause, more Nazi than German, I would argue. Theirs is an intricately developed philosophy reaching back to the time of Plato. It should never be underestimated just because some of its adherents were thugs.

"Others were outsiders: industrialists, bankers from other countries. Opportunists. If the Third Reich failed, they were prepared to appropriate whatever was of value and move on . . . to play the same game on an even grander stage.

"Well, now we have the Cold War. So convenient. Again, there is still a kernel of science—physics in this case, the undeniable power of the atom. The threat of nuclear apocalypse is used to manipulate the fears of legitimately patriotic Americans and Russians.

"War, instability, change, it is always good for someone. Mister Fowler and I know this very well. If you affect history at a high-enough level, there is no end to what you can gain. So you must realize we are about to try to take something of great value from the most dangerous men in the world. If we are successful, there *will* be consequences . . ."

Voss stared intently at Fowler, then focused on Nicole, communicating directly with them even as he spoke the same words to everyone. "This question of the ends justifying the means needs to be carefully weighed. We have a certain set of ends we wish to achieve . . . and so do they."

CHAPTER 23

IT WAS THE third afternoon out of Talcahuano when they spotted the plane. The sliver fleck winked in the sky, almost invisible against the thin tissue of cloud.

"You see, there it is!" Ihaka Waretini was off watch, but he pointed a thick brown finger at an area roughly 45 degrees above the northeastern horizon. Fowler took the binoculars from Jack Johnson and held them to his eyes.

"Well?" Jack demanded.

"Definitely a plane," Mike said. "How long has it been there?"

"Either he's flyin' a wide circle without ever overtaking us, or there's a hell of a lot more air traffic out here than I think likely. Nikos saw something early this morning. It was there, it was gone. Now here we go again."

"So, what do you think?" Johnson asked. "We can't head southwest forever."

Johnson was right—they had lost a day or more compared to simply sailing straight down the coast. Call it two days. Two additional days where Skorzeny's men would be able to search for the U-boat . . . A month ago Mike would have considered such a number inconsequential but, this close to their goal, it seemed a serious concern. It was also two days lost before Fordyce began searching for them. Fowler could feel his options diminishing like the sand in an ancient navigator's hourglass.

A gray and lonely figure stood amidships looking out at the sea. Fowler pinched his fingers together and whistled. Anton Voss looked around and Mike waved at him to come closer.

"Did you see the plane?" Mike pointed at the sky.

"Yes, yes. He is back. I believe we should slow down."

Mike wasn't sure he heard that right. "Slow down?"

"We will lose them in the weather. You see the sun? By midnight there will be a storm."

"*Blimey . . .*" Johnson muttered. Frowning, Fowler turned, but the Australian was staring into the sky. He shook his head. "A dinkum seaman, that one."

Mike looked up. "You see the halo, mate?" Johnson asked.

The high clouds were feathered by the wind, but around the sun there was a hazy ring, looking for all the world like a great bright eye. "The old codger's right. Eight out of ten, we're in for a blow!"

Voss climbed the ladder; he paid no more attention to the plane or the sky. "Captain Johnson, we do not want our friend above to notice, so you must slowly reduce our speed. Then, as soon as there is cloud cover, we will turn and run toward the coast."

Jack Johnson stepped inside the wheelhouse and checked the barometer. "Hmph!" He reached over the console and nudged the rheostat that controlled the big electric motor that turned the prop shaft. "Koji, back that off another five revolutions in twenty minutes, then another five in forty, okay?"

"Hai!"

Jack grabbed the microphone and hit the 1MC switch. The PA system hummed, and his voice blared throughout the ship. "Secure for weather. Nikos! Out of yer rack and put those new drongos to work. We've got to lighten the bow, so get some of that diesel off the foredeck and top off our tanks. Repeat, secure for weather."

Leaving Johnson and Voss to their plans, Mike dropped down the ladder to the main deck and tapped on Nicole's door.

"Oh, hello. That announcement . . . is something wrong?"

"Not at all. There's a plane keeping track of us, but there's also a storm coming. It's a good bet we can shake them if it lasts long enough."

"A storm!" Nicole was willing to sun herself beside a hotel swimming pool, but she tended to eye any body of water larger than a soup bowl with suspicion. She had faced down enemy soldiers, but somehow the sea provoked a primal fear that Mike had never understood.

He laughed. "Men have been sailing for thousands of years. I think we'll manage to stay afloat. Right now, I've got a project, want to help me out?" He led her down the amidships stairs to a steel door on the corridor that led forward to the hold.

Earlier in the day Johnson had passed along the key to what had been the *Bushranger*'s armory. With Sobek and Paluso feeling that they were losing control of the mission, and the promise of more bad news in the future, Fowler wanted to secure his weapons and explosives.

It took a number of trips and more than an hour before they finished organizing the weapons and loading magazines. By that time the movement of the ship was becoming more and more noticeable. Nicole reached out to grasp a shelf and steady herself. She shook her head and yawned. Fowler stuffed a double handful of heavy brass M19 shells into his pockets. He slung his Browning shotgun across his back.

"What's next?" Nicole asked.

"We need to unpack the clothes and other supplies I sent along. In a couple of days our Australian friends are gonna start to feel underdressed. You too for that matter."

"I'll have you know, Mr. Fowler, that I came prepared. Whatever you packed will fit me like something made by Omar the tentmaker!"

They stepped through the door and Mike set the lock. He glanced over to see Nicole staring down the corridor as it tipped up, and then down. One hand gripped a nearby pipe. Her knuckles were white. The structure of the ship creaked slightly as the bulk of the wave passed beneath them.

"You okay?"

"I—umph . . . I think I'm going to be sick!"

He took her hand. "Upstairs and be quick about it. You need fresh air!"

They barged out onto the boat deck and she collapsed toward the rail, grabbing on as the ship dropped down into another trough. She stared down at the churning waters and moaned.

"Just look at the horizon and breathe deeply," Mike said. The sun was setting, and black clouds were piling up to the southwest. "I'll be back in a moment." He climbed the stairs to the wheelhouse. Ihaka was at the helm and down in the chart room Johnson and Voss were reviewing their course. Mike unslung the shotgun and wiped it down.

"Where can I stash this?"

"Secret stash? Under the seat," the big Māori hooked a thumb at the low bench against the rear wall. Fowler cocked the gun and thumbed shells up into the magazine. Lifting the cushion, he found an ancient set of blackout curtains that must have dated back to the war. He pulled back the first layer and stuffed in the Browning and a few loose shells.

When he returned, Nicole was clutching the rail. She looked at him with haunted eyes. "I think if I could throw up, I'd feel better," she mumbled.

"It looks like they are about to make their turn for the coast. You'd better go below and get some Dramamine from the galley. It could get rough!"

"And this isn't?" She gulped.

"Not yet." He helped her inside and watched her totter unsteadily toward the galley and its supply of medications.

"Here we go . . ." In the chartroom Jack Johnson grinned and switched on the PA system. "Alright, mates, check the schedule, radar is off. We'll be running lights-out so pull your curtains and rig for red."

Johnson stepped up into the wheelhouse and snapped off the deck illumination and running lights; then he took the wheel and Waretini headed out to the bridge wing with a pair of binoculars. After a moment Anton Voss turned to Fowler . . .

"There. We will not be interrupted for a few minutes. I think it is time that I show you the nature of our plan." He led Mike over to the nav station. Beneath the plastic panel was an Admiralty chart of the southern Chilean coast. Their noon position was marked in grease pencil, as were the adjustments that had been made to their speed. Anton made a note of the time and heading, then looked at Mike.

"We are going to the southern archipelago." He indicated an area roughly 54 degrees south latitude, just past the western edge of the Drake Passage on the approach to Cape Horn. "This is not the ship for the kind of weather we will find down there. So, we will enter here"—He pointed to a gap in the shattered line of barrier islands farther up the coast—"at the Nelson Strait and take the Smyth Channel down to the Strait of Magellan. Captain Johnson was intelligent, he bought charts from a variety of sources, but look . . . this is the best of them and even today the coast is still unknown!" Voss gestured to the map.

Fowler peered at it in the dim light. Much of the coastline was indicated by dotted lines and shaded areas rather than the hard boundaries that appeared elsewhere. Only a few of the high points, the mountains or cliffs, appeared in reassuring black ink. A caption read "The coast from Dislocation Harbor to Charles Island is claimed to be from 1 to 1½ miles farther to the westward." It truly was terra incognita.

Mike had a hundred questions but there was only one he thought he could get away with. "Anton? The map you got from Captain Seegers . . . do you actually know where we're going?"

Using Voss's Christian name was intended to get his attention, and Voss looked Mike dead in the eye. "Yes . . . I do now."

"And the map book . . . have you got it locked up?"

"No. But do not worry, there is no X-marks-the-spot. Until it is necessary, I will keep that exact location to myself. My insurance policy, yes?"

Fowler understood; in the pocket of his coat he had an electronic insurance policy of his own. It was like they were all cursed, forced to play an invisible chess game with one another. He wanted an enemy he could punch or shoot, not to suspect the person he had once relied on more than anyone in the world. Mike had another question, and it wasn't going to make the situation any better.

"What happened to Seegers?"

A trace of sadness flickered across Anton's eyes. After a moment he said, "You must realize, Michael, the stakes are very high. More than a simple financial reward."

Was that an answer? Was Voss justifying that he had, in fact, murdered the old captain? Mike's head spun. And there was something else . . . Had Voss just admitted the real goal of their mission had nothing to do with a missing cache of Reichsbank bullion?

"One of us has to tell Jack," Mike growled.

"Tell him *what*?"

Now it was a challenge; Voss was not going to make this easy. Fowler leaned close. "That there's no goddamn *gold*!"

Voss silently appraised him and the moment of vulnerability was gone.

Fowler leaned in even further. "Sobek and Paluso can rot in hell, but Jack is my friend."

"And you would like me to tell him this *now*, with a storm about to break? Will he react favorably to that news?"

Mike hesitated, and Anton's pale eyes flamed.

"What if we are too late? Can we afford the time to settle a dispute that could spread to the whole crew, to Sobek and Paluso? If what we seek is not there, or if it is unrecoverable, none of this will matter! If we are caught, ignorance could be the path to his survival . . . The less everyone knows, the healthier they will remain. *I* will do what is necessary when the time is right!"

"Do not screw with me, Anton. We tell him together, and soon, or I'll do it myself. That 'ends justifying the means' thing? This had better be worth it, because you're putting every friend I have in the world in danger."

Mike was tired of the cryptic games, but he knew that Nicole was right: if he pushed things too far before they arrived it would limit everyone's options with Fordyce, her people, or whatever Voss had planned. He was trapped between honesty and survival.

The storm battered the *Bushranger* for another three days. And Anton Voss—Kapitän zur See Anton Voss—had been correct: the little net tender was not designed for the harsh weather that circled the globe in the latitudes known as the "Furious Fifties."

The fixed cranes that formed her odd dual bowsprit gave her a heavy prow and the gunwale, the waist-high steel wall that would normally help prevent seas from swamping the foredeck, had been omitted, replaced by a removable barrier of pipes and rope. In the *Bushranger*'s wartime role this had allowed large sections of antisubmarine nets and buoys to be easily serviced, and it created an effective work area during a salvage operation, but it was far from the best configuration in a storm.

Torn between manning the helm and the intricacies of navigation, Johnson had finally released the wheel to the German . . . and then became reluctant to take it back. Even in the dark Voss seemed to have an innate sense of what the sea around him was doing.

Mike shared the twelve-to-four watch, day and night, with Ian Ward, one of Johnson's new divers. Situated on the bridge wings they scanned the horizon, as much as they could see, for any hint of light or motion.

Fowler was just coming off watch, heading downstairs to the lower passage, when he ran into Mel Paluso. The man was covered in grease and the skin on his knuckles was torn and bloody. The Italian grinned. "Ya wanted hot water. So, I fixed the boiler. It wasn't easy . . . Stuff keeps movin' around while yer workin' on it!"

A hot shower was just what the doctor ordered, but even as Mike thought about it the ship heeled over and there was a long shuddering impact, then a splintering of wood somewhere above them. Fowler and Paluso stared at each other, then bolted for the internal ladder up to the main deck.

"Come on! That's the lifeboat!" Ihaka Waretini emerged from his cabin and grabbed Paluso, propelling him toward the next level. Fowler scrambled to keep up. Mike could hear Johnson bellowing curses from the wheelhouse above.

"We're on it, boss!" Ihaka yelled, and Mike cracked the hatch on the lee side of the boat deck. He pushed out into the gray maelstrom of wind and water and headed aft. The boat mounted on this side of the ship was large, a 27-footer designed for salvage work. Thankfully, it sat tight in its cradles. They edged past, clinging to the safety line that ran back to the area once occupied by the net tender's three-inch gun.

Spindrift tore around the aft end of the superstructure. As soon as it died away, Fowler stepped out, getting a look at the damage. The forward lifeboat davit had sheared off and the smaller boat was loose, dangling nose down from the remaining lines. The *Bushranger* tipped forward, and the rushing water caught the bow of the lifeboat and smashed it into the side of the ship. Shards of planking whirled away into their wake.

"That boat is no good. Mike, I hold you. You cut it free. Okay?" Waretini passed him a knife.

Mike nodded. The Māori grabbed his left wrist in a hand nearly the size of a catcher's mitt and wrapped his other arm around the safety line. Again the boat crashed into the side of the ship. While it was pinned there, Mike edged out along the tilting deck. He hooked the blade around the falls still connected to the aft davit and cut, sawing back and forth. He was so intently focused he lost track of what was happening around him.

The *Bushranger* plowed down into the foot of a huge wave. A deluge of water washed back along the flank of the ship. The deck shuddered, and the lifeboat line finally parted. The rope ripped through the pulley and struck the back of his hand like a whip. He dropped the knife and it and the ruined lifeboat were torn away into the storm.

A blast of rushing water swept Fowler to his knees. Ihaka held on even as a series of metallic impacts rang through the steel of the deck. The cargo lashed to the foredeck had come loose and drums of diesel and reels of air hose were carried off into the waves only to be washed back, colliding with the hull. Heaving Mike to his feet, Ihaka pulled him back to the safety line. "Like old times, eh?" he bellowed.

. . . And that was when they realized someone was missing.

Mel Paluso was down, struggling in a collapsing torrent of foaming white. He struck the aft railing, frantically grabbing the steel pipes, then wrapping his legs around one of the uprights. But none of that saved him from the gout of water pouring down the deck. The gangster's head disappeared below the surface, and then one of his hands pulled loose.

Fowler didn't hesitate. The port and starboard safety lines converged at the gun emplacement and Ihaka wedged himself into the juncture and again took Mike's wrist in his powerful grip.

Nearly blind from blowing spray, Mike forced himself outward. He bent and grabbed Paluso's leg. The Italian was almost completely over the edge, barely hanging on.

Mike pulled, his injured back straining, and dragged Paluso to safety. Slowly the pitching of the deck fell into a more regular motion. Beneath them the *Bushranger* was settling into a new trough, once again in relative harmony with the waves around it.

When the hatch was finally dogged shut behind them, they stood there, soaked, frozen, and battered. Electric lights glared in the caged fixtures. Warm air circulated through the passageway. Their journey out into the elements had extended no more than thirty yards.

Fowler looked at the water pooling around his feet. He shook his head. "Damn! Can you imagine this on a sailing ship! Fighting your way around the horn!"

The Māori had no choice but to stand up for his own people. "Yeah? Well, *you* imagine paddling to Easter Island in an open canoe!" Mike snorted and punched the big man in the shoulder. Waretini punched back. It was like being gently struck with a kauri stump. The two of them began to laugh.

Paluso looked from one to the other and shook his head. "You guys are crazy!" he said. "You don't get it . . . I can't *swim*!"

Ihaka turned to Mike, struggling to be serious—then gave up. He exploded, the guffaws coming in great coughing gusts. Mike shook his head and slapped Mel Paluso on the back . . . and then they were all laughing. Laughing with the realization that lies behind all humor: you laugh at death; you laugh because whatever it was didn't kill you.

Fourteen hours later the weather cleared, and the Nelson Strait yawned before them. Waretini held to the middle of the passage, noting the high profile of Isla Virtudes, a warning to shift southward to skirt a collection of rocks menacingly labeled "Grupo Lobos" on the map. The Smyth Channel, their route south to the Strait of Magellan, lay just beyond.

After confirming their new course, Johnson joined Fowler on the port bridge wing. For a moment they stood in silence, looking out at the fractured and mist-shrouded landscape. To the southeast the maze of islands and waterways stretched for hundreds of miles, a coastline crushed and torn between the earth's great tectonic plates.

Jack turned and pointed to Anton Voss, who could be seen pacing the foredeck not far from where the drums of diesel and reels of air hose had been before the storm ripped them from their lashings and washed them away.

"You want to bet that cobber's thinkin' the same thing I am?"

Fowler thought for a moment. "You mean, 'Do we have a plan B?'"

Johnson nodded.

The best way to recover the U-boat was to tap into each of the boat's ballast tanks with a separate air line. They would then use the *Bushranger*'s compressor and a set of valves to carefully control the process of blowing the tanks from as safe a distance as possible. The Type XXI Unterseeboot was 251 feet long and displaced 1,819 tons. That was two and a half times the size of the *Bushranger*.

"How much hose do we still have in the hold?" Mike asked.

"Fourteen hundred feet. Maybe a bit less. Divide that by four or five?" Johnson shook his head. "It's not enough. Too little hose if . . . say, she comes up stern first. And we'll be right on top of her if she drags her anchor and starts to drift. A ship that big's a hell of a lot of meat on the hoof, and we're gonna be a thousand miles from nowhere."

Mike didn't like it either. "There's always the German plan . . ." he said.

The original method for recovering the U-Null required using the conning tower as a half-baked air lock and hoping there was enough pressure left in the sub's tanks to blow the ballast. It was an elegant solution but, in typically Teutonic style, it relied on the perfect alignment of several variables. It might have made sense for a boat that had been sitting on the bottom for six months to a year . . . but not for a decade and a half.

Jack laughed. "Not even *I* would come up with an idea that crazy. You get in there, you have trouble, there's no way anyone can get you out! If you want to try it, you're as mad as a cut snake!"

Mike Fowler nodded. They weren't out of options, but lurking in the back of Mike's mind was the fact that in the end they might not actually have to raise the sub . . . All they had to do was find it.

Fordyce's transmitter was still hidden in the shell of the little transistor radio. In fact, he could feel it, tightly zipped into his jacket. And whether they used it or not, Fordyce was going to come searching for them . . . probably with a U.S. Navy destroyer in his hip pocket. The big question was whether Fordyce would honor his end of the deal.

The only one who might get left in the cold was Nicole . . . but Mike Fowler was under no illusions. He would defend Nicole with his life, but his loyalties were not to the Mossad . . . unless the Israelis were willing, and able, to give his friends all the help they needed.

CHAPTER 24

THE WAY SOUTH lay close between forbidding granite slopes. The channel was a strip of dark water so clear and still that it was hard to tell the difference between the rocks below the surface and the reflection of the cliffs above. The clouds drifted low and, like the reflections, it was difficult to tell where they ended and the craggy snowcapped peaks of the southern Andes began. They floated through a strange netherworld where the contradictions of land and sea and sky merged into one.

Occasionally, other passages connected to the rest of the coastal labyrinth, but these were off-limits for through traffic. The well-traveled routes were carefully documented, but the rest of the area was shrouded in mystery. It wouldn't be until they had made their way south of the Straits that they would have the advantage of Captain Seegers's folio of secret and supposedly more accurate charts.

In the long twilight they dropped anchor in a bay surrounded by the barren slopes of tall islands. A semicircle of brush-covered rocks, some barely awash in the shifting tide, enclosed the southern end. Tomorrow they would make the risky sixty-mile run down to the Sea Reach, the western mouth of the Magellan Strait.

After dinner, the first hot meal in several days, Fowler relieved

Ian Ward, who had been on watch. He took a turn around the deck, familiarizing himself with the skyline before darkness closed in. Then he went forward and climbed the narrow steps up the starboard boom. At its end, high over the water, he turned and sat, his back against the cold metal of a huge pulley.

Belowdecks the service generator grumbled quietly, and amidships a small pump emptied water from the bilge. The ship was showing its aft anchor light and not much else.

Around nine o'clock a flicker of illumination spilled across the deck, and a slight figure emerged from one of the hatches. A moment later Nicole spotted him and made her way to the foot of the boom.

"Come on up," he said.

She hesitated, then, gripping the handrail tightly, she climbed the dozen steps and sat on the rectangle of metal just below him. He put his arms around the waist of her jacket, and she slid her hands over his. They remained there silently, relishing a rare moment of privacy, away from the others, away from all the secrets and unspoken tensions that divided the various factions aboard the *Bushranger*.

"Look . . ." Mike pointed to the sky. "Give it a minute, let your eyes adjust."

The constellation of the Southern Cross soared above them, yet it was but five out of a thousand, or maybe a hundred thousand, stars sprinkled across the night sky.

"Enjoy it while you can. I don't know if we'll have much clear weather from here on."

"It makes you feel small. The ocean . . ." She gestured above them. "The distances. Whatever caused all this—" She shivered slightly and pointed at the monstrous crags and shattered rock that surrounded their anchorage.

"Yeah. It kind of keeps things in perspective." There were other things he was thinking, things that needed saying. But they had too much to get through first, too many barriers of patriotism, politics . . . and the dark forces that kept reaching out from the past. It was better, more comfortable, to remain silent . . . and, thankfully, when Nicole spoke, she asked a question that had nothing to do with the two of them.

"Why do you call him Buckets?"

"Who, Johnson?"

"Uh-huh. When the two of you talk, sometimes there's so much argot, um . . . slang I can barely tell what you mean, but every once in a while you call him Buckets."

Mike laughed. "It's an Australian thing. There was an outlaw named Ned Kelly. He became a folk hero, like Billy the Kid in America. He made himself a suit of armor and a helmet. I guess he hoped it would be bulletproof, and it was . . . somewhat. It sure didn't keep him from being hanged later on, though.

"Anyway, as a kid Jack used to play like he was Ned Kelly. He would stagger around the farm with a tin bucket on his head. Of course, he couldn't see out, so I guess it was pretty amusing. His brothers named him Buckets. It's also why this ship is the *Bushranger.* That's Aussie slang for outlaw."

"I understand," she said, ". . . and I understand why you want to tell him what we're really doing."

"As soon as possible," Mike said. "I know you have your reasons; Anton said some of the same stuff . . . but I'm not going to wait forever."

He could feel her nod, and they sat there silently in the dark with the sky all around them.

"So, what's on the sub?" he asked. "Documents? A working reactor? The easier it is to get out, the faster we can get away."

"I can't tell you." She frowned then shook her head in sadness and frustration. "I'm sorry, those are my orders. I can't say anything until we actually find it."

He understood. But it didn't make the situation any easier. "Well, be ready. There's going to be a lot of confusion when we have to admit what we're actually up to. I've got no idea what Voss is planning, but yours isn't the only offer on the table."

She turned her head, breath close on his cheek, her eyes searching his. "Other offers?"

He was under no orders, had no reason to be as guarded as she did . . . or so he thought. "CIA. Or some other faction of American intelligence. It's hard to tell."

"Oh." For a moment her body turned tense and hard, then she drew a breath and let it out. "I must ask you something. It's not fair. I know it's not fair. But when you decide you*'re* going to tell some-one . . . *anyone*. I need you to let me be there. Okay? I need to make my case before things go too far."

Mike nodded, but he fought down a swell of frustration. It seemed inevitable that their loyalties would constantly come between them. Nicole saw her cause as righteous, and he feared she'd always see him as the money-grubbing arms dealer. Yet after a career dealing with the flunkies of many regimes, he had come to the realization that he agreed with Anton Voss: militaries, ministries, and various departments were not governments, and governments were not countries. He even took it a step further: no organization deserved the loyalty given to one's friends and brothers-in-arms. His was a cynic's patriotism, nuanced and mistrustful.

Clouds had begun to move up from the south, dimming the starlit sky, and Mike gave Nicole's shoulder a squeeze. "You'd better go in. We need to make it easy for everyone to mind their own business around here." It was an excuse, but he didn't want her to ask him for anything else.

Before dawn the *Bushranger* hauled in her anchor and started south. As the sky lightened, they traveled under a low, dank overcast that made it seem like they were sailing down a gigantic tunnel. They were pressed, top and bottom, between the gray planes of ocean and cloud, while to either side were broken walls of earth and stone. The bow of the ship eased the still water aside in perfectly rounded wakes that stretched away like a gathering of soft fabric.

Johnson took charge of the wheelhouse, bringing along a cup of coffee as well as his best chart and a crib sheet of the lights and buoys they would expect to see. Ihaka Waretini manned the helm. Ian Ward stood watch out on the heavy boom of the starboard bow crane, with Fowler and Voss on lookout on the bridge wings.

It was just south of Punta Peligrosa that Mike noticed something angular and gray that seemed out of place against the distant backdrop of low, wooded hills. It had begun to drizzle, and he wiped the lenses of his binoculars and looked again, this time making out the last thing any of them wanted to see: the familiar profile of a military vessel.

He stepped into the wheelhouse and pointed. "Warship! South-southeast, two miles!"

Voss snatched the glasses out of his hands. He cursed in German. "Steer for 205 degrees!" he ordered.

"Boss?" Waretini looked at Johnson.

They were closing in on Summer Island. A half mile wide and a hundred feet high, the rock was the most prominent of a dozen obstructions that split the channel in two. On the east side was the passage known as Canal Mayne, while to the west was the far more treacherous Canal Gray. Voss was heading them directly into the teeth of Canal Gray.

"We cannot afford an inspection!" Voss snapped. "If we take the more difficult route, they will be less likely to follow. Perhaps they will believe we have a local pilot." Legally, the *Bushranger* was just over the tonnage that would require them to take on a Chilean pilot.

"Do it," Johnson said, and Waretini adjusted his helm.

Fowler moved quickly to the bulkhead and, grabbing the microphone, clicked on the main circuit. "Miss DeMaes to the wheelhouse, immediately. Um . . . wear something colorful."

Everyone stared at him . . . then Johnson began to laugh. "Be careful, mate. Down here they're liable to stop us just so they can see a woman up close."

There was a tapping of feet on the chart room stairs and Nicole poked her head through the doorway to the bridge. She had a red-and-green scarf tied around her hair. "What in the world is going on?"

Sobek and Paluso were hot on her heels. "Yeah, that's what I want to know!"

"Patrol boat. We need to look very innocent, take their minds off what a ship like this is doing down here. Get rid of that jacket. Go up top." Mike pointed at the roof of the wheelhouse. "When we get across from them, take that scarf off and let 'em see your hair."

She peered out the forward portholes. The Chilean gunboat was closer, but their courses were now beginning to angle apart. Mike thought it looked like a converted U.S. Navy tugboat. The name *Lientur* was stenciled on the bow. "I've got a better idea," Nicole said. "How long do I have?"

Fowler looked at Johnson. "Two minutes," the Australian said.

"Boss, they're slowing down!" Waretini called out, eyeing the patrol boat's motion against the background.

"Are they going to board us?" Sobek fumbled for his wallet, and Mike shook his head. If they did, it wouldn't be like a traffic stop. Certain officers might accept a payoff, but it would take more cash than Paul Sobek had in his pockets.

"Shut up or get off my bridge!" Jack Johnson scowled at him. "We're alright. He's just threading the needle, there's some foul ground over there." He readjusted the chart. "Captain Voss? Take a look . . ."

Voss glanced at the map. "Ja! We must make another course correction immediately."

Jack said, "Ihaka, take her to 220—no, 222 degrees. Give it half a mile, then dial her back by ten revolutions." They were following the course indicated for the approach to Canal Gray, but they were also barreling straight for the southern tip of Isla Orlebar.

"Ready!" Nicole reappeared.

"Perfect!" She had changed into a tight-fitting red sweater and—Mike grinned—she was carrying a camera. "Get up there and take some pictures." In an instant she was out the door and heading for the ladder to the top of the wheelhouse.

"Got to get me one of those," Johnson murmured. "Where'd you find her?"

"Egypt. She was trying to kill me."

"Well, yeah, there *is* that . . ."

Johnson hurriedly flipped through his book of sailing directions for South America. Until the gunboat had shown up, they had planned for the eastern route, Canal Mayne. Now he was scrambling to skim through the pages and make notes on the new course.

"'Black can buoy marked Gray Norte . . . west side,'" he read, and scanned the shoreline. "Okay, got it. Mike, there's gonna be another buoy, a red cone, port side."

Fowler glassed the waterline. He saw nothing. "Ian!" he shouted down to the bow. "Red buoy. Port. Anything?"

The oncoming patrol boat was putting on power; the white curl of a bow wave was visible. In just a few minutes they would pass each other, and then they would know if the officials of the Chilean Armada intended to investigate. Because of the current, and the narrowness of the passage, the farther they got the less likely it was that the patrol would go out of their way to follow them.

Mike ran down the stairs to the boat deck for a clearer view of the water. They were motoring into a gap less than a thousand yards wide. But, if there was a buoy, it marked something dangerous, and that meant the way was narrower than it seemed. In a minute or so the islands would be between them and the Chileans. That was good, but they would also be blind to whether the gunboat was coming after them.

He glanced up to see Nicole casually pretending to snap photos from the rail on top of the wheelhouse. As if on cue, she let the camera dangle from its strap and pulled off her scarf—and then the wind pulled it out of her hands and blew it away.

From a mile off came the blast of a ship's horn.

All eyes were locked on the Chilean vessel. Mike's hands squeezed the binoculars hard enough to turn his knuckles white.

Then, cool as a cucumber, Nicole waved and lifted the camera to snap a picture of the gunboat.

Had she overdone it? Even if they had no suspicions, it would be just like a gallant Chilean to follow them in order to rescue a lady's scarf from the water.

"Red buoy, coming up," Ward called out. Then, "*Aww hell!* Sheer off! Sheer off! It's washed up on the base of those rocks!"

"*Hold starboard!*" Fowler yelled. Ward was pointing toward a rock. The red cone was lying on its side in a pile of kelp with the current breaking around it. Beneath the water more and more of the slick black stone was suddenly visible.

Waretini spun the wheel and slowly the *Bushranger* started to correct. However, instead of coming neatly around, the ship slewed sideways. The tide had turned, and the current was carrying them ever closer to the rocks.

They were clear ahead, so Fowler ran to the port rail and watched as the distance narrowed. Whatever it was that justified the buoy, it was a lot closer than anything he could see. Masses of kelp, indicating shallow water, rippled in the increasing pull of the tide. He clenched his teeth, fearing the grinding of steel on rock . . . but what he felt instead was an increased throbbing from below. Waretini had pointed them onto a safe heading and increased power. In a moment they were heading back out into the widening channel.

Nicole came down the ladder behind him. She retied the scarf, this time around her neck. Fowler laughed with relief. "I thought you lost that."

"The railing caught it. Are we safe?"

"For the moment. If they are coming after us it'll take them a few minutes to turn around."

But the patrol boat seemed to have continued on and, half an hour later, in a blowing squall of rain, they rejoined the main route down the Smyth Channel. Giving Shoal Island a wide berth meant they were again gripped by the tide, and Johnson was forced to pour on the power. He got an earful from Colin McLeod in the engine room, but off to the east below a high promontory, Fowler could make out the rusted bow of a wrecked freighter protruding from the water, a stark reminder of what the local currents were capable of.

By afternoon the *Bushranger* had emerged from the Smyth Channel and into the western end of the Magellan Strait, the innermost passage that allowed shipping to bypass the tempestuous seas off Cape Horn. To the north, the rocks along Tamar Island, Roda Pass, and the Tamar Peninsula formed the shattered upper jaw of the strait and had become a graveyard for every ship driven off course by the wind, waves, or current. Through the heave of surf and explosions of spray all that could be seen was a jumbled mass of rusting hulls and bleached timbers.

The most convenient anchorage was Port Tamar, but Anton Voss demanded they press on as long as they could. It was still midafternoon, and he hoped they could make it down into Long Reach, the next section of the Strait, before darkness fell. Voss was right; there was no telling when they might accidentally alert the Chileans or run into the Brotherhood, the CIA, or even the Soviets. But with the day waning, Mike feared their chances of finding a safe anchorage were running thin.

As the sun sank in the west the higher cloud formations began to blow away, illuminating a panorama of fantastic beauty and grandeur. Ocean-filled canyons led off in all directions. Shimmering veils of rain or talcum-fine ice crystals blurred the distance and then collapsed, revealing monumental saw-toothed mountain ranges capped with snow. Occasionally, streams gushed from the high cliffs. Black-and-white Commerson's dolphins arced through the water just ahead of the bow, and small bergs of ice floated past, slowly melting in the warmer temperatures carried in from the Pacific.

There was more traffic in the strait than there had been in the Smyth Channel. In all they spotted half a dozen small craft as well as a freighter. Some were underway, but it also meant that the few bays along the coast of Desolación Island and the Córdova Peninsula were already occupied. They found nowhere they could lay up without attracting attention. There was no choice but to grimly sail on, ever closer to the crags and fierce currents of Crooked Reach.

Night turned the blue of the sky to black, and they continued southeast under a river of stars. Eventually, Johnson was forced to make a decision: they had to accept the next stopping place they found, occupied or not. Because it was across the channel from the next navigational beacon, a spot named Field Anchorage seemed the easiest to locate. It was a great relief when Fowler spotted a distant glow that slowly resolved itself into the automatic light on Radford Hill. Soon they were making a turn to the north.

"Come to seventy-two degrees, and reduce revolutions," Johnson ordered.

Waretini put the helm over. "Seventy-two and dead slow, boss." They carefully entered into the mouth of a shallow bay bracketed by slopes that rose more than a thousand feet into the darkness. A small island blocked their way and, rather than attempting to explore a route around it, Johnson let go his port anchor. Once he had run out a certain amount of chain, he dropped the starboard one as well.

Everyone breathed a sigh of relief. They were out of the main passage and safe for the night . . . or so they thought.

Johnson again posted a lookout, with Fernando Zúñiga taking the first turn. If another patrol boat showed up, they would need to appear as innocent as possible. On the other hand, should they be discovered by Skorzeny and his men . . . well, an entirely different response would be called for.

During the previous two days Fowler had quietly pulled aside Johnson, Frank Jano, Fernando, and Koji Yamada, and run them through the manual of arms on the FG 42 automatic rifles, requiring them to repeatedly demonstrate the peculiarities of its operation. Mike wasn't entirely sure about the newer members of the *Bushranger* crew, but the Japanese seemed quietly competent and he handled the exotic German weapon with the confidence of a professional.

Throughout the day Nicole had made it a point to help Clarence Benham prepare and serve their meals. Her seasickness had passed, and she was able to deliver sandwiches and coffee to the bridge and engine room, even in the heavy rollers at the mouth of the Sea Reach.

"I could have a career as a ship's cook," she said as she placed a stack of clean dishes into their storage rack and Mike filled a thermos of coffee to take to Fernando. "Where I come from, we make meals for big families and the food is very boring!"

He laughed, although he didn't know if she was talking about Poland or Israel. Pulling on his jacket, he headed outside into the blustery night. When he came back Nicole was gone. Glancing up the passageway, Fowler saw someone blocking the door to her cabin.

Mike felt his senses sharpen, felt his thoughts drop away. A mumble of voices came to him as he closed in. "—listen, chickie, if you want a shot at what's on that sub, first you're gonna have to find a way to satisfy *me* . . . you catch my drift?" Then, "Hey! Don't watch me, jackass! Close the door and watch the hallway!"

The man in the doorway turned. It was Iannucci, and Mike fired a high right that snapped his head back. The tall man went down in a pile. The latch had just clicked shut but Mike stepped back and kicked the door alongside the knob. The panel exploded, splitting in two . . . and just as he stepped through the gap Paul Sobek began to scream.

Nicole had his right wrist gripped in one hand and was viciously bending two of his fingers backward in a joint lock with the other. Sobek tried to pull her off balance and strike with his other fist, but she turned without loosening her grip, forcing his elbow straight with her hip. She twisted his fingers further and drove him to the floor.

There was a clatter of running footsteps and Fowler turned, ducked under a punch thrown by Eduardo Suarez, and came up inside. He got a couple into the diver's gut but took one on the shoulder and then the ear. It was a stunning blow, and he raised his arm to block another, then hooked a thumb toward the man's eye. Suarez lurched back and Mike slammed a knee into the side of his thigh.

"*Rummy!* Hold up!"

Mike broke off as Suarez staggered away. Someone stepped past him, and Mike recognized Johnson forcing the diver back against the bathroom door. Sobek let out another bleat and Jack pointed at him. "Mate! Stop struggling! Sheila's gonna break your fingers *and* that wrist!"

Fowler realized someone else had entered the cabin. Nikos Cacoyannis had gotten past him while he was busy with Suarez. Nicole had cautiously circled away from the Australian diver, the move that had caused Sobek to cry out. Mel Paluso stood in the passageway, looking on in an amused fashion but not making any move to enter.

Johnson looked at Nicole. "You can let him go now. I think we have this under control."

After a moment she relaxed, releasing her hold on Sobek's hand. There was a moment of silence. A breeze buffeted around the superstructure and the ship rocked on the small waves coming in off the strait. Sobek carefully got to his feet.

Once he had fully straightened up, Nicole pivoted with a speed the eye could barely follow. A delicate foot, clad in a not so delicate boot, smashed into the gangster's crotch.

Sobek tried to cry out and suck air at the same time. He bent over and then rolled to the floor. Every man in the room winced, and there was silence as Nicole DeMaes, or whatever her name was, glanced around as if to see if she had any other challengers.

Jack Johnson snorted, choking back a laugh. He shook his head in mock sadness.

Then there was a throbbing impact, the deck under their feet tilted, and the *Bushranger* swung, coming up short at the end of her chains with a bang.

Everyone staggered, Paul Sobek collapsed, and throughout the length of the ship there was the clatter and clash of unsecured items hitting the deck.

A shuddering roar tore along the flanks of the vessel, a blast of katabatic wind howling between the stanchions and through the wire rigging. Mike and Jack locked eyes as the deck heeled over even farther.

A faint cry came from outside. *"Man overboard!"*

Fowler and Johnson nearly collided in the doorway, Fowler dodging aside so Jack could go first. Everything was still at an angle as Johnson grabbed the rail of the ladder and heaved himself upward, while Mike tried to force the hatch to the deck. It opened an inch or two, then the icy gale slammed it back. Nicole joined him but, at barely more than a hundred pounds, she was little help.

"Move aside, sister . . ." Mel Paluso put his shoulder to the hatch and pushed. The metal panel opened a foot, then two, enough for Mike and then Nicole to squeeze through. Mike ran forward, the force of the wind nearly taking him off his feet, while Nicole had to pull herself along, hanging onto the inboard rail.

"Mr. Fowler! There!" Koji had somehow managed to throw a life ring over the side. But the wind had carried it thirty yards away from the churn of white water where someone was struggling to stay afloat in the darkness. Mike started to strip off his jacket only to have it pulled from his shoulders by Nicole. He handed her his pistol, then slipped between the chains that formed the foredeck railing. The williwaw nearly tore him loose and spray lashed his face and body like birdshot. He bent his knees and dove toward the black water.

It was like hitting frozen iron. Cold and hard and black as sin. He came up swimming, a pattern ingrained in his muscles. As soon as his head cleared, he tore a ragged breath into his lungs and aimed himself at the pale line that was the rope connected to the life preserver. Getting a loop of it under his arm, he struck out in what he hoped was the right direction. Then a hard bar of white lanced through the night, a searchlight on the *Bushranger*. In its beam was a body, still feebly struggling.

Mike's clothes and boots pulled him down, every move made clumsy and inefficient. The shock of the cold was wearing off. He had a few minutes, just a few, before hypothermia got its claws into him, sucking the life from the core of his body. Until then he was going to make the most of it, swim while he had the chance, do what he had to do.

The rope paid out, then tightened as the life ring banged against his arm. Fowler rammed a hand through it and slowed, positioning himself behind the drowning man. He got an arm around the man's chest and started back. After a moment the rope attached to the life ring tightened as the men on deck began to pull.

The cold hit him, really hit him, as Koji, Ian, and Clarence struggled to haul Fernando—it was Fernando Zúñiga, of all people—out of the water. Another ring was lowered over the side, but when Fowler finally got a hand over the flared edge of the deck, he was shaking so hard he could barely hold on.

As soon as they had him inside, Johnson lifted him up, helping to strip off his clothes. Mike tried to speak but his teeth were chattering and his breathing wasn't right. They rolled him in a blanket and took him to Nicole's cabin where it was warm and the lights were dim. After a moment she crawled under the covers of the bunk, hugging him from behind as Anton Voss pushed a hot-water bottle wrapped in a towel against his chest.

Mike Fowler accepted all of this. He would recover. He knew that as long as he had the energy to shiver, he would be okay. An hour went by, and he found his body relaxing, the spasms of shaking passing. That felt so good he drifted off to sleep.

He dreamed of different worlds. Of San Diego before the war, a time so simple and pure that poverty was seen but not felt. His father, never more than a dollar ahead, always confident, at least in front of his son. The Pacific with its bright sun and puffy clouds, its floating bodies and bloody beaches. History changed by a flash that put the sun to shame. Time divided before and after "the bomb." African soldiers, uncomfortable in their surplus boots, awed by the cannon he was teaching them how to fire. Cannon that, no doubt, had fought at the Somme in 1916 . . . and again in 1940. Struggling Europe, rebuilding brick by brick, tanks at checkpoints, circling bombers, steaming missiles, and hidden away on a mysterious island, the future that Fordyce promised: peace, gleaming towers, flying cars. The land of tomorrow, tranquil and sanitary. Science fiction. A possibility that at once existed, and did not, impossible and yet . . .

. . . a movement woke him, brought him back.

He watched through slitted eyes as Nicole quietly moved about the cabin. The glowing red ring of a portable heater was the only light, but he could see her picking up fragments of wood from the broken door and placing them in the wastebasket. She set her chair back onto its feet, then placed his revolver on the seat. Picking up his down jacket, she slipped the shoulders over the back of the chair . . . and paused.

Feeling something in the inside pocket, she pulled out the shell of the transistor radio that Fordyce had used to disguise his special transmitter. She stared at it and, though it was too dark to tell, Mike thought she was frowning. A well-trained operative, she was probably wondering why he was carrying a cheap AM radio in a place like this . . . it wasn't like he could tune in and catch a ball game. He stayed very still, waiting to see what she would do. The type of radio was more common in the U.S. than Europe, but if she was familiar with it she'd realize it was a bit heavier than it ought to be. She shook it slightly, glanced back at his supposedly sleeping form, then replaced it in the pocket. A moment later she was climbing back over him and into bed.

CHAPTER 25

EAST OF SANTA INÉS ISLAND,

fourteen hours later . . .

THE *BUSHRANGER* SPENT all afternoon creeping ever deeper into the gloomy labyrinth along the Bárbara Channel. At the narrowest point they were careful to wait for the few minutes of slack tide. Then, with just enough speed to maintain steerageway, they eased through, making liberal use of the ship's echo sounder. They were only a few miles south of the Strait of Magellan, but that was already beyond the rim of the world as defined by the commonly available charts.

Since they had left the wind-torn bay at Field Anchorage, Anton Voss had been annoyingly secretive about the course they had to follow. He paced the bridge trapped in a fog of tobacco smoke, constantly turning pages and rereading sections of Seegers's book. He gave directions to Jack Johnson with only a few miles to spare, always time enough to execute the required maneuver, but never allowing for a moment of relaxation.

Even as Fowler and Fernando Zúñiga were recovering from hypothermia, tensions aboard the *Bushranger* were running high. In the dim hours of the previous morning, probably not long after Fowler witnessed Nicole examining his transistor radio, Anton

Voss, Jack Johnson, Ihaka Waretini, and Colin McLeod had conducted a raid.

Sobek and his henchmen had finally gone beyond the stage where Jack was willing to tolerate their presence as an armed, and intermittently hostile, force aboard the *Bushranger*. Packing Jack's and Anton's pistols, the four had ambushed the two gangsters, as well as Iannucci and Suarez, as they slept. Rousting them out of their bunks and confining them to a corner of the compartment, Johnson searched each man as well as their baggage and confiscated a variety of weapons.

Once Fowler was awake Johnson and Voss reported what had happened, "I told 'em, if there's any more trouble, someone's gonna get to play Robinson Crusoe . . . 'less of course he finds himself dead in the troublemaking process."

"They will be more compliant once we arrive at our destination," Voss said . . . and he fixed Mike and Nicole with an intense look, as if they all shared a secret for the same reason, as if he couldn't guess that each might have their own agenda.

Mike glanced over at Nicole, but she didn't blink. She was as good a poker player as Anton.

"We found a few pistols," Johnson said. "More than I imagined, and there was also an M3!" The Australian was referring to a compact .45-caliber submachine gun. Its crude but effective design had led to American soldiers dubbing it the "Grease Gun" during World War II and in Korea.

Fowler laughed. "No kidding!"

"Strewth. They hid it in with their diving kit. Now those bludgers have had their fangs pulled, I think we can worry less about any bad behavior." Johnson handed over a pile of clothing, and he and Voss left the cabin.

Mike began to dress. As he pulled on his shirt Nicole laid a hand on his arm. "It will be okay. Just a few more days, then you can tell Jack everything," she whispered.

His silence felt like betrayal, and she knew it.

The *Bushranger* pressed ever southward through a wilderness of watery passages. Johnson ran with lookouts at the top of the wheelhouse and on the bow, sharp eyes alert for the kelp, turbulence, or underwater shadows that indicated a hazard. Each channel had to be chosen with careful attention to Seegers's charts. Some were dead-end fjords, others flowed back into the mainstream but had openings between the scattered rocks that were far too narrow for anything but a canoe or rowboat.

Late in the afternoon, Voss ordered them to make an abrupt turn to the west, into the blowing rain. At first it seemed they were heading for a large cove, but the gap opened deeper and deeper, becoming a widening three-mile-long path that led to a bay strewn with breaking reefs and low islands.

Wind thundered through the gap and Waretini increased power as the *Bushranger* plunged forward against the gale. Two hours later they were confronted with one last challenge. To reach the marked anchorage they had to steer an S-shaped path between a pair of offshore rocks and a fingerlike spit of sand. The map book described it as a Schiebetür, a sliding door, that cut off access to the protected part of the bay.

"Steer three hundred degrees. Reduce revolutions." Voss gave the orders, but Ihaka still waited for Johnson's nod.

"Aye-aye, three hundred . . . hold on . . ." The Māori added a spoke to compensate for the wind. "Okay, three hundred. *Oh, hell, mate!*"

The cloud cover had been shifting and suddenly, in addition to the eye-tearing wind, the sun appeared. In an instant they were driving straight into a blinding reflection off the water, and the storm-scummed portholes of the wheelhouse turned as white as frosted glass.

Johnson leaped for the port wing and Anton and Mike scrambled to the opposite side, crowding in behind Koji, who was squinting between the barely parted fingers of one hand. The *Bushranger* was plowing into a narrow gap and at the point they would have to turn, there was barely two hundred yards to spare.

"Koji! Sonar!" Jack bellowed.

As the Japanese slipped inside, Fowler stepped into his place. There were rocks to the right of them and the island to the left, with more rocks less than two ship lengths ahead. Their speed was barely enough to make the rudder bite and now the wind was pushing them closer and closer to the shore.

"Rocks starboard! Port your helm!" Koji yelled. The sonar stylus scratched frantically. Then, "Rocks ahead! *Rocks ahead! Turn port! Turn!*"

They hit, a long grinding impact that reverberated throughout the ship.

The *Bushranger* drew around eleven feet, and deep within the hull steel scraped and moaned. Stone was visible beneath the water and Mike saw a plume of debris drifting away. A sea monster raking them with its claws.

"*Attention! Attention!* Ready for the new heading?" Voss was holding the pages of the map tightly, so they didn't tear in the wind.

"No time like the present . . . damn you!" Johnson yelled out.

"Two hundred fifty degrees! Two. Five. Zero. Schnell! Schnell! Halt! Good! Stay at 245."

Waretini held the wheel tightly and, as the ship straightened, Fowler was aware that Voss had perfectly assessed the wind and the torque effect from the prop, correcting himself even as they changed course.

The grinding stopped.

"There! We are free. Give us one thousand yards, then steer three hundred degrees."

"Aye. One thousand yards, then three hundred."

Everyone exhaled. Johnson whispered a string of curses that began with the mundane and ended with the exotic.

Twenty minutes later one anchor splashed down, then the other. They were in the middle of a protected bay surrounded on all sides by distant mountains and low dark islands.

Johnson got on the engine room intercom. "Finished with engines. Colley, meet me forward, we gotta check for damage!"

He headed downstairs and the lights flickered as the service generator fired up. Waretini called Frank Jano, asking him to take the first watch and to wash the wheelhouse portholes. Then he put the charts away and went below.

Mike Fowler remained on the bridge, gazing out at the primeval world that surrounded them. Except for a pair of cormorants winging low over the water, it was a place devoid of life. Giant slabs of wet and angled stone dotted the surface of the bay. In the distance, glacier-capped ridgelines receded to infinity in all directions.

The setting sun produced a massive shimmering rainbow that stretched from horizon to horizon. Mike wasn't sure if the sight was appropriate or ironic. God's promise that the world would never again be ended in a deluge hung over a rain-drenched and flooded landscape. And if there was a pot of gold at the end of that fading multicolored arc, they were definitely headed in the wrong direction.

In the main deck corridor Fowler found Paluso waiting for him. "Hey, pal, something's up. I think you need to be a part of it."

"What?"

"You'll see. Just don't tell us to shut up until we've had our say."

Paluso led him down the passage toward the wardroom. They were joined by Nikos Cacoyannis, who was bringing a package down from the chartroom, and at the end of the hallway Johnson and Voss appeared. Jack's clothes were greasy, and his shoes and the knees of his trousers were soaked with dirty water. Fowler waited for them at the door.

"Serious damage?" Mike asked.

"We checked the sounding pipes," Johnson said. "The bilge is okay, but there's water in the forward ballast tank, a lot more than there should be. We got the pump running but . . . I don't know. Come morning, I'm gonna put one of my guys over the side to have a look." Johnson cursed. "That damn tank top's rusty, I don't like the idea that it's all there is between me and Davy Jones!"

The wardroom was crowded. Flanked by Iannucci and Suarez, Paul Sobek glowered at the group from a seat in the front corner of the room. Paluso walked over to stand beside him. They had kept a low profile since the events of the previous night, but now something new was clearly brewing.

Voss took a seat, looking warily around. With Waretini at his side Jack Johnson pushed forward until he was an arm's length from Paluso. It was his ship, and he wasn't going to be upstaged by anyone.

Clarence Benham and Colin McLeod watched from the pass-through to the galley. That was wise; if fighting broke out, they wouldn't be in the thick of it. Nicole had positioned herself against the back wall. Fowler could see that her right hand was buried in the pocket of her jacket. He had no doubt she was gripping the butt of his Remington .380. Mike's Smith & Wesson was back in its holster in front of his right hipbone, but he didn't get the feeling they were headed for violence . . . This was some new kind of trouble.

"Okay!" Paluso got everyone's attention. "Paul and me, we put a bunch of cash into this caper. So, now we're out here, sneakin' around in the middle of nowhere, and you—" He pointed at Voss. "—you're keepin' us in the dark. We want to know where we're going, and we want to know *now*!"

Everyone turned to look at Anton.

Without a flicker of expression, Voss said, "Yes. I appreciate that you and your associate have made investments. Your aid has been irreplaceable and very soon you may have a further role to play. I recommend you do not rush things."

"There's some of the rest of us, we want to know, too," Nikos spoke up. "We've come halfway around the world, been shot at with machine guns, maybe we're accessory to crimes. We want to know how much farther we have to go."

He pulled something off the console behind him and placed it on the table. It was Captain Seegers's map book and a pile of

Hydrographic Office charts. Cacoyannis turned to Johnson. "Boss? If you know, show us. If you don't, let's find out. All of us."

Fowler was watching as Jack's eyes narrowed. Cacoyannis's performance had definitely taken him by surprise. In his corner Sobek smirked to himself. Had he wound up this toy just to see what would happen? Was he looking to get an angry response that would polarize the rest of the ship's company in a way he could exploit?

The veins in Jack's neck bulged, and he took a breath, ready to blow Cacoyannis's hair back . . . then he shifted his approach.

"Just who is this 'we' you're whinging on about? You part of a *group*? Have you thrown in with these . . . passengers?" Johnson gestured toward Sobek, Paluso, and their two goons. He then looked over at Koji, who shook his head, and back toward the galley where McLeod rolled his eyes and looked disgusted. Ian Ward, on the other hand, stared at his shoes.

Cacoyannis stood his ground. "No, mate. It's just the question of the day, innit? They've got their concerns, but I'm just sayin' what's got to be on everyone's mind."

Johnson tacked again. "Did you take that book from my chart room? You know the rules: when something goes in there . . . it does *not* leave!"

Nikos tried to stare defiantly at his captain, but he was not quite up to it. Jack Johnson's cold blue eyes cut right through him.

"*Say* it!"

"Yeah. I took it. But it's time we—"

"—Mr. Cacoyannis, go replace Mr. Jano on watch. I'll deal with you later."

Nikos hesitated, but his new friends weren't coming to his defense . . . and it wouldn't matter if they did.

"Now!"

The diver took a step back and then shuffled from the room.

Fowler kept an eye on Sobek and Paluso. He remembered how Nikos had slipped past him during the fight in Nicole's cabin. Had he been going to Sobek's aid? *That* was an interesting question.

When the door closed Anton Voss started to rise . . . but Johnson wasn't through.

"Hang on! Now that's over, *I* think Mr. Paluso has a point."

Voss froze, and Sobek sat up in his chair.

Johnson went on, "We took some damage back there, and I'm not going out into the dog's breakfast they call weather down here till I know the extent of it. We lost one of our lifeboats back in that storm, and nearly two thousand gallons of diesel went over the side . . . more than half of our air hose, too.

"Assuming we can get what we came for, the next problem is how we get away. We've got enemies. So, Chile and Argentina, we don't stop there if we can avoid it. That means as soon as I can break radio silence, I gotta reserve as much fuel as I can at Port Stanley in the Falklands. The more I know, and the sooner I know it, the happier I'm gonna be. And right now, Mr. Voss, making me happy is a priority."

Voss glanced at Fowler as if expecting some kind of support. But Anton had been digging this hole for quite a while. Mike was no longer ready to go to war simply because he had been told the two of them were working toward a common end. Based on his unquestioning trust in Anton Voss, he had gotten himself, Jack and his crew, and even Nicole into this mess.

Fowler held Anton's gaze. "Mr. Voss, it's time to 'fess up. You show us where we're going. Believe me, it's the *least* you could do." Mike let that last sentence lie there . . . like a threat.

Johnson pushed the map book across the table and for a moment it looked like Voss might dig in his heels. But after a moment he drew a long, controlled, breath. Moving Seegers's book aside, he unfolded one of the large U.S. Hydrographic Office maps labeled "South Extreme of America, Sheet II."

As everyone gathered around, he pointed and said, "This is where we are. Please take the opportunity to look carefully, I do not wish to repeat myself. Tomorrow we must head southwest again. We will cross Stokes Bay and proceed like this . . . through the

Wakefield Channel . . ." He indicated a passage between a vaguely delineated landmass south of Isla Santa Inés and the broken line of the Grafton Islands, the last shred of land between South America and the distant frozen wilderness of Antarctica. "Then we will turn northeast."

"But . . . ?" Sobek could easily see the problem. Voss was pointing at a spot well within the mountainous center of Santa Inés Island.

"You are thinking, it is an odd place to hide a U-boat, ja?" Voss raised his finger, lecturing . . . "I will argue it is the *best* place to hide a U-boat!" He reached for the book of German maps, flipping through the thick pages.

"Here!" Konstantin Seegers's carefully drawn chart snapped the entire southwest coast of Santa Inés into focus, revealing it to be a deeply fissured landscape completely unlike what was presented on the Hydrographic Office publication. "We are going here." Voss was now pointing just east of a long narrow waterway that nearly split the land in two. He indicated a fjord that forked, with one of the channels leading to a cul-de-sac below a glacier-filled valley.

"It is less than one hundred kilometers. So, tomorrow. Depending on the weather, depending on everyone's cooperation, we will arrive. *That* will be the moment of truth."

Mike looked down at the carefully inked shorelines, the tick marks that indicated latitude and longitude, and the fancy old-fashioned compass rose with an added circle in degrees. The mountain slopes were beautifully rendered, and there were elegant frames displaying silhouettes of the relevant horizons and hand-lettered captions written in Sütterlin, the eye-punishing script eventually banned by Adolf Hitler.

It was the craftsmanship of an earlier generation. A secret map to a hidden treasure, not of gold, but of something else. Something the CIA, Mossad, the KGB, and the consortium of postwar industries created by Universal Tabulation and Processing, once the beating heart of the National Socialist state, thought was the most valuable thing in the world.

Leonid, the mysteriously crippled scientist, had implied the theory that made fusion possible predated the Nazis. Anton Voss suggested the financial powers behind the Invisible Reich had their origins in the era of chaos at the end of the Holy Roman Empire. And Yaron, the Israeli officer who might or might not be Nicole's superior, had pointedly asked about a nearly forgotten Greek god, one of fertility . . . or accident.

Mike Fowler shook his head in wonder. In just a few days' time layers of history were going to be laid bare. And then they would have to make a deal with a variety of devils . . . or run for their lives.

CHAPTER 26

THE SOUND EMERGED from the drumming of rain on the deck. It was about twenty minutes after Cacoyannis had gone down to make the final repairs on the *Bushranger*'s hull and at first the distant roar of the jet engines could have been mistaken for wind or thunder.

Mike Fowler was kitted out in a dry suit made of green rubber. Underneath he wore long underwear, a thick sweater, and a knit cap, all made of wool. The suit went on tunnel-style, with the diver stepping into the lower part of the suit through a hole in the chest. He then ducked his head and upper body into the top and wrestled his way into the sleeves and hood. A dusting of cornstarch was used to lubricate the tight openings at the wrists. The "tunnel" was then gathered up doubled over and tied off with several lengths of rubber tubing. A weight belt, tank and dual hose regulator, fins, and a mask were laid out so that he could quickly gear up and dive. If anything went wrong, it was his job to effect a rescue.

The close-fitting hood made it difficult to hear, so Fowler's first indication that something was wrong was when he glanced up and saw Nicole. She had been watching the operation from the boat deck, her head covered with one of the crew's sou'westers. Out of the corner of his eye he noticed that she suddenly swept off the oil-cloth hat and was turning one way and then the other, scanning the sky. That was when Mike heard it. The sound grew closer, passing overhead, echoing off the mountainsides and rumbling through the black-bottomed clouds. The plane remained invisible, but it was a ghostly reminder that they were not alone . . . or forgotten.

Voss scowled at the sky but then returned to pacing from one bridge wing to the other. A moment after the sound faded Paul Sobek appeared, followed by Iannucci. Both looked wildly around, as if they imagined the next step might be a strafing run. Fowler wouldn't have put it past Skorzeny, providing that the aircraft was his. But Mike's first thought was that it had been the Agency Canberra that Fordyce had promised would regularly overfly the area, searching for his signal. The B-57 Canberra was a compact twin-engine bomber that had evolved to take on high-altitude reconnaissance and electronic warfare operations. Fordyce had suggested they wouldn't come in low enough to be noticed unless they received his signal, but Mike had no idea if the CIA man could be trusted to stick to his plan . . . or even if he was still in charge.

The jet did not return. The *Bushranger*'s radar was turned off, and Fowler hoped the aircrew had no other way to detect their presence. Then he got that feeling of eyes boring into the back of his head. Mike turned. It wasn't Sobek, or even Iannucci, who surely owed him one for the punch he'd received two nights before. It was Nicole. She was hunched in her parka and her breath steamed in the cold, obscuring her face. Was she staring at him, suspicious that he was involved with an agenda that included the mysterious aircraft? If so, he didn't know if she was right or wrong.

His first inclination was to shrug, to indicate that he was as mystified by the unseen plane as she was . . . but he stopped himself. That was what he wanted to communicate to the woman he cared about, but she was also the agent of a government he wasn't the least bit certain he could trust.

Mike Fowler had long ago made his peace with the idea of drowning, being shot, stabbed, or blown to pieces. The idea that stress might give him a heart attack or ulcers or something of the sort was an entirely new problem. There was only so much he could do, so he simply turned away and walked back to where Koji and Ihaka were tending the carefully organized network of ropes, hoses, and wires that hung over the ship's side.

Ignoring her suspicions was a mistake . . . but he didn't realize that until later.

Johnson and Fowler had gone to find Cacoyannis after the previous night's meeting had broken up, and Mike had been interested to see how Jack handled this particular disciplinary problem. In the old days Mad Jack Johnson would have given a disobedient underling a thorough dressing-down, the sort of thunderous course correction provided by drill sergeants worldwide. Mike was relieved to discover a more mature Jack Johnson had a different strategy in mind. Their little crew didn't need any more internal strife than it already had.

"There's a minor breach in the forward ballast. I don't like what you did just now, but you're the best wet welder I've ever seen. So, come daylight, you get down there an' make the repair . . . Do that and I'll take it into account."

Cacoyannis looked like he was about to cut loose with some self-righteous objection, but he swallowed it and said, "Yeah, boss."

"And you leave Sobek and those others alone. Rummy here's known them for years and they are *bad* bloody news!"

Given the temperature of the water, the work had to be broken up into carefully organized shifts. Ian Ward had been first over the side. He wore a dry suit, fins, weights, and a Jack Browne–style free-flow mask. The tight-fitting triangular face mask enclosed the diver's mouth and chin and allowed him to breathe air supplied through a hose from the *Bushranger*'s compressors as well as to communicate topside through a telephone cable. Ward's job was to scout the damage to the boat and make an assessment of the necessary work. The dive only lasted about fifteen minutes.

"How was it down there?" Johnson asked as soon as Jano shut down the compressor.

"Damn cold! She's dented up pretty good, but I tested it with kapok, and I could only find one breach. It's about so long . . ." Ian indicated a space of about six inches with his fingers. Fowler was amused; the kapok trick was one he had learned during the salvage operation at Pearl Harbor. A diver spread handfuls of the cotton-like fluff in a suspect area and watched to see if the suction from the ship's pumps drew it into a break.

"Alright," Johnson said. "You work with McLeod. Get a patch cut and shaped. Meanwhile Koji'll prep the area."

The *Bushranger*'s derrick mast swung a diving stage over the side and Koji Yamada carefully adjusted a flip-down welding shield over the straps of his mask, then arranged and tied off his tools: a pneumatic grinder and drill, wire brush and hammer, and finally the heavily cabled stinger, the pistol grip that held the wax-insulated welding rods. The diver's lifeline, air line, and comms wiring were all bundled together. Coiled separately were the additional air line for the power tools as well as the electrical wiring for the arc welder.

Koji's first job was to tack-weld a pad eye, a section of steel with a hole drilled in it, on either side of the worksite. These would allow the divers to secure themselves when the pull of the tide or the pressure of the wind caused the ship to drift.

The speaker crackled. "Go hot!" In the machine shop Frank Jano closed a heavy copper knife switch and sent direct current to the stinger so that Yamada could begin welding. He would then hook on and go to work cleaning the hull down to bare steel. The next step would be to drill a hole at either end of the tear in the metal of the ship's hull. This would keep the split from spreading should the area be subjected to additional stresses.

"Send down patch."

Johnson and Fowler glanced at each other; the plan had been to have Nikos test-fit the patching plate. Koji had been underwater for twenty-eight minutes. Jack hit the switch on the comm box. "You gonna be okay down there?"

When they had planned the repair the night before, Fowler and Johnson agreed that a half hour was the maximum amount of time they could allow a diver to remain in the frigid water.

"Yes. Yes. Be quick."

A moment later Ian Ward came jogging up from the shop, a foot-wide patching plate in his hands. Waretini quickly tied a rope around a bolt welded to the center and carefully lowered it over the side.

The minutes ticked by . . .

"Okay! Up!"

The winch rumbled and the diving stage surfaced. Koji Yamada was sprawled on the grating, clutching the steel plate to his chest. His hands were shaking and when Waretini pulled his mask off Koji could barely be heard over the hiss of his air supply.

"Got to bend . . . b-bend more."

Finally it was time for Nikos to work his magic. "Make it hot!" Cacoyannis's voice echoed through both Waretini's comm box and the speaker in the shop. Nikos tacked on the plate to hold it in place then called topside for an adjustment in the current. Slowly, carefully, he began his root pass, the initial watertight weld that would join the two pieces of steel together. Maintaining the angle of the electrode was critical, but to do so floating in the dim water, only loosely connected to the ship's hull, required the utmost in concentration and physical control.

"Cold!" Nikos called for Jano to cut the current as he changed out his depleted rod, then went back to work. Once he completed the initial weld and cleaned off the slag, he added additional passes, building up the size of the joint—or fillet—between the two pieces of steel. As the chill crept through the layers of rubber and wool the diver was wearing, the stiffness and shivering began, and the sort of deliberate movements necessary to perform a perfect weld became harder and harder to manage.

And that was the moment when everyone topside heard the plane. After it passed, after the sound disappeared into the insistent drumming of the rain, Johnson glanced at his watch, aware that, just like Yamada, Cacoyannis was pushing the limit they had agreed on.

"What do ya think?" Johnson asked.

Fowler shook his head. "We didn't see them. Maybe they didn't see us." He nodded toward the water. "He's at thirty minutes, you've got to bring him up."

Waretini flipped the switch on the comm box. "How're you goin', mate?"

"Nearly got it. Just inches now." The tinny voice sounded strange, words spoken through a jaw clenched against chattering teeth.

Johnson leaned over his first mate's shoulder. "Nikos, we got to pull you out."

"Two secs! Two secs! Okay?" Fowler looked over the side where bubbles, a combination of exhalations from Nikos's mask and the furiously arcing electrode, boiled along the ship's hull. Flashes like underwater lightning lit up the edges of the staging and the diver's lines.

"Now! Come up, or I'm sending Mike in to get ya!"

"C-cold!" Fowler wasn't sure if that was the order to turn off the juice or a reaction to the temperature. But then Nikos spoke again. "I'm just gonna c-clean this—"

Hydraulic Jack Johnson had had enough. "No, you are *not*! Get your bum on that stage! If I can't pump out the tank, I'll send you back down, but this dive is *over*!"

After a shuddering Cacoyannis was helped into the heated section of the shop and smothered in blankets, Waretini, Jano, and McLeod went to work securing the derrick and diving stage. When Johnson returned to the foredeck Anton Voss planted himself in front of the Australian. He tapped his watch.

"We must put to sea. All this equipment can be taken care of while we are underway. You heard the plane. You know the risks as well as I!"

"We're not moving until I know the status of that repair. When I've sounded the tank and everything is locked down, we'll get underway. I *do* know the risks! *All* of them!"

The *Bushranger* weighed anchor just after noon. They headed south, slowly picking their way between the scattered rocks and breaking shoals. An hour later Johnson increased the power, driving them into the blasting wind and heavy rollers coming down the Wakefield Passage. The conditions they faced were only a fraction of what could be found just a few miles to the south where the currents and weather were funneled into the narrow gap between Tierra del Fuego and Antarctica's Palmer Peninsula, the only point of constriction along the entire 60th parallel.

As the vague afternoon light dwindled, Voss indicated a nameless bay that appeared to starboard. "It is time. We must steer to sixty-two degrees."

Again they slipped into the looming embrace of Isla Santa Inés and the waters calmed. Ahead a glacier-capped peak intermittently appeared through veils of low-hanging cloud. Soon the path they sailed led between a scattering of islands and a series of channels leading away to the various points of the compass. Then they were in a fjord several miles wide. Then a mile. On the map the space was marked with an illustrated anchor denoting an Unterkunft Platze, an approved place to hide a warship . . . but still they sailed on. Finally the width was less than half a mile and darkness was closing in around them.

"Five hundred yards, steer to zero degrees," Voss ordered. "Captain Johnson, we are going to need light!"

Ian Ward fired up the three big searchlights mounted atop the wheelhouse. Fowler squinted into the night. Dimly, at the extreme range of the beams, a gap in the fjord wall appeared. It resolved itself into a narrow crevasse fading away into darkness.

"Ihaka!" Johnson called down into the chart room. "The tide? When's she gonna turn?"

"Maybe thirty minutes, boss."

"What do ya think?"

Anton Voss stepped to the door and flicked a cigarette butt overboard. "The passage is constricted for just over three kilometers, about two miles. But there is no time to waste. We *must* proceed!"

"Yeah, yeah. Yer soundin' like a broken record," Jack Johnson muttered under his breath. But he adjusted the rpms and cranked the wheel a few spokes to port. The walls closed in, and the ship moved forward, a bubble of artificial light in an unknown, and unforgiving, landscape.

Voss was squinting at the map. "There are two narrow sections. Hold to the west side of the channel for both."

"How narrow? How shallow? Got any idea? This is a bloody dead end and that tide's gonna be pouring in right behind us."

Voss looked over the rims of his glasses. "In 1945 we succeeded in an Unterseeboot with deep draft and little maneuverability. Use your sonar, do not hesitate!"

"Koji? How are we going?" Johnson called down into the chart room.

"Seven fathoms . . . now fifteen fathom. Go slow, we have rough bottom."

"Go slow. Great . . . bloody great!" It was an unavoidable reality that, when not moored or at anchor, a ship is either underway or dangerously adrift. Slow might be appropriately cautious, but too slow meant a complete loss of control.

Fowler went down to the boat deck. He couldn't help with navigation, but it was his job to be prepared for another type of problem. The Blindicide rocket launcher and an FG 42 automatic rifle were wedged up against the flag locker. If they ran into any hostile force, it was his job to respond in kind.

The engine rumbled and the wave at the *Bushranger*'s bow rustled. Long fingers of white stretched into the darkness, reflecting off looming walls of moss-covered stone and penetrating the still water, refracting into the depths to reveal the debris-filled crescents of ancient landslides and schools of fish that darted away like windblown leaves.

Mike eyed the darkness ahead with trepidation. He didn't relish the idea of appearing on the other side of this water-filled canyon lit up like New Year's Eve in Times Square. On the other hand, he agreed with Anton: the time for waiting was over.

"Get your lights down in front!" Johnson yelled, and in the bow Waretini swung an arm, indicating how Johnson should steer. As they pressed onward into what seemed to be a huge black lake, Ihaka pointed in the opposite direction, taking them around some obstacle invisible from where Fowler stood. Then they were through, sailing out into an area where their searchlight beams seemed to reach into the darkness and simply end. There was no sign of anything, no mountains or cliffs ahead. Johnson throttled back the engines and cut the lights. He switched the wheelhouse over to the low-wattage red bulbs. They floated in almost complete darkness. No starlight. No civilization for hundreds of miles.

Mike and Ihaka climbed back to the bridge, and Yamada warmed up the SO-1 radar. He ran three careful sweeps before shutting it down again. If they faced a truly sophisticated opponent, the radar was almost as much of a tip-off as the searchlights. The quick scan showed hillsides surrounding them with a low point just ahead and a distinct gap opening to the northeast.

"That is it! We must proceed into the passage until it divides." Voss tapped the compass repeater.

"Just hold your horses." Johnson took up the map book, peering at the page in the dim light. The map showed that they were in a large oblong pool, a mile and a half in length, and the opening briefly displayed on the radar did indeed eventually split into two short sections, each the remains of a glacial cirque.

Johnson turned to Fowler and Voss. "You think we're alone?"

Mike nodded.

Voss lit a cigarette. "There is no one is here. We are the first, so let us stop wasting time."

Fowler and Johnson shared a look. Anton's attitude clearly was getting on Jack's nerves.

Johnson turned toward the door to the wheelhouse. "Ihaka!"

"Yeah, boss?"

"Slow ahead."

After about twenty minutes Johnson stepped out on the bridge wing and called up to Ward, "Port and starboard, aim those lights to eight and four o'clock an' fire 'em up." By aiming the lights backward Jack was trying to orient himself in the narrow fjord without blinding everyone.

Dimly the steep walls appeared on either side. Mike could see Waretini adjusting his helm, keeping the ship in the middle of the passage. Then he heard Koji call out something from the sonar station. The words were indistinct, but the engines slowed.

"Light up forward!" Johnson called out.

The big center-mounted searchlight clacked on and Fowler squinted into the glare. They had reached the end of the fjord, or near to it. The channel was split in half by a triangular peak that rose out of sight into the darkness. On either side the water ended in glistening blue rivers of ice, arms of the central glacier, patiently grinding their way down to the sea. In the distance the sound of a small waterfall could be heard. Other than the mutter of the ship's engines, other than the distant whistling of the wind, the narrow rift of rock was full of nothing but water . . . and silence. Mike glanced at Anton, and the German drew a ragged breath and nodded.

"Ja . . . ja. Wir sind angekommen . . ." he whispered.

They had finally arrived.

"Captain Voss?" Johnson spoke softly. "Come see this . . ."

Koji adjusted the echo sounder, cranking a clean stretch of paper into the window. When he was ready Jack nodded. "Alright. Hit it . . ."

The rollers on the echo sounder began to turn and the stylus raced up and down, printing out a rough representation of the bottom in spikey, squiggling lines. It was an abstract picture, one that clearly required a practiced eye . . . but then a smooth form printed its way across the paper, a streamlined rectangle and, with that as a reference, other details emerged . . . a roundness here, an angle there.

Anton Voss swayed as if they were in a rough sea. He gripped the edge of the hatch frame.

The view was somehow warped, distorted, completely unlike the clean lines of a photograph or blueprint, but it showed what was certainly the bow, the conning tower, and the tapering tail of a submarine.

Jack clapped a big hand to Mike's shoulder, holding on and shaking it gently. A silent congratulations.

In the dim light of the cabin Mike caught a glance from Nicole, a look full of something . . . was it fear, anticipation, cautious triumph? He couldn't tell.

They had found it, the U-Null, a vessel so secret it never had a name or number, the last U-boat of Hitler's Third Reich.

CHAPTER 27

SANTA INÉS ISLAND,

dawn . . .

FOWLER CHECKED HIS watch and flexed his shoulders to settle the harness holding the tanks on his back. Beside him on the diving stage Anton Voss, Eduardo Suarez, and Jack Johnson were also gearing up. Above them the sky was a narrow slot of bluish gray outlined by the steep black slopes of the fjord. Their breath fogged in the morning chill.

Ihaka Waretini, wrapped in a supersized navy deck jacket, made the rounds, checking and rechecking their equipment. Mike Fowler nodded to Johnson, who grinned and adjusted his mask. They were about as far as you could get from the sun-dappled waters of New Guinea but for a moment it seemed like old times. Fowler stepped backward into the water.

He bobbed up to the surface as the others splashed in around him. Mike eased a finger past the rubber rim of his hood. Pent-up air escaped, and the suit sucked down against his body. Treading water now, he reached up to grasp one of the magnesium torches Waretini was distributing. A rush of flame jetted from the end of the three-foot pipe.

Mike slipped his mouthpiece between his lips and blew to clear his tubes. Turning, he dove deep, exhaling to reduce his buoyancy and kicking with his long rubber fins. The pressure closed around him, squeezing against his suit and the layering of insulation beneath it. It was only once he was well below the surface that he inhaled, insurance against the possibility of the regulator icing up. Behind him his three companions descended into darkness, specks of light, their flares streaming a maelstrom of bubbles in their wake.

There was a saying in the business that there were three kinds of divers: careful, lucky . . . and dead. It was also said that unless you were careful, you didn't stay lucky for very long. Fowler didn't worry for a minute about Johnson; he had a reputation of taking on tough jobs and stretching the limits of his contracts, but he wasn't reckless when it came to the details of working underwater.

Mike was no longer an expert; he hadn't worn tanks and a regulator in two years, and though he was confident in his knowledge, he was glad Johnson was watching his back. What he was less sure about was their companions. There was no question that Anton had to go in order to accurately appraise the condition of the sub. But he was over sixty, and the depths they headed for were much more dangerous than the recreational diving he and Mike had done along the Spanish coast.

With the temperature limiting the amount of time they spent at any depth, decompression wasn't their main worry. But the cold, and the dark, and the age and physical condition—the mental condition—of the divers were significant considerations. It would be easy for anyone to become disoriented and a mistake could spiral into disaster very quickly. An extra few minutes, the *wrong* minutes, spent trying to solve an unforeseen problem could become fatal.

In the beginning, back when they had first boarded the *Bushranger*, Sobek had insisted that he would be in the first group to go down, to be a part of the discovery. He had some experience skin diving in the Bahamas, but having seen Mike and Fernando pulled from the water in the aftermath of the explosive williwaw back at

Field Anchorage and watching the divers, hunched and shivering, over their electric heaters following the repair to the hull, Paul Sobek had decided discretion was the better part of valor. He had volunteered Ed Suarez to go in his stead. That was okay with Mike—he didn't like the Cuban, and the feeling was mutual, but the man had used a dry suit and knew the amount of weight he needed to carry on his belt . . . and, on top of that, he was certainly more levelheaded than his boss.

Fowler proceeded downward; his sense of direction oriented off of the fact that the *Bushranger* had dropped anchor just aft of where the echo sounder had located the abandoned sub. The water below them was as black as ink and Mike glanced at his depth gauge, unwilling to go too deep until he was actually over his target.

The chill pressure forced the suit tightly against his body and bothered his ears, so he exhaled through his nose. With the rim of his hood overlapping the edge of his mask, that allowed a little air to escape into the suit. That gave him a bit of buoyancy and somewhat relieved the squeezing effect. To control his ascent on the back way up, he would have to repeat what he had done on the surface: open the seal of his hood or wrist to allow air bubbles to escape. A dry suit was never entirely dry, but it was a lot better than the alternative, and wool underwear was almost as good an insulator when damp.

A menacing shape loomed suddenly out of the greenish murk. The brutal streamlined profile of the Type XXI's conning tower, its antiaircraft guns jutting toward him like the horns of an oncoming bull. Fowler tucked in and scissored his legs, bringing himself to a stop. On either side the others did the same. Now that he knew where to look, he could vaguely make out other details fading off into the darkness. Canted slightly to starboard, the rusting and weed-draped carcass of the U-boat stretched beneath them, a decaying monster from a bygone age.

Mike glanced over at Voss. The secrets he had guarded for so long, the mysteries that had cost the lives of so many, were now just meters away. Had Anton truly planned on someday returning? Was this the real reason he hired Mike so many years ago? Or was their entire adventure the result of a roll of the cosmic dice, the cat in its box randomly getting its first whiff of fate or that peculiar poison, the smell of money? There was no answer. Anton's expression was sealed within the rubber and glass of his face mask, nothing visible except a dark oval.

Johnson gestured with his flare, indicating that he and Ed Suarez were heading aft to complete their first task. The two of them would search out the steel cleat Voss had told them was on the hull just above the rudder. Once there, they would mark the stern with one of the torches and a tethered lifting bag.

Fowler and Voss swam forward, following the U-boat's angled antenna cable from the side of the conning tower to the point where it was attached to the deck. Fowler forced his flare into a vent in the submarine's outer hull and then he untied a small lifting bag from his weight belt. The canvas bag was linked to a spool of light line. Motioning Voss closer, he held the mouth of the bag over the stream of bubbles coming from the regulator at the back of Anton's neck. The bag rose faster and faster as the air expanded. When the spool stopped turning, Mike tied the line to the end of the submarine's antenna wire. Then he and Voss started back.

At the forward end of the conning tower Voss wedged his torch into the gap between the gun turret and the fairing. Unlike the open bridge found on earlier submarines, the top of the XXI was sleekly enclosed to reduce drag underwater. There were three openings in which the members of the watch could stand with their heads and shoulders exposed above the steel casing. The foremost of these, and the closest above the hatch leading down into the tower, was partially blocked by what looked like a pelorus, a compass ring and bearing circle used for navigation and targeting. For a diver wearing tanks or heavy gear that gap was too congested for comfort. However, slightly farther aft, were two rectangular holes that were a bit larger.

Johnson and Suarez arrived, and Jack set about rigging another lifting bag to mark the location. Mike noticed that he struggled trying to tie the line; his numbed fingers made the fine work difficult. As the canvas balloon shot to the surface, the flare Suarez was holding sputtered and gave out. Fowler immediately looked forward and aft, getting one last read on the size of the submarine before all three of the remaining torches dimmed and failed. It was big. It was one hell of a big boat.

Darkness closed in around them. Fowler unhooked a brass flashlight from his belt. He twisted the switch. They were almost out of time, but there were still a few things left to do. He leaned over the fairing into the nearest opening, and his yellowish beam weakly probed the enclosed area of the bridge. Anton Voss peered over his shoulder.

The hatch down into the conning tower lay open, inviting . . . and potentially deadly. Fowler had never wanted to try to enter the submarine while it was still underwater. But now that might be their only way forward.

Voss slipped over the fairing, but Mike reached out and held him back. It was his job to go first, and to do so cautiously. Sucking air against the resistance of his regulator, Mike moved past the periscope housing, carefully shining his light around the enclosed space. He had to exercise caution to keep the network of speaking tubes and conduits on the overhead from snagging the hoses attached to his regulator. Because the submarine rested at an angle, the thin rime of mud was deepest along the right side and Mike's movement caused it to rise in a smoggy haze, dimming the beam of the flashlight.

He gestured to Anton, who swam past him and assumed a kneeling position at the edge of the hatchway, pulling his legs out of the way so that Fowler could approach with the light. Together they peered down into the tiny compartment, their only portal into the sealed hull of the submarine. The sound of their bubbles echoed inside the casing.

There was a blinding flash as a blur of white leaped toward them.

Mike jerked back and, with a clang, his tanks collided with the steel above him. Something shot past, three somethings . . . fish. Just fish that darted by and out the opening behind them. Fowler glanced at Voss, but the older man had barely twitched.

Mike squeezed his fists against the cold and checked his watch again. They had a minute or two, but that was all. He examined the hatch mechanism. The hinge was frozen, coated with rust and speckled with barnacles, but the locking wheel moved slightly. Voss motioned for him to shine his light down into the round metal opening.

The inside of the conning tower was many times smaller than the finlike section of the outer hull that surrounded it. A sealed cylindrical compartment sitting on top of the main control room, it functioned as the submarine's attack center. Although the view aft was obscured by the ladder and the housing for the periscopes, it looked to be about ten feet long and maybe six feet wide, room for three or four men at most. Immediately below was a second hatch, this one tightly closed. It led down to whatever fate awaited them within the body of the pressure hull.

From behind him Fowler heard a sound . . . the burbling of a boat engine from up above. Waretini was on his way to pick them up. Then Johnson tapped on the fairing with his flashlight. He pointed at his wristwatch and then to the surface. Mike nodded and bit down on his mouthpiece to control the wave of shivering that pulsed through his jaw. It was time to go.

Bolted to one of the wardroom walls was an eraser-smeared chalkboard. Well before noon it became covered with drawings and calculations as Johnson, Voss, and Fowler struggled to lay out their options to the crew . . . and to explain them to Sobek and Paluso.

Johnson indicated a rough sketch of a submarine. "Our original plan was to cut away sections of the outer hull so that we could install fittings in the main ballast tanks. The *Bushranger* could then stand off at a safe distance. From there we'd control the air our compressors pumped into the sub." Jack put a large X over the diagram that showed a set of air lines leading from the *Bushranger* to a series of buoys and then down to the sub. "But that was before we lost most of our hose."

Sobek pointed at the chalkboard. "So, don't you have to open something? How do you get the water out of the sub's tanks . . . the ballast tanks?"

Voss made a motion with both hands as if he was grasping something cylindrical. "The main ballast tanks on undersea boats surround the pressure hull. Inside of that is where the crew operates the boat. These tanks are simply open at the bottom, and they have large capped-off valves at the top. When you wish to dive, you open the caps. This releases the air pressure and water rushes in from below. As long as you have some air left when you close the caps, you stop the dive. When you wish to surface, pressurized air is blown into the ballast tanks from reservoirs inside the boat; this forces the water down, out of the tank. That is the simple version. The reality is a complex dance, a series of critical compromises."

Fowler twisted in his chair, uncomfortably stretching his aching back. Nicole sat quietly in the corner of the room closest to the galley, and Mike was happy to see she was protectively flanked by Frank Jano and Fernando Zúñiga.

"Okay." Sobek scribbled something on a folded sheet of paper. "So now you say we don't have enough hose . . . but the bottom is only a hundred and thirty feet down. How much do we really need?"

"More than we've got." Johnson indicated his drawing. "These air lines risk having nearly a thousand tons of *Bushranger* on one end and close to two thousand tons of submarine on the other. We need a lot of slack. I don't want to be anywhere near that thing when it comes up. And because it's attached to an anchor, it's gonna pull away from us as it rises. And that's if it comes up level, doesn't swing on its hook, doesn't get caught on something, doesn't break the anchor line . . . *and* if there's no tide. We have to stay connected, compressors pumping all the time, if we want this to work. If we blow a hose, if it pulls a connection loose or breaks something, things can go sideways, and I mean *literally* sideways, pretty damn quick."

"There's got to be some middle ground here." Sobek sounded like he was trying to negotiate a deal. "You said something about maybe filling two tanks at a time. You could use two longer hoses rather than four shorter ones."

"I *did* say it, mate, but I was just spitballing. Pumping in a limited amount of air, going tank to tank, is slow. That's a lot of cold dives to switch over the hoses, and I don't want that sub starting to move while I've got a diver working on it."

"We don't have the time for this," Anton Voss said quietly.

"You're right about that, buddy," Paluso grumbled. "Those Nazi scumbags are searching for us, and we're trapped in a dead-end street."

Jack turned to Voss. "Look, mate, you're the one that wanted her brought up in one piece. Give me the word and I'll cut that tin can wide open!"

Voss started to object, but Mike stood up . . .

"No." he said. He knew what he was about to suggest was a bad idea. But he didn't want Anton telling any more lies that they would both eventually have to live down. "He's right. Mr. Voss and me, we're going in."

Johnson shook his head. "You don't know what you're gonna find in there."

"Look, the worst case is that the boat's flooded. Under those conditions we couldn't lift her anyway. So we come back out and reconsider our options. Best case? There's enough pressure left in the air reservoirs and we bring her up, just like they planned in 1945."

"I should go with you." Sobek was suddenly back on that kick. "I'm the financier of this expedition. We all go in together."

If it had even been a real possibility, the idea of Sobek—a wild card in any environment—making the dive with them would have made Mike very concerned. As it was, he simply laughed.

Sobek's face turned red. "What are you laughing at?" he snarled. "You laughing at *me*?"

"Did you ever wonder if I wanted to kill you?" Mike asked.

"What the h—" Paluso shifted his feet, ready for a fight but looking at Fowler quizzically.

"I *have* thought about it," Fowler said. "But you're safe. Do you know how you can tell you're safe?" Mike glared at him. "Do you—"

Paluso broke in, rescuing his partner's pride. "—Why don't you tell us?"

"—Because there is *no way* I would *ever* take you into that godforsaken hulk." Mike paused a moment then let it all out, everything that had been gnawing at the back of his mind.

"That damned U-boat is a death trap. I have never heard of anyone even *thinking* about doing what we are about to. If you have grandkids you can say, 'I was *there* when it happened!' We are going to seal ourselves in a flooded conning tower, try to drain the ten tons of water in there into the submarine's bilge, and then if, *if* we can get through the lower hatch at all, that boat is going to be filled with poisonous gas and traps—"

"Traps? Gas?" Sobek pulled back, as if he could already smell the fumes.

Fowler gestured to Voss to take over.

"Yes. There are a variety of materials in the boat that will have broken down and become toxic. There will be fungus, possibly in considerable amounts. If seawater has made its way into the battery casings, it will release chlorine gas. If that has escaped, if the seals have deteriorated, it could be very bad. And then there are the traps that we set . . ."

Voss smiled thinly. "You see, the living spaces on either side of the zentrale, the control room, are sealed with watertight hatches. Before we left, we piled everything that would rot—floor matting, bedding, food, clothing—into those areas, which already had wooden paneling, and wet it all down. The idea was to create hydrogen sulfide—sewer gas—which is both toxic *and* flammable. The next watertight compartment going forward is the torpedo room, and aft is engineering. Both have been rigged with explosives. I am afraid the U-Null is a pharaoh's tomb of dangers."

"Right." Mike took over again. "*Then* we are going to try to blow the ballast on a ship that's been on the bottom for sixteen years. Do we have any control? Do the explosives go off? And if any of that happens, or none of it does, can we still get out? I have no idea. So, Paul . . . do you *really* want to come along?"

Paul Sobek couldn't hold his gaze, and while Mike doubted they would have to face all the hazards he had outlined, any one of them could be fatal. At the same time, he was beginning to get that quiet feeling, the calm, the focused resignation that came before a battle. For a salvage diver, this would be like riding a rocket into space, winning a championship game, or being the first to climb Mount Everest . . . complete insanity, but also the adventure and challenge of a lifetime.

The main engines were rumbling as Johnson glanced at the clock, calculating the time until the end of slack tide. Ihaka raised the port anchor and the *Bushranger* slowly reversed until they were a safe distance from the markers that floated on the gray surface of the fjord.

Johnson keyed the intercom mic. "Let go aft!"

Ian Ward knocked loose the stopper and a third anchor, its chain fed from the stern, splashed into the water.

Gently powering forward, Johnson set the flukes of the stern anchor. With the propeller barely turning over, Jack eased his way alongside the three lifting bags that indicated the position of the submarine. Once he was well forward of the bow marker, almost to the rocky shallows where the fjord split in two, he dropped the port anchor again and waited.

Nicole tiptoed up to the door to the wheelhouse. "May I?"

Jack nodded, and she joined Mike, who was watching the action from just inside the door to the bridge wing.

"What's going on?" she whispered.

"Jack is setting the anchors. When he's done, we'll be locked in place, parked right over the submarine. But when we have to raise it, we can move out of the way just by adjusting our chains."

Clank, clank, clank. Waretini released more links of the port chain as the *Bushranger* pivoted to starboard, carried by the changing tide. Slowly, they swung almost perpendicular to the fjord, the bow edging closer to the eastern slopes.

"Slow up, and . . . *stop*! Alright, let go starboard." Fernando Zúñiga swung a maul and stepped back. In a cloud of rust and dirt, the right-side anchor chain rumbled up out of its locker, across a stretch of the deck, and down the hawsepipe.

Nicole drew Fowler out onto the bridge wing and pulled the door closed.

"Is it very dangerous? You weren't just trying to scare that—well, I'll be polite and call him Mr. Sobek?"

Mike looked at her, not quite knowing how to explain. "Like a lot of things, it shouldn't be too bad if everything goes as planned. But once we're in there—" He shrugged. "Well, it's for damn sure no one's getting in if we need help."

On deck, Waretini started the port windlass, drawing the *Bushranger* back toward the three lifting bags. Zúñiga blasted the incoming chain with a hose to clear it of mud. Johnson mumbled into the intercom and the engines shuddered as they shut down. In the vast silence that followed, each small sound—a metal tool, the slam of a hatch—echoed distantly from the walls of rock and ice that surrounded them.

She shook her head. "This is crazy. How in the world did we ever get here?"

"Hell, *you* tell *me*! That old guy we met on the beach . . . he was working on something with Voss and Elizabeth Adler. Something everybody, including your people, seems to want."

"Leonid knew Voss?" She frowned.

Mike wondered if this was something beyond her official need-to-know. "Elizabeth, the woman in the photograph with the castle, was Anton's fiancé. Do you know what he told me?"

"Leonid?"

"He said I should take you and get away. He seemed to think whatever is down there is seriously bad news."

". . . And I was informed it's the answer to all our prayers."

"Yeah. Well, I've heard that one, too. Clearly, the 'answer to everything' is so valuable it's very dangerous . . . to someone." After a moment of thought he said, "Maybe to everyone."

CHAPTER 28

Koji Yamada took the first dive after the ship was moved into position, going down to clear away the temporary lifting bags and attach a more substantial rope guideline to an equally heavy duty buoy. He then descended again with a bundle of hoses and cables. This included an air line to run the tools, a cable for light, and two hoses. One was a water jet and the other a more rigid tube of larger diameter that connected to a pump. The suction from this would help keep the water inside the bridge and tower clear. The better everyone could see, the faster the job would go.

Taking the next three shifts were Ward, Cacoyannis, and then Iannucci. Their job was to begin the work of cleaning the rust and shells from the hatch mechanism using a hammer, files, and a wire brush. Until Fowler and Voss made their move to enter the pressure hull, the divers would all use the Jack Browne masks with air piped down from the surface. In the cramped confines of the submarine's bridge tanks were an awkward liability, and the Jack Browne system would allow them to communicate topside if they needed to.

At lunch Voss barely touched his meal, but he harangued everyone with the necessity to proceed with caution. "These surfaces are metal, but you must treat them as if they are delicate. Like an archaeologist excavating an ancient pot."

"What are you talking about? How delicate?" Iannucci asked.

"You cannot go banging away and risk damaging the hatch. The tolerances must be respected."

"Can I bang lightly?" The Italian diver sneered. "It *is* rusted open, right?"

"Mein Gott, how do I make this clear—"

"—Just take it easy knocking those shells loose," Mike broke in. "You don't want to have to tell your boss you're the reason we're going to be here for an extra month, right?" He didn't know if they had a month, or even a week, but it made a good threat.

After noon Johnson and Fowler suited up. Their goal was to check the progress on the hatch but also to see what could be done about cleaning out the inside of the tower. Mike dove using an Aqua-Lung and tank; he wanted to practice the maneuver of getting through the hatch with Johnson there to help and without Voss, or anyone else, being in the way.

The cold closed in with its rubbery pressure as Mike slid downward into the darkness. He had left his fins on deck; for this part of the operation there was little swimming required and they would only be in the way. Jack was waiting just inside the rectangular opening in the bridge casing. His triangular rubber mask contained a microphone and earpiece, and Mike could faintly hear him talking to Waretini up above.

The hatchway rim was looking better than it had any right to and the locking wheel turned, thanks to Cacoyannis's careful ministrations. But the hatch itself was still rusted open. Bracing himself, Fowler gave it a tug and then both of them took ahold and tried to move it back and forth. It didn't budge, but they had yet to break out the heavy tools.

Fowler held up a hand, signaling Johnson to stop. He didn't want to waste time on a job they couldn't complete. Mike motioned that he was going to practice taking off his tank. He slipped his arms out of the harness. Then, biting firmly down on his mouthpiece, he rotated the tank upward. Bracing it against the side of his head, he exhaled and guided himself downward through the hatch. No doubt it would have been easier to take the whole assembly off and then blow his exhaust hose clear of water once inside the tower. However, once they entered the submarine, the fewer chances they took of inhaling a hoseful of foul air, the better.

In the darkness of the conning tower's attack center Fowler stuck a leg through the ladder to hold himself in place and struggled to get back into the harness. The awkward position and the slick green fuzz that coated everything got him turned around. He tried to stabilize himself by bending his knee and realized his leg had slipped out from between the rungs. Then his tank clanged against metal, and his head came up against a hard surface in one direction while something clipped his ear in the other. His first thought was that he was trapped but, trying not to overreact, he carefully stroked backward away from whatever it was.

When he looked up, he couldn't see anything. Not the faint light that had been filtering through the hatch, not the ladder that couldn't have been more than two feet away. He reached out and felt nothing, then a slimy surface, he couldn't tell what it was, the wall, the ceiling, the floor—claustrophobia clutched at Mike Fowler's throat.

He groped for the flashlight at his belt and twisted the switch.

What had been black suddenly became a dingy brown. His thrashing around had stirred up the silt that had settled into the chamber.

Okay. Focus. You've been here before, he thought. But back in the ruined battleships he had usually had his feet resting on something, anchored by forty-pound brass boots, and a lifeline that indicated the way he had come. This time he couldn't even tell which way was up . . .

Bubbles! He rotated slightly until he could feel the bubbles from his regulator brushing past his ear. Okay. That was a start.

Mike reached out and touched steel, fingers closing around the ladder. Somehow it was now to his left. Then above him the sludge was suddenly a little brighter and everything snapped into perspective. Jack had dragged over the work lamp and was dangling it down through the hatchway. A moment later he felt movement, a current flowing upward. Johnson was using the suction hose to draw away the dirty water.

Mike forced himself to relax. Too many memories, he thought, or just a touch of the narks. Nitrogen narcosis, an effect of breathing air under pressure, could be a bit like having one or even a few too many whiskeys. For a moment there he had become lost in a tin can the size of a residential bathroom.

Swimming down through the circulating crud Fowler felt his way along the floor of the attack center, verifying the location of the drain valves that led to the bilge. If they could seal the upper hatch, this was how they might be able to empty the water from the tiny compartment. It was a plan that could only be attempted once or twice before the added weight began to affect their ability to raise the boat.

From there he moved upward until an octagonal wheel fell under his hand. He braced himself and gave it a turn. It didn't move. He tried constant pressure, then a series of sudden hard twists. Nothing. Taking his heavy diving knife from its sheath, he slipped it behind the wheel and used its brass pommel to tap at a spoke while turning. He struggled, trying to use his feet to lock himself into position. If he wasn't perfectly braced a hard twist was more likely to spin his body than have any effect on the valve. He twisted one last time . . .

The wheel turned!

He rotated the valve all the way open, then shut it again, opening and shutting the gritty first quarter turn until it smoothed out. That was a big step. The conning tower's flood valve was now operational. If they weren't able to bring the sub to the surface, refilling the tower would be the only way to escape.

Johnson pulled the light out of the way and Mike returned to the ladder, pulling the tank off and guiding it back up through the hatch. In the brightness of the work light and the clearer water, even the cramped enclosure of the bridge was a welcome relief.

Now it was Jack's turn. The big Australian forced himself down into the tower while Mike managed his lines, then passed along the water jet. This was basically a fire hose, but McLeod had adjusted the pump to operate at lower pressure, enough to stir up the silt and blast free the softer marine life but not so much that it would do any damage or propel the diver around in an uncontrollable manner. Even so, Jack stuck both a leg and an arm through the ladder before he opened the valve . . . and that was the last Mike saw of him for several minutes. The view down into the compartment exploded in a maelstrom of muck and Mike edged the suction pipe farther into the circular hole, trying to draw as much of it away as he could.

Mike worked the fingers of one hand then the other, feeling the trembling in his core become a constant thing, the involuntary attempts of his body to stay warm. After checking his watch for the second time, Fowler tugged on Johnson's lifeline, letting him know, if topside hadn't already, that it was time to go.

Ten minutes later they were stripping off their gear and warming themselves with the blankets that Nicole had left draped over the machine shop radiators.

Johnson held his toes in front of one of the electric heaters that added even more warmth to the curtained alcove. He frowned at Fowler. "I know you like a challenge . . . but you sure you want to do this? Go in there?"

Mike snorted and shook his head, "Seems like the wrong moment to back out. You want to go instead?"

"Hell no! I think you're insane. But it's why I believed you. When someone decides to do something, and you know they *know* better . . . you gotta take 'em seriously. Am I right?"

Mike didn't say anything. It angered him that he was starting to think like Anton Voss, lying, keeping secrets, and playing those around him like pieces on a chessboard. Establishing what Voss called "superpositions." They were all like rats in a scientist's maze, or cats in a booby-trapped box. The moment was coming when someone would have to step up and make sense of all the agendas, ambition, and avarice. Mike feared that responsibility was going to be his.

Outside the porthole they could see Koji loading the diving stage with a scissor jack and some blocks of wood. He was also taking down a pry bar and a single-handed sledgehammer. Even though Jack had specifically chosen the Japanese because of his fierce attention to detail, they could hear Anton Voss repeating his cautionary lecture about not damaging the hatch.

Johnson turned back to Fowler and rolled his eyes. "Your partner needs a drink or two, something to take the edge off."

Mike nodded. They were working as fast as they could, but he had no idea if it was fast enough. In the outer part of the shop Suarez was getting a last-minute lesson from Frank Jano on managing the Jack Browne mask and the bundle of lines that attached to it. The two of them would take the next half-hour shift, continuing to clean the interior of the conning tower with the water jet and suction hose. Then, if everything went according to plan, Ian Ward would go back down to carefully fit one of the new gaskets Mike had shipped from Spain into the dovetail on the upper hatch.

Voss paced the deck, questioning each diver as he came up, a pile of soggy cigarette butts growing at the base of the starboard bollard. They worked long into the dim twilight. Their only hope was to keep moving forward, to stay ahead of whatever forces were gathering beyond the horizon.

In his dream the P-38 Lightning dropped down out of the heavens, the bright sky giving its bizarre double fuselage the brushstroke silhouette of a Chinese character. The symbol for expendability or betrayal. Fire tumbled from its wings, turning the palms of Itu Aba into blackened trunks, leaving patches of napalm burning on the waters of a once peaceful lagoon. The dead were incinerated or blown to pieces, the unintentional survivors sworn to secrecy.

Mike Fowler awoke in the crew's fo'c'sle of the *Bushranger* surrounded by cold metal and sleeping men. He stared at the dimly lit ceiling. It was little different from the half dozen navy transports that had carried him to other distant and deadly places. The clock on the bulkhead clicked its way past three A.M., the long hour between very late and very early.

From head to toe everything ached. He had been pushing too hard, too hard for a middle-aged guy who had been shot, slugged, and pursued around the world. And there was nothing like swimming and working underwater to stress and strain every muscle in every imaginable direction.

Fowler's body might be tired, but his mind was going a hundred miles an hour. The moment of truth was fast approaching, and it wasn't a comfortable feeling. His parka hung from a hook welded to the frame of his bunk. In its pocket was the magic box given to him by Anson Fordyce. The box he had been told was an answer to all their problems. The critical signal that would call in the cavalry . . .

But promises had no doubt also been made in order to draw those Japanese businessmen, their briefcases bulging with mysterious contracts, to a remote atoll in the South China Sea. What was it that had been so threatening, and to whom? A lot had been invested in the world never being able to find out.

He slipped out of the bunk. The bed below, the bed where Anton slept, was empty. He touched the sheets. They were cold; Voss hadn't been sleeping very well. At night he roamed the decks, the ghost of a ship's captain.

Clipping his pistol into his trousers and carrying his boots, Mike went forward along the passageway. Climbing the stairs to the main deck he paused, listening for movement from the deck above, the chart room, the wheelhouse, the captain's quarters . . .

He heard nothing but the clicking of the radiators and the hush of a fan. To his left Nicole's door had been fixed, replaced by the panel from Clarence Benham's cabin. Ian Ward had the watch, but that meant he was outside, bundled up against the chill, and spending most of his time aft, looking back the way they had come.

If there was ever a time to install the CIA's transmitter, it was now. The device lay over his heart like a ticking bomb. There was a part of him that yearned to be naïve, to simply do as he had been told, to hook up the beacon and trust that it would all turn out okay. But the last time he had blindly accepted orders from Fordyce, he and Jack had nearly died.

On the other hand, he had also trusted Anton Voss, a man who had been like a father or at the very least, a mentor. But Voss was rapidly turning into someone Fowler didn't know or understand. Not "turning into," Mike thought. This is who he always was. Voss had been planning from the first day they met . . . planning to return to this place or planning in case he *had* to return to this place.

Fowler didn't go on up toward the chart room and its radios. Instead he sat on the stairs and pulled on his boots. Then he let himself out into the night and closed the hatch. He needed to do some thinking. He needed to do a lot of thinking.

Mist filled the fjord, invisibly embracing the ship. It gave the air a wet taste and left droplets hanging from the cables and railings. Fowler made his way forward, avoiding the deck gear by memory and a brief touch here and there. His toe felt something and in his peripheral vision he caught sight of a railing in front of him. The diving stage was set up, ready to be boomed over the side. In the morning they would find out, or they would begin to find out, if any of what they planned was possible.

Behind him Fowler heard a click and rasp. He turned. Back of the foredeck winches, under the protective overhang of the boat deck, a flame wavered, and a cigarette glowed.

"So, you cannot sleep? This makes two of us, yes?" Anton Voss stood in the darkness.

Speak of the devil, Mike thought. But he replied, "It's just as you said it would be. Now all we have to do is get in."

"And then *all* the secrets will be revealed." There was a mocking tone to the older man's voice, a twist of irony, but Mike couldn't tell who it was aimed at.

"Well, sooner would definitely be better than later . . . before we go down there, in fact."

"Perhaps. But the explanation is complicated. If I must say, 'The ship does not carry a certain cargo,' it is critical that I immediately show them, not just tell them, what it *does* carry." It was a good argument. But Voss always had an explanation. Fowler wondered how many of them had ever been true.

"Mr. Voss, there've been too many lies and too many secrets." Mike was tired and his feelings slipped out around his words.

"True. I am guilty of this," Voss countered. "But you are hardly innocent yourself, yes? First it was the Israelis. However, if you had actually sold us out, I suppose they would not have sent Miss DeMaes. So, who else have you been speaking with?"

"You're interested *now*? You could have asked me days ago."

"There are priorities. If we did not arrive here, nothing else mattered. Now, *who was it?*"

"American intelligence." Fowler was tired of pussyfooting around. "Specifically, our friend from Alexandria."

Something about that rattled Voss more than Mike expected. "They have been watching you all this time?"

"No. But it's pretty clear what you're looking for isn't as secret as you think."

Voss sucked in hard on the butt of the cigarette, causing it to glow brightly, then he flung it to the deck and rubbed it out with his heel. "What did he say? What did they tell you it was?"

"A reactor. Some form of advanced atomic generator." Mike kept it to a minimum; he didn't want to embarrass himself if he got any of the details wrong.

"Is that *all*?"

"All? I don't know, they seemed pretty excited about it." Mike wondered if he had missed something, or if Voss was just being sarcastic. "Don't you even want to know what their offer was?"

"Of course, of course. Tell me."

"Six million dollars, protection from Skorzeny, immunity from prosecution . . . and we get our business back."

"And now that you have delivered the message they gave you, do you believe them?"

"Maybe. I don't really know if they are capable of delivering. And they might be just as motivated to do away with us as anyone."

"Very astute."

Mike had the uncomfortable feeling that Voss had slipped inside his guard yet again. His tendency to trust in Anton's intelligence, if not his honor, was a weakness.

"Have you got a plan? It would sure help if you told me what it was!"

"The plan has not changed. We retrieve various items, destroy everything else, and escape without being caught. From the perspective of salvage, you are better off . . . We will not have all that bothersome gold to slow us down."

Mike stepped in closer, whispering, "Anton, that is *not* what I was asking! What are we going to do with . . . *it*? How the hell do we survive this with the whole world breathing down our necks?"

"When the time comes everything will be revealed."

"Oh, come *on*! The CIA knows you had Aleixandre book you a bunch of rooms in Cape Town. They are pretty sure you're planning an auction."

Voss was silent for a moment . . . "Well, then it is working—"

"*What?* What's working?"

"The plan."

Mike felt his eyes narrow. He knew how Anton's mind operated. "Cape Town's a distraction . . ."

"It is . . . whatever we need it to be. If we allow our adversaries to think they can simply purchase what I am after, who knows, it might encourage a certain amount of laziness. Any lack of motivation on their part is to our advantage."

"Fordyce is *not* going to wait! That plane we heard was probably his."

"Then we must hurry . . . but there is a precise order in which we must act." There was a vague glint of light on silver. Voss tucked his cigarette case into his pocket and sighed. "We need you. But sometimes I wish you had remained behind in Spain or Argentina. Fate, however, is ambivalent to our feelings, so now we must see this through to the end." He turned and started aft.

"What do you mean?" Fowler stopped him, a hand on his arm. But before he could say anything, before he could ask the questions that might allay his anger and suspicion, Voss gently pulled free.

"Enough! This is sentimentales Gerede. Tomorrow you and I will be taking our lives in our hands . . . and the morning will be here before we know it."

The hatch closed, and Mike stood there, fog wrapping close around him. Voss had not admitted the details of any plan, and Mike had not told him about the transmitter. He and Anton were circling each other . . . like sharks. There was no blood in the water, but he feared there soon would be.

Mike Fowler awakened to the grinding of the winch that raised and lowered the diving stage. After a hot shower he pulled on long underwear and a sweater, then had breakfast. It was a quiet meal, just he and Voss with Clarence Benham bringing them their plates in the wardroom.

As they got up to leave, Benham called out from the galley, "Rummy . . . you be careful down there."

By the time Waretini and Yamada were helping them into their suits Mike could hear the clanking of the anchor chains. Johnson was already repositioning the *Bushranger* to avoid any potential collision should they succeed in their mission. The workboat was lowered over the side and its outboard burbled softly as Jack and then Anton climbed into it.

"Michael . . . Mike!" Nicole caught up with him on deck. She had left her jacket behind, and the chill breeze ruffled her hair and put goose bumps on her skin.

She shook her head, and he couldn't tell if the tears forming in the corners of her eyes were from emotion or the wind. "You know I don't want you to do this—" she whispered.

"—Except you do."

She blinked, hurt. But he hadn't meant it like that.

"*You'd* go, if you could, right? Look, you want this damn thing. And I don't think any of us are safe—including you—as long as we're sitting right on top of it looking guilty as sin to whoever shows up. There's only one way to keep from being buried down here. And we've got to get it done quickly."

She threw her arms around his neck and kissed him. "I'm sorry. Go. Get us out of this place. But please, please, be careful!"

Johnson took them out to the buoy. Clouds hung low along the gray stone slopes and the waters of the fjord were as flat as a pane of black glass. The three men sat silently while Anton finished a cigarette. Then they stood, slipping into their harnesses and carefully examining one another's equipment, verifying that everything was as it should be. Mike pulled on his mask and adjusted the edge of his hood.

"You cobbers ready?" Behind Jack, the ship was a distant outline in the drifting mist.

There wasn't anything more to say, so Fowler and Voss crouched and tipped backward off the gunwale, bobbing to the surface momentarily before venting their suits and abandoning themselves to the depths. Silver bubbles vanished above them, merging with the faint light as the guideline led them down into darkness.

In the gloom-filled bridge Mike Fowler switched on his flashlight and looked around. The only remaining connection to the surface was the line leading up to the buoy; all the other cables and hoses had been cleared away.

Anton Voss swam under the casing and forward to the hatch. Mike followed. Then Mike switched on another light and dropped it into the attack center. Taking a deep breath, Voss slipped off his tank, removed his mouthpiece, and pulled himself through the hatchway. Mike handed down the tank and waited until he could see Voss was back in his gear and bubbles were again emerging from his regulator. Then he followed, sinking down into the crowded compartment.

After checking that all his tools had been placed where he wanted them, Mike took ahold of the ladder and, reaching up, tugged on the locking wheel of the hatch. The springs kicked in and it slammed shut with a heavy thud. The retaining dogs clicked down over the interior rim. In the stark yellow light, he and Anton shared a look, meaningless and blank, neither able to read the other through the glass ovals of their masks. Mike spun the wheel and locked the mechanism, sealing them in.

Fowler positioned himself near one of the bilge valves. He twisted the wheel, but it got him nowhere, so he slipped a screwdriver between the spokes and pulled. The additional leverage did the job. The valve opened but he couldn't feel any suction at the drain. He closed it again.

On his side of the tower Voss was tapping away, working to loosen his valve. After a moment the wheel turned, and Anton's light picked up a flickering of motion, a disturbance in the dirty water . . . His drain was functioning!

Fowler made a rotating motion with one finger. Voss closed the valve and Mike turned his all the way open. Earlier that morning Ian Ward had tightly lashed a large air bottle to the periscope trunk. Mike reached out and cracked the attached valve. A solid jet of bubbles thundered into the cramped space, increasing the pressure. After another few moments he shut the valve and when he did, he could hear it . . . the gurgle of water pouring down a pipe.

Fowler pointed to Voss, who reopened his drain. The water level dropped. A foot, two feet. Fowler again signaled that they should close their valves. Now was the critical moment. Would they be able to escape? Mike reached up and twisted the flood cock. A hard, dirty stream shot down from the nozzle. After it turned clear he rotated the wheel and waited to be sure the dripping stopped.

A few minutes later they had taken off their weight belts and were sloshing around in calf-deep water, the sound of their movements and the beams of their flashlights reflecting crazily in the metal drum of the tower. The last of the water drained away.

Voss approached the lower hatch and Mike motioned to it, suggesting that Anton should do the honors. After slipping a three-foot crowbar between the spokes Mike stood back and Anton pulled, slowly increasing the pressure.

Suddenly, the mechanism gave way and Fowler had to grab the older man to keep him from falling. He cursed himself for not being more careful. An accident in here could quickly turn into a disaster.

Removing the bar, Fowler motioned for Voss to turn around. He then changed out Voss's air bottle, and Voss returned the favor. If anything went wrong Mike preferred to have a full supply before they opened the polluted body of the submarine.

They were ready. Mike nodded to Anton and, after twisting the lock, the two of them bent, straining at the hatch. It lifted reluctantly with a coarse grinding of hinge and springs, and then a wet tearing sound as the aging gasket peeled away. The spring tension kicked in and it locked open, leaving the two of them staring down into the black hole at their feet.

CHAPTER 29

ANTON VOSS PEERED through the hatchway into his past, the ship that had carried him away from the collapsing ruins of the Third Reich, the ship that contained the mysteries that demanded he compromise everything in order to return. All Mike could see was nubbed steel flooring. The short tube of the evacuation skirt blocked most of his view.

The skirt was designed to be a submariner's last desperate hope. If the U-boat was damaged beyond repair, the control room could be flooded and the hatches locked open. The skirt, which was welded on beneath the hatch, would trap a pocket of air along the ceiling where a sailor could survive for a moment or two before ducking under the edge of the tube and attempting to swim to the surface. Fowler thought the idea sounded like a long shot, but sometimes that was all you had.

Voss fumbled with the waistband of his tank harness, but Fowler grabbed him and shook his head. Taking up a scraper and a wire brush Mike began to strip the torn and decomposing gasket out of the hatch assembly. If they could make the sub watertight again, they could come and go by flooding and draining the tower as they just had. First things first. He wasn't going anywhere until the possibilities of retreat and counterattack were adequately covered.

Eventually, Fowler made a final pass with steel wool and a rag doused in solvent, then he mounted one of the new gaskets into the dovetail. As he began to pack up his tools, Voss gestured vehemently. He wanted to get down into the control room.

"Mm-okay! Okay!" The words were garbled by Mike's mouthpiece.

Voss took his place on the lower ladder and, while Mike held his tank, he slipped out of the harness. As he went down rung by rung, Mike rotated the air bottle, carefully managing the distance to keep from pulling on the hoses and Anton's mouthpiece. With the upside-down tank braced against the side of the escape skirt, Anton was able to get one arm through the harness and let the tank drop into place on his back. Then Fowler handed over the canvas sack of tools and a pair of fresh flashlights and followed him down.

He wasn't exactly sure what he had expected, but what he saw was confusing. At first glance the control room seemed relatively well-preserved, familiar yet unfamiliar, the German version of the two American fleet boats he had briefly been aboard. A closer look, however, revealed the ravages of its time on the bottom.

As Mike moved his light the shadows stretched and twisted. Moisture had condensed on the cold metal surfaces, leaving behind peeling paint and a coating of rust on anything made of steel. Seat pads had rotted, splitting open to allow the swollen horsehair stuffing to spew forth like entrails. Dead patches of mold lurked in the shadows. Had it simply used up all the air or had chlorine gas leaking from the batteries killed it? Mike didn't want to find out.

Voss followed the yellow beam of his flashlight aft, past the controls once used by the diving-plane operators. Standing in an alcove formed by several valve-studded manifolds, he studied the complex banks of piping, each lever and knob labeled with a metal tag. Anton reached out and touched the controls as if trying to assess exactly what he wanted to accomplish.

While Voss investigated the air system, Fowler checked over the watertight hatch leading forward and then, stepping through a doorway into the boat's compact galley, the one that led aft. Both were tightly sealed.

Voss turned to the tool bag and pulled out a diver's slate. "Ready?" he wrote.

Mike looked around. He had thought there would be more to it but, of course, the sub had been prepared for this very moment. He nodded.

Voss took hold of a large wheel at the top of the manifold. Slowly, stiffly, the wheel turned a few degrees. There was a powerful hiss that cut off abruptly. Shifting to a different section, Anton worked another control; it hesitated and then, as he added more pressure, suddenly opened.

Air rushed and shuddered through the system. Somewhere deep in the boat a pipe groaned, and something let go with a sound like a muffled gunshot. In the dim light Mike saw the needle in a tarnished gauge jump.

Alarmed, Anton tried to close the valve. It stuck, and a rumbling like an approaching subway train roared into the ballast tanks. Frost hazed one edge of the manifold . . . and then Voss used all his weight and the sound stopped.

Fowler looked around, still fearing the screaming of a ruptured pipe . . . but the last of the pneumatic clicking and moaning simply trailed off. The system on the other side of the manifold seemed to be holding pressure. For a moment the iron monster that surrounded them had come alive.

The two men stared at each other, and then there was a hollow exhalation, the breath being released from the tubes of their Aqua-Lungs.

"Okay . . . one more time," Voss mumbled.

This time he opened the valve carefully and the charge of air pushed into the system more evenly. They waited, Voss with his head cocked, listening, his knees bent in order to feel the cant of the deck, ready . . . ready.

But nothing happened.

Anton Voss opened the valve farther, then even farther. Instead of increasing, the hiss of air diminished.

"Nein. Nein. Nein! *Nein!*" Voss hammered his fist against the bole of the valve.

As Mike had feared all along, the U-Null had not been able to retain enough pressure in its reservoirs to force the water out of the ballast tanks . . . not by a long shot.

Voss twisted every knob in the bank, carelessly throwing them all open then, savagely, he laid into the master control again. A pitiful whistling diminished to nothing. Cursing incomprehensibly in German, Anton turned and grabbed a pair of valve wheels. He shook them violently, shook them as if he could rattle the entire U-boat free of the sea floor, as if he could punish or threaten it into obedience . . . but all he could do was slam his own body back and forth. It was an outburst of frustration and anger unlike anything Mike had seen in the many years they had worked together.

Mike reached out; he didn't want Anton smashing his faceplate on any of the protruding valves—

The valves! Now, that was something worth thinking about—

Fowler's hand closed on Voss's shoulder and the older man whirled, eyes flaring, a fist cocked.

"Whoa!" Mike let go to block the punch but, as Anton turned, his rubber-clad foot slipped on the greasy surface. He went down. His tank crashed into the floor and his head impacted the edge of the aft diving plane console with a solid thunk.

Anton Voss did not move.

Mike quickly knelt. A moment passed before he heard Anton's lungs pull on the regulator, then release. Thank God. His gear was intact and functioning, but Voss was out cold.

That was not the only problem. Through a split in the older man's hood Mike could see blood soaking into Anton's hair.

"Oh, hell . . ." Cold flickered through the pit of Mike's stomach. If there was one thing he had come to respect, it was how rapidly trouble could spiral out of control.

First things first . . . try to stop the bleeding. Fowler unsheathed his diver's knife and cut through Anton's harness, laying him flat on the floor with the tank resting on his chest. Everything inside the sub was filthy but the rag he had used to wipe down the hatch was by far the cleanest thing they had available. He folded it and worked it into the hood, pressing awkwardly on the wound while trying to stabilize the other side of Anton's head.

Fifteen minutes minimum. He had to keep up enough pressure to stop the bleeding while trying not to make any other injuries, if they existed, worse.

Then what? There were two narrow hatchways and nearly a hundred feet of water between them and the surface. Could he go by himself and come back with help? Voss only had so much air. To make things worse, he worried that Anton would try to pull out his mouthpiece if he began to wake up.

The dead whispered from the dark corners of Mike Fowler's mind. The people he could have helped, the people he should have helped. His father was first and foremost, but there was also an abalone diver, bent and writhing with decompression sickness, soldiers and sailors in the Pacific . . . a vivacious young girl and a crippled old man in Argentina. What should he have done? And what part had Anton Voss; this helpless man who lay beside him, played in *that* disaster?

Thinking back over the years, of their struggles and success, he had to wonder: had Anton given him wealth and a future or used him to further his own ends? Did it matter?

He cursed, and he prayed. He prayed that Anton would come to, unscathed. Because no matter what, no matter how mysterious, deceitful, or infuriating the man could be, it was Mike's job to keep Voss alive. His sense of honor would not allow him to leave his partner to die alone in this reeking steel box at the bottom of the ocean. He cursed again, this time specifically at Anton. Loyalty did not preclude anger.

Mike adjusted his position, trying to relax, to clear his mind. The walls, the narrow steel tube, gripped them tightly. Two cats in a gas-filled box.

Clink.

What the hell—?

The ship had been as silent as a grave since the air pressure gave out. The ghostly sound continued, and then the pattern repeated. A single watery tap, then a pause and three taps, distant but decipherable. Then four more . . . and one.

It was the knock code taught in military survival schools. If the alphabet was divided into a five by five grid then row one, column three, stood for the letter C and row four, column one, was Q. "CQ" was the radio shorthand used to call a station, to call anyone listening. Someone was banging out a message on the hull of the *Bushranger.*

Fowler carefully set Anton's head on the deck and stood. He was desperately thirsty. It was time to figure out what to do and get the hell out of this mess.

Taking a hammer from his kit, he found an exposed stretch of hull. Struggling to imagine the graph of letters he tapped out T B L, an abbreviation for "trouble." Then W R K I N G, O N, I T.

"Roger" came the coded reply. Then, "Report later."

Mike Fowler looked around at the decaying control room, the unconscious man, and his bag of tools.

"Alright," he said aloud. "It's time to sort this mess out." There was a world full of possibilities just above his head. He needed to get back up there, and he needed to do it *now.*

From his bag, he pulled a roll of cloth-backed tape. It took several strips to seal the gash in Anton's hood and a few more to secure the Aqua-Lung's mouthpiece as well as his mask. Then Mike loosely taped Anton's wrists together. He had work to do and, if Voss came to, he wanted to be sure the man would think for a moment before he did anything stupid.

Ducking under the hoses that curled over his shoulders, Fowler slipped out of his tank. Gripping his mouthpiece firmly between his teeth, he pushed the tank up the evacuation skirt as he mounted the ladder. Crawling out onto the floor of the attack center, he felt around for another of his flashlights and, after switching it on, found the coil of rope he had brought in case they needed an additional guideline. With the rope in hand and the tank harness hanging from one shoulder, he reached up and fed half the length of rope over the rim of the locking wheel at the center of the hatch that led out to the submarine's exposed bridge. It was a straight drop through the lower hatch, and he let both ends fall to the floor of the control room. Then he had to take the damned tank off again in order to make his way, rung by rung, back down through the evacuation skirt.

The first time he tried it while hugging the steel cylinder to his chest. That didn't work. But it might with Voss. The old man was taller, but he had a slighter build.

Back in the control room, Fowler tied a loop in the rope. He got this under Anton's armpits with the rope in front, then tied on the tank. Mike dragged Voss over and propped him against the ladder.

He pulled on the loose end of the rope until it was taut, running from Voss and the tank all the way up to the wheel of the upper hatch and then back down. He ran a twist around the side of the ladder just under the first rung. Voss weighed a good 180 pounds plus his gear, but the twist of rope around the foot of the ladder would act as a brake. As long as Mike kept it snug, it should create enough friction so that he wouldn't have to hold Anton's full weight at every moment.

In order to keep Anton's neck straight he taped his head to the line leading up into the tower, then raised Anton's arms to full extension and taped them up too, giving him the arrow-shaped posture of a man about to dive into a swimming pool. That would keep him centered and, with luck, stop his shoulders from hanging up on the skirt.

"Alright," Fowler mumbled. "Let's get out of here!"

He hauled on the rope and Voss limply rose to a standing position. He tightened up the slack below his improvised brake. Then, taking the rope over his shoulder and bracing one foot against the base of the ladder, Fowler pushed off, leaning into it. Voss straightened and his feet left the ground. Mike tightened the rope and did it again. Anton's head and arms vanished up the evacuation trunk.

Mike took a fresh grip and a deep breath and pulled once more. Now it was just Anton's hips and legs that were protruding beneath the evacuation skirt.

"Again!" He lunged forward, hearing the steel of Anton's tank grind against the hatch combing. Progress! But—

No matter how hard Fowler pulled, the body would not move. The tank, the rubber suit, whatever he was wearing under it, somehow he was stuck, plugging the hole. Mike had to be sure Voss was centered in the ring of the hatch.

Mike pushed Anton one way and tried tightening the line. Nothing happened. He pushed the other way—

Damn it! Nothing about the man was ever easy!

Holding on to the rope as tightly as he could, Mike crouched, positioning himself with his shoulders under Anton's knees and clamped part of an arm across the man's ankles. With Voss almost sitting on his shoulder, Fowler rocked back and forth and tried to straighten up. His back felt like someone had painted a stripe of fire down one side and his wounded leg shuddered. His breath drew on the regulator in ragged gasps.

"Go . . . Up . . . You lying, miserable old goat! *Go!*"

Something happened. Anton's body rotated and came loose. He popped upward. Mike desperately pulled on the rope. He could feel its roughness scrape past his cheek. Bracing himself against the ladder he pulled and pulled. Anton's feet swung as they passed his face. He pulled until he could pull no farther. Anton's hands were jammed against the upper hatch. He had to give up a few inches to tie it off, but the escape trunk and the hatch were clear of everything except Anton's feet and ankles.

Mike crouched, gripping the ladder, gasping for breath.

Gasping—

Gasping —

"Oh, hell!" He had emptied his air tank.

Yanking on the wire to his J-valve, he released the reserve and took a breath. The remaining amount of air was just enough for a diver to get himself to the surface. But he was still sucking wind, and he couldn't take a moment to rest.

He gathered up his tools and cut off the loose part of the rope, then tied one end to the handles of his tool bag and the other around his waist. He slipped out of his tank harness and, pushing Anton's legs out of the way, made his way up the evacuation trunk and through the hatch.

Reaching out, he dragged over another air bottle and, taking a deep breath, unscrewed the valve and pushed the used one out of the way. Bracing the fresh tank with one knee, he mounted the valve and tightened it down. There was a blast of odd-tasting air and a moment of light-headedness. He blew out immediately and took another breath, this one pure, or as pure as the *Bushranger*'s compressors could provide.

Fowler staggered to his feet. He still didn't know how he was going to float Voss out of the upper hatch. He was just pulling up his bag of tools when he heard a noise, not the signaling from the *Bushranger*—something different. He shook his head; the ghosts of the USS *West Virginia* were thousands of miles away and twenty years in the past.

Then something touched him on the back.

"*What the—!*" Visions of the dead, both mournful and terrifying, loomed up. He turned . . .

. . . just as Anton Voss tried kicking him again. "Akk—Verflucht! Get me down from here!" he mumbled.

Mike Fowler relaxed his fists.

A few minutes later Voss sat propped against the wall of the attack center. Fowler had changed out his air tank and Anton groaned as the circulation painfully returned to his arms that had been constricted by the rope. Mike thought one pupil was dilated more than the other, but Voss turned his head out of the light before he could be sure.

Fowler reached over through the mess of spilled tools and spare air tanks and fished out the slate. *Can you swim?* he wrote.

Voss tried to lift his arm, but it limply collapsed. He pointed to his watch and made a circular motion. He needed more time. He gestured for the slate. Gritting his teeth against the pins and needles that coursed up both arms, he wrote, *A disaster!* His usually precise script was a child's scrawl.

Maybe not . . . Fowler thought. They had come this far and giving up wasn't really an option. If they didn't succeed, or at least get into position to make a deal, their lives would be forfeit.

"You just sit there." In case he wasn't understood, Mike indicated Voss should stay put. "I'll be back." Then he stood and, taking up the bag of tools, got ready to return to the black void of the control room.

Once again, the lower hatch was sealed, and a coded signal had alerted Johnson to come pick them up.

"You ready?" Fowler asked Voss.

The old man flexed his fingers and tried to square his shoulders. He looked beaten. "Get us out of here!" he ordered.

Fowler twisted the flood valve, and the chamber began to fill with water. It came to their knees, their thighs, higher and higher. Mike climbed the ladder and turned the wheel on the upper hatch. The increasing air pressure slammed it up to where the dogs caught it, and huge bubbles belched past him as freezing water rushed in. When everything had equalized, he twisted the handle to release the catches. Then he descended to tie on the tool bag, take off his tank, and thread his way back up and out into the cold but far less claustrophobic waters of the bridge.

Moving very carefully, he helped ease Anton's tank, and then his body, out of the hatch. Moments later they were slowly following their bubbles up the guideline. The surface glowed like the light of heaven.

Jack, Nicole, Sobek, and Koji were all waiting in the workboat.

Yamada was kitted out for a dive just in case anything went awry. Under a low overcast the snow-spattered mountains looked unbelievably tall and a blustery wind blew down the fjord, kicking up choppy waves and blowing spray. It was a dismal day, but it looked like the first of June after the interior of the U-boat.

They pulled Voss and then Fowler awkwardly over the side. Anton pawed the tape and mouthpiece away and ripped off his mask. He sucked in lungfuls of clean natural air. Nicole embraced Mike, seemingly unconcerned about the water soaking into her jacket as she helped him strip off his equipment.

Jack cast off from the buoy and the outboard roared to life. He turned the boat in a wide circle. Sobek peered at Fowler. "No luck, eh?"

"Just get us to the ship, okay? I could drink a gallon of water, and Mr. Voss is going to need stitches."

"Well, you got in once. Can't you figure a way to get the gold out?"

Mike almost lost his temper, but Voss glared at him, and he bit back angry words that might have revealed too much. After a moment he said, "We have several options, some of them a lot easier than others, just keep your shirt on."

Nicole looked alarmed. No doubt she, like Voss, was worried he was going to blow their story. This wasn't the time or place for that argument, but as far as he was concerned it had grown completely stale. Mike Fowler had had it.

When they reached the *Bushranger*, the others went aboard, then Jack and Koji swung out the diving stage so that Voss wouldn't have to climb the cargo netting they had hung over the side. During that moment alone Anton gripped Fowler's arm and whispered, "Say nothing, understand! Nothing!"

Mike was disgusted. He reached out and removed the hand.

While Voss was hustled to the cabin that doubled as a sickbay, Fowler changed into a pair of dungarees. By the time he made it back to the main deck Anton had been peeled out of his dry suit and placed in the barber's chair that sat across from the examination table. Using scissors and liberal amounts of peroxide, Johnson began to carefully remove the blood-encrusted rag. On a tray nearby Frank Jano was organizing a set of needles and sutures.

Suarez, Ward, Benham, and Paluso all crowded around the door, peppering Fowler with whispered questions: "What happened?" "What now?" "What was it like in there?" Mike didn't answer; he didn't even bother to remember the questions.

Nicole delivered two aluminum tumblers of water, one for him and one for Voss. Mike finished his in two big gulps, then Paluso pulled him aside. "Seriously, if that didn't work what the hell are we going to do?"

"Look, just take it easy! I've got a different plan and it's going to solve all our problems." He looked around for Nicole to hand the cup back. She had been there a moment before but, suddenly, she was gone. Mike pushed past Suarez but nearly ran into Fernando, who was headed toward sick bay.

"Señor Fowler! You are okay!"

"Yeah. It's Mr. Voss who got banged up. Have you seen Nicole? She was here a minute ago."

"Oh, sí, I think she is looking for you . . . She is on deck with your jacket."

He didn't need his jacket; he needed a damn shower—and she knew where he was—

Oh, *hell*!

Mike Fowler turned away from Fernando, slamming through the hatch and out onto the deck.

Forward, all he could see was Yamada stowing their gear. Aft? At the far end of the deck his down jacket was draped over one of the stern bollards. Its sleeve fluttered in the wind. Mike began to run.

When he came around the corner of the deckhouse, he saw Nicole crouched over. She was prying at the plastic case of the transistor radio with her fingernails. It came apart, the two halves clattering to her feet.

"Nicole! *Stop*!"

She whirled. There was a look in her eyes he hadn't seen since she tried to stab him in his Alexandria hotel room.

"What *is* this? Is this your new plan, the one that's going to solve all our problems?" she hissed. White-knuckled, her fist clutched Fordyce's transmitter.

"You know what it is. Hand it to me." He started toward her.

"No. I can't let you—"

"Let me *what*?"

"Stay back!" Her right hand slipped into her jacket pocket and emerged with his .380 Remington. Her thumb flipped down the safety. "I can't let you give it to them."

"No one is *giving* anything to anyone."

She took on a boxer's stance, the gun held almost at shoulder height but close in, where she could defend it. What she wanted to do was throw the transmitter overboard but, unless she just tossed it blindly over her shoulder, she wasn't in a position to do that.

"Stop!" she demanded.

Mike Fowler was *done*. He was sick of Paul Sobek and Mel Paluso. He was sick of Anson Fordyce, and Otto Skorzeny, Heinrich Hartmann, Peter Anhaldt, and all their Nazi pals. But more than anything he was angry that his attempts to protect Voss, and Nicole, and Jack Johnson had all three relationships dancing on the edge of a precipice. And he was fed up with being led around, with taking orders, being used as a pawn or as cannon fodder for one supposedly greater agenda or another . . .

. . . so he didn't stop.

"Don't! Michael, no matter how I feel about you . . . I *will* shoot you."

"No, you won't."

That got to her, something about the flat certainty in the way he said it. She backed up a step and shook the little gray box at him,

"The CIA won't share what's on that submarine. I have my orders. This is it. This is the mission!" Though her eyes filled with tears the gun tracked straight and true.

He looked at her coldly. He knew exactly how he felt about her, but he wouldn't be thwarted. "No, that is *not* your mission. Get your head on straight. That transmitter *has not been used.* Those people are *not* my friends. But if Anhaldt and Skorzeny show up, or if we cannot raise the sub, it just *might* be an insurance policy. It could save our lives, understand? So, that decision is not going to be mine alone. And it's sure as hell not going to be *yours*!"

"You have to think about *us* . . ." she said.

That slowed him down. "Us? You and me?" It also made him angry. "You mean that's the price? That's your *price*?" He stared at her. He had already paid too much by keeping his mouth shut. He didn't owe her anything, and he didn't owe Anton. They had both asked for more than they deserved.

She could see it wasn't working. "You have to understand! I—I was asked to take this mission for Israel. But I chose . . . I came to protect *you*."

"Good for you. I'd do the same." He meant it and this time he believed her. It didn't change his mind.

She had shown him the Israeli laboratory in the dunes. She had warned him about the hat that would help her people tail him in Italy. And if she had been ordered to maintain a relationship with him to have an inside line on the international arms trade . . . well, it had been totally unproductive, because from the beginning, he had never shared the details of a single deal, and she had never asked. He was done fooling around; whatever she chose to do was a risk he was willing to take.

He put out his hand.

Her finger tightened on the trigger.

"Hand it over!"

Her eyes wavered.

"There's been too much plotting and too many secrets. We're *all* going to get to the bottom of this mess, and we're going to do it right *now*. So, trust me, or shoot me, because I'm taking that damned transmitter!"

A tear streaked her cheek.

But she lowered the pistol . . . and then handed him the gray box with the wires wrapped around it.

"Come on," he said, and turned away to pull on his jacket. He was cold and he wanted to get this over with before it was too late.

CHAPTER 30

When Fowler returned to the crowd near the sick bay door Anton Voss had a patch of hair shaved off the side of his head. It was marked with an angry red line dotted with tied-off stitches. Johnson taped a gauze pad over the wound and handed Voss a pair of bottles, penicillin and Demerol. Jack looked up and Fowler caught his eye.

"Meet me in the wardroom," Mike said, then looked around. "That goes for everybody."

"What now?" Sobek grumbled.

Voss seemed to sense that the situation was about to go critical. He closed his eyes and clenched his jaw. Well, that was tough. What came next wasn't going to be pleasant for anyone.

Mike grabbed the dripping tool bag he had left near the doorway and started down the passage with Nicole following close behind.

Entering the wardroom Fowler went to the pass-through and spoke to Benham. "Could you round up the rest of the crew? I want to explain what's going on."

The others filed in, and Anton Voss unsteadily took a seat in the back corner. He had been losing weight since they left Talcahuano, and now he looked like death warmed over. Mike expected an objection or at the very least a hostile glare, but what he got was more veiled.

Paul Sobek fidgeted with a highball glass. "So what's this big announcement?"

There was no way to sugarcoat it, and Mike didn't want to.

"There is no gold," he said.

In the back of the room Voss lowered his head into one hand. For the rest of them the news took a moment to penetrate.

"Wait! You mean somebody got here first? *Who?*" Sobek seemed to think Fowler and Voss had been able to search the submarine.

"No." Mike made it a challenge. He was angry, angry at himself for letting things get so out of hand, angry at Voss, at the whole situation.

"Whaddya mean, no?" Paluso demanded. "What the hell happened to it?"

"You've been lied to." Mike turned to Jack, his friend. "I lied to you."

"You mean—" Iannucci was still working it out.

This time Mike put some extra force behind his words. "There never was any gold! No gold. *Understand?*"

Sobek lurched to his feet. "Oh, no! Don't you try and con me! We—we get our end. That's final! If this is some kind of scam—" He frowned, realizing that he didn't fully understand the situation. He pointed to Nicole. "She said there was! She said—"

"I lied, too," Nicole stated flatly. She might have enjoyed tormenting Sobek, but now they were neck-deep in the exact situation both she and Voss had tried to avoid.

"Really?" Jack Johnson took a grip on Fowler's jacket and spun him around. Muscles bulged in the Australian's arm. "You'd better explain . . . *carefully*. And don't give me any of that 'I tried to warn you' rubbish. You suckered us into something seriously bloody crazy!"

Waretini growled. There was a shifting of feet and a change in attitude from the crew of the *Bushranger*. Cacoyannis glanced at Ian Ward. "Great, just great . . ."

"I'll crucify all of you!" Sobek was breathing hard, and his voice slipped into a higher register. "Do you know where the money we gave you came from? There won't be anywhere you can hide! Nowhere!"

Mike almost laughed. If Sobek had compromised himself by using mob money to finance their expedition . . . Well, he was going to have a hard time feeling bad about it. And as for the threat, Meyer Lansky could get in line. He was the least of their worries.

The mobster went on, "If we don't deliver what *you* promised, there's gonna be hell to pay!" He lunged toward Voss, but Paluso held him back. Sobek was shaking with anger, or possibly fear. "I'm not—"

"What you're doing is blathering on like a wounded galah!" Johnson pointed toward Nicole and Voss. "*Think!* We've got Mata Hari and the Great Mastermind on board. We didn't end up down here for nothing." He glared across the room. "So, what is it?"

Neither spoke up.

Johnson turned on Mike. "Alright, mate, your turn . . . *just what in bloody blazes is going on*! Speak up, because I'm losing patience very, very, quickly!"

Mike Fowler felt the stress of the last few weeks lifting away, Jack had the right to hate him for what he'd done, or hadn't done, but at least he wasn't lying anymore.

"It's about nuclear power. There's some kind of secret information on that U-boat," he said.

Jack Johnson, then Mel Paluso, then Paul Sobek . . . and the whole crew of the *Bushranger* turned to stare at Anton Voss.

Voss sighed.

"It is more than that," he admitted. "The U-Null was the world's first atomic submarine."

Anton's statement hung in the room.

Mike Fowler blinked in surprise. That was a new and astounding fact: a secret German project completed a full decade prior to the launching of the USS *Nautilus* . . . but while it might be an interesting historical detail—or an attempt to derail their anger—it wasn't particularly meaningful unless what Voss was after, and what Fordyce, the CIA, and the Mossad *thought* Voss was after, were the same thing.

"Tell them the rest," Mike challenged. "Go on."

"It is a unique technology, significantly more advanced—"

"Atomic fusion." Mike drove him back to the actual point. Then he gambled and repeated a word he remembered from that night on the beach in Israel . . . "Tychon."

Voss looked like he'd been hit with a brick, like his partner had betrayed him instead of the other way around.

"We've got atomic submarines, right?" Paluso challenged. "If you listen to the news, everyone's building them."

Voss shook his head as if to clear it and winced in pain. "It is not the *what*. It is the *how*. When *you* think 'atomic submarine,' whether you know it or not, you are imagining a fission reactor. Now remember the term Mr. Fowler used, 'fusion,' yes?"

"So, you're saying it's a different process . . . ?" Johnson asked.

"Indeed. A much more elegant process."

Paluso scowled. "You showed us a photograph with gold bars. You were in it!"

"Yes, yes. Gold bars from the Reichsbank. We used several hundred kilos to construct shielding for the second generation of experiments. Anyway, it was convenient that I still had the photograph."

"*Convenient?*" Sobek exclaimed.

Johnson released an exasperated breath. "Why didn't you tell us, eh? How is this more secret than . . . well, stealing stolen gold?"

"Gold . . . is only money. This is harder to explain. If I had admitted what I was after, one of you would certainly have asked questions, done research. This would have led to exposure."

"So you swindled us!" Sobek shook his head as if he had never contemplated an unethical act of his own. "I need to hear 'thirty million dollars'! Without that we're *toast*. You made promises . . . so *I* made promises."

Paluso held up a hand, quieting his partner. "Okay, wait. You say it's 'unique technology' . . . Is there money in it?"

For just an instant Mike caught a flicker of Anton's cunning smile. "There is certainly money. A great deal of it, if handled correctly."

"And you knew all about this?" Johnson turned on Fowler. "You played right along."

Nicole suddenly spoke up. "Michael didn't know anything about the actual cargo until he got to Israel. We told him very little, and he didn't believe us." She was defending him, but she was also looking at him with almost as much suspicion as Jack. "But somehow he now knows a good deal more."

She let them consider the implication.

"I was picked up by the CIA in Bariloche. They gave me this beacon"—Mike tossed Fordyce's gray box onto the table—"and they made me an offer."

Voss looked at the transmitter as if it was a poisonous snake. Was he disturbed that Mike had been carrying the damn thing around all this time, or because he hadn't realized how easily a betrayal might have been engineered?

"So, what's the offer?" Johnson asked.

Nicole swallowed, bracing herself.

Fowler laid it out. "Six million dollars. Protection. Help with the cops and the courts, the banks . . . maybe Jack's shipyard problem. All we have to do is locate the sub and hook up the transmitter, no need to salvage."

Johnson nodded slowly. "Well, it's not thirty—"

"It's not enough." Sobek turned to his partner. "We can't go back without—"

Paluso shook his head. "*You're* the one who couldn't keep his mouth shut. *My* reputation is based on whatever I deliver. I didn't promise them a bank!"

"That's not the only offer . . ." Fowler broke in. He couldn't have cared less about Sobek's problems, but Nicole was treating him like the opposition. Nothing could be further from the truth. He just wasn't automatically in the bag for her bosses.

They all turned to look in her direction.

Her back was straight, resolute. "I can't do better. If this is the way it has to be—I can only guarantee half of that. Up to three million, depending on the exchange rate. If you need protection I can provide citizenship, new identities."

Mike still hadn't told them everything. "There's a problem with the American proposal." He glanced at Johnson and arched an eyebrow. ". . . It comes from Anson Fordyce."

Jack Johnson froze, shocked by that name from his past. Then he erupted, a volcano of profanity ending with "No! No! No! Ab-so-lutely no!"

Ihaka Waretini and Colin McLeod shared a look. Fordyce was a name they remembered from Johnson's and Fowler's war stories . . . the kind that were told when the booze ran out and all that was left were the bad memories.

Sobek and Paluso looked at each other in alarm. "What's going on? Who's this Fordyce character?"

"*Don't!* Don't even say his name!" Johnson insisted. "That snake! Rummy and I—he almost killed us. And I'm not talking *accidentally*!"

Now it was Nicole and Anton's turn to trade a look; they both knew Mike despised and distrusted the dapper operative, but they had never been told why.

"There is no way in heaven or hell I'll make a deal with that maggot! You can take that transmitter and shove it!"

"Aaand that means you don't want the six million dollars?" Paluso asked.

Mad Jack Johnson just growled.

"I want to remind everyone that Anhaldt and Skorzeny are still looking for us," Mike said. "And I've been told that if we don't get in touch, Fordyce is going to treat us like a liability rather than an asset."

The room quieted. Everyone was looking at their hole cards and finding they were unhappy with the result.

Mike looked over at Anton. He hadn't come all this way without a plan. He always had a plan. "Alright, Mr. Voss," Mike said, "it's about time you tell us what you're thinking."

Voss took a moment, gathering his energy.

"We must make the best deal possible, yes? And we must live to collect it." He turned to Fowler. "So, a regulated fusion reaction . . . did they explain why this is a good thing? Perhaps you will tell us what they said."

"Fordyce seems to think it's the solution to mankind's future. Endless power, no pollution, advanced manufacturing, an economic miracle for everyone."

Voss glanced at Nicole. "What do you think? What will happen if it goes to Israel?"

Her response was immediate. "We become a scientific power competitive with the most advanced countries in the world. Our security is guaranteed. Israel must act now, in the open; there is no incentive for keeping secrets."

"Is that *all*?"

Mike and Nicole glanced at each other, but neither spoke.

"Very interesting. Either your friends in so-called intelligence have kept the most important details to themselves . . . or they are as ignorant as I hoped they would be."

"You mean there's more to it?"

"Of course there is. The Manhattan Project? Did you think that was the *end*, that it was something only *Americans* could do? Do you think this sort of progress simply stopped, just because we no longer hear about it?"

Voss pinched the bridge of his nose right where his glasses had long ago worn a crease in his skin. "The beginning of the twentieth century was an extraordinary era in the study of physics. Immediately after the Great War, when I first contemplated an advanced degree, it was thought that all atoms were made of electrons and protons. Such is the conservative nature of science that to speak of anything beyond this 'two-particle paradigm' was considered reckless and disruptive. Then, in just a short period of time, five more of what we now call 'subatomic' particles were either identified or mathematically postulated.

"For those arrogant enough to think they understood the nature of the universe, it was humbling. If you were to add in the earlier discoveries of photons and alpha particles the picture had become more complex than could be tolerated by the existing theories. Scientific work exists to be disproven, but there was a joke that anyone who proposed yet another aspect of what we called the 'inner-atomic realm' should be punished for adding to the confusion.

"But you know the outcome: we now live in an age of miracles and wonder. We can heat our food with microwaves, treat cancer with radiation, transmit moving images across the planet, look within the human body, understand the cosmos, and map the microscopic world. At the same time, we developed nuclear bombs, and the most paranoid have attempted to solve their dilemma by building monuments to that paranoia, true doomsday weapons. We are faced with the waste products of nuclear industry and our primitive reactors. Humility is required because of one great truth: everything in existence also contains its opposite, the blessing as well as the curse.

"In the torpedo room of that U-boat there are thirty-two stainless steel drums. They contain the archives of a series of highly classified experiments. Experiments that were able to discover many things . . . things that should not exist. Miraculous things. *Dangerous* things.

"The device that made this science possible was called 'Die Glasglocke,' the Bell Jar, because of its shape and the aspect of isolation that was part of its function. The rest of us called it the 'Bienenstock,' the Beehive, because of the noise it made . . . and because its swarm could harm whoever was not careful.

"The initial investigations were performed near the Reichspost facility in Miersdorf and the results far outstripped the capacity of our sensors. It was war, so this was not cautious research. Mistakes were made.

"Before I became aware of the project, five of the seven original scientists had died. The second generation of workers were much more careful. But even that was not enough." For a moment Anton Voss closed his eyes, perhaps remembering . . . or trying to forget.

Finally, he went on, "My responsibility was to develop advanced naval technologies. In this case a propulsion system for Unterseeboots that did not require them to surface to recharge their batteries. It so happened that the first useful product of these experiments was a negatively charged elementary particle. They named it the Tychon, after an ancient god of accident. But from what I understand it was not an accident, and by no means was it the only discovery.

"To produce a stream of the newly discovered particles we constructed a carefully tuned version of the original laboratory equipment. This was focused on a target volume of deuterium, which was electrolyzed from heavy water, in a reaction chamber. For a subatomic particle the Tychon was quite massive, and once it was induced to take the place of the electron in an atom of deuterium, the increased mass would cause it to orbit much more tightly around what was now the Tychonic-deuterium nucleus. Thus, these atoms are drawn more closely together, close enough so that . . . voilà, the nuclei fuse, and when they do, a substantial amount of heat is released. Steam can then be created to power a turbine and produce an abundance of electricity.

"The process is called 'catalyzed fusion' because hydrogen atoms *are* able to fuse naturally. However, this is a rare and isolated event. Only in the heat and gravity of a star does it become a naturally self-perpetuating occurrence. But add a stream of targeted Tychons to the mixture and the probability greatly increases. All of this occurs at much more reasonable temperatures. No stars are needed."

"What about radioactivity?" Nicole asked.

"Pfft! Nothing at all like a fission reactor. There are very few liabilities. Except . . . well, it is a *catalyzed* reaction, so you would not want to lose control of the process, allow it to run away and become so energetic the hydrogen simply begins to fuse on its own."

"You're saying that's bad?" Paluso asked.

"It is a thermonuclear bomb."

"So it could be a weapon?" Johnson asked.

"A poor one, quite heavy. Given the state of technology in 1945 it was too big to be the warhead of a missile or be delivered by aircraft. But, yes, it is a clean hydrogen bomb, vastly more powerful than those dropped on Japan, yet with no long-term radioactivity. Nothing to make a mad dictator, or anyone else, think twice about using it, if they could only figure out how."

Anton Voss looked around the room. He was exhausted . . . but his eyes burned like pale fire. "Look, you must realize the Tychon particle was only one of *many* discoveries, the easiest to turn into a functional technology. Whoever takes the information from the U-boat, it will be like Prometheus stealing fire from the gods, Pandora's box, all the trouble in the world . . . and all the hope, too. Fusion power was merely the first gift, the enticement. The value of the entire archive is astronomical."

"Okay, we understand, this is a big deal, big enough to put us all at risk. What do you think we should do about it?" Fowler pushed him to get to the point.

Voss shot him a look from the corner of his eye and his voice took on a sly, testing tone . . . "The safest course would be to destroy it all and return home. But then each of us would still have to find a way to pay our various pipers."

Mike glanced at Nicole, who clenched her jaw, then Jack who shifted his feet and looked away. "Not a chance!" Sobek spoke up. "This sounds like the opportunity of a *lifetime*."

Anton hesitated, then said, "Alright. So, here is *a* plan: we raise the boat. I will extract just enough of the documentation to suit our needs, enough to be worth what we will ask but not so much anyone feels they must kill us to control it. I will preserve the science, not the engineering, the what, not the how. Then we burn the rest.

"The power plant of the U-Null has many similarities to the test equipment that enabled these discoveries. Even without the archives, a careful study of the engine room could reveal much of what we wish to control. That must be completely destroyed with explosives.

"As quickly as possible we will then make our way to Cape Town where"—Voss gestured toward Fowler—"our associate Señor Porras has set the stage for an auction. If all went according to plan, the list of guests was sent out several days ago. They were carefully selected to maintain a balance of power and our survival. The USSR, companies from the U.S., France, and the United Kingdom—I picked these for obvious reasons. Sweden was invited because of their industrial capacity and because they are neutral. I have included South Africa so that they, as hosts, do not feel slighted."

"And we already have an emissary from Israel with us," Mike stated. He was not asking Anton's permission.

Voss gave a slight nod. "In the past the rules have been that I would reveal limited amounts of information. This would be interspersed with rounds of bidding. The result was always a 'winner take all' affair. This time we will do things differently. Once everyone has paid in, they will all receive a copy of the entire package; the information will not be exclusive.

"Simultaneously, we must break the story to the major newspapers of the world. There will be no more secrets, so there will be no use in silencing us."

"How much?" Sobek was not going to let it go.

"Israel has three million," Nicole said.

"Look, doll, even if everyone matches you, that's not enough. If this is the biggest thing in history, we've got to up the ante."

Nicole glared at him, then she said, "As soon as we are out of here I'll need to use the radio."

Johnson cleared his throat and moved on. "Alright, raising the boat . . . that job sure hasn't gotten any easier."

"Jack?" Mike was glad Johnson was back in the game, but raising the sub was still the best option. "We need to get the hell out of here before someone corners us. I can bring her up. One hose. The *Bushranger* will have enough clearance, twelve to thirteen hundred feet, and it'll be a *lot* faster."

Mike reached down into the tool bag he had used inside the submarine. He lifted out the core of a ballast control valve he had pulled from the panel while Voss had been recovering.

"What the hell?" Sobek murmured.

"We're going to run an air line from the *Bushranger* right through the sub's hull and into the high-pressure manifold. Then Mr. Voss and I are going back inside, and we're going to blow the tanks and drive her straight to the surface!"

Johnson didn't speak. He looked deep into his friend's eyes and Fowler held his gaze. This idea was no less crazy than the one they had just tried . . . but whether he ever regained Jack's trust or not, they still had a job to do.

"Alright . . ." Jack finally said. "Alright. You tell me what you need. We'll get 'er done."

The evening sky was a mottled gray, and a lower level of clouds was scudding past the surrounding peaks. Ripples formed around the *Bushranger*'s anchor chains, and flecks of ice followed the turning tide.

Nicole and Anton, Jack and Ihaka, Mel Paluso and Paul Sobek stood at the stern railing. Each had come to a decision, committed to a course of action. And even though they didn't necessarily trust one another, they had decided that there was only one way forward.

"Are we all agreed?" Mike Fowler asked.

Nicole nodded and hugged her coat tighter against the wind. She was getting most of what she wanted, but she didn't look happy about it.

Anton, standing beside her, just arched an eyebrow. He was worn out but still appraising his errant partner.

"Do it. The last thing we need is someone else cutting in on our action," Paul Sobek growled.

"Just chuck the blasted thing before that miserable ponce shows up to take it back!" Jack turned away and headed forward.

Mike wound up and threw Fordyce's transmitter as hard as he could. Far out on the water there was a small splash. Then it was gone forever, and with it went any temptation to change their fate. Mike hoped it was the last secret that existed between the members of their expedition . . . but deep down he didn't believe that, not at all.

CHAPTER 31

By dawn the *Bushranger* was already bustling with activity. Winches rumbled as Waretini adjusted the ship's position, moving back to the buoy that marked the location of the submarine. Breath steaming in the cold air, Frank Jano laid out rolls of cable for the welding and cutting equipment and Koji Yamada serviced the compressors, purging their tanks of moisture. No one was happy, but they were all hard at work.

In the machine shop Colin McLeod hunched over his bench, magnifying spectacles perched on his forehead. He was making careful measurements of every aspect of the valve core Fowler had brought back from the U-Null. He would then compare the measurements to a grease-smeared set of reference books. Only once he was certain of the precise dimensions would he cut the threads that would marry a stretch of air hose to the ballast-control manifold of the submarine.

Though Anton Voss should have stayed in his bunk, he appeared for breakfast. But rather than eating, he demanded a pencil and a large sketch pad. Soon the table was covered with detailed drawings of the inside of the U-Null's conning tower as well as a section of its exterior.

When Johnson appeared, Mike beckoned him over to the table where Voss was working. Setting aside whatever tension remained, the three of them pored over the stack of plans, discussing exactly how they were going to modify the side of the conning tower.

"You will cut through here." Voss pointed to a spot on an interior elevation. "The outer deck is like this . . ." He penciled in an arc that struck the wall of the attack center several inches above the floor line. "It is not intelligent to remove all this material. Whenever we enter, a small amount of water will have to drain to the bilge . . . I will go down and mark the spot for you to cut—"

"No, you will *not*." Fowler brought that idea to a halt. "Do whatever drawings you need to. But I'll mark it. You need rest. You're not going back in the water until we're ready to bring her up."

"Are you now my commanding officer, or my caretaker?" Voss snapped. "I know what I'm capable of!"

"I'm not taking any chances. Without you, we're all up this particular creek without a paddle. You made this mess, Anton. Until we can see our way clear, you're going to do what I say!"

Johnson looked from one of them to the other, assessing how their relationship had changed. Fowler caught Johnson's eye and inclined his head toward the door.

In the corridor Mike said, "We're sitting ducks. I'd like to post sentries, forward observers, make sure we're forewarned if someone finds us."

"Where?"

"In that narrow passage where the tide almost caught us, or the hills above the big pool just inside."

"Who were you thinking of? My men are gonna be needed."

"Paluso and Zúñiga."

"Right. Do you think the two of them'll do it? I'd say trust is in short supply around here."

Fowler shot a skeptical glance at his friend. No matter what, Jack was going to bust his chops every chance he got. "Zúñiga isn't going to be a problem. Paluso? I don't know. We'll have to find out . . ."

"Not a chance!" Paul Sobek spoke up immediately. He turned to where his partner was lying on his bunk. "These liars are trying to divide and conquer. And if my guys and I are out of action, you're gonna get left behind. They're not—"

Fowler interrupted. "Every minute we sit here increases the possibility we end up with nothing, go to prison, or get shot and dumped at sea. There are days of work ahead . . . maybe weeks. I need someone down there who can stand watch and give a shout if anyone comes our way." Mike looked directly at Paluso and went on, "Cool heads, who won't do anything suicidal if it's a Chilean gunboat or the U.S. Navy but can figure a way to help out if a bunch of Nazis show up."

Paluso sat up and stretched. "You know, I've been feeling like a fifth wheel," he said. "How's this gonna work?"

Sobek threw up his hands and stalked out.

"Waretini will take you down in the workboat. He'll help you set up an observation post, then he'll come back."

"Nope." Now it was Paluso's turn to object. "You give us the boat, a month of supplies, and weapons. I'm not getting stuck down there without a way back. And I'm not getting stuck down there without a chance of making it out if you mugs abandon us. I'm ready to be useful, but I'm not stupid!"

Fowler looked at Johnson; it was his boat.

Jack shook his head. "You can have an inflatable, a Seagull outboard, and thirty gallons of petrol. That might get you somewhere, but I need the workboat."

"Throw in a couple of paperbacks and it's a deal."

By 9 A.M. they'd set a diving plan, and Ian Ward was already at work preparing the side of the submarine's conning tower. For this job the divers would be wearing heavy gear, the old-style suits of rubberized canvas, weighted boots, and the bulbous Mark V copper helmet that Fowler remembered from his days in salvage.

It was a safer setup and better for working in deep water. The primary advantage was that additional layers of insulation could be worn. By the time they had removed enough of the outer plating to install the air line they would be down past one hundred feet. That meant they had a total of twenty-five minutes to get down to the worksite, do what they could, and return to the surface. If anything went wrong and decompression stops were needed, the extra insulation might be the difference between life and death. Additionally, when a diver was handling heavy scraps of freshly cut metal the protection of the tough canvas was a significant advantage over the thin rubber of the dry suits.

Along with the three younger divers, Johnson, Clarence Benham, and Fowler would each take at least one shift a day. Suarez and Iannucci, neither of whom had any experience cutting steel, stood ready to go down wearing an Aqua-Lung and fins if there was an emergency.

Once the work had begun, Johnson left Waretini in charge and he and Fowler packed the inflatable boat with camping supplies, binoculars, and an AN/PRC-10 field radio. Then Paluso and Zúñiga waited as Mike unlocked the door to the ship's magazine. He gave Fernando an FG 42, a bandolier of loaded magazines, and one of the Browning pistols. Paluso took his .357 Python and the M3 submachine gun.

"You be careful down there. We're just looking for a warning, not heroics."

Paluso nodded, then he stuck the pistol in his belt and shook Mike's hand. Ten minutes later Paluso and Zúñiga climbed down into the rubber boat and headed south.

The divers spent three days cutting away sections of the U-Null's outer hull. Three days of short, cold shifts interspersed with intervals for recovery. Three days that seemed to drag on and on. The pressure and constant immersion in the freezing water caused a cascade of bodily reactions and overworked kidneys. The lavatories stank, and to compensate for dehydration and combat hypothermia, they drank hot tea by the gallon. After his second dive Benham began to feel dizzy and weak. Fearing the bends, Johnson completely removed him from the schedule.

By the end of each day the men looked at the icy water with dread. The fatigue, the awkward conditions, and the slow pace of the work all took their toll on morale. To make matters worse, the temperature dropped, bringing in rain and powerful blustering winds that made everyone fear a return of the vicious williwaws they had experienced at Field Anchorage. The various factions on the *Bushranger* all performed their duties, but the growing camaraderie of the last couple of weeks had dissolved.

Anton Voss seemed to be recovering yet he kept to himself as much as possible. That wasn't difficult; no one was interested in talking to him except, ironically, Nicole, who was also looked upon with suspicion. Ever since their showdown on the afterdeck, she had been avoiding Mike. He couldn't tell if she was still angry, or embarrassed. Whatever her problem was, he suspected she'd get over it. She was an intelligence officer; pouting wasn't in her job description.

On the third day Fowler did not suit up until evening, and when he did he climbed back into his dark green dry suit and one of the Jack Browne face masks. An hour before, Johnson had announced that Koji Yamada was back on deck and that he had succeeded in removing the last section of outer plating. The next job—Fowler's job—would require as much maneuverability and dexterity as he could manage.

Alone in the workshop, Waretini helped Fowler gear up. Under the big man's supervision Mike smoothed out his wool long underwear and sweater before pulling on the clingy layer of rubber. The pressure at a hundred feet left an itchy welt anywhere the fabric bunched or folded.

"You always knew what to do."

Mike turned to look at Ihaka, wondering what he was talking about.

"Back in New Guinea, if there was something too heavy, too dangerous, trapped under wreckage, buried in a ship's hold . . . you were the one who figured it out.

"We was Mad Jack's crew, wild men who thought they could salvage anything." Waretini handed over the suspenders and an extra-heavy weight belt. "Before you left, you taught us how to do all that and survive. You turned Mad Jack Johnson into Hydraulic Jack Johnson, the name on the business card. You made us a success."

"I was just trying to make a living, same as you."

"Well, you taught us. I know you're a good man. You thought this would be a chance for everyone. It would have been better if we had known the truth, but diving, she's always risky . . . We accept that. Some of them might be angry, but I understand. So does Jack. So do Collie, and Frank, and Clarence. We knew you then; we know you now, okay? Just remember, we want to be rich . . . but we also want to go home."

Waretini helped him tie off the tunnel in the front of the suit, then handed Fowler the bag of tools he would carry with him on his dive. The last thing Mike picked up was a diver's slate where he had scratched a series of numbers, the dimensions Voss had calculated from his drawings.

As they headed for the deck it wasn't just the extra-heavy belt that weighed Mike down.

He descended in darkness. The surface and the hull of the *Bushranger* became invisible almost as soon as the water covered his head. The tinny vibration of the winch followed him down.

"Alright. Stop here." The microphone was a silver knob attached to the triangular glass between his nose and mouth. A rubber-covered headphone pressed against the hood over his left ear.

The diving stage ground to a halt, the lights affixed to its sides revealing the top of the Type XXI's conning tower. Mike ducked into the enclosed bridge and gathered his lines before swimming forward. He dropped his tool bag through the open hatch, then eased his way down into the now familiar confines of the attack center.

In the dim glow of a flashlight, he began making careful measurements, identifying a spot on the wall opposite the rear edge of what Voss called the "Fruit Machine." This was a large mechanical computer that did indeed look a bit like an old-style vending machine. In wartime it was used to program the sub's torpedoes. After consulting his notes, Fowler made a mark about fifteen inches off the floor, then another twelve inches above that.

Bracing himself against the periscope trunk, he picked up the pneumatic drill, planted both feet on the pressure hull, and placed the bit on the upper mark. He pulled the trigger.

Bubbles rushed past Fowler's mask and rattled off the overhead. He leaned in, applying pressure. A minute went by, then another.

The bit broke through and ran free. He shut it down.

"You there? Five minutes." Fowler must have missed Waretini's first call.

"One more job and I'm on my way," Mike said.

He pushed a bolt into the hole he had just drilled then gathered up his tools. Wriggling up out of the hatch he got everything back onto the diving stage.

"Take me down," he said.

Mike lay on the platform and used his feet to hold it away from the side of the tower as he descended. With a strip of its external skin removed, the submarine had lost some of its sleek menace. It was beginning to look like just another wreck. Anton's memory, however, was fantastically accurate. Protruding almost exactly halfway between the steel ribs that had connected the inner and outer hulls and ten inches above the line of the deck was the tip of the bolt.

"Stop!" he called out. His fingers were numb and unsteady, so he grasped the bolt firmly and twisted a nut onto the threads to hold it in place. Then he unwound a string tied to a heavy grease pencil and attached it to the bolt. Using this as a guide he marked the hole that Cacoyannis would cut with his torch.

"Okay. Ready to come up."

Nothing happened.

"Hey! Anybody listening?"

The stage didn't move and the comm line hissed impotently. Fowler's chest tightened as he restrained a new spasm of shivering.

Then suddenly the stage started upward, grinding against the freshly cut steel along the side of the conning tower.

A voice whispered in Mike's ear . . . not Waretini's mellow tones but Johnson's harsh Queensland accent. "Mate, don't be alarmed. We're going lights out. I'll explain when you get on deck . . ."

The gray-green bubble of illuminated water around him collapsed, but the platform continued winding its way upward into blackness.

Waretini pulled Fowler onto the deck using a red-filtered GI flashlight. Mike yanked off his mask and dropped it, hissing air, to the deck.

"What happened?" he demanded.

"Come on!"

Mike unbuckled his weight belt and followed the Māori to the machine shop door. Waretini knocked twice. The door opened, but all was dark inside. Frank Jano dogged it tight behind them then turned on his own flashlight, holding the lens cupped in the fingers of one hand.

"Guys . . . what *is* it?"

"We've been spotted . . . maybe," Ihaka said.

Jano shut off the compressor, then used the muted beam to illuminate the interior door. "Jack's aloft, monitoring the radio."

Mike went up the steep stairs two at a time.

Jack Johnson wasn't the only one in the chartroom. Sobek was there, as were Voss and Nicole. Koji Yamada stood in the corner.

He was keeping out of the way, but he wore a bandolier of magazines and one of the FG 42 automatic rifles was leaning against the radar console.

Mike pulled the rubber hood off his head as Jack turned away from the radio. "There was another plane," he explained. "Paluso heard it. He radioed in using code, clicking his mic on and off in case they had scanning equipment. It wasn't clear what he was doing at first, so I don't know if we got our lights shut down fast enough."

"Damn! That's not good."

Johnson held up a finger. Above the buffeting of the wind, the moan of an engine could be heard. "Hear that? That's the second pass."

Jack pushed past Nicole and Voss, climbing to the step below the closed door to the wheelhouse. He nodded at Koji, who switched off the red battle lights. They all followed, feeling their way through the door then out onto the bridge wing.

The sound came from the north, near the peaks that marked the center of the island, but it had the unmistakable burble of a set of piston engines. "That's no jet," Fowler said.

"Right. Is it one group with two planes, or two different groups? And what are they doing down here, at night, in this weather, if they're not searching for us?"

There was no answer to his question. Off to the northeast a bat-like shadow flickered between the moonlit layers of cloud. The sound was lost in the wind and did not return.

"Did they spot us?" Sobek whispered.

"No telling . . ." Johnson murmured. "We're pushing our luck, that's for sure."

"We're ready," Mike said. "Cacoyannis can make his cut as soon as you want to send him down."

"Right," Johnson said.

"How long?" Nicole asked. "How long do we have to stay here?"

Mike glanced at Jack, his form dark against the blue background of the glacier. When Johnson didn't speak up, he said, "A week. If we're lucky a bit less."

Voss grumbled something in German, and Sobek said, "That's too damn long!"

Mike Fowler agreed, but there was nothing any of them could do about it.

CHAPTER 32

WITH A RUSH of water, the diving stage broke the surface. Dressed in heavy gear, Cacoyannis gripped the frame to steady himself, one brass-bound boot positioned atop the circle of steel he had cut from the side of the conning tower.

Mike Fowler moved in, clapping the Melbourne Greek on the shoulder then bending to untie the safety line connected to the precious chunk of metal. As Waretini helped Cacoyannis out of the copper helmet and weights, Mike lugged the heavy disk into the machine shop and dropped it on McLeod's bench.

"How long?" he asked.

"Well, there's the shapin' of the overlay an' the installation of the various and sundry bits." He gestured to the collection of valves and electrical connections arrayed on a shelf nearby. "You canna rush it, but I'd say three hours."

It was more like five. Finally McLeod announced the patch was complete and the connections that passed through it had been fully tested. This time it was Fowler and Yamada who went down to do the installation.

Mike again dragged his air hose through the hatch and down into the tower, while Koji manhandled the thick piece of metal up to the outside of the hole Cacoyannis had cut.

McLeod had attached a slightly larger disk of metal to the one that had been removed. This created a flange that would allow it to be easily welded back into place. In the center of the plug were the critical parts, a valve to let water in or out, and the fittings for air as well as a vent that could release any excess pressure to the surface. Additionally, there were sockets for communications and electrical power.

On the inside, the air manifold was split into two paths, one that would be directly hooked into the open valve in the U-boat's ballast control panel, and another that passed through a pressure reducer so those inside could breathe through hoses connected to the Jack Browne masks.

Mike swam down, positioning himself on the floor of the cramped compartment. With a foot braced on either side of the hole, he bent forward and took hold of the protruding valves, pulling the assembly tightly against the outside of the submarine.

"Hot! Go hot!"

With Fowler holding everything in place, Yamada fired up his arc and began tacking the disk onto the hull. It was the first step in a long and arduous process.

The next morning was cursed with intermittent rain, but as soon as Cacoyannis announced he had finished building up the weld, Ian Ward went down pulling a long loop of high-pressure air hose that slowly unspooled from the first of the reels they had removed from the *Bushranger*'s hold. After it was attached, along with a set of electrical and communication wires, they cleared the deck and Waretini worked the anchor winches, edging the ship away from the sunken U-boat while slowly paying out the bundle of lines hooked to the sub. Buoys kept as much of the umbilical on the surface as possible.

In the shop Fowler and Voss geared up, then waited. Voss paced, going through cigarette after cigarette. The choking haze of smoke made Mike want to strangle the old German, so he stepped outside to get away. He took a deep breath of the cold wet air and found that his senses were humming with anticipation.

His friends, the men of the *Bushranger*, would be hard-pressed to forgive his omissions or Anton's lies. He had a woman whose business was secrets yet seemed offended he had kept one of his own. He was relying on a partner who had likely killed an old friend . . . and might very well consider the rest of them to be equally expendable. But none of that mattered. He was headed into action, making a move so desperate that any other salvage operator would think he'd lost his mind. The arms trade might seem exotic to some, but in the end a lot of it was office work. *This* was swimming out into the night without knowing if you'd ever come back. It was something a man couldn't do from behind a desk.

Half an hour later they huddled in the workboat as Johnson circled the buoy. They all shook hands. There was a certain forced civility to it, but they were each counting on the others in order to survive. Then Fowler and Voss went over the side. Once again, the cold press of water surrounded him and once again Fowler slipped out of his tank harness and followed Anton Voss through the conning tower hatch into the confines of the U-Null's attack center.

A moment later the hatch slammed down, and Voss turned the wheel, sealing them in. Fowler opened the external drain, then turned on the air. The head of pressure in the line from the *Bushranger*'s compressors blasted into the tightly packed cylinder of the conning tower. He backed off the knob slightly. When the air had forced the water down to the level of the newly installed plug, he cranked both shut. Silently they waited. Everything seemed to be holding. The two men looked at each other. Water sloshed around their calves and dripped from the overhead. Fowler shrugged.

He stripped off his diving mask and the mouthpiece to his Aqua-Lung, then picked up one of the Jack Browne face masks. He jacked the air line into a Schrader valve and plugged in his phone line. He turned the knob to verify that the air was flowing and handed the other mask to Voss. Then Fowler opened the valve leading to the submarine's bilge, draining the rest of the water and equalizing the pressure between the two compartments.

"Comms check?" Fowler adjusted the headset, getting it directly over his ear.

"Reading you loud and clear." Jack's voice crackled in his ear. "Captain Voss, you there?"

"Yes. The system is working. We are ready to open the lower hatch."

Voss unlocked the hatch and pulled it open. He started to straighten up but paused, bracing himself for a moment. Mike hoped he was up to this; they were both the worse for wear, but the trip south had aged his partner in ways he didn't completely understand.

After lowering two work lights into the control room, Anton started down. Mike fed him his lines, then lowered their tool bags and wrestled the stiff high-pressure air hose through the hatch. One end of this hose was attached to the patch they had installed in the wall of the conning tower, the other held McLeod's carefully machined fitting.

Finally Mike descended into the control room. Even with all their hoses and cables it was a lot easier than trying to negotiate the narrow hatchway while manhandling an air tank.

The Type XXI's zentrale hadn't improved any. Mike's imagination played tricks on him; he felt he could smell the mold and rotting canvas even through his mask. Their first job was to attach the air line to the body of the valve Fowler had removed from the ballast control panel, essentially connecting the compressors aboard the *Bushranger* directly into the submarine's air system.

It was not an easy job. The hose was barely flexible and had to be arced clear around the narrow confines of the control room in order to approach the valve at an angle that allowed it to line up. It was trial and error, attempting the alignment over and over again.

"Got it! Yes!"

Voss twisted the adapter until it was finger-tight, then put a wrench on it and carefully turned, feeling the tapered threads bite. Fowler handed him a two-foot pipe that slipped over the handle of the wrench so that he could ever so gently apply additional torque. If they damaged the finely machined piece of brass, everyone would have to wait while McLeod made another.

They were both breathing hard and sweating heavily inside their rubber suits by the time the connection was tight.

"Alright. Topside, we are tied into the manifold," Fowler reported.

Voss closed all the valves but verified that each could easily open should he need it to. He looked deliberately around, running through a mental checklist.

"Now," he said. "It is time."

Dragging his lines, Mike crawled back up into the attack center. He bent, squatting in front of the welded patch. "Ready?"

Mike twisted the knob. The heavy hose barely moved but, suddenly, there was a perceptible tension in it. A powerful muscle ready to flex. More than two thousand pounds of air pressure was being compressed into the line. If anything broke, things would get messy, fast.

"Open!" He almost whispered it into the microphone. There was no forgetting the way the U-Boat's air system had reacted last time . . . and that had been merely the last gasp of its depleted reservoirs.

As if following his train of thought, Voss said, "First, we will try charging four of the high-pressure flasks. That way we have some compressed air onboard for additional control. I am going to test them one at a time."

As Mike dropped back into the control room Voss opened a valve. He held up a hand, listening carefully. Air hissed along the pipes. In the bowels of the ship something rumbled. He closed that wheel and moved on.

Bang!

The sudden concussion was followed by a high-pitched shriek that diminished into a low moan that echoed beneath them. Mike felt like his ears needed to pop.

Anton quickly shut off that particular line. "There! You see, condensation has rusted through the pipe. We must leave that closed." Finally he settled on which flasks to charge and began the process, one at a time.

They had hours to wait. Hours with no food or water, trapped in their uncomfortable suits and long underwear, breathing the oil-and-rubber-smelling air that came down from the compressors on the *Bushranger*. Mike tried to keep his eyes on the floor and to breathe regularly. Once upon a time he had been used to working in cramped spaces. However, there was something about the decaying walls and overhead, and the way the mask hissed and clutched at his face. Dwelling on it was unhealthy. They were filling the third flask when Voss held up a finger then mimed raising it to his lips.

From his tool bag he extracted a heavy diver's knife. He dropped it in behind the panel that had once indicated the status of the U-boat's hatches. "There are various kinds of tools," he said. "Some we store away in case we must do a certain job."

Mike nodded.

Checking his watch, Voss finally decided they were finished charging the air reservoirs. Stepping back into the alcove of pipes and valves, he redirected the air from the *Bushranger*'s compressor into the main ballast tanks. Slowly the pressure built. Ghosts muttered in the sealed sections fore and aft and rustled outside the walls of the pressure hull.

Voss had just sat down on the bench in front of the bank of valves when a shudder ran though the boat. There was a dull sense of turbulence from beneath them.

"Aha!" Anton leaped to his feet and closed the main valve. He spoke to whoever was monitoring the other end of the comm line. "Topside? We will need the observer in the water. *Now!*"

"Righto," Johnson spoke up. "We're headed to ya."

With a portable compressor mounted in the workboat, Ihaka would maneuver as close to the U-Null as he could get. The limiting factor was how much phone cable they still had. Then Jack, suited up in heavy gear, would descend just far enough to be able to see the submarine.

"Okay, I'm on station." Jack's voice was laced with static.

Voss turned the wheel again, and after a moment or two the bubbling, rushing sound reappeared.

"You're makin' a plume of silt! It's on the other side though. I can't get 'round there without disconnecting the phone line."

"Stay where you are," said Voss, and opened the valve wider.

Tap. Tap. Tap-tap. Tap! Fowler grimaced as the steel around them reacted to the stress. Somewhere something fell onto a hard surface and rolled. For a moment the noises stopped . . . then the hull moaned, straining with buoyancy for the first time in years. However, there was no upward movement.

Voss blew out a breath and cranked the valve closed. He put a hand to his head. "So . . ." he said, "we are stuck."

"What? What does that mean?"

"The water *is* being pushed out the bottom of the portside tanks, but we are stuck in the mud. If I continue, the imbalance will become more serious." He glanced around and shook his head.

Fowler said nothing . . . letting Voss think it through.

"Okay. We are going to blow forward, see if we can peel her off the bottom." He worked the knobs and after a moment silence closed in again.

Nothing happened. Mike wished that he could hear the noise of the compressor, anything to get a sense that progress was being made.

"Captain Johnson? How is the visibility?"

"Not much. The sun's gone behind the mountain."

"And the tide?"

"Almost slack. You've got a few more minutes."

Once the tide started to go out, the sub, if it came up at all, would have a tendency to drift dangerously around at the end of her anchor cable. And that was providing it didn't break loose completely.

Anton turned to Mike. "I do not want to spend the night in here, do you?"

Mike shook his head.

"I am directing the compressor back to the main tanks." The ballast panel hissed, then quieted. "Now we are going to use the air from the onboard reservoirs to blow forward again . . ." Voss turned the wheel, turned it more aggressively than he had before. There was a rushing in the pipes.

The U-boat trembled. Then the noise of straining metal and scraping rock. The angle of the deck, slightly higher toward the bow, suddenly increased.

"Something's happening, mate!" Johnson broke up, the amplifier overmodulating. "There's mud everywhere! I can't see—you're bow up! You're up—!"

"Get out of the way!" Voss commanded.

Through the phones Mike heard Johnson cursing, and then he was not paying attention. The deck tilted, tilted to the point where he had to grab the rotting back of a diving plane seat. A grinding roar echoed from somewhere aft.

"Quickly!" Voss snapped. He was hanging on to one knob and turning another. "If I say so, open this valve!" The rising bow was constrained by the anchor line. As it tried to rise, the stern was being dragged forward.

"Come up! Come up!" Voss was firing shots of air into the after tanks, desperate to get it off the bottom yet unwilling to lose control. Something rolled and crashed. The stern of the two-thousand-ton submarine was taking a lunatic roller-coaster ride across the sea floor.

"Hold on! *Hold on!*"

Thud!

There was a sudden concussion from somewhere in the bow. Fowler looked quickly to Voss.

"That was one of the Sprengfallen, the explosives!" Anton cackled insanely. "Not to worry, if it was serious, we would know it!" he shouted.

Then they were free, and for a moment, Mike had the sensation of riding an elevator in a New York City skyscraper. The floor pressed against his feet, and they went up, and up, and up.

Kapitän zur See Anton Andreas Voss turned, an alien being in a triangular mask, tethered to the outside world through rubber hoses and electrical cables. "Your wheel! Open your valve now!"

Like an underwater eruption the U-Null broke the surface on a tidal wave of displaced water. Then they were falling as the boat bobbed, then settled ponderously. Fowler's tool bag crashed from the navigation station to the deck and the work lights suddenly went out.

"You made it! You bloody well made—" Johnson's voice cut off.

The U-boat rocked as the waves it had created rebounded from the sides of the fjord. Somewhere water gushed, and Mike hoped it was simply moving from one part of the bilge to another rather than coming through a breach that would carry them back to the bottom. He felt around in the darkness and his hand closed on Anton's shoulder. Twisting on his flashlight he passed it over. Voss bent to the controls. Air hissed and chirped as he tested the system.

"We are alright!" Voss yelled from inside his mask. "We still have pressure from the compressor. Feel the boat. You can tell she is riding on the surface."

"That explosion?" Mike asked.

"She is built to take depth charges. We are still alive. Hope for the best."

Then metal rang loudly against the hull.

Clang. Clang. Clang.

Johnson or Waretini was pounding away with some sort of tool.

"You see! Go up top and tell me how she sits in the water."

Fowler scrambled up one ladder, then the other, turning the wheel to release the pressure then flinging open the hatch onto the bridge. He yanked at his lines until he could stand, then pulled off the face mask, taking a deep breath of the cold, clean air.

"Oi! Rummy! You did it! Bloody hell! You did it, mate!"

Mike leaned over the fairing. Waretini and Johnson waved at him from the workboat. The deck immediately below the tower was exposed, though marred by muddy outcroppings of mussel shells and patches of rust. The bow rode high and seemingly without damage, while aft the curved hull trailed away below the waterline. All along the shore the waves caused by their rising splashed against the rocks yet again.

Across the water someone let loose with a long blast from the *Bushranger*'s horn, a sound that echoed off the cliffs and was likely heard by Paluso and Zúñiga miles down the fjord.

An hour later they were back aboard the *Bushranger*. The U-boat's hatches were left open, but Fowler had rigged both of the heavy manila lines that secured the two ships to each other with coils of Primacord. If the sub began to sink or anything else went wrong a detonator could be fired and the explosive rope would immediately sever the connection.

Both Mike and Anton were dehydrated and hungry . . . and ready for a hot shower. Afterward, dressed in fresh clothes, they collapsed into chairs in the wardroom and tried to eat as the rest of the crew peppered them with congratulations and questions.

With their prize finally floating alongside, it seemed a lot of the tension that had haunted the voyage south had eased, at least momentarily. Sobek poured everyone drinks, and Nicole sat close by Mike's side. Even Mel Paluso signaled his approval, cautiously clicking the message through the microphone of his radio.

The only one who didn't seem relieved was Anton Voss. If anything, he was even more restless, running on adrenaline and possessed by a new level of intensity. "We must go back, open the aft compartments. The ventilation system and pumps need to be activated. There is no telling what could be wrong. She is not sinking, but we could still lose her."

Fowler squinted across the table at Voss. He held up a hand. "Wait. You're talking about opening up the engine room?"

"Yes, yes. There are condenser banks used to start the Tychon generator. To run the electrical system, they must either be re-formed, or I must bypass them entirely."

"That means we have to deactivate some of your booby traps, right?"

"Correct. It will take some preparation."

"And a steady set of hands, which I barely have at the moment. You ready to tell me what we're up against?"

Voss took a breath, and the answer came out in a rush. "The engine room and the torpedo room, each has three stick mines . . . an obstacle course. The prize is a torpedo warhead on a timer."

"A torpedo—! Anton, are you *kidding* me?"

A G7 torpedo carried more than six hundred pounds of Hexanite, an explosive only slightly less powerful than TNT . . . It was literally a charge big enough to sink a battleship.

"Opening the hatch more than a few centimeters will pull the safety pin and activate a clockwork time fuse. We will then have three minutes to deal with the mines and remove or stop the timer."

Johnson spoke up. "Are there trip wires? Can we just cut them?"

"The fuses we used on the mines will fire if they are either pulled *or* cut. You must lock them on 'safe' with a pin."

"You're talking ZuZZ 35s?" Fowler suddenly had an inkling about the explosion they had felt.

Voss nodded.

Mike gritted his teeth. It was the German disease all over again. The ZuZZ 35 was brilliantly complicated and thus had a reputation for killing combat engineers.

"We did not make this impossible. Herr Könnecke and I timed ourselves getting to the torpedo and deactivating it. If you know what to do, where to step . . . it can be done. Of course, I was fifteen years younger . . . and I never really expected to come back and have to do it under pressure."

"Or while dealing with some sort of air supply!" Fowler's brain was running at a mile a minute. After all this time there was no telling what condition the fuses would be in. And Mike knew that the only thing worse than a sensitive detonator was an unpredictable one.

What made it doubly difficult was that the job would have to be done while managing the awkward bulk of an Aqua-Lung. Dragging the air line from a Jack Browne mask through a pitch-black minefield choked with machinery seemed like the definition of a bad idea.

CHAPTER 33

"I'M GOING, TOO," Nicole announced. She was examining the diagram Voss had drawn of the U-boat's engine room.

"No, you are not! You've got no idea what you're talking about!" The words were out of Mike's mouth before he even realized he had spoken them.

"And that's why I intend to go. I want what's on that submarine as much as anyone here! More than some, in fact! Now I want to see it, and I believe I can help."

"Miss DeMaes, be reasonable. This is going to be both difficult and potentially deadly," Voss objected.

"Dr. Voss, I have set quite a few bombs in my life. Both your countrymen and the British were on the receiving end. And I am smaller and much more agile than either one of you!"

The argument went on for quite a bit longer but eventually they were forced to agree that, if she could manage an Aqua-Lung and mask, she might indeed be an asset. Though it bothered him to admit it, Fowler discovered he was more confident about going through the engine room door with her at his side than Voss. The old man was tired. He was smoking too much and looked like death warmed over.

A careful study of the diagram revealed several areas of concern. While they called the compartment they were planning to enter the "engine room," that designation was no longer accurate. The diesel engines on the U-Null had never been installed and the space was extensively modified to accept the bell-shaped Tychon device, a tubelike particle decelerator, a convoluted web of plumbing carrying liquified deuterium, and the thickly insulated reaction chamber.

On the other side of the next partition were a steam turbine, the electrical generator, and the motors that drove the boat. Their goal, the torpedo warhead and its attached timer, was just inside what Voss called "Section Two." It was less than thirty feet from where they would enter, but the path was a complex maze of machinery, piping, and conduits, ill-suited even to the men who had been trained to work there.

Immediately above the torpedo Voss had drawn a small circle. "This is an external hatch. It leads to the deck, and it is also connected to an additional fuse mounted on the warhead . . . one that is set to fire the charge with no delay. Von Pollnitz, our engineer, truly had an aptitude for this sort of thing."

"You might try being a bit less proud of the guy," Johnson grumbled. "There's still a chance he could kill the lot of you."

The U-Null's galley was separated from the zentrale by a conventional door, but access to the crew's quarters, the next compartment aft, was blocked by a circular waterproof hatch about four feet in diameter. What greeted them on the other side was a fetid and rotting mess far worse than the control room. It was the foul remains of all the fabric, food, wood, and paper that had been left aboard the submarine. The crew had doused it in fresh water in order to produce a toxic environment full of explosive hydrogen sulfide . . . sewer gas.

"Oh my God! This is *disgusting!*" The words were mumbled into the mouthpiece of Nicole's Aqua-Lung, but Fowler understood what she was trying to express. She had come to a stop, momentarily frozen as she confronted the decaying swamp that filled the passage between the bunk rooms. The mere sight of it turned the stomach.

After fifteen years what remained was a passage calf-deep in reeking muck surrounded by fungus-riddled paneling and a ceiling scabbed in stalactites of rust. Where previously they had worn the rubber dry suits to stay warm in the icy waters, they now wore them in order to stay clean and so that the filth they had to slog through could be hosed off once they reemerged from the U-boat.

At the end of this twenty-foot stretch was an identical hatch leading further aft . . . into the even deadlier territory of the engine room.

Nicole awkwardly climbed through the circular hatchway. She was still conditioning herself to the claustrophobia brought on by the cramped compartments, the rubber suit, as well as her mask and the need to draw air through the Aqua-Lung's regulator. Behind her came Anton Voss, wearing a Jack Browne mask and pulling an air hose. He carried the square box of a speaker hanging from a strap around his neck. Frank Jano had wired up this contraption so that anything said over the comm system would be broadcast loud enough for Mike and Nicole to hear. Voss could speak to them even if it was more difficult for them to say anything back.

They picked their way through the muck and debris toward the next barrier. The moment of truth had arrived. Once they cracked the far door a wire would trigger the time fuse and three minutes—just one hundred and eighty seconds—later the torpedo warhead would detonate. It would blow a hole in the hull the size of a Buick and would likely kill anyone inside the U-boat.

Voss checked his watch. "Topside? We will be ready to go in . . . four . . . three . . . two . . . *one*!"

He pulled the locking lever, swung the heavy steel hatch open, and stepped out of the way.

Fowler glanced upward. A rusting wire ran aft into the darkness. An instant later he saw it go slack. The safety pin on the timer had been pulled.

"Three minutes!"

Nicole directed her light to the left as Mike pulled himself through the circular opening, getting his feet up onto the rim. The yellow glow fell on a black cylindrical outline, an ominous shape he remembered from the beach in Israel. Unlike that drawing, this device was surrounded by a cage of electrical conduits. At nearly the level of the hatch, just as Anton's drawings had indicated, the upper and lower portions of the cylinder were split by a heavy flange of metal held together by a series of bolts.

Mike balanced himself against the weight of his air tank . . . and jumped. He hit, and his rubber-clad feet scrambled for purchase on the flange even as he reached out, his hand closing on a conduit.

Edging backward around the bell-shaped particle generator, Mike banged into something with his tank. That was as far as he could go. He switched on his flashlight, trying to see exactly how the first trap was set.

Inside the hatch four steel steps led down to a narrow walkway. He could see that the lower bolts of the rusted stairway had been removed. No doubt that would allow the stairs to shift so that the stick mine—a stake topped with a charge of explosive surrounded by a layer of shrapnel-impregnated concrete—could be detonated.

With Anton's help, Nicole was climbing into position. Mike did his best to illuminate the side of the bell where she would have to grab on.

Bending at the knees, she let go of the bar above the hatch and sprang outward . . .

She hit, and Mike grabbed a fold of rubber near her shoulder. Her feet found the ledge. "Two minutes thirty seconds! Look at the light!" Voss moved the beam of his flashlight up and down the walkway well back from the stairs. "Do you see it?"

A thin line of shadow danced against the mottled steel. If a man had known enough to jump past the booby-trapped stairway, his momentum would carry him directly into the trip wire that ended somewhere within the forest of piping just to the other side of the compartment.

There was about three feet of safe space. Mike carefully lowered himself, then helped Nicole down. There was barely room to turn. Getting a light on the wire, he cautiously stepped over it then helped Nicole to do the same.

"I cannot show you from here, but the last mine is on the right, just beyond the deuterium feed-metering console. You now have two minutes."

The steel pathway jogged a yard to the left, squeezing past a series of cylinders festooned with valves and gauges. The trouble was that Anton's diagram had made the whole area feel bigger than it now seemed. All around them was a chaos of piping and electrical panels. In the awkward suits and tanks, with their face masks fogging in the moist air, Mike dared not move too quickly.

The walkway narrowed. In the gloom Mike spotted a watch station with the distinctive gauges and ceramic-coated stainless steel piping Voss had described. He put out a hand to make sure Nicole didn't get in front of him.

Where the hell was the wire?

Nicole tapped him on the shoulder and pointed . . .

There!

Ten feet farther on was another set of four stairs leading up and through the doorway to the compartment that held the submarine's steam turbine . . . and the torpedo warhead. The thin cable was almost chest high, and, from his point of view it had been perfectly, and invisibly, aligned with the edge of the top step. Once he moved a bit he could see it clearly. This time they went under, crawling up the stairs on their bellies, their tanks missing the wire by less than two inches.

"Ninety seconds! Ninety seconds! Tell me when you have it—immediately!"

They scrambled up the damp steps, tumbled through the doorway, and stopped.

Upright on the floor in front of them was the nose cone of a G7 torpedo. It had been unbolted from the long tube that held the propulsion and guidance system, but Mike was still amazed at the effort it had taken to maneuver the heavy warhead from one end of the boat to the other. Its base had been set in what looked like a pool of tar to hold it in place. Nearby lay the safety pin attached to the wire they had pulled loose when they opened the hatch. The standard trigger from its nose was missing and a dark metal device the size and shape of a wineglass had been installed.

A thin grinding noise could be heard as the clockwork gears turned.

Nicole focused her light on the timer.

"Damn it!"

Inside the top of the timer was a shallow rotating cup that Voss had said would be marked with numerals and that contained a small hole near the outside edge where a different-sized pin could be inserted to stop the countdown. But the dial was full of greasy green scum—verdigris caused by the slow corrosion of the copper dial.

Mike pulled an old 35mm film canister out of his tool bag and unscrewed it; inside was a selection of folded cotter pins of different sizes. He set it on the deck then tried to wipe the green gunk away with a finger. It just smeared across the etched numerals. No hole was visible.

"One minute!" Anton's voice was distant now.

Mike tried another swipe. Nothing. The crud was thick and grainy. He tried to stop the timer by holding the dial. No luck. The grinding of the gears continued. When he let go, the spring-loaded dial snapped forward, no doubt to tell you exactly how much time you had left . . . bloody Germans!

Mike pointed at the film can. "Be ready!" He couldn't tell if Nicole could decipher his words, but she got the message. Locking the flashlight under her arm she bent to pick up the can . . .

. . . and knocked it over.

As Nicole desperately tried to pick up the pins, she dropped her light.

She scrambled after the rolling flashlight, and Mike took a deep breath. Forcing himself to be calm, he pulled a rag from under his tools. By feel, he wiped the dial, then sopped up some moisture from the deck and wiped again.

The light was back. Nicole extended her hand; in it were two cotter pins . . . both the same size. He spotted the hole, grabbed a pin, and pressed down. It only went in about an eighth of an inch. Not enough! He worked it back and forth. It didn't catch.

Nicole tapped him on the shoulder, handed him the other pin. She had pried the two halves apart with her fingernails, so it was now thinner. He stuck it in, felt something lock.

The clock, attached to a striker, aligned to hit a percussion cap, affixed to the detonator for six hundred pounds of high explosive, stopped.

The pin did not, however, fit very well. The bomb was not deactivated.

"Hold that." Mike took Nicole's finger and pressed it on the top of the pin. Then he deactivated the second fuse, the one wired to the exterior hatch overhead. Using another wrench, he unscrewed the timer. Aware that they could be surrounded by explosive gas, he opened the barrels of both fuses and removed the percussion caps.

Finally Nicole released the timer pin, throwing it to the deck and examining the deep white dent it had left in her fingertip. The timer counted down: tich, tich, tich—*snap!*

She grabbed his arm and held on tightly. They had only had four seconds.

Moving back through the doorway into the engine room, Mike located the chest-high wire and traced it to the stick mine. Nicole had found more of the cotter pins, and he slipped one into the safety hole and bent the ends to lock it there. He extracted the fuse and, as before, removed the cap.

From the hatchway Anton caught sight of them and clasped his hands over his head, signaling victory. The speaker hummed, "Congratulations! Congratulations! Herr Jano is coming to help with the electrics."

Mike and Nicole continued on, securing and then disconnecting the mines. As soon as it was safe to use the stairs Voss and Frank Jano began their attempt to restore the onboard power.

Because of the amount of current required to initiate generation of the Tychon particle, more than half the sub's electrical storage capacity had been converted to an enormous bank of condensers, units similar to a battery yet capable of a near-instantaneous discharge. Before the system could be used, every connection had to be checked and any damaged component bypassed. An electrical accident could be almost as dangerous as setting off the torpedo.

On the deck of the *Bushranger* Mike held Nicole as Waretini blasted them with seawater from a canvas fire hose. It was a strange embrace; they stood with the glass of their masks pressed together, still breathing canned air, as a layer of filth was washed away. Inside, they washed their hands thoroughly and wiped them down with peroxide. Nicole playfully flipped a towel at him, and they wrapped themselves in warm blankets to keep their damp long underwear from getting chilled.

There was something different about her; it was like a switch had been thrown. Maybe her pride had recovered, or maybe it was the closeness to death as the timer ticked down. She seemed younger, not as burdened by the weight of her mission. They stopped outside her cabin, where the stairway headed down, belowdecks.

She smiled. "Well, I guess we can't say we do that every day." There was a strange edge to her voice, a memory of a past life.

"No, we can't . . . Well, I'm going below to hit the showers."

She opened the door to her cabin and provocatively peered around the edge. "Why don't you use mine?"

He blinked. "Uh, I . . . I don't think there's enough room in there."

Nicole laughed. “One at a time, silly!” She batted her eyes. “I’ll go first. I promise not to use up all the hot water.”

Defusing explosives might be dangerous, but on the other hand it was a reminder of what was really important. She had spent several days looking at him as if he was on the other side of a political or ideological divide, as if his allegiances were suspect. But what she greeted him with once he got out of the shower was definitely not suspicion.

CHAPTER 34

FROM SOMEWHERE ABOVE him Mike Fowler heard a voice, an incomprehensible static-filled whisper. He blinked and then was fully awake.

He could hear the muted rumble of the *Bushranger*'s diesels. They were running at well over half speed, generating the power needed to recondition and recharge the submarine's electrics. Bolted to the wall, the radiator clicked and tapped; the heat was always inadequate, even though it was technically summer. Beside him, Nicole breathed softly.

All as expected . . . but something was wrong.

The sound came again. He couldn't make out the words, but they *were* words. He heard feet hit the floor, the floor that was also his ceiling. A door creaked open. Jack Johnson was awake.

Fowler pushed himself up and out of bed. He yanked up his trousers, pulled on a shirt and his jacket without bothering to button either.

"Wh-what's happening?" Nicole sat up.

"I don't know. We're getting a radio message. Voice, no code. Whatever it is, that's not good. You'd better get up."

He stuffed the holster with his .44 into his belt, grabbed his boots, and went out the door.

In the chart room Jack was pacing back and forth. He looked up as Fowler entered. "Something came over the radio, mate. But I couldn't tell which one."

Both of the ship's standard receiving units and Fowler's AN/PRC-10 had been left on. Any traffic other than Paluso's occasional mic clicks could indicate trouble. Mike turned up the volume on each. A low electric hum filled the room.

Johnson stepped outside. A cold breeze stole the warmth from the room. The predawn sky glowed faintly beyond the mountains. Mike pulled on his socks and boots.

"Nothing. There's nothing out there." Jack closed the door behind him. He wasn't relaxing. The phantom radio call had him keyed up, ready for action. Footsteps ascended the metal stairs. Nicole entered.

"What is it?"

"We don't know." Johnson glared at the radio equipment.

"FORWARD OBSERVER TO *BUSHRANGER*!" The blaring of the field radio made them all jump.

"WE ARE UNDER ATTACK. GROUND FORCES. SHIP HAS CLEARED CHANNEL. HEAVY WEAPONS. OVER." There was a sound that might have been gunfire.

Mike grabbed the handheld and mashed the transmit button. "*Bushranger.* Forward Observer. Message received. Message received. Get out! Report when possible. Over."

They waited. Minutes passed, but there was no response.

Johnson switched on the main circuit. He lifted the mic. "All hands, all hands. Prepare for attack. Blackout. Red light only. Yamada and Jano, report to chart room."

Johnson snatched up a pair of binoculars as he stepped outside. Mike was right behind him.

In the dim light the narrow cut of the fjord was visible, but mist cascaded down the mountainside, obscuring their view beyond a mile or so. Johnson didn't lower the glasses.

"Anything?"

Jack shook his head.

Koji Yamada raced up the stairs with Jano on his heels. Jack pointed at Mike. "You're on, mate."

"Okay . . ." Mike was thinking as quickly as he could. "Distribute weapons. Our people first. Each of you take an automatic rifle. Bring one to Jack. Koji, set up forward here on the boat deck, use the winches for cover. Frank, you do the same in the stern, and haul the rocket launcher back there too. Any questions?"

The two headed off.

Waretini and Voss climbed the external ladder from the main deck.

"Tell me, boss." Ihaka was only wearing an undershirt and shorts.

Johnson brought them up to speed. Mike grimaced; their tactical situation stank to high heaven.

"Get dressed," Johnson said. "I want tools set out to break those anchor line shackles. Toot-sweet, you follow? With that damn submarine alongside we're locked in here. Pull the electric and get us unhooked."

"Hold on . . ." Fowler broke in. "Whoever is out there, the sub is our bargaining chip. Whether we hand it over or sink it again, we're going to need to get in there!"

"Okay, okay, belay that," Johnson said. "But cut loose the starboard and stern anchors so we can move as quickly as possible."

Paul Sobek appeared in the chart room doorway; his eyes were bloodshot, and a robe was tightly belted around his paunch. "Where are they? What's going on?"

Johnson scowled at him. "Just simmer down. We don't know yet."

Voss winced as he straightened his back, and the bandaged side of his head shone white in the dim light. "Who is it going to be? This is the critical question."

"They attacked Paluso and Zúñiga out of the blue," Fowler said. "I'm betting it's Anhaldt."

"And they put men ashore," Nicole spoke up. "That means they think they have more than they need."

Fowler turned to Voss. "This isn't a good place for a fight. You got any ideas?"

"The U-boat," Anton agreed. "You are correct. Our diving gear is still aboard. When the time comes, you sever the ropes, but do not disconnect the air or communication lines. I will enter it and dive. If they cannot immediately take it from us, if I can threaten to permanently sink it, maybe we will be able to buy some time."

Johnson grabbed up the intercom. "Ward. Meet Mr. Voss in the shop. Help him suit up to dive."

"I'll be the one to negotiate," Sobek said.

"No, you will *not*!" Mike barely glanced at Sobek. "Get some damn clothes on. Collect those two thugs of yours, and button up the main deck. No one gets inside—that's your job."

Sobek opened his mouth to argue, but Mike grabbed him by the collar and shoved him toward the stairs. The gangster fought back, flailing. "Get off me!"

"Move it!" Mike ordered, and Sobek finally seemed to get the message.

Out on the deck the winches were grinding away as McLeod and Benham located the shackles connecting one section of anchor chain to the next. McLeod drove out the pin on the starboard side and stepped back as the loose end roared down the hawsepipe.

Mike looked at Voss. "Get going. We don't have much time." Stepping up into the wheelhouse he opened up the bench and pulled out his Browning shotgun. He slung it across his back, then stuffed his right-hand pocket full of shells.

In the distance something moved through the swirling fog. Fowler took the binoculars from Johnson. He adjusted the lenses.

The high prow and low deckhouse of a large fishing trawler were momentarily visible. A low gantry supporting outriggers for nets straddled the foredeck. Handing the glasses back, he spoke to Nicole. "Well, it's not a military vessel . . . Two guesses what that means."

Yamada reappeared, leaning an FG 42 between the radar unit and the wall and dropping the bandolier of magazines on the floor nearby. He went out the far side of the chart room to set up his own position on the forward part of the boat deck.

The trawler nosed its way out of the veil of mist. Whatever they were planning, they would have to approach carefully. Not too far beyond the *Bushranger* the fjord turned into a dead end full of ice and boulders.

The fishing boat was still nearly half a mile off and seemed to be slowing. Johnson raised his binoculars. A yellow flame flickered on the trawler's foredeck.

"Oh, hell!" Jack Johnson dove, sweeping Fowler and Nicole down to the deck.

SSSH-CRACK! SSSH-CRACK! Thump-thump. Something screamed through the air just above where they had been standing. The distant concussion was the gun going off.

"Take cover!" Johnson bellowed.

Like the blows of a supersonic jackhammer, heavy slugs slammed into the steel wall. Above them the wheelhouse windows shattered, ricochets and slivers of metal flew.

Mike knew that sound even though he had never been on the receiving end. Ma Deuce—a .50-caliber M2 machine gun.

He pushed Nicole ahead of him and they scrambled inside, Johnson slamming the door to the chart room behind them. If the trawler got much closer the walls would be no protection.

From the forward boat deck Koji opened up. Mike stuck his head up, peering through the single porthole. He saw the tracers fall short, then lift as the Japanese tried to correct his aim. He ducked back down.

"That thing's good for a thousand yards. They can do a lot more damage to us than we can do to them."

The jackhammer was back, pounding away at something farther aft. Impacts rang through the hull.

Johnson pulled the FG 42 into his lap. "Can you hit them with that bazooka?"

Fowler glanced at Nicole. "Too far—but we'll give it a try."

Voss and Ward were crouched at the base of the stairs. Anton was tugging his heavy sweater into place and Ian had the suit peeled back ready for him to insert his feet. A burst of .50-caliber bullets stitched the nearby hatch, leaving a line of thumb-sized dents. All four instinctively ducked.

Voss looked up. "And I was hoping they would wish to talk!"

Fowler laughed.

"I will wager you it is Skorzeny out there. This is his style: send a gift before inviting you to the party."

"Get ready but stay under cover. I'm going to try to knock out that gun."

Mike and Nicole ran aft. Exiting on the safe side of the ship, they found Jano had set up at the rear of the deckhouse. The overhang of the boat deck created a shadowed pocket, and the area was protected by the steel gunwale and the stern winches. Six 83mm rockets had been laid out alongside the assembled Blindicide.

It was getting lighter, and the trawler's momentum had carried it forward, exposing its flank. But now Mike saw a white wave curl up at the fishing boat's stern. They were reversing, keeping their distance and bringing the heavy structure and narrow profile of the bow around to face the *Bushranger*.

Fowler was suddenly sure Voss was right. Otto Skorzeny was aboard. Their enemy knew from the speedboat crews back at Talcahuano that they were armed with a rocket launcher . . . They knew, and they were smart enough not to get close.

Thud-thud-thud. The big machine gun smashed away at the wheelhouse and bridge wings.

As Mike loaded a rocket he spoke to Nicole. "When I pick this up, you release the safety, here. Then you get right up against my back, understand? If you end up behind this, you're dead!" He glanced over at Frank. "You ready to cover me with that thing?"

Jano snapped off the safety on his FG 42. "She's no Bren gun, but I'll do my best!"

"Now!" Fowler grabbed up the Blindicide.

Jano steadied the automatic rifle against the top of the gunwale and fired. The range was extreme, but the goal was simply to force their enemy to take cover.

Mike felt a tug at the end of the tube and then Nicole grabbed him around the waist. "Heads down!" he yelled at Jano, then steadied himself, held the enemy ship in the bottom of his sight, and pulled the trigger.

Bang! For an instant the heat of the rocket blast blew away the cold.

The big projectile cut into the water about ten feet short.

Regardless of the incoming fire, whoever was behind the M2 didn't lose his nerve. Even as Mike and Nicole dropped behind the cover of the winch a storm of copper-jacketed lead blasted divots in the wall beside them. A jagged chunk of metal whacked into the back of the Blindicide's blast shield, and another tore a bloody cut in Jano's arm.

"Ow-ow-ow!" Nicole squirmed as a hot fragment burned her neck.

Then Koji or Johnson fired back, and the gunner changed his aim.

Mike had the sickening feeling he was missing something. Skorzeny could sit out there all day and pound them with his heavy gun. But at over a thousand yards, even a .50-caliber wasn't going to beat its way through the sides of a warship, and that's what the *Bushranger* was. Inside of five hundred, he could turn everything above the deck line into a sieve. But inside of five hundred Mike could rip that fishing boat apart with antitank rockets . . . and Otto Skorzeny *knew* that. He knew his weapons as well as Mike Fowler did. Skorzeny had sent scouts over land to discover and wipe out Paluso's observation post. Skorzeny was no fool.

The gun on the trawler fell silent. They were almost certainly reloading. Nicole tapped Mike's ankle; Voss had crawled up, joining them behind the winch. He was wearing his shoulder holster over the rubber dry suit.

"Go now?" Anton pointed up the deck toward where a ladder had been roped from the rail of the *Bushranger* down to the deck of the submarine. With the exception of a couple of open scuppers the path forward was covered by the gunwale, but Voss would be completely exposed as he went over the rail.

"No—wait!" Had he been ready a moment earlier it might have been the opportunity they needed, but suddenly every sense Fowler had was screaming at him. He twisted around, looking at the steep slopes that loomed behind them.

The damned trawler was a distraction. There was an attack coming, but it wasn't by land.

"Nicole! With me. Frank, Anton, watch the deck on this side." Mike was pretty sure Skorzeny's men wouldn't come aboard where their own gunner might hit them, but they might. He slipped the shotgun off his back and, crawling to the corner of the deckhouse, peered down the far side of the ship.

Two frogmen in black rubber were struggling out of their tanks and pulling submachine guns out of waterproof bags. Two more disappeared into the nearby hatch. A grappling hook and rope hung over the rail. One of the attackers raised a flare pistol over his head and fired, a signal that they had made it aboard.

Fowler came to his feet. The Browning Auto-5 hit his shoulder and he fired three times as he ran forward. The result was like a hand grenade going off. Two men down, dead or dying. One moved and Mike pulled the trigger again. From the hatchway a dark figure fired at him, once, twice, a bullet nipped the fabric at his elbow. The door slammed closed.

Without lowering the shotgun, Mike dropped his right hand to his pocket and shoved a shell up into it. From behind him he heard the sharp crack of a pistol. Nicole killed an attacker as he came over the gunwale. Another hook hung nearby. Mike leaned out. There was a second black figure climbing the rope.

This one was ready. He fired the automatic that was already in his hand. Mike ducked back. Without exposing himself he shoved the gun out, angled it slightly into the hull, and pulled the trigger. The ricochets hugged the steel plating and the man cried out, falling into the water, his tanks pockmarked, suit a shredded mess.

Mike expected to hear fighting from inside, but the noise must have been lost in the confusion. On the other side of the ship Johnson and Yamada were shooting at something, and the sledgehammer blows of the .50-caliber were back, pounding the hull. Then Nicole fired forward, past his shoulder. Three more soldiers had come aboard in the bow. One of them dropped to a knee and raised a weapon. Mike's shotgun slammed and he bolted back into the cover of the deckhouse, dragging Nicole with him. A burst of submachine gun fire ripped into the deck.

Again, Fowler topped off the Browning. Jano triggered a burst down the port side of the deckhouse, and someone returned fire. That meant there were more attackers in the bow. Time was running out. If they didn't get control of the submarine, they'd have no options at all.

Then three half-inch holes tore through the steel of the gunwale. Frank Jano's body was wrenched by an invisible force as the huge slugs crashed through him and hit the side of the winch. Nicole had flattened herself to the deck, and Voss pulled Fowler undercover. Blood, Frank's blood, stuck to Mike's hand.

The heavy machine gun fired again, and a bullet bounced, howling off the steel above him. The next two punched clear through the wall. The trawler was moving closer, and the gunner was firing much more carefully now. The M2 fired a short burst at the *Bushranger*'s bridge. Someone roared in pain.

"Stay in front of me!" Mike grabbed Nicole and slid her up against the cover of the heavy wire-wrapped drum.

They had been outmaneuvered. Skorzeny's men had gotten inside and were certainly moving aft.

Fowler awkwardly reloaded the Blindicide, removed the safety, and lunged to his feet. He was exposed, but that damn .50-caliber was too close, and it would be the end of them if he didn't do something.

The distant muzzle flamed, and jacketed lead crashed and howled around him. Aiming just below the looming prow, a couple of feet under the gun, Mike held his target and squeezed the trigger.

There was a flash of flame and, from behind him, a scream. Then the foredeck of the trawler bulged, and the explosion ripped skyward. The net gantry that straddled the trawler's beam toppled; torn metal flew. At his knee, Nicole suddenly twisted and emptied her pistol at someone.

A figure clad in smoldering rubber collapsed on the deck, the wall beside him scorched by the rocket's exhaust. Voss lunged to his feet.

"Now! I must go now!"

Fowler tossed the tube aside. They weren't going to get another chance. He looked up at the narrow portside deck. Their enemies had taken the bow and soon the fishing boat would be within accurate rifle shot. Keeping Voss alive once he was on the ladder was going to be a trick.

Anton grabbed him by the shoulder. "Not up there. I'll go over the side here! But you must cut us loose." The igniter that would fire the Primacord and sever the ropes tying the sub to the *Bushranger* was taped to a stanchion halfway up the deck.

"Okay." Mike handed the shotgun to Nicole and, edging around the winch, he pulled the automatic rifle from under Frank Jano's body. He yanked out the partial magazine, slapped in a fresh one, then stuffed another in his hip pocket.

Sticking his head above the gunwale, he quickly took in the situation. The trawler had drifted sideways; its foredeck was a scorched mess and a few of the bridge windows had been blown out. The .50-caliber was gone, and the ship's diesels were throwing up clouds of smoke. It was being handled roughly, but someone was bringing it under control, maneuvering it in closer.

From inside the *Bushranger* came the dull bang of gunshots. Mike raised the automatic rifle, aiming up the deck. "Go!" he said.

Voss slipped over the top of the gunwale and let go. Mike heard him hit the water just as he saw movement, a black shadow near the forward edge of the *Bushranger*'s deckhouse. He fired and someone fired back. Bullets whined off steel.

Mike stepped over Frank's body and ran forward. Every couple of steps he fired a short burst, trying to keep the attackers under cover. Ejected brass bounced off the wall on one side, bullets from the trawler slammed into the gunwale on the other.

Just outside the midships hatch he dropped and slid to a stop. Nicole had followed close behind, guarding his back. He dragged her down, under cover.

"What the hell are we doing?" she yelled.

He reached up, ripped the igniter free, and jerked out the safety. Pushing the fuse end over the edge of the rail he pulled the ring. The Primacord detonated with a bang. Burning at twenty thousand feet per second, it tore forward and aft, its tightly wound loops blasting through the heavy hemp lines connecting the U-Null to the *Bushranger*. Smoke drifted down the deck.

Fowler changed magazines, armed the FG 42, and stood. Voss was dragging himself out of the water and up the submarine's hull. Just in front of him the impact of a bullet sent up a small explosion of rust and broken mollusk shells. The gunfire was coming from the stern deck of the trawler. Mike caught sight of a rifle barrel, the motion of an arm working the bolt. He put his sights on the shape and fired. The man went down. A bullet smacked into the steel beneath him, then another. He searched for a new target. Firing, he drove the second gunman under cover. Beside him the shotgun roared, Nicole shooting toward the bow.

Voss ran forward toward the cover of the conning tower. Bullets smashed around him, around Fowler, around Nicole. Mike returned fire. Something tore through the fabric of his jacket. Down stuffing mixed with blood.

Nicole tugged at his leg. "Get down! Are you crazy?"

Not crazy. Just doing his job.

Two dark shapes came over the side of the submarine, alien-looking in their old-fashioned triple tanks and masks. He lined up on one of them, then a stunning impact knocked him backward ripping the gun from his hands. Mike tripped over Nicole and crashed to the deck. The automatic rifle was bent. His shoulder was pocked with shards of wood and metal.

Fowler struggled to his feet. Bullet fragments caromed off the inside of the gunwale, one of them tearing at his pant leg. Nicole fired the shotgun empty. He drew the Smith & Wesson from his belt.

One of the frogmen tackled Voss, driving him to the deck; the other struggled to clear his weapon from its waterproof bag. Just as Mike raised the pistol the hatch behind him banged open. Someone slammed Nicole into his back. He twisted, but the revolver was torn from his grip. A fist came at him, and he ducked—not far enough. The blow stunned him.

He tried to get a grip on his attacker, but his hands slipped off the man's slick rubber suit. Then Nicole was dragged out of the way and another frogman swung the butt of a submachine gun. It took Mike in the gut. He folded forward, collapsing onto the deck.

In the fog of his peripheral vision a bristle-headed cyclops appeared. Heinrich Hartmann striding down the deck, a bloody bayonet in his right hand.

"So, cowboy . . . now you are truly in the devil's kitchen, yes?"

He swung a boot, and the world around Mike Fowler went dark.

CHAPTER 35

ANTON, MIKE, AND Nicole were dragged to the bow of the *Bushranger*. Their hands were tied. The bodies of Frank Jano, Koji Yamada, and Eduardo Suarez were piled nearby. Ian Ward had been stabbed and lay unconscious and bleeding on the deck. Ihaka Waretini had been shot but was still able to stand. Jack Johnson had a broken leg. Clarence Benham and Nikos Cacoyannis were there but Colin McLeod was not. The bodies of their attackers, both dead and wounded, were being transferred to the trawler. It was cold comfort that there seemed to be more of them.

Mysteriously missing were Sobek and Iannucci. Mike wondered about the lack of resistance from inside the deckhouse, but at the same time, Ed Suarez had taken a burst of machine gun fire to the chest. Whatever had happened, Sobek's crew had at least one casualty.

After half an hour or so a motorboat made its way up the fjord and Fernando Zúñiga, shivering and bruised, was lifted aboard the *Bushranger* and laid beside Ward. It turned out that he too had been shot, but the wounds in his hip and shoulder had been bandaged. He tried to talk, but one of the guards kicked him until he passed out.

Hartmann strutted back and forth, looking down on his handiwork. He spoke to his men in German, but they talked to one another in Spanish. Mike gathered they were part of the crew of divers that had been searching for the sub, but the fact that Anhaldt had at his disposal more than a dozen men capable of an underwater assault was impressive.

"These"—Hartmann pointed at the dead—"over the side." One by one the bodies splashed into the water. He peered at Zúñiga. "Can you stand?"

Fernando tried to get to his feet but barely managed to sit up.

"This one, too."

"Que? No! *No!*" Zúñiga struggled, then jerked loose and fell.

"Hey! Hey! Damn it, stop this!" Fowler struggled to his feet, but a black-suited frogman shoved him back down. Then the man backed off and fired a burst from his MP 40 over their heads.

"*Abajo!* Everybody down!"

Kicking and screaming, Zúñiga fought. Stepping close, Hartmann drew a heavy ballpeen hammer from his belt and swung it. Fernando's body stiffened and collapsed. A moment later it splashed into the water.

"Here!" Hartmann indicated Ward's comatose form. Nicole choked back a sob and averted her eyes. The hammer swung again, and he too went over the side.

"You bastard! Come on, I'll fight you just the way I am!" That earned Johnson a kick directed at his damaged leg. Mike Fowler didn't waste any more breath. If he lived long enough, he swore on everything holy he was going to finally kill Heinrich Hartmann.

Voss was looking out toward the trawler and Fowler followed his gaze. On deck a large figure paced back and forth. Otto Skorzeny was clearly waiting for something and a few minutes later they discovered what it was.

With a familiar rumble, a large three-engine seaplane passed over them then banked to land in the fjord. The motorboat helped the aircraft tie up and then brought its passenger and Skorzeny across to the *Bushranger*. The passenger was Peter Anhaldt.

As Hartmann briefed Anhaldt, the big Austrian lit up a cigarette. Beyond him, Fowler could see Sobek and Iannucci being ushered forward. The two were clearly prisoners, but their hands were bound loosely, and they seemed little worse for wear.

"Those pukes!" Waretini whispered to Johnson. "As soon as Suarez was killed, they surrendered and let these others in."

Paul Sobek looked down on Fowler and Voss and arched an eyebrow. "I told you I'd be the one to make the deal."

Anhaldt and Hartmann finished their discussion and joined him. Sobek shared a glance with his new associates, demonstrating that he was an insider of some sort.

"Make a deal?" Anhaldt frowned. "Heinrich . . . they have useful information, but we only need one."

Hartmann snorted, a laugh kept mostly to himself. He swung his hammer, breaking Iannucci's knee and sending him screaming to the deck. Sobek went white.

Heinrich "Kuvalda" Hartmann exploded in a frenzy of motion. Grunting as he swung, the heavy tool arced downward. Over and over it crushed ribs and hips and shoulders. Anhaldt watched, leaning forward, fascinated. Hartmann paused for a moment to admire his handiwork before ending it all with a blow to the forehead.

Paul Sobek moaned. He dropped to his knees gasping for breath.

Anhaldt clasped his hands together in a soft dry clap. "There," he said. "Now, I'm *certain* we will be in agreement."

Hartmann removed a handkerchief from his pocket and fastidiously wiped the blood from the rounded end of the hammer and dabbed at the drops that had hit his face. Then he lifted the shaking gangster to his feet and pulled him toward the motorboat.

Peter Anhaldt tugged up his trouser legs and squatted down to look Anton Voss directly in the eye. "You have misread the times, Kamerad. We live in an age of institutions . . . not heroes. You should have signed the contract I offered, joined with your brothers, been a part of the"—he smirked—"solution rather than the problem. Now you have done all the hard work." He gestured at the U-boat. "Yet we shall reap the reward. So shortsighted."

Fowler couldn't allow the man to gloat. "We set a beacon in the hills. The CIA is headed here right now. You'll pay for this, so I wouldn't waste too much time congratulating yourself."

A flash of irritation crossed Anhaldt's face, and he swiped a lock of glossy gray hair off his forehead. "Spare me. The American ship was spotted north of the strait yesterday. They will not find us. This good weather will only hold until tomorrow, and by then we will be gone.

"You have been inside the submarine; you must have some idea of the magnitude of the prize." He winked at Voss. "Once we have adequately explored its potential, perhaps our friends in the American government will wish to cooperate with us, just as they have in other things. If not, it will be someone else. The world can be quite a resource if you are the primary arbiter of progress . . . or the balance of power."

He turned to Johnson. "Are you the owner of this vessel? I want to offer you a chance to continue living. Are you interested?"

Jack glanced at what was left of his crew. After a moment he nodded.

"Good. This fishing boat is well-known in these waters; for that reason, we have used it for reconnaissance. Our salvage tug and the experts I have hired remain at Puerto Montt, several days away.

"My goal is to tow this submarine to a . . . facility. I want to do it *now*, before we are trapped by the weather. Our two ships can manage the job, especially if there is someone who can operate the systems of the submarine. Captain Voss, I will make you the same offer . . . It will be the price of your life."

The two Germans stared at each other.

"It seems I have little choice." Anton's tone was guarded.

"Correct. You have no choice at all."

Anhaldt stood and motioned for Skorzeny to join him. "Otto, Mr. Sobek has mentioned that the archive canisters in the torpedo room were rigged to explode. Dealing with that seems both a pressing and dangerous task."

"Use that one to take the risks." The big commando pointed at Fowler. "Voss set them; he can advise from a safe location."

"Good. Captain Johnson, tell me what these other men do." Anhaldt pointed specifically at Nikos.

"Diver. Ship's officer."

"And this one." Clarence Benham was singled out.

"Cook. Assistant engineer. Works topside during diving operations."

Anhaldt pointed at Waretini.

Jack paused an instant then said, "Chief engineer . . ." and Mike had to restrain himself from glancing around, wondering where Colin McLeod had disappeared to.

"Heinrich!" Anhaldt turned to his henchman. "We should give them another reminder that everyone must cooperate. Who would you pick?"

Hartmann strode forward and, before Fowler could get his feet under him, the German had dragged Nicole from the group.

A black-suited frogman lunged forward to hold Mike down. He fought and got free but took a blow to the ribs. Mike kicked out and then rolled on top as the man fell to the deck. He smashed a hip into the frogman's face and was feeling for an eye socket when Otto Skorzeny stepped forward, drawing his Luger. "Herr Fowler. Do not move. Or I will not allow just one to die, I will kill several." He thumbed down the pistol's safety.

Behind him Nicole was dragged to her feet. She got her balance, and bravely tried to kick, but Hartmann was inhumanly fast. He caught her foot and twisted. She crashed face first to the deck. Hartmann laughed, booted her in the ribs, and flourished his hammer, clearly enjoying the moment.

Johnson growled, Waretini tried to stand, and Mike lunged against the younger man who was struggling to restrain him. The diver was forced back, trying to keep control. Mike met Skorzeny's crazy, intense glare with a look of his own and a flicker of understanding passed between them. No matter who had the guns, the ex-SS officer was about to lose control of the situation.

"Scharführer!" Skorzeny barked.

"Jawohl!" Hartmann almost came to attention.

"Pick a different prisoner. This one may be useful."

Peter Anhaldt turned to frown at the back of the big man's head.

"Your chivalry gets the better of you, Otto. But yes, entertainment aside, I fear the time is coming when we may need leverage over her masters." The slender man placed a hand on Hartmann's shoulder. "Heinrich, I do not believe they will need a cook."

"Now, wait a minute!" Jack struggled to stand and Waretini helped him up. Hartmann spun the hammer and Clarence Benham backed away, eyes wide with fear.

Skorzeny sighed, a man tired of foolishness. Barely turning his head, he nonchalantly shifted his aim and shot Benham in the heart. The old man dropped to the deck.

"There is your example. Now let us get to work. We have wounded to treat, and a great deal to do. We cannot be trapped here if anyone else arrives."

Two at a time, their captors escorted them below decks and locked them in the forward hold. They remained tied but one of the guards poured peroxide over the bullet wounds that pierced Waretini's side and taped bandages on, front and back. Another crudely set Johnson's leg and bound it in splints and they let Fowler pick the splinters out of his shoulder. When they were all in place, the lock clicked shut and the lights went out.

Mike felt Nicole try to straighten up. Until they reached the narrow stairway, he had carried her. She inhaled sharply as she felt her ribs.

"Are you okay?"

"Nothing's broken. I'll live."

That was the question. How long would any of them survive once Anhaldt and Skorzeny no longer needed them? From what they had just seen, it would be minutes, not hours.

The darkness of the ship's hold was complete. It was cold, and around him he could hear the ragged breathing of his companions. Nicole's back pressed against his side, and for all her bravado, she was shivering.

Mike Fowler felt like he had finally swum too far and the tide was dragging him even farther out to sea. He had been taken in—by Voss, by his desire for a mission, by the sheer momentum of events. He had greatly overestimated their chances of success. He had led his friends into a trap.

He had only just met Yamada and Ward, but Fernando Zúñiga had helped to drag him from the surf. Frank Jano, Clarence Benham, and Colin McLeod . . . once upon a time they had all been young men diving for scrap in the graveyards of the Pacific . . . No, not McLeod . . . back on deck Johnson had lied.

There was no indication anyone was listening in, but Fowler didn't want to make any more mistakes. "What's the situation with *engineering*?" he whispered. "Any damage?"

Johnson didn't speak immediately, but then he said, "No damage . . . 'less the problem is, you know, *hiding*. In that case, there might be *surprises* if someone pounded on the hull." He reached over and tapped out the old "shave and a haircut" riff on Mike's arm.

Well, that was something. McLeod was a veteran, even though he had fought his war in the engine room of a battleship.

"Anybody got a clue what happened to Paluso?" Johnson asked.

No one had an answer to that one.

"We're not gonna make it," Cacoyannis mumbled.

"You're *wrong*." Fowler couldn't stand the idea of losing any more than he had already. "We're going to get one chance. They want to deactivate the explosives, then move the sub. It's afterward, as soon as they feel like they've got the situation under control—*that's* when we have to worry."

"The U-boat will never leave this place," Voss stated. "If I am allowed to again go inside, I am going to kill it."

"Kill it? That might be a bit optimistic, mate."

"Jack's right. We've got to concentrate on getting out of here," Fowler agreed.

There was silence. Then Mike heard Voss move, turning toward him in the dark. "A long time ago, I made a promise. A promise to myself that I did not keep—I could not keep . . . until now."

"What are you talking about?" Mike demanded. Voss spoke as if this was something he ought to be familiar with.

"I am talking about why I am here . . . why *we* are here. Do you remember when Peter Anhaldt said he knew I had worked with Konrad Zuse?"

Mike struggled to remember the conversation. Barcelona seemed like years ago. "The computer guy?"

"Yes. I told you of the experiments at Miersdorf, the tragedy with the Bell Jar device. In one afternoon, it killed five of its creators . . . and a few others."

"This was, what . . . before the war?" Mike tried to remember what Voss had said.

"Before your part of the war, in 1941. There was a team assembled to investigate, to analyze the data and decide if it was possible to continue the program. They achieved very little until one of them, a young mathematician, asked to be introduced to Konrad Zuse.

"Zuse, you see, had built a programmable twenty-two-bit electromechanical calculator. Today it would certainly be called a computer. Through my department at the Reichspost Research Institute I was recruited as the liaison between the two of them. For security purposes my responsibility was to divide the work into sections, to make it incomprehensible to Zuse and his staff. The mathematician was Dr. Elizabeth Adler, the woman you have asked me about. This was the beginning of my work on Projekt Glasglocke."

"And a personal relationship with Dr. Adler, correct?" Nicole asked.

Voss took a long breath, then he said, "We spent a great deal of time together, she and I. So, yes, the working relationship became a good deal more than friendship. Those were exciting times . . . intellectually, emotionally.

"One of the first things the Zuse calculations were able to isolate was the Tychon particle. Soon after, I was placed in charge of building a power plant. We called this 'Der kleine Bienenstock,' the little beehive, an iteration of the Bell design specifically focused on the production of fusion energy.

"Just this one discovery could change . . . everything. Elizabeth believed our program might lead to the end of want, the end of war. And not just our war, all war. The obsession of all empires is resources. We had at our fingertips an unending supply of almost free energy. If one element could be converted to another, then the days of looking at the world as a zero-sum proposition—that whatever one has gained must automatically be something another person, another country, has lost—were over. Perhaps we had uncovered the secrets of alchemy, the ability to perfect both physical matter, and also our souls.

"These were beautiful thoughts. But by 1943 the realization that we were damned was quietly spreading throughout Germany. Our drive southward to seize the Ukraine and the Russian oilfields in the Caucasus was failing. Stalingrad had become a frozen disaster. The government declared Total War. This meant every hour of labor, every ounce of food, of chemicals, of metal, the lives of every man, woman, and child were owned and controlled by the Fatherland.

"Because of repeated air raids, we were ordered to move the laboratory south into a complex of protected facilities beneath Fürstenstein Castle and an abandoned mine some distance away. Until then, none of us who were newcomers to the project had ever seen it . . . the original device, Die Glasglocke."

In the dark Voss moved, and his breath caught. "It was a monster. And just as in the stories, the monster now lived in a cave. We had constructed a gateway, a lens, for looking into the abyss. Galaxies and time were hidden within its heart. But as the saying goes, if you are at it long enough, the abyss always looks back. And that is the great sin of science: the truth you are pursuing is like touching the hand of God. No matter the cost, I do not believe any of us would have denied ourselves that opportunity. We could not stop.

"There is a story that the men of the Manhattan Project feared their atom bomb might set the atmosphere alight, destroy the world. Yet they went ahead. Our people truly confronted such existential risks on a daily basis."

"Destroy the world?" Nicole asked. "You mean . . . an experiment . . . could just kill everyone, everywhere?"

Voss made a noise that resembled laughter. "Oh, no. It is much worse than that! We assume our universe is stable, the laws of nature, of physics, these are certain. But maybe—quite possibly—the forces that have allowed existence of any sort, from the microscopic world to the cosmos above us . . . maybe this is only a local phenomenon, a bubble. Create a hole in that bubble and it collapses into a vast, completely unknown state of being. For his part, Dr. Zuse had the beginnings of an idea—that we existed within a 'rechnender raum.' An ongoing calculation, and the creation of high-entropy events such as our extreme voltages or perhaps atomic explosions, might disrupt the process.

"Some of the team at Fürstenstein were convinced we were on the edge of a catastrophe, that our experiments carried the possibility of creating just such a collapse. Our machine was like an ancient god, demanding of respect and only vaguely understood.

"After the move, during the reconstruction of the device, we discovered that its base, a plinth made of the finest steel weighing many tons, had mysteriously developed an unnatural brittleness as well as gas bubbles. Mysteriously, impossibly the device was cannibalizing itself.

"At the same time, back in Berlin, Allied air raids destroyed one and then the other of the computers we had used. There would be no more fine-tuning. Yet we were given no choice but to push forward. There was a desperate hope that our research could create a weapon, a dozen different weapons. Something that would save us from the disaster we had brought upon ourselves. Talk of saving the world came to an end.

"More and more my responsibilities required me to remain in the shipyards while Elizabeth continued with the theorists, attempting to make further discoveries. Research had moved beyond the simple Tychon. There was no retreat; we were as tragically bound to our objective as soldiers in the field.

"I traveled back and forth. In Danzig we worked under a constant rain of destruction. But even in the south at Castle Fürstenstein safety was not assured. The little beehive we built for the U-boat was quite docile, but the *experimental* device, Die Glasglocke—it was not.

"For many nights after a test Elizabeth could hardly sleep. She developed cramping in her calves and ulcers in her mouth. Bear in mind, these health effects were quite minor; we thought our new safety precautions and the work with the computers protected us from the deadly results suffered by the original team."

"You thought?" Nicole asked.

"We were wrong. But I will get to that.

"I was only present for a few of the experiments. The Bell had its own chamber blasted out of solid rock, a space insulated with ceramic tile and rubber matting. Each run of tests exposed special photographic plates, cloud-chamber particle detectors, and highly classified instruments constructed on-site.

"Though thirty meters of rock separated us from the device, we donned protective suits, and those manning the controls were required to wear a wire, grounding themselves electrically to the consoles. After the cooling system was activated and the device brought up to speed each experiment was over very quickly. Perhaps a minute, or a minute and a half. The lights flickered, I had the sensation of pins and needles in my hands. My mouth felt like I had tasted an old coin. Then, after so much preparation, all the test elements were removed for analysis.

"The Glasglocke systems continually suffered from equipment failures, malfunctioning electrical components, broken connections. However, this sort of issue was rare with the simplified Bell

Jar we used in the U-boat. Our failure to comprehend what that meant was a tragic mistake.

"A mysterious deterioration, like the gas bubbles we had discovered in the plinth, was affecting *everything*. It was as if infinitesimal pieces of our equipment, perhaps even ourselves, were being transferred . . . elsewhere. There were many failures. Some of them were human.

"The end came as they were preparing for an experiment. The power was on, the motors that turned the cylinders within the Bell were up to speed. Once the chamber was sealed, a timing circuit connected to the condenser banks would be activated. This caused a cascade of discharges. In previous tests, it had been discovered the most sensitive detector plates needed to be shielded until the last minute.

"One of the scientists, a Hungarian who had been with the program from the beginning, was mounting the plates when lights appeared on the status panel indicating the condenser circuit was live. I have mentioned that the effects of Die Glasglocke could be felt from a distance, through insulation and rock. Understand, the problem was not radiation, not as we know it . . . but certainly no one was allowed to be in the chamber during a test."

Mike felt Nicole shift position and he knew what she was thinking: Voss was talking about Leonid, the old man they had met on the beach.

"Perhaps it was trouble with the wiring . . ." Voss said, "Or a buildup of static electricity, a solar flare, the phases of the moon—" His voice caught. "Forgive me . . . I am sarcastic because no one could offer a useful explanation. When Elizabeth ran down the tunnel to warn him, he froze. She was very brave. She stepped inside and pulled him out.

"In the control room one of the operators panicked. He was too late, both of them had been exposed. But instead of disconnecting the electrical mains from the condensers, he shut down everything . . . including the cooling system and the power to the magnetically stabilized bearings within the Bell itself. The cylinders inside weighed several tons and were turning at many thousands of revolutions per minute, but that problem did not manifest itself immediately.

"I was called from my office. By the time I arrived deep underground, Elizabeth and the engineer had already been taken to our clinic. I was assured they were healthy, shaken, but healthy enough to walk to the security checkpoint. I was terribly relieved.

"As I tried to establish what had gone wrong, we heard the rumbling. It was a sound like the wobbling of a huge top as it begins to spin down. In the test chamber streaks of superheated metal appeared on the upper part of the Bell. The cylinders inside had lost alignment and, with a screaming that almost precluded thought, the device began to tear itself apart. There was a steel door. We slammed it and ran to safety. Even from the surface we could hear its death throes.

"And when I returned to the castle, I discovered that one disaster had become yet another."

Voss hesitated.

"In the early days, during the experiments at Miersdorf, they discovered the operation of Bell could cause damage to organic elements. Plants, animals . . . people. This was before we did the work with Zuse, before we moved underground. The physical damage . . . it was—I do not have the words—it began with bleaching of the affected areas. After a week or so there was sudden disintegration, the complete liquification of affected tissues.

"Elizabeth and the Hungarian engineer, within a few hours, both of them had patches of skin that were turning white, transparent—I can barely allow myself to think of it. Transportation to Charité hospital in Berlin was their only hope. The trains were running erratically at best. We finally secured an automobile. Finding just a single tankful of petrol required both bribery and coercion.

"The trip was less than four hundred kilometers, yet it took more than two days. Two days of Elizabeth knowing she was dying. Two days when I knew she was dying. There was no blood, no infection.

But for both of them the bandages were weeping and underneath, the shape of their flesh seemed to collapse.

"North of Dresden the roads were clogged with soldiers moving to the front and civilians fleeing south. Towns were bombed to rubble and a damaged train had been tipped completely off the tracks to clear the line. When we arrived, the hospital was a madhouse. Elizabeth was in agony and the engineer was unconscious. I saw her once more . . . when they put what was left of her in the ground."

Voss paused, and the blackness that surrounded them closed in. "For the first time since I was a child I went to church, an abandoned place, surrounded by destruction. There were lessons we should have learned, lessons all of us still have yet to learn. Humility before a higher power . . . that would be one. It is a worthwhile practice, and too rare among scientists.

"For days I was little better than a robot. The world was ending. Bombs rained from the sky. The Russians were on the horizon. Children were armed for a last defense. I was told the project was being evacuated and I was ordered to assist. Some documents were sealed in drums, others were destroyed. There was a plan, and I did what I was told.

"But afterward, after Elizabeth died, after the SS murdered the project's staff, after we fled to the bottom of the world, after Gunther Könnecke blew up my crew as well as his own men, after I killed him . . . after swimming in this ocean of sin, I made myself a promise . . . many promises. That thing, that knowledge . . . it will *not* leave this place."

For a few moments Mike Fowler had been carried away by Anton's story. It was clear why everyone from the CIA, to Mossad, to Anhaldt's Invisible Reich wanted to get their hands on the results of the Glasglocke experiments. With the possibility of the end of want and war at one extreme of the vast spectrum of possibilities and the universe collapsing like a soap bubble at the other, no one wanted anyone else calling the tune for future developments. The world was walking a tightrope as it was, desperately locked in a cycle of defensive reactions.

But although he was beaten, bloodied, and unsure he was ever going to see another sunrise, anger boiled up like bile in the back of Mike's throat . . . at the sick realization that Anton Voss had played him, played all of them, over and over again.

The man who had been his friend and mentor was using him. It went all the way back to the tropical ruins of New Guinea when he'd first hired Fowler away from Jack Johnson . . . a bodyguard, but also a diver.

Anton had taught him how to think strategically, to contemplate all the latent possibilities. The superpositions. In the black void of a sealed box the likelihood of whether the cat was dead or alive. But Voss had just come out and admitted his true agenda. It was tragic . . . and it was heroic . . . but it was also completely despicable.

Mike shook his head and choked out a sound . . . He didn't know where to start. There wasn't a word foul enough. In the darkness he could feel everyone's attention turning toward him, their eyes seeing nothing. Nicole pulled away, unsure of what was going on. She hadn't figured it out yet.

"You—you *played* us! We didn't come down here to find some, some . . . scientific treasure. That was as much of a lie as the gold. You played us all for a pack of fools."

"Mate? What are you going on about?" Johnson spoke up.

"He knows how to *build* it . . . the Glasglocke! He always did! It's not some secret nobody knows! He knew enough to pull Elizabeth Adler's equations apart and put them back together. He spent years engineering the system that went into the U-Null."

Mike was having trouble catching his breath. "Damn it to hell, Anton! You were lying the whole time. You could have auctioned the theory behind the Tychon from your office in Barcelona! But *no* . . . you made me sell my friends on how we were all going to make a fortune!"

Voss sighed. "To be precise, I didn't make you. You offered."

"Men *died*! I *trusted* you!" Mike struggled to keep his voice under control. "They weren't even given the honor of knowing the mission!"

He lashed out and his bound hands connected solidly with Anton's shoulder. The old man grunted in pain.

"I'd have done it! Don't you understand? I didn't need some fake reward! All you had to do was *ask*!"

"I had to be sure. We required a crew. We needed a cover."

"Rummy? What are you saying? If he knew, what the hell are we here for?"

"Jack, he just *told* you! Hell, he almost told us a bunch of times, but all we could think of was the money, or who was after us, or a mysterious, marvelous, dangerous future. We're not here to salvage the Glasglocke archive. That was all an excuse and a distraction. We're only here so that he can destroy it!"

CHAPTER 36

"DESTROY IT?" NICOLE sounded bewildered.

Voss said nothing, so Fowler went on, "Jack and his crew were here to do the hard work with no reward. Sobek and Paluso were scumbags to be used and discarded. The only one stupid enough to follow him out of loyalty was me! That damn auction in Cape Town was just a—a diversion!"

Mike shook his head. "How was that going to work, Anton? Were we going to burn the archives, destroy the reactor, and *then* you were going to say you'd accidentally dropped what was left of the greatest scientific discovery of all time overboard? And if we had nothing to offer, and no money, how the hell were we going to defend ourselves from, I don't know . . . every intelligence service on the planet?"

"You are only seeing what is in front of your nose!" Voss snapped. "The United States is surrounded by oceans, protected by the most powerful economy in history, yes? For the first time in hundreds of years, Russia is defended by geography, safe behind a barrier of satellite nations. Yet both are developing missiles and building hydrogen bombs as quickly as possible. Scientists are breeding diseases and dream of tearing apart human DNA. There is Sputnik and spy planes. There is no reason for any of this, and yet insanity reigns to the point where only the threat of nuclear fallout keeps the peace."

"Wait a minute." Nicole sounded like she wanted to laugh but couldn't. "Suddenly you're the idealist who is going to save the world from itself? *You?*"

"*Yes!* The Glasglocke discoveries, they are the most dangerous thing on the face of the earth. Releasing this information would be like throwing gasoline on the flames of the arms race. Simply repeating the experiments could risk everything in existence."

The bitterness in Anton's voice dripped like acid. "So, with whom would you suggest I share them? Your Israelis? Has tragedy turned them into moral supermen? I think not. The Soviets? They find themselves tormented to paranoia by everything that moves. The Americans? The same government who built its CIA around my countryman Generalmajor Reinhard Gehlen's spy network? Far too many of *his* merry band have been playing both sides . . . likely at the behest of those who have taken us captive. War is good business; the fear of war is even better. I should know, yes?"

"Wait a minute," Johnson spoke up. "Is this what you were blowing on about when you gave us that lecture about the ends justifying the means?"

"Of course! Does *anyone* believe Herr Anhaldt and his associates—these Nazis who no longer even have the courage to declare their ideology—should control the sort of technology I have described to you?"

No one replied to that.

Above them there was the sound of feet moving across the deck. Voices called back and forth.

Mike Fowler tried to swallow his anger. "We don't have time for this. Pretty soon they're going to make the two of us disconnect the torpedo room explosives. Then Anton will be needed when they try towing the sub. That's it. Those are our chances to escape. Skorzeny's men will be spread thin, distracted . . . and"—He dropped his voice to a whisper—"we can't keep McLeod in hiding until we're at sea. He might not wait for the signal."

"These are also the opportunities I will have to destroy the U-boat." Voss cleared his throat. "However, that creates some . . . difficulties."

"You think you're gonna try to sink it? Reset the explosives?" Johnson turned toward Anton's voice. "How the hell are you gonna do that and make it out? We get a chance, I'm not waiting, understand?"

"I will dive the boat, yes. If you act quickly, that should create the needed diversion. But I will not fire the torpedoes. That would simply lead to a more ambitious recovery operation. Listen . . . you hear the engines, yes?"

Distantly the humming of the *Bushranger*'s diesels could be heard. "I have repaired and reformed the condenser banks. Since last night they have been recharging. With luck I can start the Tychon generator. Do you remember what I said would happen if the process was allowed to run out of control?"

Nicole spoke up. "It would turn into a nuclear bomb?"

"A *thermonuclear* bomb."

"You're thinkin' you can set that up to go off?" Johnson asked.

"Aww, come on! We're gonna escape an H-bomb now?" Cacoyannis's voice rose. "H-How in hell are we supposed to do that? I've seen the pictures. You get burned into the pavement!"

"Be quiet!" Voss ordered. "On a street in Hiroshima, maybe . . . but think of where we are. Escape is possible. The mountains will block most of the blast. In open country at ten miles the overpressure would probably break windows. If you were exposed, outside the structure of the ship, the heat would cause severe burns. But this is not open country, and sightseeing would be a bad idea. Even seven miles might be survivable. The great risk will be the tsunami, displaced water either from the explosion itself or the collapsing cliffs and glaciers . . . Anywhere in the fjords could be a deathtrap. You must retake the ship and be ready to move immediately.

"This is . . . well, it's a *bad* idea . . ." Nikos mumbled.

"I am going to try," Voss insisted. "You can stop me. You can inform our captors if you wish. I am sure it will prolong your miserable life for a few more hours."

"Hold up . . . let's say it's our best bet. What about radiation?" Johnson asked.

"I have told you! This is *pure* fusion, not one of these crude military devices. You will have the steel of the ship to protect you from the initial explosion. After that it is not a concern."

Fowler took a breath and packed away his desire to strangle Voss. Diving the U-Null *would* provide a significant diversion. And Voss was still in his dry suit, so if the sub went down with open hatches he might even be able to escape without dying of exposure. But once they started down to the narrow passage to the outer fjord there would be at least two of Skorzeny's men on the sub, one to watch Voss and another to relay commands to the control room. As unexpected as it would be, the knife that Anton had stashed behind the control room's status panel hardly evened the odds. Voss wasn't going to make it. And there was something else . . . something about the way Anton was speaking. Mike had the distinct feeling he was missing something.

"If they let you into engineering, how long does it take to set up the power plant to explode?"

"Several minutes, at least. The boat was not designed to self-destruct."

"And you can rig some kind of delay, so that we can get all get away?"

There was silence in the darkness.

"Anton?"

"No, Michael. That is not possible."

Cacoyannis muttered a curse. "So, you're just gonna, what . . . blow us all up?"

"With luck I will not have to set it off immediately. The question is, Can I kill whoever they send with me? The question is, How long will I be able to breathe? Once there is no air—"

"Mr. Voss, you and me we may need to have a reckoning," Jack replied. "But maybe we just try retaking the *Bushranger* without a diversion. We get out of here, *all* of us. I'm not happy these blokes are gonna claim their prize but . . . this feels like the moment to cut our losses."

Mike Fowler discovered that his hands were tingling. He could sense what was left of his father and the damning forces that called him to swim in the dark of night. He felt the stillness that overtook him right before a mission. He might have a dozen angry reasons to slap Anton silly, but his body still knew what had to be done.

Voss had deceived every one of them, made them all a sacrifice to his obsession. Mike had no doubt what awaited his friends at the hands of Peter Anhaldt. And if he wasn't careful, Anton Voss might also kill them all just as quickly. The more control Voss had over events inside the submarine the longer he would likely wait before he did whatever he was going to do to the reactor.

"Mr. Voss is right," Fowler said. "Jack, be honest . . . assuming no one dies when we try to break out, how long to dump the anchor and get her turned around and underway?"

Johnson didn't answer right away. Then he said, "Fifteen minutes. Ten if everything goes right . . . which it won't."

"Okay. Mr. Voss can't take on several of them by himself. If we make our move when he and I go in after the explosives there will be two of us. We know the layout of the sub and Anhaldt's men don—"

Suddenly everyone, including Voss, was objecting at the same time. Nicole grabbed his shirt and yanked on it as if she was trying to shake some sense into him . . . but he knew what he had to do. He had brought these people to this place; he had held back the truth. Even Nicole wouldn't be here if he hadn't gone to Israel or if he had insisted that they put her ashore in Talcahuano. If he could get them out . . . well, he owed them that.

"Shut up! Shut *up*!" Mike wanted all the conflicting feelings in his own head to shut up, too.

"There's no better distraction than if Anhaldt thinks his precious submarine is sinking, and if the two of us can take down our guards, well . . . there's however much air we bring with us plus the partially empty tanks we left behind. That could give us more than an hour if we're careful. The question is: Can you get far enough away in that amount of time?"

Far off they heard a heavy engine fire up, and then the more staccato sound of an outboard. Whatever their fate, they weren't going to have very long to think about it.

Fowler blinked and lowered his head as the lights snapped on. Squinting, he peered into the glare to see Skorzeny and Hartmann standing in the doorway.

"Voss. Fowler. Get up. It is time to work."

Even as Mike staggered to his feet Nicole clutched his hand, holding on tightly for a moment. Her eyes were wide, and he turned away . . . He had to concentrate, no one was going to get more than one chance in what was about to happen.

Skorzeny brought him up short at the door, a powerful arm barring his way forward. The man's piercing eyes bored into his . . .

"I know you. This is where you do something brave . . . and foolish. Well, not today." He glanced at Hartmann. "Bring the girl. Get them both dressed."

Fowler took a breath, violence boiling in his gut, his entire body ready to explode.

Skorzeny leaned forward and casually struck him across the ear with the back of his hand. Mike staggered and the big Austrian planted a finger in his chest.

"Say nothing. Just do what you are told."

"Michael!" Nicole's eyes bored into his. "We *must* do as they say. It is the only chance . . . for *everyone*." He couldn't imagine allowing her to sacrifice herself. But if he objected everyone else would lose their chance to escape.

They were hauled up the stairway and into the machine shop. Once there both Mike and Nicole were ordered to change into dry suits. They struggled to pull the rubber arms and legs over their clothes. Anton, who had been in his suit since the attack, sat on the diver's bench. He wouldn't meet Mike's eyes and didn't look at Nicole. Her presence on what was about to become a suicide mission hadn't been considered by any of them. The only question left was whether they died at the hands of Anhaldt's men, or they went out on their own terms.

Outside, Fowler could see that the U-Null had drifted away from the *Bushranger* and was now loosely tied to the bow of Anhaldt's trawler. Several of the submarine's deck plates had been pried up and two men were at work disconnecting the anchor cable. Just aft of the trawler's damaged forward deck, someone in a rubber suit was being hosed down. Muck from inside the submarine sluiced over the side of the boat.

Farther out across the water the trawler's motor launch delivered Peter Anhaldt to the airplane and started back. After a moment the engines of the aircraft turned over and then, with a puff of smoke, came to life. Soon it was beating its way across the waves to disappear down the fjord.

Mike Fowler took a last look around him. This place was bleak, but it was also beautiful, its austere perfection marred only by the battle-scarred ships. He felt the breeze in his hair. He took a deep breath and smelled the cold sea and the icy shore.

"Attention!" Heinrich Hartmann had the well-scrubbed look of a man who had recently bathed. "It is time for bomb disposal!" He was also dressed in a dry suit but the belt around his middle carried a knife and his ballpeen hammer. He had carefully taped down his eyepatch.

Mike shot Nicole a look, and it seemed she understood. They were going to die . . . but Hartmann was going to die first and, if it was in his power, Fowler was going to be sure he realized the magnitude of his failure.

The launch scraped alongside the submarine and one of the crewmen from the trawler caught the bow with a boat hook. Hartmann held Nicole back until the two Argentine divers he had brought with him were standing on the hull, making it clear that she was a hostage.

They were forced up the ladder on the outside of the conning tower. At the hatchway, Voss balked. "Wait! The air in the U-boat—"

Hartmann laughed. "Just hold your breath. In the zentrale we will give you the apparatus . . . if you behave." He wiped a finger covered with slime from the ladder across Nicole's cheek. She twitched her head away and he finished up by carefully wiping his palms on the rubber of his suit.

From the set of her hands, Fowler imagined Nicole was fantasizing about applying a joint lock like she had used on Paul Sobek. He was glad she didn't try. Mike had half-blinded the bristle-headed German in Spain, and he had put a bullet through the man's abdomen in Argentina. If Heinrich Hartmann wanted to kill you, he wasn't going to be deterred by pain.

One of the divers went first. Then Voss. Fowler caught a breath and descended. In the dim light of a flashlight, he was pushed to his knees so that the hoses of an Aqua-Lung could be dropped over his head and the tank strapped to his back. He stood. He exhaled. The small amount of air in the mask held the foul taste of rot.

When Nicole came down the diver wisely allowed Fowler to help her into her tanks and regulator; she was already getting a bit wild-eyed by the time Mike pressed the mouthpiece between her lips. "Breathe out," he mumbled.

Hartmann was last and he was handed one of the two Jack Browne masks Mike and Anton had used during the raising of the sub. The other was worn by Voss. Both were still connected to the compressors and intercom on the *Bushranger*. As soon as Hartmann got the hose situated under his arm, he began speaking in German, reporting back to Skorzeny. The two South American divers were outfitted with the triple tank setups they used during the attack.

Someone had repaired the comm line and discovered the speaker that Frank Jano had rigged up. Hartmann jacked a lead into it.

"Herr Fowler, turn to your left," he ordered. Laid out on the navigation station were a flashlight, a diver's slate, and a shoulder bag with a selection of tools.

He had to get Hartmann to move. The man was between Voss and the status panel . . . the spot where the knife was hidden. Fowler grabbed the slate and scratched out, *Cotter pins?* He hoped Hartmann would step forward to look at it . . . but he didn't.

Mike picked up a roll of wire and shook it. "This is garbage! Useless!" He struggled to make himself understood through the Aqua-Lung's mouthpiece.

"No! Use what you have!"

"Okay. Okay," Fowler mumbled. If he'd been serious, he would have pre-cut sections of wire so that he could use them like the cotter pins they'd had in the engine room. However . . . he was beginning to get an idea.

Taking the slate and the bag he started forward. One of the divers levered open the big circular hatch and stepped into the foul slop on the other side. The muck came up over his ankles. The man carried a flashlight, and he gestured for Fowler to go ahead of him.

Hartmann gave an order in German and the taller of the two divers stepped behind Voss and reached up to grip his air hose right where it entered his mask . . . as effective a way of controlling him as any other. Then Hartmann drew his knife and manhandled Nicole toward the hatchway.

Wading forward, they stopped at the final pressure hatch, the entrance to the torpedo room. Hartmann was keeping Nicole close, a hostage and a human shield. It was a careful move . . . He just didn't realize none of his captives expected to live.

"Open it! *Schnell!*" Hartmann's voice rasped through the speaker.

Fowler gritted his teeth. Nicole stared at him in the dim, wavering light. Going through that door was insane. As soon as he succeeded in disarming the bombs, *if* he succeeded, he and Nicole would be killed. There was, however, one last thing he could try . . . but everything depended on how much he could accomplish in three minutes.

"Damn it, we need cotter pins!" he yelled into his mouthpiece. He pulled out the slate and wrote: *Tres minutos! 300 kilos TNT!*

He had no idea if the young diver knew what sort of trap had been set on the other side of the door, but he figured *now* he certainly wasn't going to take it lightly.

Then Mike twisted the lever and yanked open the door. "*This is crazy!*" he yelled, and dramatically threw down the slate.

The black four-foot hole gaped . . . and he just stood there, challenging them to imagine what was happening in the darkness. Somewhere inside, the timer, connected to the G7 torpedo warhead, started counting down. The young diver flinched back. He glanced over at Hartmann, then down the filthy corridor toward the questionable safety of the control room.

The instant his eyes shifted, Mike whipped the heavy waterproof flashlight out of his bag and swung it, smashing the diver across the side of the head. As the man fell, Mike saw Nicole twist and drop to her knees, away from Hartmann's knife.

Mike threw himself at the German, barreling in on top of him even as Nicole pulled one of his legs. The three of them crashed to the filth-covered deck. Hartmann's blade went in through the shoulder of Mike's dry suit, tearing rubber before cutting clear and arcing back as the man pushed him away to stab again.

Something—Nicole—jerked free of Mike's legs. She kicked out to take down the diver as he staggered back to his feet. Then the flashlight went out and Mike was fighting by feel alone.

Both his hands gripped Hartmann's knife wrist. He drove a knee down behind the German's thigh, locking himself in, and tried to jam a shoulder into the man's throat. Fowler's right hand slid, slipping off the arm of Hartmann's slime-covered suit. The blade thrust closer; Mike could feel the point of it tickling the skin just over his left eye.

Sweat popped from every pore. He forced, forced, forced the knife back. His feet flailed at the decking. He rammed Hartmann's head up into the rotting paneling that covered the wall. He could hear Skorzeny shouting into the earphone of Hartmann's mask, demanding to know what was happening. Then someone tripped over his legs, and he lost his grip.

Fowler felt the blade catch on the hose from his Aqua-Lung and he had one last instant to draw a deep breath before Hartmann ripped through it, cutting off his air supply.

Mike jerked to one side, but the blade didn't cut him—it was jammed in the frame that held his regulator! Instead of abandoning the knife Hartmann yanked on it, struggling to get it free. Mike shifted his position, trying to force his arm between them. Hartmann struck out, smashing an elbow into his ribs, again, and again.

"Breathe, damn you! Make this your last breath!" the German gasped. He didn't know who he was dealing with. If there was one thing Mike Fowler had trained for, it was this.

Then Fowler slipped a hand between Hartmann's air hose and his body and ripped upward, pushing the free flow Jack Browne mask up off his face.

There! Let's see how *you* like it!

The edges of Fowler's consciousness were drawing inward. His mind was screaming for air. His body was begging to give up. But he knew . . . he *knew* he always had something more in reserve. His hand pressed against Hartmann's face, his thumb found the eyepatch, the empty socket.

Somewhere in the dark the mask hissed and bubbled in the muck.

Hartmann twisted his head, straining to hold in a scream. He tried to set himself to throw another punch, but there was something indecisive in his grip . . . He could kill, or he could reach for the mask and live.

Fowler's muscles exploded into that indecision. He drove himself over, on top of Hartmann, flipping him face down into the sewage that filled the corridor and slamming himself hard into the man's back. The German bucked and lunged, but Mike leaned in, his back locked, his legs ramming into the slick floor, until he felt the man involuntarily take a breath, an oozing lungful of filth and chemistry. Choking, Hartmann struggled to turn. Trying to fight, to live, to cough, to breathe, to vomit, his body convulsed. Mike held on, held on, as vertigo spun the blackness around him, until Hartmann's muscle-bound body clenched then relaxed one last time.

Mike fell sideways onto Hartmann's sputtering mask. With numb fingers he pressed it to his face and waited, waited, for the flow of air to clear any gas away, then took a breath. Another. Coughing, he straightened. More breaths. Something was wrong. Something bad . . .

There was motion farther up the passageway. Nicole clubbing the diver over the head with a flashlight. He wasn't moving, but she didn't stop. Something bad—

The torpedo!

Fowler slewed around and nearly fell. He yanked the straps of the mask down over his head. He caught the edge of the hatchway and steadied himself.

There was no time.

Fowler grabbed the handle and pulled. Slowly the heavy hatch hinged closed and he pulled the locking lever.

"Anton!" he gasped into the microphone. "Button up! We're going down!"

CA—*WHAM!*

The explosion kicked him clear down the corridor. He thought he could see the walls bend. Was that possible? Was he out? Had he been out? He came to on his back. In his mind he was screaming, *Jack!* It was time for Jack to make his move. Now. Now. Now.

Then his head cleared. The deck was already tilting downward. He scrambled to his hands and knees. Nicole grabbed his arm. The bloody flashlight was in her hand. He pointed toward the zentrale. "Go!"

The hatch to the torpedo room was holding, but something else was spilling water. A sprung vent? A damaged bulkhead? He didn't know what injury the sub had taken. Fowler grabbed the Argentine diver by the tanks and heaved him over the threshold of the control room hatch. The man was probably dead, but they were going to need the air he carried. A few more minutes of life.

Mike pulled in his air hose, yanked the inner door shut, and dogged it tight. He collapsed back on the floor still sucking wind. The second diver lay collapsed over the helmsman's chair, the dive knife they had left hidden protruded from his back.

Anton Voss slid down the ladder from the conning tower and gently pushed Nicole out of the way. At the ballast control panel, he opened the valves and air boiled through the tanks that surrounded them, surrounded the pressure hull of the U-boat. Water rushed, and gurgled, and flowed.

Through the earphone in his mask Mike could barely hear the word . . . *"Dive!"*

The boat went down like eighteen hundred tons of stone . . . and then the bow snagged on something. With a groan it rebounded while the stern kept going, down and down and down. It hit, scraping and grinding along the bottom. They hung there, a twenty-degree angle to the deck. The bow of the submarine moved strangely, heavy but dancing to what felt like waves even though they must be many feet beneath the surface.

"So . . ." Voss tried to steady himself against the bank of valves. "It would seem we are still tied to the trawler. That cannot be good . . . for them." Sounds of distress, mechanical and otherwise, drifted down through the water.

Nicole mumbled a question.

"We're a lot bigger ship than they are," Fowler said, loudly enough that she could hear through the faceplate of the mask he had taken from Hartmann. "They are lucky we didn't pull them under."

A blast of frantic German crackled in the headphones. To Fowler it sounded like a mixture of questions, demands, and threats.

Voss paused a moment then said something . . . telling them to wait, delaying.

Fowler bent over the diver Nicole had clubbed and began stripping off his equipment. "We need to get these tanks ready." He tapped his Jack Browne mask and made a gesture like a pair of scissors to indicate that in a minute or two Skorzeny was going to wise up and cut off their air supply.

Voss nodded.

Then faintly they heard the thump-thump of gunfire. Jack and McLeod were making their move. A hand closed tightly on Fowler's arm. Anton Voss leaned close, his voice whispering through the comms channel. "You can still go," Voss said.

"What?"

He gestured toward the conning tower, then glanced at Nicole. "Leave your tanks for me. Save her. Try to live."

Mike felt his throat tighten, something, some words, some powerful feeling trying to get out. He couldn't see clearly. An hour ago he'd been ready to strangle this man.

"Anton . . . ?"

"I used you. I never wanted to, but yes, I did. You have gotten me this far; the rest is *my* mission. Alone."

Mike hesitated—

"Get out of here, Verdammt nochmal! The more air you leave me, the greater everyone's chances."

Mike Fowler swallowed and heard himself say, "Nicole! Get up there." He pointed up the ladder.

She frowned at him and shook her head.

He spoke louder. "We're going! Now!"

"What? How?" The mouthpiece kept her from more complicated questions.

"We're going to swim."

"No. *No!*" She shook her head, her fears overwhelming the certainty of death if she stayed.

"I'm going to tell you what to do. Do you trust me?"

After a moment she nodded, then slipped out of her tank and pushed it up through the evacuation skirt.

"Do you know what it is I most want right now?" Anton said. "A smoke. Find my cigarette case and lighter. Promise you'll have one for me, yes?"

Mike couldn't speak. He just gripped Anton's hand tighter.

"Go!"

Fowler dropped his air tank and followed her. Then, as Voss slipped into the dead diver's Aqua-Lung, Mike hauled up the Jack Browne mask. He handed it to Nicole. "Hold your breath and put this on. Tank off, quick!"

As she struggled free of her harness, Mike lowered the partially filled tanks they had left behind during previous trips, then Nicole's. He dropped to his knees and grasped Anton's hand for the last time.

The fierce, obsessive energy that had possessed the man since the night he had shot Hanno Wuttke in Barcelona was gone . . . he was old, and gray, and fragile. Then Voss stepped back, leaving Mike looking down into empty darkness.

Fowler pushed himself to his feet and slammed closed the lower hatch. He cranked the valve to flood the tower. Water poured in, covering their feet, then their ankles. Nicole shuddered.

He took her firmly by the shoulders. "Just listen," he said. "As the room fills up, and pressure builds, it's going to get harder to breathe. After I open the hatch, we are going to take off our masks, and I am going to go first. On the way up, you have to breathe out or you will rupture your lungs and die. You cannot hold your breath . . . Say it!"

"I-I cannot hold my breath." She was hyperventilating, sweat ran down her face inside the mask.

"Blow out slowly, slowly. You have to make this sound, 'aaaahhhh,' all the way up!" He moved his hands up to her chin looking right into her eyes. "Say it!"

"Okay . . . I will blow out slo—"

There was a hum and the comm line went dead. Either one of Skorzeny's men had cut the line or the *Bushranger* had torn free and was already moving to escape.

Mike tried to suck in a gulp of air but only got a wisp. He yanked off his mask and grabbed the wheel to unlock the upper hatch. It caught on the safety latches as dollops of compressed air ballooned past him. He couldn't wait. He let the hatch slam open and the air blasted him through. He hit the fairing above and rebounded. Stunned, he pushed himself back and reached in, taking hold of Nicole, peeling off her useless mask and pulling her out.

She took his hand, and he guided her up, out of the enclosed bridge. Water flowed into his suit through the cut from Hartmann's knife. It was a freezing stream weighing him down, but Nicole's suit was big enough for a man, and the air in it carried them both upward. It expanded, bubbles blowing past the seal around her neck.

But not from her mouth!

Fighting the ballooning suit, he caught her around the middle and squeezed. She struggled for a moment and then he heard it, a sighing exhalation. Bubbles blew away from her face. It was a long, long breath, expelling the last of the air from their lungs as they swam upward toward the dim light, escaping from the deadly gas-filled metal box of the submarine and into another world of noise and confusion.

CHAPTER 37

Mike Fowler's head broke water. Nicole drew a shuddering breath, then a wave smacked her in the face. She choked, coughed, and spat. Fowler got an arm under her chin. He bent his back, used his legs to force her body and the buoyancy left in her suit to spread out on the surface.

Nearby, the trawler's damaged bow was almost underwater. It lay half over on its right side, the stern high and exposed, the propeller thrashing. A sailor with an axe braced himself, prepared to cut the heavy Manila lines tied to the U-boat's submerged bow. Another man was screaming at him to stop. They didn't want to lose the last connection to their prize.

Fowler took a quick look over his shoulder. Black smoke poured from the *Bushranger*'s stack; someone had cranked up the diesels and left them running full out, but the ship wasn't moving.

A moment later what was left of the forward anchor chain poured from the hawsepipe. Someone had released the bitter end from inside, cutting the ship loose. Fowler stopped trying to see what was happening and concentrated on his swimming. As soon as the *Bushranger* got underway, they would be out of luck. A section of cargo netting still hung from the port bow. Fowler aimed for that.

From somewhere came the throbbing sound of the trawler's motor launch. Mike craned his neck, caught a glimpse. A boarding party was headed to reinforce Skorzeny or whoever was left aboard the fleeing net tender.

Mike and Nicole were low in the water, and no one had seen them yet. But that wasn't going to last. It didn't matter. There was nothing else to do. Just swim. He tasted salt, gulped cold air. Then someone in the launch yelled. A man stood, unlocking the safety of a machine pistol.

Another sound ripped through the water. A high-speed engine, a small outboard. Approaching from down the fjord, a black inflatable raced toward them.

The gunman on the launch looked up, tried to shift his sights. The whine of the outboard died for a moment and a staccato hammering ripped into the wooden boat. Heavy slugs smashed through the hull, cloth, flesh, and bone. The man with the machine pistol twisted and fell. The hammering went on and on, five long bursts.

Fowler could barely scissor his legs; his flooded suit slowed every movement. He gasped for air. Their savior coasted into view: Mel Paluso changing out the magazine on his M3 Grease Gun.

"Hey, buddy. Need a lift?"

Paluso pulled Nicole into the boat but Mike, with his suit full of water, was another problem altogether. A bullet skipped off the surface nearby, then another. Someone was shooting at them from the trawler. Mike was shuddering with cold and fatigue, but he wrapped an arm around the inflatable's grab line and yelled, "Don't worry about me. Go!" Paluso's thumb mashed down on the throttle, the bow came up, and the little engine howled.

Salt spray blasted into Mike's face, and he held on for dear life. The *Bushranger* was drifting, and they got her between them and the marksman on the trawler. As Paluso cut his motor, Fowler heard another gunshot, this time from inside. Nicole caught the cargo net and pulled the little boat close.

"Knife! I need a knife!" Fowler whispered. Paluso pulled out an old Marine Corps blade and passed it over. After cutting slits in his rubber suit, Mike was able to pull himself into the boat.

Paluso went up the netting and rolled onto the deck. Nicole followed. Soaked and freezing, Mike joined them near the machine shop hatch. No one was in sight.

Mel Paluso reached under his jacket and pulled out the Colt Python. He handed it to Fowler. He pointed back and forth, indicating the ship as a whole. "What do we do?" he whispered.

Just then there was a jolt and the noise from the engines changed pitch . . . The *Bushranger* started to turn, but it was not moving down the fjord—it was heading slowly toward the trawler!

Fowler passed the knife back to Nicole and said, "Up to the bridge. Quick and quiet!"

Creeping under the line of portholes, they reached the ladder to the boat deck. Mike went up first, then Nicole, with Paluso covering the main deck, then joining them.

A rattle of gunfire rang inside the steel walls. Glass broke, and then all was quiet again. Mike risked a quick glance through the porthole in the chart room door. One of the Argentinians was crouched in the cover of the doorway at the top of the stairs to the wheelhouse. Beyond him was the black-suited shoulder of another of Skorzeny's divers, who was at the wheel. Whoever they were shooting at—it had to be Jack or his crew—seemed to be trying to fight their way up the internal stairwell.

Mike heard a noise, the scrape of a foot on metal, and ducked down. Paluso snapped the submachine gun to his shoulder, finger tightening on the trigger. Aft of them, beyond the bulk of the workboat, a large figure moved. Mike touched Paluso's shoulder and shook his head. It was Waretini.

The Māori looked at them in shock, three people he probably never expected to see again. He grinned ferociously, but he was clearly suffering. His dungarees were soaked in blood from the bullet wound he had received earlier in the day. He carried a bloody axe. Mike thought quickly. They were closing in on the trawler and in another moment their position would be revealed to the rifleman who had shot at them earlier.

He pointed Paluso and Waretini at the chart room door and indicated that there were two men in the wheelhouse. On his signal Paluso would provide covering fire from his M3, while he and Nicole entered through the door from the bridge wing, flanking the men inside.

Nicole went up the stairs ahead of him. This door to the wheelhouse opened out and forward. She crouched, gripping the handle.

"Now!" Mike yelled. An instant later Paluso's submachine gun roared, and Nicole yanked open the door.

Fowler went in with the big revolver up and ready. But there weren't two men in the wheelhouse, there were four!

He fired into the first body that offered itself. He didn't aim, it was just metal on meat and pull the trigger. The .357 Magnum produced a stunning concussion and a blue-white fireball the size of a grapefruit. The bullet tore through the man, blasted a spoke from the ship's wheel, and carried on through the far porthole.

Fowler stepped past someone he barely registered, and shot the sailor who had stumbled away from the wheel. Mike pulled the trigger again, following the man down. Paluso had killed the man in the doorway, so Mike pivoted to see Otto Skorzeny pointing his old Luger, its barrel two feet from his face. Instantly he dropped to one knee, under the gun, the Colt coming up punching into the big Austrian's hard gut . . . but he didn't shoot.

Nicole had stepped in behind Skorzeny. She had a hold on his jacket collar and Paluso's knife tickling his kidney.

Skorzeny glanced down at Fowler. "Hmpf! Well, it would seem this is the correct moment to surrender, yes?"

He disarmed the pistol and handed it over. After a moment, Johnson levered himself up into the wheelhouse.

"Bloody hell, Rummy! Didn't expect to see you again."

"We've got to move, Jack! Voss is down there and he's going to blow it up!"

"Crikey . . . and that's passin' for *good* news?" Stepping over the dead men Johnson put the helm over and dialed up the revolutions. The ship turned, gathering speed as it headed down the fjord.

As they passed the trawler, they could see men peering at them from the angled deck, men unsure if they were friend or foe. One of them was Paul Sobek.

"Hey! Hey, what's he doin'—?" Paluso stepped out onto the bridge wing. The two partners stared at each other, but they were moving in opposite directions. Fowler pulled Paluso back, afraid that the crew of the trawler would start shooting again. "He picked the wrong side. I'll explain, but we've got bigger problems."

Leaving those men to their fate gave Fowler a hollow feeling in the pit of his stomach . . . out of all of them, Sobek was the only one who might guess what was coming. But they had made their choices, and Mike didn't have much sympathy for anyone who now, decades later, considered a Fourth Reich to be a path to the future.

He glanced at the clock. It was 3:17 in the afternoon.

He had lost track of time but, if they were lucky, they might have an hour. An hour to live. An hour to get far enough away so they could continue to live. Seven miles or they wouldn't even have a chance. Ten was better, but the most *Bushranger* could do was maybe fourteen knots and that was straight ahead in clear water. In a few minutes they would have to slow down to negotiate the treacherous passage to the outer fjord, and for that they needed all hands on deck, wounded or not.

He sent Nicole to get cleaned up and then to sick bay with orders to do what she could. Cacoyannis had taken a bullet in the leg and had three broken fingers. Waretini needed his bandages changed at the very least. McLeod was everyone's hero, yet as he shuffled around the engine room his back seized with spasms. On Johnson's orders he had hidden in the narrow space behind an electrical panel, unable to move for hours.

While everyone was busy, Fowler gathered their enemies' weapons then ran below to wash and find clothes that weren't sopping wet. That was easier said than done. The cabins and crew's quarters were a mess. Anhaldt's men had ransacked every corner.

It wasn't long before Mike could feel the *Bushranger* slowing and adjusting course. He finished dressing, grabbed a jacket that had belonged to Suarez, and dragged himself back up the stairs. The next few minutes would decide whether they lived or died.

The narrow crevasse leading to the outer fjord looked less menacing now that they could see it by daylight. Two arcing arms of rock restricted the entrance. They were barely awash but thankfully clearly visible because of the low tide.

Captain Seegers's charts were nowhere to be found but all they had to do was reverse the process they had used when they came in. If they maintained the right angle of approach, held to the southwest side, and proceeded slowly, they should be fine. The trouble was that sometime during the afternoon the depth finder had taken a bullet, and Johnson wasn't slowing . . . much.

Jack leaned forward intently studying his approach. He knew that as soon as Voss pulled the reserve on his last tank of air the fjord behind them, as well as this winding passage, was going to turn into a giant gun barrel. The explosive charge at its base would be many times that of the Hiroshima bomb.

At seven knots they'd risk ripping a hole in the *Bushranger*'s hull, but at four they might still be trapped in the inner fjord half an hour from now. Was that too long? How many breaths did Anton have? How fast was his heart beating? How much physical work was it going to take to rig the U-Null to explode?

They angled closer to the rocks and Fowler clambered to the top of the heavy fixed crane on the port side of the bow, getting as far out in front as he could. Gusts of wind forced him to hold on with both hands. The speed with which they were sliding toward the rocky entrance didn't *look* impressive, not if you were used to driving a car. But the *Bushranger* was a seven-hundred-ton ship that had no ability to come to a complete stop and, if it went too slowly, couldn't even steer.

Below him on the starboard side was Cacoyannis, leaning on a chair and hollow-eyed, his left hand and right leg heavily bandaged. Mel Paluso stood by to help if needed. Waretini clutched the railing of the bridge wing ready to relay their signals to Johnson. They moved past a line of boulders that barely broke the surface then nosed into the channel itself. Fowler signaled a turn to port.

"Slowly . . . *slowly*!"

Johnson ignored the advice. The bow came around . . . further . . . further. They were fighting the wind this time rather than the current. As soon as they had a straight run for a thousand yards Jack dialed up the power.

Another adjustment, a few degrees to the southeast, was coming. Their momentum diminished, then Jack increased his revolutions, kicking them into the turn just as a powerful blast of wind pulsed down the passage.

Too far! Steel ground on rock as the stern made contact with something beneath the surface. There was a long dragging scrape, and their forward movement slowed. Pinned by the friction, the ship began to pivot. Mike could see white water frothing up from the propeller as Jack poured on the power, trying to correct their heading. But until they could straighten out, the wind was forcing them sideways.

There was another scrape, a release, then a solid impact. Mike looked down. It had been right under his feet. Fowler couldn't see anything except drifting mud. The rock was hidden under the angle of their bow. Mike signaled Johnson to reverse.

From the wheelhouse he could hear a stream of profanity. Were they stuck? No. The prop thrashed. They edged backward.

There it was! A single rock like a shark's tooth, barely visible beneath the surface. With the tide out, the west side of the channel wasn't as safe as they had been told.

Adjusting the rudder, Johnson powered the ship forward, increasing speed heedless of danger. All the care he had shown earlier was thrown to the winds and, with a rending growl, the *Bushranger* scraped across another shelf and shouldered into the final stretch. The snow-flecked slope across the outer fjord appeared and they plunged into the main channel, turning, heeling over like a destroyer chasing a sonar trace.

The wind was now pouring across their beam. Fowler slipped and lost his footing, hands clamping down on the railing. The foaming bow wave curled beneath him, the ship slamming through the choppy surf that came in from the distant sea. He got his feet back on the narrow stairs and, not trusting the slick metal a second time, made his way down to the deck by edging along in a sitting position. Safe again, he ran for the wheelhouse.

The clock read 4:03.

Jack had the nearly useless Hydrographic Office chart spread out on the bench behind him, a set of navigating dividers holding it down. He looked up as Fowler entered. His eyes were haunted. "I don't know if we're gonna make it," he said.

"It doesn't matter," Mike said. "We keep going full ahead. Get to the bay. Pray the mountains shield us. I'll keep her headed in the right direction. You and the others get below the water line."

"Me? Not a chance!"

"Look, we don't know what's going to happen, but we might need someone up here who can move fast." Mike nodded at Jack's leg. "Right now, that's not you. Go on, batten down every hatch, disconnect the radio antennas, and shut down all the electrics you can. Be ready with fire extinguishers."

Johnson shook his head, not quite knowing what to say. "Mate, we've been up the track together . . . done a lot of things that shouldn't have been necessary."

"Yeah. Let's just try and get out of this alive. After it goes off—if it goes off—this ship will have a new set of problems and we're going to need you . . . badly."

Jack turned, carefully lowering himself down the short staircase into the chart room. “Alright!” Mike heard him say. “Get this Kraut off his butt and down those stairs!”

A moment later Fowler was alone. It was 4:06.

A blustering westerly wind forced him to carefully mind the helm. Just behind them was the dim slot of a short fjord leading off to the east. Were they still too close? Mike worried that maybe they should have tried to hide in its upper reaches and hope for the best. But any sailor preferred open water; land could kill you quicker than the sea.

A mile or so ahead the fjord opened up. The nameless bay lay streaked with sunlight slanting in under the clouds. It was beautiful, but it was also 4:10, and he was aware of every breath he drew into his lungs. In. Out. Even as a diver he had never appreciated what that could mean.

Anton would be doing whatever he had to do to bypass the fail-safes on the Tychon generator, filling the reaction chamber from the tanks of deuterium, preparing for the last moments of his life. His last breath.

The bay was just a few minutes ahead. Seven? Ten? It wasn't safe, but it was better than here. Mike heard a sound from the chart room.

“Couldn't do it, mate. I couldn't wait down there,” Jack stood in the doorway. Behind him was Nicole.

Fowler gave the helm to Johnson. He and Nicole pulled open the seat cushion and quickly started snapping the canvas blackout curtains into place. Before he hung the last one Mike used Jack's knife to cut a foot-high slot so that Jack could see forward. Now the only thing they could do was press on, hoping they would know what to do when the moment came.

It was 4:15 and they couldn't have much longer, unless—unless the joke was on them. Unless Anton couldn't get the power plant to blow up. Unless he was going to die for nothing. Unless—

It was like a flashbulb as big as the sun.

Several flashbulbs. A reflection off the clouds, the hillsides, and the water ahead of them. A landscape impossibly seen *through* rubberized black canvas. The outline of the curtain edges seared into their eyes; the slot Mike had cut was a punishing window of blazing white.

"Duck!" Fowler pushed Nicole through the doorway into the chart room.

"Help me . . . I can't see!" Mike grabbed Jack and pulled him along. Together they crashed down the stairs. Jack yelled in pain as his splinted leg hit the deck. A bolt of heat went through them, through the ship, like an electric shock.

Mike took Nicole's hand. He looked at Johnson, the man who had been his friend for more than fifteen years. "You ready, Jack?"

His friend nodded his head. "See you on the other side, mate."

"Open your mouth! Cover your eyes!" Mike yelled.

The outward wave of super-compressed air ricocheted along the sheltered canyons and exposed hillsides like a solid thing, a thunderclap the size of Texas, an echoing staccato explosion. It was a sound that blew in the glass from the *Bushranger*'s portholes. A sound that punched like a fist into Mike Fowler's ears and lungs.

The *Bushranger* tipped forward, bow driving down into the water. The steel of the walls bent. The straining rivets crackled with a sound like machine gun bullets.

Then the wave reversed, the wind sucked backward, rushing, pouring in to fill the hellish vortex.

The ship was rising. In panic Mike scrambled to his feet. His head swam. The floor pressed upward, and he could see the bow, the two heavy cranes like the horns of some mythical animal emerging from the sea. The decks shed water, steaming from where the flash had singed the hull. The air was full of burning paint and canvas and rope.

Nicole was struggling to get her breath, but she was alive.

Jack was coughing blood, but he was alive.

Mike tried to take a step and staggered. On more than one occasion he had felt the raw electric concussion of a battleship's sixteen-inch guns. That was . . . *nothing*.

There was something, something, he had to do. If he could just think . . . Think!

Fowler staggered up into the ruins of the wheelhouse. The ship pitched and rolled. They were emerging from the fjord into the scattered islands of the bay.

He verified that the engines were still running. The rudder still worked.

Light, alternating between angry and orange and a diffused and blinding glare, shot shadows and ghosts and rising streaks of impossible brilliance across the landscape.

The shuddering concussion had passed, and he realized he wasn't deaf. But from somewhere, everywhere, a crackling roar filled the air. It shook in his chest and numbed his eyes.

Mike opened the door and stepped out onto the bridge wing. The ship's gray paint was blistered and peeling. Fires burned on the slopes around them. Fog, melted snow, vaporized water, whirled ahead and around them like wind-torn phantoms. Behind and to the west, a vast dark column blasted upward. A volcano of rock and debris that looked like the trunk of a gigantic tree. It seared a hole through the clouds then, after a margin of empty sky, the roiling cap, like the head of a mushroom, expanded in all directions. Inside the curling dome of ice crystals was a pulsating ring of fire, a living demon of energy that swallowed the moisture at its edges and converted it into even greater expansion, upward and out. Its shadow raced toward them. Surrounded by a halo of black the blistering white and purple and yellow of it reached for the stratosphere, thundering higher and higher.

Something tugged at his arm. Nicole holding on, looking aloft with wide and horrified eyes. Jack clutching the door frame, squinting and blinking, straining to see in the hellish light. Below him the hatch to the deck had opened and Paluso, Skorzeny, and Waretini stepped out, staring in unsteady wonder.

It was one heck of a way to go out. Mike's eyes watered and it wasn't just the wind or the drifting smoke. Anton Voss had devoted half his life to keeping a Pandora's box of secrets. When that was no longer possible, he had goaded one of those secrets into destroying all the rest. He had told them what to expect, and he hadn't been wrong. He had told them—

Oh, hell!

"Get—get off!" he yelled at Waretini. "Get off the deck and cl-close her up!" Mike was still having trouble forming words.

"Jack!" He turned, his heart slamming in his throat. "We've got—we've got to get out of the channel!"

"Wha-what?" Johnson frowned.

Like a pack of fools, they had stood there gawking at one ongoing disaster while another was bearing down on them.

"Wave! Uh, coming—!" Fowler was still sorting out the muddled picture in his mind.

Suddenly Jack Johnson straightened and shook his head. "Damn! Keep a lookout," he commanded.

Johnson pulled Nicole inside. "I can't see very well. You gotta be my eyes!" He released the wheel and turned hard to starboard, heading for the mile-wide gap between a pair of triangular islands west of the channel.

Looking back up the fjord, Fowler caught sight of something, but he wasn't sure . . . He didn't know what to expect. It wasn't a great capping wave like the surfers had ridden at Waikiki Beach. It was a froth of white water that climbed up and up the edges of the fjord, an endless flood pouring toward them, into the bay, radiating outward. A moment later he could again feel the deck of the *Bushranger* lift. The tsunami wasn't a high wall of water, it was a swell . . . but it was deep, miles deep, and it was still coming.

The ship rocked as they shot forward on the swirling tide. The shores on either side of them shrinking, the sea around them rising ten feet . . . twenty feet? Mike Fowler's sense of scale was completely gone.

Johnson cursed and spun the wheel back and forth. It made little difference; the speed of the water was outpacing the motor that drove the ship's propeller.

"You see that?" he demanded.

Just over a mile ahead was a long, low set of rocks split by pools and channels. Fowler dropped down into the chart room, yelling down the stairs to the main deck, "Brace yourselves! We're going aground!"

They glided over the tops of trees, between boulders, past a moss-covered slope . . . and then they hit.

The hull tore across the rock with a grinding roar. Dozens of separate impacts jolted them left and right. The deck tipped. Nicole stumbled forward, cutting her arm on a shard of glass. Mike held on, pulling her back as the ship slewed sideways to the current, wedging into a hollow, bow down, the ongoing rush of water carrying over the deck, sluicing past them in thick streams. Another, higher, wave or flood ripped past them, and he could hear it pouring through the broken portholes. He could hear the cries of alarm from their crewmates on the lower level as tons of water poured through the passageway and down the stairs to the deck below.

Finally the flow slackened. The tormented sea receded. Bruised and bewildered, McLeod, Waretini, Paluso, and even Skorzeny climbed to the chart room to look around at their plight. Cacoyannis was unconscious. The ship was completely out of the water, off center, and firmly jammed into a jumble of boulders, each the size of a house.

They wandered, speechless, around the remains of the deck. The wind whistled through the broken glass and torn metal. And then the rain began to fall. Muddy rain, pouring from the unnaturally shaped clouds. Mike caught some of it in his hand and he prayed that Anton Voss had been right . . . that, for all its fury, uncontrolled Tychon-catalyzed fusion did not produce radioactive fallout. Because, if he was wrong, their problems were only beginning.

CHAPTER 38

MAGDALENA CHANNEL,

twenty-four hours later . . .

MIKE FOWLER STARED at a gray-painted wall. The air smelled of oily dust, and he could hear the muted hum he remembered, without fondness, from his days in the Pacific. In the bunk beneath him Jack Johnson snored. They were aboard a small warship . . . what the United States Navy used to call an APD, the sort of fast transport that had been used by the Underwater Demolition Teams. This one was modified to support a forest of antennas and a flight deck big enough to accommodate a compact helicopter housed in a bulbous waterproof enclosure. Besides the crew, he had seen both a small number of civilians and a squad of Marines.

Mike stretched and his body hurt, but the dazed feeling that had plagued him throughout most of the previous day was gone. They had all been in bad shape, struggling to tend to their wounds and stay warm in the wreckage of the *Bushranger*. Cacoyannis remained unconscious, Waretini was feverish, and Jack's leg had begun to swell. McLeod could only walk crouched over, and Nicole had bruised ribs, a knot on her forehead, and a bandage wrapped around her wrist. Once the adrenaline wore off, Mike paid the price for several severe beatings. He could move, but it was slow and painful. The only two in reasonable shape were Paluso and Skorzeny.

After a couple of hours, they cut off the ropes that bound the Austrian's wrists. They were on an island, halfway to Antarctica, and it had become obvious that as strong as the old commando might be, he wasn't going to run anywhere. He'd smoked one too many cigarettes, probably back before Fowler and Voss had ever met him.

There was also something about the apocalyptic orgy of destruction they had just witnessed. For the moment they were all humbled. It was like God had shouted at them. Whatever their fate, they were resigned to it.

The following morning strange figures had appeared on the rocks surrounding the ruined ship. They wore protective hoods, masks with huge dark eyes, heavy jowls, and oval snouts. The camouflage patterns printed on the capelike smocks seemed more suited to a jungle than this world of snow-dappled rock and wind-bent trees. One of them swung a metal box, moving it back and forth in an almost ritualistic pattern. Two others flanked him, each fingering a sleek black rifle with upraised sights and a tapering handguard.

Fowler and the other survivors were taken into custody, to warmth and relative comfort, but not before they were closely scanned with that metal box, a Geiger counter.

By afternoon the APD was powering through increasingly violent seas, although where it was headed remained a mystery. Mike guessed that, now that they had the only loose ends firmly in hand, whoever was in charge wanted to put some miles between the scene of the crime and anyone else coming to investigate. Their wounds had been expertly treated in a surprisingly well outfitted ship's hospital, they were given the opportunity to bathe, and food had been delivered directly to the cabins where they were confined.

The rest was desperately appreciated, but before long the door was unlocked by a petty officer.

"Mr. Fowler? Please follow me."

They went down the passage and then up a deck. Farther along the corridor the PO stopped and discreetly knocked on a varnished panel.

"Come!"

The man sitting at the desk was not a military officer. It was Anson Fordyce. As usual he was impeccably dressed, togged out in heavy trousers and a shirt with rolled-up sleeves. A winter coat that had probably come from Abercrombie & Fitch was slung across the back of his chair.

"Mike Fowler! All I ask is that you activate a simple beacon, instead you send up an eighty-thousand-foot pillar of fire. Well, I must say . . . you're getting easier to track!" Fordyce pointed across the office. "Pull up a couple of chairs, there are two others joining us."

Fowler did so and was waved to a seat. "Before they get here," Fordyce said, "I am going to give you an opportunity you really don't deserve." Fordyce arched an eyebrow and waited, forcing Mike to ask if he wanted to be informed of his fate.

"Go ahead."

"Remember all those promises I made . . . back before you *didn't* do what I asked?"

"Vaguely."

"Well, this is your lucky day. You do realize that I've had to take an oath, allegiance to the Constitution of the United States, and all that? But because of my role in our faux pas so many years ago, I find myself, let us say . . . additionally careful. Especially when it comes to you. There are, however, sometimes things that simply have to be done. You follow me so far?"

"Not at all." Fowler suspected that he was about to get railroaded into something. Fordyce had almost apologized, and that didn't come without a cost.

"Alright, some background. There are people back home who profited greatly from the war. I don't hold it against them, it's possible I've even helped. What I *don't* like is when they aid a vanquished system in reasserting itself. I'm in it for America.

"Recently, the man who used to be my boss was . . . retired. Among other things, like a bad relationship with the new president, he was not sufficiently motivated when it came to keeping our old enemies in their place. He was in it for America too, but this game is not a simple one. For better or worse, a good deal of our intelligence on the Soviet Union is collected by his colleagues in the Reinhard Gehlen Organization. I'm sure quite a few of them are loyal Germans . . . but to which Germany?

"On top of that, there're Nazis, even SS members, ensconced in government agencies and in boardrooms all over the world. There are quite a few in prestigious positions in the U.S. They appear on children's TV programs. They sign autographs. Some have become true American patriots. Others . . . well, you know them better than I do.

"Because of the severity of what just happened"—Fordyce mimed a rising mushroom cloud—"We have an opportunity . . . a chance to send a message, to show our ex-Nazi friends that while they have some influence, our patience is . . . limited. I want to trim the weeds, so to speak. But I can't do it myself. I'm going to need a gardener."

Fowler knew better than to relax around this man. "And something about that is supposed to be lucky . . . for me?"

"What you did for your country on Itu Aba . . . I want you to do it again. I want you to clean up what happened here. I think we have about ten hours. Do what I tell you and I'll uphold an . . . abbreviated version of my previous offer."

"Define 'abbreviated.'" Lives had been lost. Jack's business had been destroyed. Fowler needed to know that his friends would be taken care of.

"Mike, you're either in or you're out. If you're out, I throw you to the dogs. *All* of you. Your choice . . . but it's not really a choice." As usual, Fordyce wasn't making any promises.

"When this is over are you going to try to kill me to cover your ass?"

"That wasn't me, old boy." A cynical smile flickered across Fordyce's face. "I like to retain an asset . . . for as long as possible. So? Yes or no."

Fowler sighed. "Alright. What's the op?"

Fordyce stood and walked to the door. Cracking it open he said, "Send them in." Turning to Fowler, he said, "Listen carefully, I believe you'll catch on . . ."

A moment later Otto Skorzeny appeared in the doorway.

"Herr Standartenführer!" Fordyce grinned and gestured across the cabin. "Please, come in and have a seat."

The next person to enter was Nicole. She ran to Mike, and they embraced. Then she looked up into his eyes and, taking hold of his upper arms, she shook him as if to assure herself that he was really there, all in one piece.

Fordyce cleared his throat. "This is charming, but we're on the clock."

They sat, and Nicole shot a venomous glance at Skorzeny. Mike guessed she regretted not stabbing him when she'd had the chance.

"So, Otto, old boy, I understand this U-boat you were all so entranced with was about to be transferred, towed somewhere. Give me that location."

Skorzeny smirked . . . or something. His scar distorted the expression. "Please, may I have a cigarette?" He reached out as if Fordyce had already offered him one.

"No." There was nothing in the word except a flat denial. "I want to know where that sub was going. I want to know where Peter Anhaldt is. And I want to know *now*!" Anson Fordyce— five-foot-four, pink-faced, and perfectly shaven—stared into the eyes of the commando who had rescued a dictator, blackmailed a nation, and caused Eisenhower, the most powerful general in Europe, to go into hiding.

"Alright. I'm going to mention some names," Fordyce said. "Hans-Ulrich Rudel, Günther Rall, Gerhard Barkhorn—all decorated members of the Luftwaffe. Panzer officers Hans von Luck, Otto Carius, and Franz Bäke. I'll add a few more: Siegfried Milius and Hans Jüttner. How would you describe these men? Heroes of the Reich? Personal friends? Admired colleagues?"

"Of course, they are known to me," Skorzeny snapped. "But I am not falling for some trap. Say what it is you have to say."

"If you give me the location of this facility and the tactical situation there, I will buy you a plane ticket to any city in the world. If you do *not*, I'm going after every Nazi on that list. I will contact our reporters with the wire services, prosecutors, police forces, private detectives, and every intel agency in Europe and South America. I will make their lives a living hell. I will hound them to the grave. *And* I will let the world know that their misery was because of you.

"But *before* I do that, I will turn you over to the Israelis. Miss DeMaes here will shepherd you through a very public trial, one that will make it seem like Adolf Eichmann got a vacation. And if you don't believe there is evidence for an adequate amount of war crimes and perversion . . . just wait. What I can't dig up, I *promise* to manufacture.

"Now, make your decision. Are you going to support some insane fantasy of a Fourth Reich . . . or the honorable soldiers you respect and fought beside?"

Otto Skorzeny's jaw clenched and his face reddened. He shifted in his chair. Mike didn't know if he was on the verge of lashing out or having a heart attack.

Fordyce wasn't waiting. "Let me make it easier for you. I'm going put your wife's name on that list. She's a player in our great game. But, unlike *you*, she tends to fly beneath the radar. In particular, the French press will be interested in all that we can tell them."

Skorzeny sounded like he was choking on something he thought he'd swallowed long ago. "Get me a map!" he croaked.

"So, we have a deal?"

"Get me a map, damn you!"

Fordyce spread a chart on the desk and Skorzeny stabbed a finger at it. Fowler leaned forward; the spot was on the northern shore of Skyring Water, a huge inland sound. A narrow channel connected it to Seno Otway, yet another almost completely enclosed body of water.

"There! The residential compound is maybe five hundred meters from the waterline. There is a warehouse on a pier. It was built so that once the U-boat was discovered it could be hidden and dismantled."

"Personnel?"

"At this moment, minimal. Perhaps ten. Six will be workers, guards, a cook; they have their own residence, closer to the water. Is that all? Are we done here?"

Fordyce laughed. "In our business we're never *done*. You know that. But we're done for now."

He snatched up the telephone on the desk. "Get us to Seno Otway. Let me know when you have an ETA. Then send someone to collect Skorzeny."

When the door closed and it was just the three of them, Fordyce leaned back in his chair. "What I want to do isn't exactly authorized. It comes more under the heading of, uh . . . showing initiative. The kind of initiative that requires deniability."

"You need a fall guy."

Fordyce shrugged.

"You're in this, too?" Mike glanced at Nicole.

She nodded. "Whatever intelligence we gather will be shared with Mossad."

Fordyce tapped the spot Skorzeny had indicated on the map. "Weather permitting, my men will perform reconnaissance and secure the site. All I require is that the three of you clear the main residence. There are to be no survivors."

"The *three* of us?"

"This is my day for granting dispensations."

SKYRING WATER.

eight hours later . . .

MEL PALUSO, MIKE Fowler, and Nicole huddled in the darkness behind the crest of a shallow ridge. Their faces were streaked with boot polish, their fatigues dyed black, and anything that might make noise had been left behind or wrapped in electrical tape. Below them, jutting well out across the dark surface of Skyring Water was a long, low pier, the last hundred yards or so supporting a large corrugated tin shed. Closer in, Anhaldt's seaplane was tied to a floating stage. Fowler handed his binoculars to Nicole as several men moved up behind them in a low crawl.

"We're set," Fordyce whispered. "They're almost ready to pull out. My guys will manage the foreign nationals . . . anyone down there at the bunkhouse."

There was a good-sized building situated at the base of the pier; it housed half a dozen small apartments and a commissary.

Much closer to their position was a rambling stone-and-timber lodge that looked remarkably like the place Fordyce had used as his headquarters on the shores of Lake Nahuel Huapi. Midnight had come and gone, but electric lights illuminated the main house as well as the pier. A generator grumbled inside its small enclosure, and sparks rose from a trashcan in the side yard. Anhaldt and his men were destroying evidence. Though almost a hundred miles away, the explosion of the submarine was not an event that could be missed.

In the distance a pair of dark figures were starting back up the hill. For the last hour they had been carrying cases out to the plane.

"Alright. We're going now. You ready?" Fowler asked.

"Lead off," Fordyce commanded.

Easing backward, Mike and Nicole slid through a stand of wind-mangled trees. They circled into the shadows surrounding the generator shack. Its noise and bulk covered their approach. Thirty yards behind, Fordyce and Paluso knelt among the trunks, ready to provide suppressive fire should anything go wrong.

The entire operation was sterile; all clothing had been stripped of insignias and even labels. Dog tags and identification documents were left behind. And, while the Marines were armed with experimental AR-15s—a shorter, lighter version of the Dutch-produced AR-10—none of the weapons carried any serial numbers. For their part of the job, Fowler and his companions had been issued silenced High Standard HDM .22-caliber pistols, an off-the-books handgun manufactured for OSS agents during World War II, and fragmentation grenades. Beyond that, they had to make do with weapons scavenged from the wreck of the *Bushranger*. Paluso retained his Colt Python and Grease Gun, Mike had discovered his Smith & Wesson under the desk of the chart room, and he and Nicole had MP 40 machineguns that had once belonged to Skorzeny's men strapped across their backs.

In the late afternoon they had used the helicopter, a Kaman Huskie, to ferry them north. The Marines had gone first, the last group boarding after dark. Fordyce brought with him two civilians festooned with photographic gear.

They rose, dangling from the lift of the rotors as the ship slipped away beneath them. Its lights snapped out and then they were roaring through the freezing darkness with no point of reference beyond the vaguely gray clouds above. It was a rough ride; the storm seemed to have blown itself out fairly quickly, but they were still flirting with the margin of safety for a helicopter. It was more than an hour to the drop-off point, and then a five-mile hike to the objective.

Mike and Nicole were both beaten and bruised. Soldiers had fought with greater injuries in nearly every war, but it had not been a fast or pleasant walk.

The two men came up the path. Fowler had chosen a spot just past the generator building. The warmly lit house was just ahead, and they were likely to be looking in that direction, focused on gathering up another load to take down to the plane.

He slid out of the shadows, angling in while Nicole stood back, ready to cover him should anything go wrong. Silently closing the distance, he extended the silenced pistol and fired.

One-two, one-two. He took both of them to the ground then gave each man three more rounds. With a .22 it paid to be sure. He swapped out the magazine as Nicole moved in to search the bodies. Neither carried any keys.

In a moment they were up on the porch on either side of the kitchen door. Nicole gave the knob a cautious twist. It was locked.

Fordyce and Paluso appeared out of the darkness. The intelligence officer squatted down in the corner between the porch and the stairs, his AR-15 ready. He wasn't coming in, however, not until the situation had stabilized. Paluso on the other hand carried what he called "the big key," an eight-pound sledgehammer.

The burly Italian lined up between the knob and bolt, then swung.

The door crashed open, and Mike went one way while Nicole went the other, pistols up and ready.

Mike took in tiled walls, an enameled sink, an old-fashioned icebox, a table with a cutting board in the middle of the room, and a door in the far wall. Architecturally, the house was a duplicate of the place outside of Bariloche. Nicole wisely snapped off the light.

The door was situated in a corner, and the next room was a small pantry with another room beyond it, a dangerous configuration, so he took both of them fast. They only had a moment before—

"*Hey!* What's going on in there?"

—the element of surprise was over.

A slight figure was outlined for a moment in the next doorway and Mike fired. He heard the bullet hit and there was a scream.

Suddenly a jet of flame ripped toward him. A weapon that fired so fast it was impossible to distinguish the individual shots. He dropped to one knee as bullets crashed wildly through the pantry cabinets, tore up the wall, blasted holes in the ceiling. Then the man was gone, a shadow fleeing into the next room screaming at the top of his lungs.

"Everyone okay?"

Nicole laid a hand on his shoulder and Paluso, guarding their backs, mumbled, "Yup."

There was a thud as someone collided with something in the dark, then another flash of panicked gunfire and a crash of glass. Their quarry had shot out a window. Through the ringing in his ears Fowler could just barely hear the sound of someone running up a set of stairs.

He tossed the silenced .22 aside and drew the Smith & Wesson .44. With its perfectly sculpted grips and light-reflecting sight, it was by far the better weapon in the dark. There was an office or den to one side—Nicole and Paluso split in either direction verifying it was empty—then a dining area that was open to the living room. In a glow of colored lights and shattered ornaments, a Christmas tree lay on its side.

Fowler heard a whisper of feet on the stairs and past a low partition a burly silhouette lifted a pistol. Mike fired and the man shot back. Mike pulled the trigger twice more to make sure. The body collapsed over the railing, falling onto a sideboard.

Glancing around, Fowler pointed Paluso to set up in the near corner where he could cover the bottom of the stairway. Mike and Nicole quickly cleared the rest of the rooms on the main floor. From outside there was the distant crackle of gunfire, then shouting . . . the kind that indicated a surrender was underway.

Returning to the stairwell from the opposite side of the room Fowler caught Paluso's eye. The gangster shrugged. He turned to look at Nicole; she had more training at this sort of thing than he did. The only thing worse than going through a doorway was attacking up a set of stairs.

Nicole winced; she made a throwing motion. Mike stuck his head out. The top of the stairs was dark, but he could tell there was a hallway running crosswise.

Brrr-rip!

He jerked back. There was an arc of fire and a cascade of shells pinged off the wall and railing. Across the room a lamp exploded, and a framed photograph of Adolf Hitler smashed to pieces. He recognized the gun now, a Schnellfeuer, the fully automatic version of the venerable Mauser C96 pistol. It was hard to control and good for very little except . . . something like this.

Mike slipped out of the sling to his machinegun and rotated the stock into position. He laid it on the floor. Then he fished a grenade out of his pocket. He showed it to Paluso and pointed up the stairwell. Nicole gripped her MP 40, ready to move. He pulled the pin . . .

Paluso moved in, then leaned to one side to fire a burst up into the second floor. Mike needed all the covering fire he could get. If he didn't angle the grenade just right, it would bounce off the wall and back down the stairs.

He stepped out. The lever flew clear, and he tossed the lemon-shaped metal canister underhanded. He hit the ground and rolled into a ball.

The explosion blasted dust from cracks in the ceiling, sent pieces of metal tearing in all directions. Before he could uncoil himself, Nicole sprinted up the stairs with Paluso hot on her heels. She crouched down, head and gun barrel poking around the left-hand corner at the top of the stairs.

Paluso turned right and Mike caught up with him in the hallway. The gangster didn't wait. There were two doors across from one another. He kicked in the first and went through. Only luck saved them.

The room was empty. In the cover of the doorway Mike dropped to one knee, and as he did, he heard a sound, a whimper that turned to an angry whine . . .

Brr-rap!

The door across the hall and the wall just over his head were torn by a line of flying splinters and shredded paneling. The interior walls were clearly not made of logs! Fowler fired back, three bursts from the MP 40 through the wall and door. Something hit the floor.

Mike stood, and Paluso stepped in behind him. Both were covered with flecks of wood and plaster dust. Gun up, Mike pushed open the damaged door. It was Anhaldt's flunky, the young man who had managed the contracts in Barcelona. On the floor beside him was the chunky outline of a Mauser pistol surrounded by a halo of shell casings. He was just a kid, a stupid kid.

"To hell with it!" Mike growled. He was exhausted. The beatings, the hike from the infiltration point, the pummeling from the gunfire, and more than anything, the loss of his friends. Peter Anhaldt had to pay for all the death and destruction he had caused, but there was no clean way to do this job. Mike was sick of it. Dead or alive, he just wanted to get out the other side.

He started back down the hallway. As he passed Nicole, she stood, but he motioned that she should stay behind him. As he came to each room, he fired a long burst, 9mm bullets chewing through the walls and doors. Light from inside the rooms blazed through the holes in dusty streaks.

Paluso and Nicole stepped in behind him, slamming each panel open and strafing the closets and bathrooms. By the time they were done the floor was covered with empty cases and discarded magazines, the upper half of the hallway hazed with gun smoke. There was no resistance. They saw no one.

After a moment, through the ringing in his ears, Fowler heard "Coming up! Am I clear?"

It was Fordyce. He came bounding up the stairs, then stopped, looking around at the destruction. "Good Lord! Was this all you?"

Paluso laughed. "Most of it."

From the large bathroom at the end of the hall there was a groan and then the sound of movement. Fowler palmed his Smith & Wesson and stepped through the door with Fordyce and Paluso right on his heels.

Peter Anhaldt was struggling to pull himself from a bullet-pocked cast iron bathtub. He got to his feet, swiped back his hair, and adjusted his cuffs. Three guns were trained on him but his expression barely flickered.

He nodded at Fordyce. "Oh, it's you . . . good. *Very* good. I surrender. You're a sworn officer of the United States government. I'm an American citizen and, what's more, my company has contracts with the Defense Department. You can't kill me . . . and now that you're here you can't let *them* do it either." He nodded toward Fowler and Paluso.

Fowler didn't care. He cocked his revolver. But Fordyce held up a hand. "You *are* right," he said. "Technically, we can't kill you."

He sighed . . .

". . . but *she* can."

Nicole stepped forward, raising her MP 40. "With pleasure," she said.

Three days later and fifteen hundred miles farther north, the mysteriously outfitted transport plied its way toward San Diego. After twenty years, Mike Fowler was headed home.

Until he was released in Puerto Montt, Chile, Otto Skorzeny had remained under guard for his own protection. Fordyce was rightfully nervous that Mike or Nicole might decide to finish off the old Nazi. As always, the man had found a way to turn defeat into an asset and even made jokes about the potentially nefarious deeds he might be required to perform at the behest of the CIA.

Mike was unsure what his own fate might be. Fordyce had promised to square things with the Spanish government. He would owe a few favors . . . but there was no indication of exactly what that meant. At the very least Aleixandre Porras would be able to return home, and together they could probably manage to skim enough money out of the Sistemas Militar accounts to buy Jack Johnson a new . . . well, not a ship, but something that would allow him, Waretini, McLeod, and maybe Cacoyannis to get started again.

Fordyce hadn't exactly sworn them all to secrecy, but he had suggested that they might be better off if they didn't talk too much about what they had experienced.

Mike wasn't sure that it mattered; they would hardly be believed. He imagined that years from now he would probably get a call, or two, or three. It would be Jack, or Ihaka, or Collie reaching out, looking for some reassurance that all those strange things had really happened, way back when, at the bottom of the world.

It was late in the afternoon when Fordyce and Nicole joined Fowler at the taffrail. The two of them had spent most of the last couple of days sequestered in the ship's communications cabin. Something was being hashed out between Israel and the United States, or maybe just Mossad and the CIA. Looking back along their wake, Fowler imagined the widening angle of rippling water was like all the many possibilities that had finally been focused down to this very moment. He had a lot to think about. A decision to make.

Nicole slipped an arm around his waist. "We're taking a break for dinner, come on inside."

"You two didn't get what you wanted," Mike said. "How is that going to go down back home?"

The little man laughed. "It'll be a problem, but not as much as you might expect. There are people who are scared of progress, especially the risky kind. But what happened back there proved that harnessing catalyzed fusion is possible. Just knowing that is half the battle. I have great faith. Not that I forgive you, but the wrong people didn't get it. That's what we care about most."

Nicole leaned her head on Mike's arm. "I can only say so much, but there is a deal on the table. If everyone can learn to trust one another there may be a joint Israeli and American program. The information our people collected, and the pieces Leonid knows, all in cooperation with the big American labs."

She pulled back and looked at him, sensing he wasn't the least bit excited by that idea. After a moment she sighed. "I'm just telling you what's happening. It makes me nervous, too."

"Do you remember what Anton said about scientists lacking humility? I only wish your higher-ups had been there to see it go off."

"All above our pay grade, old chum. The eggheads will do what eggheads do."

"Well, there's food on and I'm cold." Nicole kissed Mike on the cheek, then headed forward.

Anson Fordyce looked from Mike to Nicole and back again. "You two *do* make a good couple . . . I've thought so ever since I introduced you."

Fowler shook his head in mock disgust. "Oh, shut up," he said.

After they had both gone, he turned back to the rail, gazing down into the churning water. The news Nicole and Fordyce had just delivered made the next part much easier.

He reached inside his jacket and pulled out the cigarette case that had once belonged to Anton Voss.

After the fighting in the house on Skyring Water, Mike had wandered from one room to the next. His senses were dulled from the concussion of the guns. His soul was gripped with a profound fatigue. All he wanted to do was to get away from Fordyce and his plans, from Paluso, and even Nicole. The Agency collection team was already scouring the first floor photographing or bagging whatever they found. From downstairs he could hear the sound of flashbulbs popping and a mumble of voices.

Beyond a shattered door he came upon a suitcase lying open on a bare mattress. Packed up and ready to be taken out to Anhaldt's airplane was Captain Seegers's map book, as well as everything Voss had left behind when he had last suited up on the *Bushranger*. Wedged down on one side was Anton's cigarette case. Voss had asked him to have a smoke, and that was strange . . . He knew Fowler thought it was a bad habit. The man had been trying to tell him something. But what?

Shooting a look over his shoulder, Mike slipped the case into his pocket. In the days that followed, he had shown it to no one.

Now, shielding any view of it from the deck of the ship, he clicked the case open and took one last look, a reminder of the two things Anton had cared about more than anything else in the world.

The inside, like the outside, was covered in complex asymmetrical designs. The clip, which still held a few disintegrating Chesterfields, was engraved with a flowing script. Mike's German was far from fluent, but he thought it said:

> *Dearest Anton, let this be a prayer that we can build a better tomorrow.*
>
> *Yours forever,*
> *Elizabeth.*

When he looked closely, the elaborate art deco designs resolved themselves into concealed arrows and squiggles, numbers and symbols . . . the scientific notation of, if he remembered the names correctly, Stueckelberg and Wentzel. Convoluted mathematics proving . . . what? The secret of the Glasglocke? A pathway to discovering the Tychon particle? The formula Elizabeth had used to steal fire from the gods? The bubblelike collapse of all reality? Was it the most valuable thing in the world, or the most deadly? He had no idea.

What he did know was that, rightly or wrongly, Dr. Anton Andreas Voss, his trusted partner, his deceitful benefactor, had been trying to save the world from its headlong race toward scientific annihilation. Voss had been a Nazi, a murderer, and an arms dealer, and Mike Fowler was little better himself.

But he wasn't any worse.

Mike snapped the case closed, locking inside Elizabeth's message and the secret that could doom or save mankind. With a flick of his wrist, he tossed it out into the roiling waters. It splashed and winked in the fading light. Six million dollars sinking down, shifting like an autumn leaf into the blackness of the deep. It was a final good-bye. And it was what his friend deserved . . . a burial at sea.

THE END

POSTSCRIPT

THE OPENING WHISPERS of the story that became *Skyring Water* can be found in *No Traveller Returns,* my father's first attempt at a novel. *No Traveller* is a curious book, literary in its aspirations and part of Dad's extended "Yondering" universe, tying together several of the Yondering short stories as well as various elements of his early life.

A major theme of *No Traveller Returns* is that all people are connected. He illustrates this first through the roads and rails and the sea lanes that carry cargo across America and on to the rest of the world. Then, he develops a set of fascinating connections in the way the lives of the crew of the S.S. *Lichenfield* are intertwined . . . often without them even knowing. It's a wonderful metaphor for a first novel that is the jumping-off point for so many other aspects of Dad's life and career.

One of the most interesting elements connects the characters of Dennis McGuire (a stand-in for my father), first mate Borly Shannon, seaman Conrad "Shorty" Carmody, and his long-lost sister, actress Faustine Carmody, to the Carmodys' father, who left home searching for a mysterious treasure some twenty years earlier.

In a foolhardy attempt to resurrect his family's fortunes, Raoul

Carmody took off for South America in the company of several suspicious characters. Over the months that followed, his family received letters from New Orleans, then Cartagena, and finally Ushuaia, a tiny settlement at the extreme tip of the continent. The message explained that the expedition had been successful . . . but his wife and children never heard from him again.

An additional piece of the story is separately picked up by Borly Shannon. He tells of rescuing a man from a sinking sailboat well off the coast of Chile. The man was dying from exposure and several wounds, but he told a story of an ancient map and finding Spanish treasure. When greed took over and fighting broke out, he was the only one who survived . . . only to die soon after being taken in by Shannon's crew. A letter in his pocket identified him as Raoul Carmody.

Only partially finished, *No Traveller Returns* was stored away, almost forgotten, for 80 years. Eventually, I reassembled its various elements, discovered the throughline in the seemingly haphazard pile of scenes, and wrote the connective tissue needed to finally get it into print. But the story of the Chilean coast and the hidden treasure didn't end in 1938, or in 2018 when *No Traveller Returns* was published. However, to pick up that trail, we have to go back in time to the middle of the twentieth century and the books that turned Louis L'Amour into a household name.

BETWEEN 1953 AND 1958 my father wrote fourteen Western novels. Mostly sold as paperback originals, they established him as a force to be reckoned with in a crowded genre and delivered a modest level of financial stability . . . a level unknown to him before that time. At age fifty he could finally feel that his future was somewhat secure.

But Dad's writing talent had matured in the era of the pulp magazines, a time when he was often able to publish short stories in two or even three different genres in a single month. As much as he enjoyed the westerns he was selling to Gold Medal, Ace, and Bantam, his ever-active imagination was still busy creating crime stories, historical novels, and even science fiction.

His notes from the late 1950s are full of outlines, beginnings, and treatments having nothing to do with the West. He had a myriad of interests and wanted to branch out. Unfortunately, it was at this exact moment that changes in the publishing business made successfully shifting from one genre to another extremely difficult.

In the early days of paperbacks, each of the different publishers had separate racks just for their own books. Paperbacks were mostly sold like magazines, rotating through the stands in drugstores and airports. But as the phenomenon swept into bookstores, the industry realized that it needed to reorganize. Soon the various publishers embarked on a process called "integration." This meant the old individual publisher's racks were retired and content from all the various companies was intermixed on the bookstore shelves. To help customers find what they were looking for, books were strictly labeled and categorized by genre.

So Louis L'Amour was found in the Western section. Period. And the incentive from both the marketplace and the publishers was to keep authors firmly in their own lane. Dad understood this as well as anyone. Success, credibility, respect—he had fought for years to earn these things . . . but he didn't like being limited. His creativity, his *imagination*, constantly rebelled.

Besides the dozens of incomplete ideas he left behind, this was also the era in which he created *The Walking Drum*, conceived of *Last of the Breed*, and wrote what became the first draft of this novel, *Skyring Water*. None of these projects got him anywhere. No publisher was interested.

And so that was the end of it for quite a while. Bantam wanted Westerns, Dad was about to have his first child, and he had spent too much time over the preceding years writing and planning books he had been unable to sell. Fame and fortune, enough fortune to support his family, lay in the Western genre and so he completely recommitted himself to that. *Skyring Water* went into a drawer and stayed there . . . for about twenty-five years.

Remarkably, even as Westerns waned in the public's consciousness, Dad became more and more successful. By the mid-1970s, he was a superstar in *any* genre, and the fact that he was cranking out one *New York Times* bestseller after another was a given. By 1984 he had such popularity that Bantam was finally willing to buy *The Walking Drum,* then *Last of the Breed,* and then *The Haunted Mesa* . . . and that was when *Skyring Water* raised its head once again.

Because Dad was fighting a recurring case of pneumonia and hiking at high altitude was out of the question, I had been running around the southwest doing research on *The Haunted Mesa.* And whenever I was at the house, he and I spent a good deal of time talking about that book, where he wanted to go in his career, and some of his unfinished stories, including *Skyring Water.*

Originally, he had conceived of it as a straight-up adventure story appropriate to its era. But Dad had never felt it lived up to its full potential . . . and that wasn't just because he had not been able to interest a publisher. The story explored what had become a favorite scenario, that of several hard and desperate men, each distrusting the others, pursuing a treasure. But that particular plot, which he had executed beautifully in the short story "Off the Mangrove Coast," only worked well if its elements remained simple. His concern about *Skyring* was that it contained too many characters and too many complications. Additionally, there were a host of technical details that he had never been able to adequately research.

After reading it, I agreed with him. Yet with *Last of the Breed* making its way up the bestseller lists, I wondered if *Skyring Water* might become a fitting follow-up, another novel of international suspense. The way I saw it, the story had the potential to be taken in that direction.

For Louis L'Amour, a man known for his westerns, *Last of the*

Breed had been a brilliant transition into new and different subject matter. After his initial attempts to write novels in different genres had not worked out, he had pivoted to a plan of breathtaking ambition. Starting in the 1960s, Dad began to gently stretch the boundaries of what the fans and publishers would accept, moving away from cowboys and trail drives, town marshals and train robbers, Native Americans and encroaching settlers.

Over a period of decades, he incrementally altered the fundamentals of his work to include stories of the early frontier (*Sackett's Land*), contemporary mysteries (*The Broken Gun*), Europeans in the West (*Shalako*), and Westerners in Europe (*Reilly's Luck*). *Last of the Breed* took a Native American protagonist and set him down in a situation based on one of the seminal events of the Cold War, the Gary Powers or U-2 Incident.

After Dad had a major success with his historical novel *The Walking Drum* and with high hopes for *The Haunted Mesa,* his first foray into science fiction, it seemed like he might reformulate *Skyring Water* into a major novel in the suspense or thriller genre. And this time he would not require a connection to the American West in order to make it palatable to the publishers or the audience. It had been a long road, but Dad had finally attained the goals he set for himself more than twenty years before.

It didn't hurt that the 1970s and '80s were the heyday of authors like Robert Ludlum, Frederick Forsyth, Clive Cussler, Jack Higgins, John le Carré, and the incredibly prolific Ken Follett. All had made their mark writing sprawling international thrillers, moving the genre to a level of significance well beyond the somewhat tongue-in-cheek adventures of James Bond.

My feeling was that Dad should keep pushing the boundaries. Instead of trying to pare the story down, trying to make it like the elegantly minimal "Off the Mangrove Coast," he should expand it. Those big bestselling suspense novels thrived on complexity. I also reminded him of "The Goose Flies South," a short story he had written in 1947 that shared similar locations in Chile, as well as a focus on a resurgent Nazism attempting to develop nuclear technology. Incorporating these ideas might give *Skyring Water* the sort of existential punch required by the suspense genre.

So he and I laid out a strategy for the changes that would need to be made, and we discussed the sort of research that would have to be done. There were going to be a lot of aspects, various details of science and engineering, that fell more into my areas of interest and were subjects where I had useful contacts. At the time I imagined our working relationship would be much like it had been on *The Haunted Mesa,* with me going out and doing the legwork, digesting the specifics, then reporting back.

Unfortunately, around the time Dad finished *The Haunted Mesa,* we discovered that the pneumonia he suffered from was caused by a thin veil of cancerous tissue that stretched across his lungs. The scope of it was inoperable. Chemotherapy could only buy him time and not much of that. All other plans were set aside, and he launched himself into the one book he definitely wanted to complete before he died, *Education of a Wandering Man.*

After he passed away, I occasionally revisited the various subjects I would have to research to write this story. I planned to work on it someday but there were books of short stories to edit and other projects that needed attending to. As we found ways to package many of the other materials that Dad had left behind, the books of short stories, his Hopalong Cassidy novels, the Lost Treasures series, and the previous novel he and I "wrote together," *No Traveller Returns,* I began to realize that if I was going to bring his career to a close, I had best do it with a good loud bang!

And that meant a big book. As significant a piece of entertainment as I could muster and something that tried to be worthy of one of the most popular novelists of the twentieth century. I really had my work cut out for me, and it turned out to be a grand adventure through an amazing collection of subjects about which I knew very little. I met a bunch of interesting people and had an opportunity to "live" as my father and wrestle with many of the issues that he confronted on a daily basis decade after decade.

I have always felt that, if you can listen closely enough, a story will tell you what it wants to be. This one whispered in my ear continuously and I did my best to follow its directions and prayed that maybe it was my father speaking from that undiscovered country beyond the grave.

The novel you have just read is not simply a well-edited version of Louis L'Amour's original draft of *Skyring Water.* And unlike *No Traveller Returns* it is not a "time machine," a forensic re-creation duplicating my father's writing style from a particular era. Rather than either of those, it is my take on the sort of story that *Skyring Water* might have become if those dreams and speculations from the fall of 1986 had come to fruition.

It is a partnership across time that hopefully delivers the book Dad and I had so much fun planning, but that he was never able to write.

I hope you have enjoyed it.

Beau L'Amour
Los Angeles, 2025

ACKNOWLEDGMENTS

FIRST OF ALL, it is important to say that regardless of all the research I have done to create *Skyring Water,* this novel's intent is to simply entertain. It is a work of fiction and all the historical personages and situations mentioned in the book are my fictional interpretations designed to be functional to the needs of the narrative. It is my hope that anyone interested in the pieces of actual history related here will do their own investigations and come to their own conclusions.

A lot can be said about the process of creating this novel and all the wonderful people and source material that contributed to it. However, in order to make what is already a substantial volume as short as possible, I would like to invite readers to visit SkyringWater.com for more in-depth information about the story, the era it takes place in, how it was written, my research, and the details behind the role that many of those who are credited below played in its creation . . .

To start off, of course, the first and most important "thank you" goes to my father, without whom none of this, including me, would be possible! Following the rough order in which they contributed to the creative process, I wish to thank the following people:

Dr. Thomas O. Paine: Tom was head of NASA during the Apollo years, a navy diver and an engineering officer on American submarines during World War II, and the man who compiled the amazing Submarine Warfare Library (which now resides at the U.S. Naval Academy).

Mike Demetre: Mike is a close family friend who worked with the State Department and over the years added a great deal to my perception of the wider world during the 1950s and '60s. He also welcomed me into his home in Barbados while he was covering the Caribbean for USAID in the aftermath of the invasion of Grenada.

Dr. Terry Rickard: Terry is a physicist who patiently coached me on the subject of catalyzed fusion and created the concept of the fictional Tychon particle.

Bob Condon: Bob is a diver, a SEAL, and a submariner who spent many hours helping me plan the salvage of the U-Null and who provided a great deal of insight on the sort of men who joined the U.S. Navy Underwater Demolition Teams.

Leonard "Red" Bird: Red was a college professor and Marine, and one of the few men to witness an atomic explosion from roughly a mile away and live to tell the tale.

Alex Hawkins: Alex was an Australian soldier who participated in a commando mission that landed on Itu Aba.

Dan and Robert Retting: The Retting brothers owned LA's oldest gun store and were good enough to share their childhood memories and photographs of a 1960 visit to the Spanish arsenals with their father.

Angelo De Sapio: Angelo was a family friend and an architect who is well-known for his work on the modernization of Caracas in the 1950s.

Diana and John Lopez: The Lopezes have been amazing friends and incredibly helpful, connecting me to many useful sources as well as giving me valuable insights into the activities and personalities of intelligence operatives.

Justin Ruddelson: I've known Justin from childhood and he

helped out with the various languages and gave me many insights into the country of Israel.

Harry Cooper: Without knowing me from Adam, Harry generously offered a great deal of information on submarines and also referred all my crazy questions to Peter Hansen. During the time I was writing this book, Hansen was one of the last living, if not *the* last living, U-boat officers.

Dan Lajeunesse and Ryan Pote: Dan and Ryan provided remarkable stories and insight into the details of Aqualung (SCUBA) diving. Ryan is a veteran navy man who, besides being a helicopter pilot, was also a SCUBA instructor and is the author of an excellent adventure novel recently published by Berkley titled *Blood and Treasure.*

Bruce Bello, Larry Zarcoff, Angelique Pitney, Kathy L'Amour, Paul O'Dell, and Mike Plescia: All of these people, friends and family, were early readers and helped me refine many aspects of this novel.

It is important to note that the L'Amour family has just passed its seventieth anniversary with Bantam Books, now a part of Penguin Random House. With that in mind, I want to express my deep and abiding gratitude to all the incredible members of the current team as well as those in whose footsteps they tread. In particular I want to thank a recent retiree, Stuart Applebaum. Without his help and guidance, the last fifty of those years would hardly have been as welcoming, productive, or exciting. Bless you, Stu, you're one of a kind!

So, there it is. I'm sure I've forgotten a few people just as I'm sure I've messed up various technical details no matter how much research I've tried to do. Wherever any errors exist, the correct assumption would be that they are mine.

Thank you for sticking with me this long and allowing me to pay these debts of knowledge. I hope you've enjoyed the ride . . .

ABOUT THE AUTHORS

Our foremost storyteller of the American West, the late LOUIS L'AMOUR has thrilled a nation by chronicling the adventures of the brave people who settled the American frontier. There are more than 300 million copies of his books in print around the world.

BEAU L'AMOUR is a writer, art director, and editor. He has written and produced several films, including USA Network's *The Diamond of Jeru*. Since 1988 he has been the manager of the estate of his father, Louis L'Amour.

louislamour.com
Instagram: @Louis_LAmour
X: @Louis_LAmour

ABOUT THE TYPE

This book was set in Minion, a 1990 Adobe Originals typeface by Robert Slimbach. Minion is inspired by classical, old-style typefaces of the late Renaissance, a period of elegant and beautiful type designs. Created primarily for text setting, Minion combines the aesthetic and functional qualities that make text type highly readable with the versatility of digital technology.